Spies Never Lose

BANANA GIRLS
BOOK 3

Spies Never Lose

M. TAYLOR CHRISTENSEN

MOON
ZOOM
PRESS

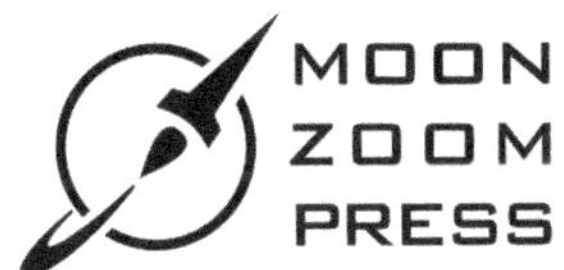

eBook ISBN: 978-1-951454-09-8

Paperback ISBN: 978-1-951454-10-4

Hardback ISBN: 978-1-951454-11-1

Moon Zoom Press - Orem, Utah

Cover Design by Myles Christensen

Copy Edit by Courtney Larkin

For My Love:

Don't look too closely at these characters. ;)

Chapter One

A LOUD BANG SHATTERED the stillness of the scrubby Georgia woods.

Even though she had expected the sound, Hannah still jumped. Normally she didn't startle easily, but something about spending hours traipsing through the forest across a floor of matted red and brown leaves, followed by another hour on her stomach watching the occupants of a small, rundown house at the end of a long dirt road had thrown her off.

But if that's what a spy girl had to do to get the job done, then Hannah McCarthy would do it.

From her hiding place behind a small copse of trees, she watched through a pair of high-powered binoculars as a man stormed away from the house and walked across the wild, unkempt lawn to an old, red barn. He had a scruffy beard and looked to be in his mid-twenties—slightly round in the middle, and very rough around the edges. He certainly fit in here in the backcountry.

With a quickly entered code, the man activated the barn door, which slid open to reveal the gleaming interior of a posh garage. Knowing that this guy was the right-hand-man of a high-level money launderer in Atlanta meant that a well-disguised garage with half a dozen new cars didn't come as a surprise to Hannah.

A matte black pickup truck sat between a silver convertible and a bright red Mustang. The man got into the truck and sped away down the dirt road, gravel churning in his wake.

Once the engine was a dull whisper in the distance, Hannah counted twenty more seconds then moved quickly from her hiding place and down the small hill to the edge of the tree line, still thirty feet from the house. She glanced at the portable video screen in her hand, checking once more that the flying micro-bots had successfully spoofed the home's security video feeds, before striding quickly across the crunchy grass to the nearest wall of the old house.

At the kitchen window, she paused, just out of sight, and watched the interior for signs of activity. Like the garage, the inside of the home stood in stark contrast to the exterior. Instead of decades-old wallpaper and tattered sofas, the room was superbly furnished with top-of-the-line leather couches and mahogany tables. Of course, Hannah would recognize expensive furniture. She remembered going with her mother to the most expensive stores, picking out the highest priced pieces. Her mother had always seemed happiest when she was spending money. But it had all been a facade. She'd had her demons to fight, and money hadn't helped. She left their family the week after Hannah turned eleven.

A young woman in her mid-twenties came into view at the far end of the family room, pulling Hannah back to the mission at hand. The woman walked purposefully across the room and lifted a small child from a bouncy seat before moving into the kitchen. Hannah slid slowly into view, hoping not to startle the woman. Hannah's movement caught her attention, and she glanced out the window.

The woman froze in place, eyes locked with Hannah's. Finally, she motioned toward the back of the house. Hannah slinked along under the shadow of the eaves until she reached the back door.

"I didn't know you'd be coming tonight," the young mother said in a thick southern drawl. "I don't have anything packed."

Hannah slid nimbly through the door into the kitchen. "Good. You weren't supposed to pack anything yet. Your husband would have noticed. That's why they sent me before the rest of the extraction team arrives."

"I'm Carissa, by the way," the woman said as they moved across the living room toward the bedrooms.

"Hannah."

"How much time do we have?" Carissa asked over her shoulder.

"About thirty minutes," Hannah said, following close behind. She nearly ran into Carissa when the young mother came to an abrupt stop in the middle of the hall.

"Thirty minutes? I can't get ready that fast."

Hannah frowned as she appraised the young woman. Hannah had packed for week-long spy missions in half that time. How long could this girl really need? "You'll have to if you want to get out before your husband gets back," Hannah said, guiding her forward with a firm hand on her arm. "Don't worry, though, I'm here to help."

Carissa stopped at the door to a small bedroom painted floor to ceiling in sky blue. "If you could pack some stuff for baby Freddie, that would be a huge help." She nodded toward the nursery.

Hannah considered the chubby little boy perched on his mother's hip, babbling. Instinctively, she backed away a half step. "Uh, actually, I don't know anything about babies."

Carissa pointed at various items. "Just grab the diaper bag, but make sure it's got his changing pad, wipes, and diapers in there. The nighttime onesies are in the top drawer of his dresser, and his warm daytime outfits are in the third drawer. Oh, and don't forget the travel crib. Unless we're staying somewhere that has one of those."

Flustered by such a convoluted list, Hannah repeated her protests. "No, really. I can't pack for the baby. Just show me where your stuff is."

"You know, it's okay to be a little nervous about babies. I was, too, when I first had Freddie."

Hannah just shook her head, hoping to convey how *not* okay it really was.

Carissa considered her for a moment. "Maybe you're right." Carissa pointed down the hall toward the master bedroom. "My stuff is in the top drawers of the dresser. There's a suitcase in the very back of the closet."

Hannah ran to the closet and grabbed the first piece of luggage she saw. She returned to the dresser drawers and started stuffing various items of clothing and necessities inside. She walked into the master bathroom and made a quick evaluation of what Carissa might need. The federal marshals would have her and Freddie in a hotel until they found a permanent place for her to live. She grabbed the makeup bag sitting on the counter along with a tube of toothpaste and both toothbrushes—she didn't know which was Carissa's, but it would serve her husband right if his teeth rotted out.

On her second trip to the bathroom, Hannah glanced in the shower and grabbed the pink razor and the flowery tube of shaving gel next to it. When she looked at the shampoos, she quickly decided that Carissa would just have to use the little bottles at the hotel. Before Hannah turned to check the rest of the bathroom, a large bottle of baby shampoo caught her eye. Did Carissa's baby take showers already? He didn't look like he could even stand up yet. The hotel definitely wouldn't have special shampoo for a baby. With a huff at the extra inconvenience, Hannah grabbed the huge bottle with the tear-free label on it and hurried back to the bed, stuffing her latest acquisitions into the suitcase.

Carissa stepped into the bedroom, baby Freddie still on her hip, and surveyed Hannah's work. Hannah glanced at the small bag on her shoulder. No wonder the young mother had finished before Hannah; she'd only needed to pack what looked like an oversized purse.

Carissa must have noticed Hannah's appraisal of the bag. "The rest of the stuff is in the hall. I didn't grab the stroller, though. Do you think we'll need it?"

Hannah shrugged as she zipped Carissa's suitcase closed. "I have no idea. But I think we just have to go with what you've got. The marshals can buy whatever else you really need."

The young mother's shoulders relaxed a little. "Oh, good. Because there's still so much more that I wasn't able to—"

The sound of a car in the distance had caught her attention.

Hannah checked the time. "Looks like the retrieval team is early."

As she glanced back at Carissa, Hannah saw the young mother's face drain of color. "Oh no. It's Eddie," she whispered.

For a moment, Hannah considered asking if she was sure, but the look on Carissa's face was answer enough.

Hannah grabbed the suitcase and flew past Carissa into the hall. "We need to get out of here." She stopped at the pile of baby paraphernalia blocking her path. "We can't take this stuff now." She looked at the suitcase in her hand. "In fact, we can't take any of this."

She pushed the nursery door open as far as it would go and shoved the entire pile inside. She grabbed Carissa's suitcase and plopped it on top before slamming the door shut. Getting away in time to avoid a physical confrontation with Eddie was the most important thing at the moment. It wouldn't matter if he found a mess in the nursery as long as they were gone when it happened.

Grabbing Carissa's arm, Hannah pulled her forward. "Let's go." She led the way to the back door and glanced outside. The treeline was at least thirty feet away, but hopefully the house would shield them from view. Hannah was grateful she hadn't disconnected the flying micro-bots yet. If Eddie happened to check the recording from his security cameras, they would still be showing the spoofed video.

They slipped outside to the sound of a loud engine pulling into the garage. It would only take Eddie about thirty seconds to reach the front door, and the backyard would be easily visible through the windows as soon as he stepped into the living room.

"Go. Run for the trees," Hannah said in a harsh whisper, pointing to a collection of tall pine trees straight back from the house.

Carissa started across the yard as Hannah pulled the door shut behind them. Not weighed down by a baby, Hannah quickly caught up and raced ahead toward the trees. Eddie was probably only seconds from opening the door, and his wife and small son were still in full view. Hannah scampered back, grabbed the bag from Carissa's shoulder, and began pulling her urgently forward. Hannah considered taking the child but decided that having a crying baby on her hands would be a billion times worse.

A split-second after they reached the cover of the tree line, Hannah heard the door slam shut. She stopped and crouched, pulling Carissa down next to her. Though the trees did offer some cover, they weren't nearly dense enough to hide the movement of two people—three, if the baby counted. From behind a pair of tree trunks, they watched as Carissa's husband stood in the living room looking around, calling for his wife. He moved to the kitchen—still in plain view of the back trees where they hid. When he finally walked through the living room toward the bedrooms, Hannah stood and pulled Carissa and the baby farther into the forest.

Hannah wondered if they could get deep enough into the trees that they wouldn't have to worry about Eddie seeing their movement. How long would he search the house? Would he find the pile of baby stuff with the suitcase on top? What would he do then?

For the third time in less than an hour, the sound of the slamming front door echoed through the quiet hillside. An angry yell followed.

"Carissa!"

Hannah dropped to the leaf-covered ground again, but when she turned around to pull Carissa down with her, she saw the young mother rooted to a spot ten feet behind her, looking back toward the house.

Hannah scurried back and pulled on Carissa's arm until she knelt to the ground.

"Maybe this isn't a good idea," Carissa said. She looked dazed and confused.

"Stay with me, Carissa," Hannah said, touching the young woman's face, and turning it to her. Her expression was wistful, almost lost. "We need to get you and Freddie somewhere safe, and that's not here."

After a few seconds, Carissa's expression hardened. She hugged the baby closer to her chest and hunched down next to Hannah. Indistinct sounds from the other side of the house reached them. Hannah had no idea what Eddie might be planning.

"What's he doing?" Hannah asked.

"He's probably checking the garage right about now. Just to make sure I haven't driven off in one of the cars," Carissa replied.

Hannah dipped her head in acknowledgment.

"Of course, it doesn't really make much sense, considering I've never driven any of his cars," Carissa whispered. "I don't even know how to drive."

Hannah couldn't hide her shock at that news. She opened her mouth to express her surprise that any woman would miss the chance to feel that kind of freedom, but Carissa cut her off.

"Eddie and me were high-school sweethearts. He was a grade older, so he got his license before I was even old enough to think about it. And after that, he just drove us everywhere," she explained with a shrug. "He said he'd always take care of me and that I didn't need to worry about getting permission from the government to drive." Her voice was wistful, as if nostalgic for some former time.

Hannah bit down on her immediate instinct to point out the irony that her husband had told her to not ask for permission from the government while at the same time he clearly expected her to get permission from him.

With a quick peek in the direction of the house to make sure they were hidden from view of the garage, Hannah stood and helped Carissa back to her feet. Hunched over, they hurried deeper into the sparsely spaced trees.

"Carissa!" Another yell, closer this time, split the silence. Eddie must have come around the corner of the house to the backyard.

Immediately, Hannah and Carissa both dropped flat onto the carpet of leaves. Carissa wasn't at ninja-level reflexes yet, but not bad considering she had a baby in her arms. The infant grunted in protest but then fell silent as his mother cuddled him close. They were far enough from the house that it was unlikely Eddie could see them—as long as he didn't see their trail into the woods and follow after them. Hannah lifted her head to look at the matted leaves behind them. The trail they had left was faint, almost imperceptible. Hopefully, Eddie wasn't an expert tracker.

"Carissa!" he yelled again from the back of the house. "You ain't got to the road yet, so I know you're out there." Loud footfalls stomped into the woods nearby. Eddie hadn't picked the path directly toward them, but he had guessed pretty close.

Clumps of scrub brush cluttered the woods between them, and Hannah hoped it would be enough to keep them hidden. The swish and clomp of Eddie's steps through the fallen leaves grew. He was heading directly toward them now. The sound stopped, then resumed, fading away as he wandered in another direction.

Hannah and Carissa scooted along the ground toward a large fallen tree overgrown with brambles and shrubs. With Eddie moving away from them, Hannah helped Carissa and the baby climb over the end of the log before scampering over behind them.

Once well-hidden in the small, branchy alcove, Carissa turned to Hannah and whispered, "If he catches us, he's gonna be so mad." She bit her lip and glanced over her shoulder in the direction of his yelling. "I can't believe I agreed to this. I never should have been snooping on

Eddie's computer. I never should have sent those files to the FBI. Maybe I should just go back and apologize."

Hannah placed a hand on the young mother's arm. "Carissa, Eddie's boss is a ruthless criminal. He destroys people's lives. And you're helping us put him away where he can't hurt anyone anymore. You're making a difference. You're saving people." Hannah paused to let her words sink in. "But when the arrest warrant becomes public, you and Freddie will be in danger. We need to save you first."

Carissa nodded slowly. "And what about Eddie?" she whispered.

Though Hannah didn't think Eddie was physically abusive, he was obviously very controlling and manipulative. Hannah couldn't understand why a girl like Carissa would fall in love with a guy like Eddie. But too much hung in the balance to argue about it at the moment. "If he cooperates, the agents will cut him a deal. But the most important thing right now is to make sure you and Freddie are safe."

With another flinch at Eddie's yelling, Carissa curled her body around the baby, rocking him gently. Finally, she nodded her understanding.

Eddie's loud footfalls and screams turned toward their hiding place again. As he approached, Baby Freddie squirmed in Carissa's arms, craning his head to see where the sound was coming from. The young mother shushed and rocked him as quietly as she could.

Eddie stopped in the clearing they had just crawled out of. "Carissa! Come back here right now!" he bellowed into the seemingly empty forest.

Hannah held her breath as Carissa silently rocked the fidgeting child.

After several seconds that felt like an eternity, Eddie turned and tromped the other way.

A few seconds later, Hannah let out a quiet sigh. If Eddie hadn't been clomping through the woods like a herd of elephants, he might have found them. The two women huddled in silence for another minute or two until they heard an engine roar to life. With the clatter of gravel hitting the nearby outbuildings, the sound of the car slowly faded into the distance.

Cautiously, they stood from their hiding place and continued deeper into the woods. Hannah pulled out her phone and tapped a quick code to connect to Club Banana, her spy girl headquarters in Midtown Atlanta. Her close friend, and Banana Girls cofounder, Anna, answered the call.

"Anna, we've hit a snag in the operation, and I could use a little help."

"Sure thing. What's up?"

"Carissa's husband came back before we were out."

Anna sucked in a breath. "Yikes. What can I do?"

"Contact the retrieval team and tell them we're going to be out on the main road. Can you see my current location?" Hannah walked alongside Carissa. Baby Freddie was happy again now that they were moving.

After a short pause, Anna answered. "Yeah, I've got you."

"We're trying to walk straight away from the house, so draw a line from the backyard to us and just extend it to the road. We'll keep going until we hit it."

"I'll have the team meet you on the road," Anna said.

"Thanks. I'm going silent again so we don't get any surprises."

"I'll message you when I know the team's ETA."

"Thanks, Anna," Hannah replied and ended the call.

After a few more minutes of walking, the terrain became steeper. Hannah did her best to help Carissa negotiate the difficult parts. They were forced to skirt the end of a small ravine because it would have been impossible to scale the other side holding the baby.

Once around the ravine, Hannah sighted their course again using a prominent tree in the distance. It wouldn't win her any orienteering awards, but hopefully the retrieval team would find them easily enough.

After the ravine, the terrain leveled out. Carissa turned to Hannah. "My arms are killing me. Can you hold Freddie for a spell?"

Hannah would've rather balanced on one foot atop the nearest log while singing the Georgia Bulldogs' annoying fight song than hold a small child. But she didn't see any way to get them safely and quickly out of danger without giving Carissa a short break. She nodded, and the young mother gladly placed the baby in Hannah's arms. Little Freddie seemed fascinated by Hannah's long blond hair because he kept getting strands of it into his tiny fists and pulling hard. It was frustrating at first, but the smile on the baby's face every time she tried to extricate her hair from his hand kept her from getting too angry. He really was adorable. He giggled and cooed all the way down the hill.

The trees became denser as they approached the main road. Hannah handed Freddie back to Carissa and told them to hunker in a small depression behind a fallen log while she scouted the road for the retrieval team. The tree line ended at the top of a short slope that bordered the small country road. Hannah stepped cautiously down the embankment to the edge of the road. She glanced both directions.

No retrieval team. She hadn't really expected them to be there yet. That type of timing only happened in the movies—and only if the agents synchronized their watches.

She sat down against the sloped berm to wait.

In the deepening twilight, the details of the road and the surrounding forests became more and more difficult to make out, and the sky started to look more purple than blue.

Right when Hannah was about ready to start walking and take her chances in the nearest town, the sound of an approaching car drifted toward her. Hopefully, a black government SUV would come around the corner any second. She scooted next to a scrubby bush to keep herself hidden, just in case it wasn't the retrieval team.

Half a minute went by, and the vehicle hadn't passed her hiding spot yet. Hannah could still hear the sound of the engine. Had she misjudged the distance? Why would someone be driving that slow?

Her phone buzzed in her pocket. She pulled it out to see Anna's brief message.

— Hang tight. Team enroute. ETA 15 minutes.

Hannah's stomach dropped. Assuming Anna's information wasn't about fifteen minutes old, it wasn't the retrieval team coming around the bend.

A distraught wail pierced the evening air.

"Carissa! Please!" Eddie must be the one driving slowly along the road.

Hannah had maybe three seconds to make a decision before his truck came around the bend. She could stay put next to the small bush or she could scramble back up the slope to Carissa. Hannah felt confident in her ability to stay hidden where she was, but if Eddie's state of mind played into Carissa's decision to see this thing through, Hannah didn't trust her to not give herself away.

With the asphalt growing brighter in the approaching headlights, Hannah scampered up the berm to the treeline where Carissa and Freddie remained hidden. She jumped over the fallen log and hunched down next to them just as the black pickup truck came into view and another cry split the peaceful air.

From the look on Carissa's face, Hannah had gotten there just in time.

"He's miserable without me," Carissa whispered. "How can I just leave him like this?"

"Hang in there, Carissa," Hannah said. "We can't give up now. The men Eddie works for won't hesitate to use you or Baby Freddie as bargaining chips against your husband. We have to get you out of here while we still can."

Carissa looked ready to cry. She nodded and held Freddie closer, rocking him unnecessarily. Perhaps more for her own soothing than the baby's.

Hannah risked a glance over the top of the fallen log. The black pickup crept along the shoulder of the road, Eddie's head hanging out the window frantically scanning the tree line.

As he pulled even with them, Eddie yelled, "Carissa! Where are you?"

Carissa squeezed her eyes shut with a quiet whimper. Hannah placed a hand on Carissa's arm, hoping to convey some strength to the wavering young woman.

Eddie cried out again, and Carissa clapped a hand to her mouth, attempting to stifle her sob. Tears began coursing down her cheeks.

How did a lowlife like that elicit such devotion from a young woman like Carissa?

Freddie squirmed at the sudden shift in Carissa's arm. Apparently, he didn't enjoy the extra pressure on his middle. He struggled in Carissa's grasp and craned his head against her shoulder.

Hannah patted the baby's chubby arms and shushed him quietly. If they could just keep him quiet until the retrieval team arrived, they could get away unseen.

Freddie grunted and then briefly squawked his frustration.

Carissa's eyes shot open wide and locked with Hannah's.

They immediately heard the sound of wheels skidding to a stop on loose gravel followed by a door slamming shut.

"Carissa, is that you?" Eddie's footsteps echoed from the road below them.

Hannah peeked over the log again. The truck was stopped about fifty feet down the road, and Eddie moved along the shoulder in their direction, stopping every few steps to look up into the forest and listen.

Hannah looked at Carissa and Freddie. Freddie wouldn't stay quiet indefinitely. And with Eddie out of his truck and searching on foot, it was only a matter of time until he found them.

Hannah had to do something. She looked down at her outfit: dark pants and a stylish black leather jacket. She would never pass as a girl lost in the woods in her spy outfit. As quietly as possible, she slipped off her jacket and untucked her navy-blue top. She considered the change. She still didn't really look like she belonged in the woods. She quickly teased a few knots into her hair and added some twigs and leaves to compliment the look.

"Stay here. Maybe I can get rid of him," she whispered to Carissa.

Carissa turned a pleading look on her. "Please don't hurt him."

"I'll try to go easy on him. But no matter what happens, you have to stay hidden."

Carissa closed her eyes and nodded.

Hannah crouched low and moved deeper into the woods, sideways from Carissa. Once she was far enough away, she stood up straight and began shuffling and clomping her feet on the dry leaf bed.

Eddie saw her almost immediately. "Hey!" he yelled up at her. "What are you doing here? Who are you?"

With a well-timed trip, she wrapped her arms around a trunk at the edge of the tree line and stared down at Eddie, trying her best to look happily dazed. "Hi," she said with a broad smile. "I'm glad you found tree . . . I mean, me." She released the tree trunk and half-stumbled, half-slid down the dirt embankment.

"This is private property." Eddie gestured to the woods behind her. "You're not allowed to be here, you stupid kid."

Kid? Eddie wasn't more than three years older than Hannah. Her inebriated highschooler routine must be working. She flailed a hand toward the surrounding woods. "My friend and I had a party . . . picnic." She slurred her words generously. "He's gone now. But I'm not." She finished with a goofy smile.

Eddie shook his head. "Stay off my property," he yelled with a wave of his arm, before continuing along the gravel shoulder closer toward Carissa and Freddie.

Clearly, he wasn't going to be distracted from his search so easily. Hannah conveniently lost her balance sideways, keeping her body between Eddie and his hidden wife. "But maybe you could help me find him." She hiccupped.

Eddie stopped and eyed her more closely.

That was the problem with drawing attention to yourself and the reason Hannah avoided it whenever possible.

Trying to remain calm under his scrutiny, Hannah took the opportunity to size him up. At a little under six feet tall, Hannah had an inch or two on Eddie. But given that he outweighed her by at least fifty pounds, she would have a hard time bringing him down unless he was within arm's reach.

Eddie opened his mouth to say something but stopped short when a loud cry came from the trees at Hannah's back, followed quickly by soft shushing. Hannah cringed. Eddie's gaze cut to the hidden child then back to Hannah, realization dawning on his dumb-looking face. He reached into his jacket, but Hannah didn't wait to find out what he was grabbing. She took two steps forward, planted her foot, and swung a roundhouse to Eddie's ear. He stumbled sideways and fell into the gravel.

As he staggered back to his feet, Hannah grabbed him by the arm and flipped him onto the ground again, a loud whoosh of air leaving his lungs accompanied the impact. She rolled him onto his stomach and pulled a pair of zip-cuffs from her back pocket.

Thirty seconds later, she had Eddie's hands secured behind his back and his ankles cuffed together. Eddie coughed and sputtered in the dirt as he tried to catch his breath. Out of Eddie's view, Hannah glanced back toward Carissa's hiding spot. She held a finger to mouth, hoping that Carissa knew to stay there a little longer. Eddie might have guessed that his wife and son were somewhere in the trees, but there was no need to confirm that suspicion. Better to let him think he just imagined it.

She dragged Eddie up to a sitting position, facing away from Carissa, and leaned down to his eye level. "In a minute, some federal agents are going to come and arrest you officially. When they do, I'd suggest you cooperate with them to the very fullest. Though you may not deserve them, your family's counting on you." She put special emphasis on the word *family*.

Eddie still looked groggy from the encounter with her foot, but hopefully he understood what she was trying to tell him.

A few minutes later, a dark SUV drove up. Several federal officers jumped out and approached Hannah, clearly confused as to why a cuffed man sat at her feet.

One of the agents stepped over to Hannah. "Agent McCarthy?"

Hannah nodded. "This is Eddie Grayson," she said curtly.

The agent frowned. "He wasn't supposed to be taken into custody until later tonight."

Hannah gave him a patronizing smile. "He got home early."

The agent rubbed the back of his neck. "Sorry we didn't get the retrieval team to you in time. They actually took a turn up to the wrong house." He glanced at the surrounding woods, now growing dark. "I assume you—"

Hannah cut in. "Your agents are welcome to use the truck"—she nodded over her shoulder toward Eddie's pickup—"to take Mr. Grayson back to his home." She cut a very deliberate glance toward the tree line.

It took three seconds too long for reality to finally dawn on the other agent. "Oh. Right." He waved to a pair of nearby agents, who lifted Eddie from the ground and dragged him back to his truck.

Once Eddie was out of earshot, Hannah continued in a lowered voice. "Eddie's wife and baby are hiding nearby. Eddie hasn't seen them, but he might have heard the baby. We'll wait until he's out of sight before moving them to the retrieval vehicle."

The agent grinned. "You seem to have everything under control. Do you often take care of entire missions on your own?"

"You have no idea," Hannah replied.

Chapter Two

Hannah always loved to treat herself after a successful mission, and as the next day was Saturday, she convinced her fellow Banana Girls to join her for a late lunch at their favorite waffle restaurant south of the Georgia Tech campus. Lately, anytime they were together, Hannah tried not to think about how much she would miss college life and the other girls when she graduated at the end of the school year.

She still felt unsettled about what her future held.

On the way back from lunch, she and Anna rode alone in the sporty BMW convertible affectionately dubbed Hot Banana. Anna hit two traffic lights just right—yellow threatening red—which meant they easily beat the other girls into the parking garage.

Hannah jumped out of Hot Banana and raced past their fleet of yellow vehicles to the high-security, private elevator to the penthouse. "C'mon, Anna," she called over her shoulder. "You know how I hate to lose."

"I'm coming," Anna said patiently, sliding through the doors just as they closed.

As the elevator rocketed toward the top floor, Hannah reached out and pressed the buttons of the floors they passed, all the while peeking sidelong at her tall friend like a mischievous child.

"Hannah, that's not very nice," Anna warned. She sounded stern, but Hannah could hear the laughter in her voice. "Just because they don't know all the best shortcuts in Midtown doesn't mean we should strand them in the garage."

Hannah huffed. "It's not like they're stuck down there forever. They just have to wait for the elevator."

"An elevator that's going to stop at every single floor, thanks to you."

"We weren't allowed to haze them; the least we can do is put the new girls in their place," Hannah replied with a grin.

Anna laughed. "New girls? We recruited Katie and Susan over a year ago. Even Mari has been with us for several months."

They walked down the hall toward the door to Club Banana. Hannah gave her best friend an innocent smile. "It can't hurt to remind them that we were the first," she said as she pushed the penthouse door open

Hannah froze in the doorway. Something smelled off.

Though they did sometimes welcome male visitors—Katie had a long procession of boys coming to study with her—the scent of this particular cologne was strong and unfamiliar.

Hannah crept along the short foyer, her body tensed for combat, her back against the wall. Anna followed right behind her, equally prepared to do battle.

When they reached the living room, Hannah saw a man standing in front of the full-wall video screen, hands in his pockets, looking around the room in awe. He was in his early-twenties—probably twenty-two or twenty-three—fair skin, nondescript dark-blondish hair, and medium build; not stocky, but not thin either. Hannah relaxed when she realized that she and Anna could take him, if necessary.

"This is a nice place you've got here." He glanced their way. "I did knock, by the way, but no one answered, so I let myself in."

Club Banana—along with all access points to the top floor of the luxury condominium tower—was completely secure. The only way the elevator would even open on the penthouse floor was after an encrypted key scan or special remote clearance plus on-site biometric authentication. It would take a ninja of the highest order to have bypassed all that. And this guy didn't appear to be that kind of ninja. Or any kind of ninja.

"How did you get in here?" Hannah demanded.

The guy continued glancing around the room in an aggravatingly casual way. "It's a simple enough process of sending the encrypted codes between federal facilities. But I must say, this one is quite high-end."

Hannah bristled. "This isn't a government facility. It's our home."

Anna held up a calming hand toward Hannah before addressing the stranger. "Perhaps you could tell us *who* let you in."

"Oh, I have my connections. My boss and your boss go way back," he said with a grin.

Though the Banana Girls weren't technically a part of any particular government agency—they were more like independent contractors—this guy was clearly alluding to their federal agency liaison, Stacia Keller. Regardless of who he got the clearance from, he must have gotten it somehow, because he was standing in their living room.

"And who exactly are you?" Hannah asked dismissively.

"HSI Special Agent Jason Briggs."

Hannah's brow furrowed. "HSI?"

"Homeland Security Investigations. It's the investigative arm of the DHS. You know, the Department of Homeland Secur—"

"We know what the DHS is, thanks," Hannah said with a withering glare.

His overall attitude was giving her major flashbacks. She shared a quick glance with her friend. They'd worked with a self-absorbed federal agent once before, and it hadn't ended well. Mostly because they had initially both been attracted to him.

Fortunately, they had learned their lesson, so that wasn't likely to be a problem in this case.

"We have a small assignment for you," Agent Briggs continued, "and it's of a clandestine nature." His delivery was even more pompous than his introduction.

Hannah put a hand to her mouth in mock surprise. "Really?! You mean like a secret spy mission?" she asked sarcastically.

Annoyance flashed across Agent Brigg's face. Hannah chalked a win in her annoy-annoying-people column.

"You know, Agent Briggs, we usually receive our assignments from Director Keller," Anna explained calmly. "Are you supposed to be a new handler or something?"

He gave her a condescending smile. "You can call me Jason. And I've never liked the term *handler*. It seems too rough." He grinned as if something funny had just occurred to him. "Not that I couldn't handle you ladies," he said.

Hannah had the sudden urge to throttle him. She glanced at Anna, who looked like she was barely holding her composure.

Jason continued, oblivious, "No, consider this a recruiting trip. Because of the nature of the assignment, we need a woman to join the team. I was told you ladies were the best, which I'm sure is true up to a point."

"What's that supposed to mean?" Hannah snapped.

"Just that you girls obviously have a special skill set. I'm sure you do a great job—within the scope of female assignments. My boss tells me that you've even helped out on a case or two."

Before the impulse to launch herself over the couch and slowly strangle this smug pile of masculinity had even been processed as a signal from Hannah's brain to her muscles, Anna's firm grip closed on her elbow. Her friend gave her a warning look.

How did Anna always know exactly when she was about to attack someone? It ruined all the fun.

Jason turned and walked away from the girls, a mistake that would have cost him a broken bone—at the very least—had they been true enemies. Hannah kept her eyes fixed on Jason as he meandered around the room. Under her not-so-cool exterior, Hannah's insides spewed lava. How dare this guy come into their condo and start making snide remarks and veiled insults!

From an end table on the other side of the room, Jason picked up a decorative fan that Katie had been given by a friend in Japan. He casually twirled it, his back to the girls. "I suspect there are other reasons why the powers-that-be keep your group active. Certain . . . shall we say . . . *intangibles*."

The sneer in his voice put her over the edge. "That's it," Hannah muttered. She moved around Anna's attempt at a body block and was three steps across the room when Anna grabbed her by the wrist, barely catching her before she pummeled the jerk who was completely obvious that his life had nearly come to an end.

"Let go," Hannah hissed.

"You can't kill our guests, Hannah. You know that," Anna whispered back.

Hannah huffed. "I wasn't going to kill him . . . much."

"Let him dig his own grave," Anna said, firmly pulling Hannah to sit on the sofa beside her.

Jason finished inspecting the fan and set it back down on the end table before turning to face the girls. "Now it's just a question of which of you *spy* girls will take the mission."

Hannah felt her blood boil at the snub.

At that moment, their three other roommates spilled in through the front door, laughing the whole way.

"That was a dirty trick, Hannah," Katie said as they entered the living room.

"How do you know it was Hannah?" Mari asked, though she sounded as if she knew, too.

The girls stopped in their tracks, either thrown off by Anna and Hannah's lack of reaction or the presence of an arrogant jerk in their living room. Or both.

"Who's this?" Mari asked, stopping behind one of the couches.

"This is Special Agent Jason Briggs of the Department of Homeland Security," Anna explained. "He's here to recruit one of us for a mission."

Susan's eyebrows shot up. "That's a new one. What's the mission?" she asked.

All eyes turned to Jason. His chest puffed out at the attention. "Though the Department of State is tasked with ensuring that our citizens and government agencies comply with the Hague Adoption Convention, it's been decided that Homeland Security—through its role in Immigration and Customs Enforcement—assign a special agent from the Homeland Security Investigations agency to—"

Susan threw up her hands in a huff. "Blah, blah. Just tell us who the bad guys are."

Agent Briggs appeared flustered for a moment before continuing. "There's a local adoption agency that we suspect is engaging in illegal activity with the children it's bringing in from abroad. We'll need to investigate." He glanced at the gathered Banana Girls. "Who would be best for the mission?"

"Any of us could do it, obviously. But you haven't given us much to go on," Anna said. "Is it undercover? What are the mission parameters? How long is the mission expected to last?"

"The cover would be a married couple trying to decide which adoption agency to use," Jason replied.

"And you would be the husband to whichever of us takes the mission?" Hannah asked.

"Obviously," he said with a self-satisfied smirk. He stood there looking from one girl to the other, apparently waiting for them all to jump at the offer.

Hannah leaned over to Anna and whispered, "I'm out."

Anna stifled a laugh with her hand. She sat up straight, facing Jason. "Given my recent mission with Prince Leopold of Luxembourg, I don't think I would be a good fit. I've been in too many tabloid pictures. Not to mention I'm exhausted." Anna turned to Hannah with a guilty look. "Sorry," she whispered.

Hannah shrugged. Anna was right; she wouldn't be good for an undercover mission for a while, if ever.

"Stacia still has me working on a small assignment for her," Mari piped in. "It's my first official one since I joined the group," she added with a note of excitement.

Hannah wasn't sure she would have picked Mari for a mission like this anyway. She was too inexperienced.

"So, Mari and I are both out. What about the rest of you?" Anna asked.

Hannah glanced at Katie, hoping she would volunteer. Two agents out; that had Hannah worried.

Katie opened her mouth to say something, but Jason held up a hand toward her. "Let me stop you right there. You wouldn't be a good fit for this mission because of your heritage. The adoptions in question are coming from rural China. Even with the best disguise, it would be too difficult to hide the fact that you're—"

All four of the other Banana Girls cut him off with simultaneous sounds of disagreement. Hannah spoke first. "If you knew anything about ethnicities, you would know that Katie's family is Japanese, not Chinese. Kinda racist of you to lump them together." The other girls nodded in agreement, which made Katie smile.

Jason stared at Hannah, a broad leer on his annoying face. "If the mission were happening in Asia, then you're absolutely right, the people involved would be able to tell that Katie has Japanese, not Chinese, ancestry. But don't assume that's because their societies are so wonderfully inclusive; it's because they tend to exclude or look down on people from other ethnicities. I don't have time to go into the details of Chinese-Japanese relations right now. Let's just say that the adoption agency is here in Atlanta, and the people involved don't have the same discerning eye for ethnicities. And yes, that might be racist, or it might just be unfamiliarity. Either way, that's the reality of the mission."

When he finished with his long-winded explanation, Hannah simply glared at him.

"Thanks, Hannah," Katie said. "But I couldn't have taken it anyway. The guy I got to tutor me after my last mission doesn't really know anything. I might have to start asking for help from the smartest boys instead of the hottest boys." She said the last part as if it was the most absurd idea ever.

With a sinking feeling, Hannah realized it was down to her and Susan for the mission. Hannah gave Susan her best pleading expression, even clasping her hands together to mimic one of Susan's favorite mannerisms. Susan smiled, a look of empathy on her face, and then shrugged an apology. "Sorry," she mouthed to Hannah.

"That leaves Hannah and Susan," Anna said, looking at the last two girls.

"I can't do it," Susan said.

Hannah immediately added, "Me, neither."

Susan continued. "That public policy elective is kicking my butt with assignments like—" Susan made a pounding sound as she acted out stuff stacking up in front of her. "And there's a team project." She made an exaggerated freaked-out face. "And besides, it's—"

Anna held up a hand. "Hang on, Susan." She turned to Hannah. "You said you can't do it either."

Hannah nodded curtly. Anna tilted her head and raised her brows.

"I'm busy," Hannah replied to her friend's unspoken question.

Anna leaned toward Hannah. "Han, you're gonna have to give me more than that," she whispered.

"I just don't want to do it, okay?" Hannah said, not keeping her voice as low as she should. She glanced at Jason, but he appeared engrossed on his phone. Probably texting some girl to insult her and then ask her on a date.

"You know that's not good enough," Anna pressed. "We all have to do missions we don't like. It's part of the gig. So, unless you have something—"

"Don't worry about trying to convince her," Jason said. "I've already sent a message to your boss about it."

"You did what?!" Hannah rose from the sofa, ready to physically escort this punk out of the penthouse if necessary.

"You clearly weren't going to say yes, so I had to take matters into my own hands."

His nonchalant attitude was absolutely infuriating.

"So, when a person clearly isn't interested in something, you, what—force them to do it?" Hannah countered.

Jason folded his arms across his broad chest and glared at her. "This is a very important mission; I can't have it jeopardized because you have . . . personal issues."

"That's it." Hannah didn't care what Anna thought about killing guests; she wasn't going to stand there and let him insult them anymore.

She lunged across the small space and caught him by the shirt collar. Her momentum, combined with his surprised flinch backward, caused them to topple onto the couch behind him.

In a flash, Hannah straddled his middle, pinning him to the cushions. She held the front of his shirt crumpled in one hand while she slowly drew the other fist back. "Now, are you going to apologize for the insult, or should I introduce you to my *intangibles*?"

Hannah must not have heard the sound of the incoming video call, because the next thing she knew, the faux wall had dissolved into a video screen filled with their boss Stacia's face.

"Hi, girls," Stacia said brightly, though her smile looked a little forced. "I see you've met Agent Briggs, so the site clearance must have gone through." Aside from a slight uptick of one brow, Stacia didn't even acknowledge that Hannah was about to clobber their guest.

But Stacia's look was enough to get the message across. Hannah reluctantly stood from off Agent Briggs and sat back on the couch next to Anna.

Stacia continued the mission intro briefing as if nothing had happened. "The Department of Homeland Security has requested that one of you girls work with Agent Briggs on this case. It is very important for international relations." A hint of a smile crept across Stacia's face as she scanned the room again.

Hannah tried her best not to scowl back at their boss.

"Based on expressions I'm seeing and the extracurricular activities I just saw, I'm going to guess that Hannah volunteered," Stacia said.

Anna let out a snort of a laugh that Hannah answered with a glare. Anna shrugged back. "Hey, it's not my fault she can read you so well."

Hannah turned to the screen. "Please, Stacia, I'd really rather not take this one."

"When was your last assignment?" Stacia asked.

"Last night. I helped get Carissa Grayson and her son out of their house and into protective custody. Her husband showed up, so I also—"

"I mean a full mission assignment," Stacia amended.

Hannah stopped mid-sentence in her explanation. She'd known that last night's events didn't really count in terms of new mission assignments. "July," Hannah begrudgingly replied.

Stacia nodded. "And are you caught up in all of your classes?"

Hannah let out a frustrated sigh. "I guess," she said.

"Then I need you to take this one, Hannah," Stacia said with a commiserating smile.

Hannah frowned and folded her arms. She wanted to huff and throw a fit and stomp out of the room, but that only worked on her father. And truthfully, it hadn't really worked on him in a few years. Finally, she nodded her agreement.

Stacia smiled. "Thanks, Hannah. Agent Briggs will bring you up to speed on the rest of the details. And I know you'll be great. You always are." Stacia spared a quick glance for the rest of the room.

"Thanks, Stacia. That was a big help," Jason said with a smug grin.

Almost instantly, Stacia's smile evaporated as she turned her gaze on Jason. "Mr. Briggs, my girls call me Stacia because . . . they're *my* girls." Her brow ticked up the way it did when she was annoyed. "You, however, will call me Director Keller or Ms. Keller. I will also accept Agent Keller, as that would still be an appropriate title." She glared through the screen at the arrogant agent. "Are we clear on that?"

"Yes, ma'am," Jason quickly replied. "My apologies, Director Keller."

Hannah smiled to herself. It was nice to see this egotistical jerk put in his place. The one thing that could be said in his favor so far was that he knew how to make a hasty and proper apology. That, and he actually did have nice hair. Not that it mattered.

"Good," Stacia said with a curt nod. "I assume you all can take it from here. Good luck, Hannah." She paused for a moment, staring at her. "At least you won't have to worry about your Rule Number One," Stacia whispered conspiratorially. A second later, her image vanished.

The Banana Girls all looked at Hannah, their faces full of sympathy and understanding. They'd all had missions they hadn't wanted. Well, maybe not Mari. Yet. Of course, she probably hadn't wanted to risk her life going undercover to save her mother, so maybe she understood, too.

"Just great," Hannah muttered under her breath. Stacia was right. Rule Number One—the Banana Girl's oft-repeated, frequently broken rule to not get romantically involved with a guy during a mission—would definitely not be a problem in this case.

Anna squeezed her arm. "Stacia's right; you'll be great."

"Excellent." Jason clapped his hands together. "Hannah, I'll forward the mission summary to you, and then we can sit down and discuss it once you've had a chance to review everything. How about lunch next week?"

Hannah couldn't believe this was happening. She stalked over to her favorite lounge chair in the corner and slumped into it, heaving a huge sigh as she did. Would this aggravating agent even realize the trouble he was putting her through?

Jason took a few steps toward her and lowered his voice. "You know, I understand that you might have overstated your class situation to Director Keller. I'd be happy to help you with any assignments you might be struggling with."

He was condescending even when he was trying to be accommodating.

Hannah's stare shot daggers. "If I'd had the excuse of falling behind in class, don't you think I would have used it to get out of doing this mission with you?"

"Fine." He shrugged. "But my favorite burger joint is near campus, so I'll be around if you need."

Jason smiled at her for a moment. Or it might have been a smirk, it was hard to say. Then he turned and walked across the living room, nodding at the other girls on his way out.

As the slam of the door echoed through the large penthouse, Hannah wondered what she had just gotten herself into.

Chapter Three

H ANNAH HADN'T BEEN ABLE to come up with a plausible reason why she shouldn't meet her new mission partner for lunch, so after putting him off for three days, she finally agreed.

She walked into the hamburger restaurant northwest of campus at fifteen minutes past twelve. The place was pretty full for a Tuesday. Groups of students sat eating and visiting at the various tables and booths. She scanned the small eating area until she saw Jason sitting at a booth in the corner. He must have already ordered his food, because only a few bites of a burger remained on his plate.

"You're late," he said with his mouth half full. "Doesn't that fancy condo of yours have any clocks?"

Hannah glanced at her watch. "What are you talking about? I'm fifteen minutes early."

"I said to meet me here at 11:30," Jason replied.

Hannah pulled out her phone and scrolled past a handful of messages until she found his. She double-checked the time then held it out for Jason to see. "It's right there in your message. 12:30."

Jason stared hard at the screen for several seconds, as if that would change the number. Finally, he sat back and looked up at her. "Must have been a typo. You know how sometimes you try to touch the same character twice but the tiny smartphone keyboard thinks you meant to do the character next to it. That's what must have happened when I tried to type 11:30." He held up his hands to indicate that there wasn't much else he could have done about it. "Did you get a chance to review the mission summary?"

Hannah slid into the bench across from him. "Yeah, and we've got a problem right off the bat. It says we'll be posing as a social media influencer couple. There's no way we can build up a social media account with enough followers to be considered influencers. That would take months, if not years." Hannah really hoped she could submarine the mission right out of the gate.

"Not a problem," Jason said as he licked ketchup from his finger.

Hannah glared back at him. "How is that not a problem?"

Jason fished his phone from his pocket. A few taps and swipes later, he slid it across the table to her. A video started playing, showing a cute couple hugging and dancing in what must have been a new home. As the couple pulled back from their hug, Hannah gasped out loud. There before her eyes, she watched herself walk through a stylishly decorated living room into a bedroom that was clearly meant for a new baby. It was the strangest feeling as her mind fought with her eyes. Even though her brain knew she couldn't be the girl in the video—she had never been in that room or that house—she couldn't help second-guessing herself. It looked so real.

Jason must have noticed her dismay. "Deep fake," he said through his last bite of burger.

Hannah shook her head in awe. "I've heard about this technology, but I had no idea it could be this realistic." She watched her doppelganger dangle a stuffed purple unicorn in front of the camera.

Jason spoke again, through a mouthful of tater tots this time. "The agency found a newlywed couple with a small social media presence but plenty of videos. The acquisition was completed in time to finish up the deep fake process and bulk up their following from a few dozen to a few million."

Hannah glanced down at the follower number. It was indeed above four million. "Are these followers all agency fakes?"

Jason shrugged. "I'm not sure how the agency works its magic, but probably so. That, or maybe they hack other people's accounts to follow us."

Hannah shook her head as she watched the digital copy of herself sit in a rocking chair, smiling around at the furnished nursery. "Wait. You said a newlywed couple. Does that mean—"

Before she could finish, the video answered her unspoken question. The camera shifted around and Jason's face loomed on the screen. He had a few days' stubble on his cheeks and his gray-blue eyes looked so happy. Hannah was forced to begrudgingly admit—only to herself, of course—that this digital version of Agent Briggs, with his sandy blond hair, broad shoulders, and athletic build, was relatively attractive. She glanced up at the real thing sitting across the table snarfing down tots. Not quite as appealing as the pretend version.

The fake Jason held the camera at arm's length and moved toward the fake Hannah. Unfortunately, Hannah realized a split second too late what was about to happen. To her horror, she watched the fake Jason bend down close and kiss the fake Hannah full on the lips. It was the most disconcerting feeling she had ever experienced—dislike and disbelief warring with a tiny spark of desire inside her. Determined to keep her emotions in check, she slid the phone back across the table to her mission partner and soon-to-be fake husband.

Jason glanced at the phone and grinned. "That's an interesting part."

Hannah wasn't sure, but she thought she caught the hint of a blush creeping into his cheeks. Unwilling to consider what he might think about the completely fabricated scene, Hannah glanced around the restaurant, trying to come up with something else to discuss. She definitely did not want to talk about the kiss they'd shared—or not shared. Her whole concept of seeing is believing had been thrown topsy-turvy.

She decided sticking to the mission was the best bet. "So, what was the video about?"

"Several of the early videos show the couple—us—remodeling that room to be used as a nursery. That's the one where they finally finish and celebrate," he said.

"And what do the rest of the videos show?" Hannah asked.

A hint of sadness crept into Jason's expression. "The overall tone of the videos goes from hopeful and optimistic to discouraged and gloomy."

Hannah realized where things must have gone if the footage could be used for their mission. "They weren't ever able to have children?" It didn't really matter, but suddenly she wanted to know what had happened to this now-faceless couple.

When Jason finally looked at her, his expression was somber. He shook his head. "No. They weren't." He took a deep breath. "But that's where our story begins. We'll approach the local adoption agency posing as a childless couple looking to adopt a kid from China."

"Why China?" Hannah asked.

"We've uncovered a few recent international adoptions that are in violation of the Hague Adoption Convention. They've all been from China," Jason answered as he grabbed another handful of tots.

"You mentioned this Hague thing before. What's that about?" Hannah asked, somewhat interested now.

"It's an agreement between countries that they will put safeguards in place to prevent children from being bought and sold for adoptions."

"So, if Chinese adoptions are breaking the agreement, why don't you just tell the Chinese government they have a problem and be done with it?" Hannah said.

Jason glanced up from his meal. "Governments can sometimes act like parents when it comes to their citizens."

Hannah shook her head, hopefully conveying that she had no idea what he was talking about.

"You've never tried to tell a parent that their kid is misbehaving, have you?" he asked.

"No," she said with a shrug. Hannah tried not to feel embarrassed about her lack of experience with children. As an only child, her interactions with kids had been limited to the elementary school playground.

"Well, it usually doesn't go well. Parents—as well as diplomatic representatives—get defensive and irrational about the flaws in their children—or citizens. Rather than cause an international incident, my superiors decided we should investigate things on our end first."

Hannah sighed. "Fine. But if you know the adoption agency that's breaking the law, why don't you just arrest them?" There had to be a way to get this mission canceled, and Hannah was determined to find it.

"Arrest everyone at the adoption agency?" Jason looked up in surprise.

Hannah rolled her eyes at his ability to willfully misunderstand her. "No, of course not. Obviously, they're not all guilty. But one of them must be. You could hold them all for questioning until you figure out which one is guilty and then arrest that person."

He gave her a look that was equal parts incredulous and patronizing. "Let me guess, your team is more the 'shoot first, ask questions later' type. Am I right?"

Hannah huffed. "Actually, we usually try not to shoot at all." He was one to talk. Hannah had already caught sight of his shoulder holster. Was Special Agent Briggs going to blast their way into the adoption agency?

"Well, we can't just round them all up for questioning. That would tip our hand in terms of the investigation. Besides, there's a chance it's not the agency at all," Jason said. "In fact, my money is on one of the other influencer couples."

Hannah sat up. "Other influencers?"

Jason cocked his head to the side. "Didn't I tell you about this agency's main clientele?"

"No," she replied with a deadpan look. He'd better not make a habit of this, or she wouldn't last a day with him as a partner.

"The adoption agency apparently partnered with a few social media influencers," Jason explained. "There's been a recent trend for popular social media couples who plan to adopt to share the process with their followers. The agency probably hoped it would bring in more clients."

Hannah frowned. "But how would it benefit the influencer couples? Would they get a finder's fee or something?"

"There's no finder's bonus, as far as we can tell," Jason said, as he popped a tater tot in his mouth. "But my bet is that someone is getting a piece of the action somewhere along the adoption pipeline. We won't know until we start investigating the other couples."

Hannah slumped back in her chair, out of ideas to sabotage her new assignment. "I don't see what the big fuss is about anyway," she muttered, glancing at a couple in a nearby booth. "The orphans would probably be way better off here in the U.S. than the country they came from."

Jason stared at her, a look of mild disappointment on his face. After a moment, he glanced at his watch and suddenly stood, tilting his head for Hannah to follow. "C'mon. I need to show you something. It'll help you understand things better."

"But I haven't eaten anything yet," Hannah protested.

Jason looked down at the empty space in front of her with a surprised expression. "What have you been doing this whole time?" Before Hannah had a chance to answer, he continued, "Actually, it doesn't matter. We have to leave now or we'll be late." He reached down, grabbed Hannah's wrist, and started to pull her out of her seat.

Fighting the instinctive reaction to reverse his hold and flip him onto the tile floor, Hannah hooked her ankle around the booth's support post and tensed her muscles. "Why are you touching me?" She whispered through gritted teeth. Despite the obvious stares of curious onlookers, she glared daggers at him.

"I'm helping you up." Based on his tone, he clearly questioned her mental capacity to figure out the obvious.

Hannah continued her struggle against his strong grip and very noticeably muscular arm. "Does it look like I need help standing up?"

Jason scowled back at her. "Obviously. Because you don't seem able to do it at the moment."

His grip on her arm was still firm, but now he apparently wanted to get into a staring contest. He had no idea who he was dealing with.

They held each other's gazes, unspoken threats flying both ways, until Hannah finally spoke. "I'm not leaving without something to eat."

Jason blinked. "Fine." Releasing her wrist, he grabbed the half-empty pouch of tater tots from his tray. "Here, you can have these. Most girls I've eaten lunch with barely touch their food anyway." He slid the pouch across the table. "But you have to eat them on the way. We need to get going."

Hannah barely caught the tots as they landed in her lap. She wanted to jump out of her seat and show the arrogant special agent what a girl could do on a full stomach, but unfortunately, she had missed breakfast, too. Besides, it would probably have caused a scene and jeopardized the mission.

She had thought working with Agent Briggs would try her patience. Now she realized it would be a miracle if they both survived.

Jason took a few steps away from the table and turned around. He held out his hands as if he couldn't believe she was still sitting. "C'mon, Hannah, this meeting is important." There was a note of pleading in his voice that softened her just a little.

Hannah slowly and deliberately stood and walked toward him. When she was close enough to whisper, she paused. "It's not my fault your fat thumbs can't push the right numbers. You don't have to be a jerk about it." She lifted her chin and brushed past him before he had a chance to answer. A moment later she called loudly over her shoulder, "And you forgot to leave a tip." A mischievous grin spread across Hannah's face as several dozen eyes swiveled in Jason's direction.

Outside the restaurant, Hannah stood on the sidewalk, popping tater tots in her mouth and staring around the parking lot with her most bored expression.

A few seconds later, Jason joined her. "You know, when the restaurant has you order from the counter, you don't technically have to leave a—"

"What took you so long? Didn't you say we were in a hurry?" Hannah popped another tot in her mouth and smiled sweetly.

Jason's mouth hung open. He blinked several times before shaking his head and walking toward a nearby car. Hannah followed him, reveling in the small victory.

She had won the staring contest and then burned him in front of the whole restaurant. Maybe this mission wouldn't be so bad after all.

Once in the car, Jason tore out of the parking lot, squealing the tires of the small, white coupe twice as he banked around tight turns. He didn't say anything intelligible—simply shaking his head, casting her side-long glances, and muttering to himself—until they were several miles from the restaurant. The stores and stop lights slowly gave way to yards and hedges.

Finally, he took a deep breath and said, "We're going to see the Phelps, a couple that recently adopted a child from China. They know I am a federal agent, so we won't need to use our undercover personas. We do need to work through our undercover relationship at some point, though, so that it can come across as authentic."

The idea of being in a relationship with this guy—even a pretend one—made Hannah's stomach turn. She put on a false smile and nodded. "I'm sure we can make up something sappy sweet."

He glanced at her, perhaps unsure which was her true personality. That was good. Hannah liked to keep guys guessing. It was much safer that way.

Five minutes later, Jason pulled into a small neighborhood of mansions. These were ten-million-dollar houses—minimum. Hannah would know.

Jason parked along the edge of the manicured driveway and got out. Hannah joined him at the front door of the beige and gray stone house. He knocked and rang the doorbell, which Hannah thought was rather presumptuous.

After half a minute, no one had come to the door, and Jason was clearly getting impatient. He pulled out his cellphone and tapped out a quick message.

"You calling in backup so we can bash in the door?" Hannah joked.

Jason glanced up at her with a scowl. "I'm texting Brandon to apologize for being late."

Hannah raised her brows, unsure whether Jason was planning to explain who Brandon was. He didn't.

A few seconds later, Jason's phone buzzed. He read the message and said, "He says they're in the backyard and we should go around the side." He set off, leaving her standing alone on the porch.

Hannah shrugged to no one in particular. Apparently, this mission was going to be chock-full of this type of interaction. She wondered if Special Agent Briggs had any idea how obnoxious his personality was.

Hannah and Jason made their way through an elaborate terraced garden overflowing with green until they reached a small gazebo next to an enormous wood swing set that was more like a castle. A young couple who looked to be in their early thirties welcomed them. Jason introduced the pair as Brandon and Kayla Phelps. Brandon was tall, easily over six feet, and very slim, almost nerdy-looking. Kayla was medium height and build. They both had beautiful brown skin, like her best friend Anna's. Their attire matched the lush surroundings of the garden and gazebo, classy but casual.

As they made small talk, a little boy ran up and nearly tackled Kayla at the knees. Brandon invited Jason and Hannah to sit, and Kayla joined them, hefting the child onto her lap. Even without Jason's explanation in the car, it would have been obvious that the boy was adopted.

"This is Jinhai," Kayla said, attempting to coax the boy out of his shyness.

"Why don't you two tell Hannah some of the story you've told me," Jason said.

Brandon took a deep breath and glanced at Kayla. "Well, I guess it starts with us trying—unsuccessfully—to have children. One of the other startup owners in my networking group mentioned an adoption agency he knew about. He said they catered to couples who could pay to have the process completely taken care of for them."

Kayla joined in the explanation. "He also told us about the family support group that the agency was a part of, and it sounded wonderful—family picnics, learning seminars, retreats. It was exactly what we were looking for."

"The adoption trip was like an exotic vacation. Everything was orchestrated leading up to the picture-perfect moment when we met Jinhai." Brandon reached over and poked Jinhai in the chest, eliciting a cascade of giggles.

"We didn't expect things to always go perfectly," Kayla said. "And we had been warned that the adjustment to a new family would probably be difficult for Jinhai." She kissed the squirming boy on the top of his head before letting him down to go play.

Hannah watched him go, knowing based on Kayla's tone that there was definitely more story between the idyllic opening and the current, happy-family-in-the-backyard scene. When she turned back, Hannah saw tears in Kayla's eyes.

"He cried himself to sleep every night," Kayla said, choking back her emotions. "For weeks and weeks . . ."

Hannah swallowed against a lump in her throat. She knew what that was like.

When Kayla couldn't continue, Brandon squeezed her hand and picked up the narrative. "Obviously, he couldn't tell us what was wrong; despite our best efforts to teach him English, he couldn't really tell us what he was feeling." He paused and smiled sadly at Kayla. "About a month after the adoption, we were at a get-together with Kayla's family, and Jinhai started playing with our niece, Anika. She's a little bit older than Jinhai, but they had fun together."

"Anika's in a Chinese immersion program at her elementary school," Kayla added. "And it was amazing to watch Jinhai open up after a few minutes of playing together. We had never heard him speak more than two words at a time, and here he was jabbering on and on. And even though we couldn't understand him, it just made us so happy . . ." Kayla trailed off as her voice filled with emotion again.

"We thought it was a breakthrough," Brandon added. "That we would finally be able to communicate with Jinhai and make a real connection. But then," he paused and shared a glance with Kayla. "After a few hours of playing together, Anika approached us with some startling news."

Hannah realized she was leaning forward in her chair, anticipating what would come next, eager and worried at the same time.

"Jinhai told her that he missed his mom and dad. Obviously, Anika thought she meant us,"—Brandon gestured between Kayla and himself—"but when she offered to go get us, Jinhai told her that he missed his other mom and dad from before. He told Anika all about his village and his parents and . . . the day he was taken away from them."

Hannah let out a long breath as Brandon's word sunk in. "Jinhai wasn't an orphan?" she asked softly.

Kayla shook her head, a tear running down her cheek.

"That's when we got involved," Jason volunteered. "Brandon called the authorities, and they put him in touch with our office here in Atlanta. We're hoping our investigation can figure out what went wrong in the adoption process and who's responsible."

Hannah nodded, trying to digest the information and what would need to be done next. "How old is Jinhai?" she asked.

Kayla lifted a shoulder. "We don't really know. The adoption agency didn't give us any information about his birthday or age. When we first saw him, we thought he was probably three years old. But I've taken him to the pediatrician, and she says that Jinhai is probably four, maybe even five. He's just very small for his age."

Hannah gazed out into the yard where Jinhai was kicking a ball around. She looked back at Brandon and Kayla then at Jason. "What happens to Jinhai now?" For some reason, the future of this little family was suddenly important to her.

The couple shared a sad look but didn't answer.

Jason blew out a breath. "We don't really know. A lot will depend on what we find out in our investigation," he said.

"We just want Jinhai to be happy," Brandon added, his voice cracking on the last word. Kayla sniffed and wiped more tears from her cheeks.

The four of them sat in silence for several moments, weighed down by the gravity and sadness of the situation. Finally, Jason thanked them for their time, telling them that he would keep them updated on the progress of the investigation. As Jason and Hannah stood to leave, Jinhai approached Kayla again, wrapping his arms around her leg and clutching the fabric of her loose pants.

"Can you say goodbye, Jinhai?" Kayla said as she put an arm around his shoulder.

The little boy smiled shyly and waved a pudgy hand at Hannah. "Bye," he said softly before burying his face behind Kayla's leg.

Hannah wasn't fully aware of the next minute or two as she followed Jason back around the house to his car. Her heart swirled with emotions. Disappointment for the Phelps. Pity for little Jinhai who had lost his family. And even a little bit of envy because of the obvious love that Brandon and Kayla had for that little boy. Hannah would have given anything to have gotten even half that much attention from her own mother.

She plopped down into the passenger seat and stared blankly out the window.

Jason slid into the driver's side but didn't start the car. After a moment, he said quietly, "This is what the mission is all about." He held out a hand toward the Phelps' home. "We're not trying to deny orphans the chance at a better life or prevent couples from adopting them. We just want to make sure that the children who have families in China get to stay with them."

Hannah gazed unfocused out the window. She took a deep breath and steeled herself for what she knew lay ahead. Then she focused on her partner again and nodded curtly. "I'm in. What do we do next?"

CHAPTER FOUR

L ATER THAT WEEK, HANNAH sat in her room in the middle of the afternoon, counting the minutes and wishing for an escape. When the penthouse door chime rang, she breathed a sigh of relief. Not because she was looking forward to seeing Jason again, but because Katie was nearly driving her crazy.

They had tried on a dozen different outfits until Katie was satisfied that Hannah could pass as a fashionable social media influencer. It wasn't that Hannah's normal style was overly shabby. She could probably thank her mother for her extremely expensive taste in clothing brands. But in Katie's opinion, the majority of Hannah's outfits were too casual, too cozy. Hannah told her it was called *comfortable chic*.

Katie had cordoned off three quarters of Hannah's closet after that comment.

Hannah didn't think there was anything wrong with comfortable.

They finally settled on a tan sweater paired with black jeans and closed sandals with just enough heel to hide their standard multipurpose tool—knife, file, saw, lock-picker—in case she needed it.

Even though it was out of character, Hannah raced to the door after hearing the bell. Normally, she let Katie or one of the other girls get it, even when she knew it was someone coming to see her. But this time she answered it because she didn't want Jason inside their condo any more than absolutely necessary. Not because she didn't trust his security clearance—she obviously did—or because his behavior wouldn't elicit a plentiful amount of sympathy from her roommates—it definitely would—but because she wanted to skip the pleasantries and get on with the mission of saving kids.

Plus, she hoped to minimize the time she was forced to spend with her partner and his aggravating behavior.

Jason stood in the hall, a small smirk on his face. Hannah slipped through the door, not even calling goodbye to her friends.

As they walked down the hall toward the elevator, Jason cleared his throat. "So, which way do you prefer holding hands when we walk together?"

"What?" Hannah spluttered.

Before she could even react, Jason reached down and grabbed her hand. "Would it be more comfortable with my hand in front,"—he switched their hands so that his was in the back—"or do you want yours in front? Or maybe—"

When he started to intertwine their fingers, Hannah abruptly pulled her hand away from his grip. "No, no, no. Definitely not like that." She pressed her hand against her leg as if she could wipe off his touch and took a calming breath as she pressed the elevator call button.

They waited in silence until the doors opened.

"I don't see why it matters." Hannah entered the waiting elevator and held the door for him.

Jason paused on the threshold before taking a deep breath and stepping in with her. Hannah pushed the button for the lobby. When she turned to continue their conversation, her partner was pacing back and forth in the small space.

"Are we really going to be holding hands that much?" she asked.

Jason didn't answer right away. Every few seconds, his gaze flitted to the digital readout above the door. He shook his head absently, but Hannah wasn't sure if it was in answer to her question or a reaction to something else.

Was Jason afraid of elevators?

The elevator came to a stop at the lobby, and Jason was out before the doors were even half open.

He took a breath and rolled his shoulders. Then he turned back to her almost as if nothing had happened. "Our cover is that we've been married for nearly five years. Don't you think a couple that's been together that long would have a very comfortable—and consistent—way of holding hands?"

Hannah filed the elevator incident away in her mind. She'd have to think about that some other time; right now, they had work to do. She shrugged in response to his question. "Maybe we're not openly affectionate."

"I guess if I were married to you, I wouldn't be," Jason said under his breath.

He immediately turned and strode across the lobby atrium, leaving Hannah behind, her mouth agape. She followed him toward the large exterior doors, completely ignoring Thomas, the front desk attendant. "What's that supposed to mean?" she asked once they were outside.

Stopping at the driver's side door of his car, Jason shook his head. "Nothing. I just mean that you might need to act not like yourself for the mission."

Hannah looked at him over the top of the car. "Same goes for you."

"Fine, we'll both need to act differently if we're going to fool anyone into thinking we're actually romantically involved."

Though she agreed with the sentiment, Hannah bristled at the implication that she would be difficult to be married to. "So, you'll be less rude and chauvinistic, and I'll be a little more warm and pleasant."

They sat down in the car, and he started the engine. "A little more?" he scoffed. "How about at all?" He maneuvered the coupe through the small parking lot. "And what do you mean 'rude and chauvinistic'?"

Hannah heaved a theatrical sigh that would have made Susan proud. "I'm not sure we have enough time in the mission for me to list all the examples."

Jason scowled and grumbled something under his breath, his hands twisting back and forth on the steering wheel as he waited to pull into traffic. Apparently, she really knew how to get under his skin. That might come in handy.

After several blocks of silence, Jason appeared to relax a bit. "Let's just say that we'll have to use our best performance skills if we're going to pull off the happy couple act."

Hannah knew he was right, so she resisted the urge to needle him again. "Agreed. We'll both need to compromise to make this marriage work."

Jason's head whipped toward her, an alarmed expression on his face.

"The mission marriage," Hannah clarified.

His face relaxed into a relieved smile. "Right. The fake marriage."

During the twenty-minute drive to the adoption agency, Hannah and Jason went back and forth on the details of their cover relationship. They were Hannah and Jason Sterling. They met in college—Georgia Tech, obviously—about seven years ago. On a whim, they married a year to the day after their graduation ceremony. They just passed their four-year anniversary last spring. They've been trying to have kids the entire time with no luck. They follow one of the other influencer couples and found out about Eastern Seas Adoption Agency.

"What got you into social media?" Jason asked.

For a moment, Hannah was about to say she hated social media—except when her pictures got hundreds of likes. She had to remind herself that he was talking about her fake persona. "Probably because I wear stylish clothing and I'm gorgeous," she said flippantly. That seemed to describe most influencers, unless they had a specific skill. Too bad she couldn't have a ninja-girl channel.

"True. But I feel like it needs to be something more unique," Jason said.

He hadn't objected or made some snide comment about her self-appraisal. In fact, he'd agreed with her. That was surprising.

"I got it. What if you started it as a hair-styling channel and then it evolved after you got married?" Jason suggested.

Hannah shook her head. "I'm horrible with hair."

Jason glanced at her hair, and Hannah suddenly felt incredibly self-conscious. "Really? It looks fine," he said.

"This was all Susan." She pointed to two simple twisted braids that Susan had used to create a hair waterfall in the back.

Jason shrugged and turned his attention back to the road. "Well, it doesn't really matter. You could fake it. Or you could come up with something else. I doubt anyone at the adoption agency is going to ask how you became an influencer."

They drove on in silence for a few minutes before Hannah had an unlikely, though terrifying, possibility occur to her. "We won't have to actually adopt a child together, will we?" She playfully wrinkled her nose to show that she was joking—mostly.

Jason looked dumbfounded. "Uh, no. That's not really possible."

Hannah hid her smile by glancing out the window. "Good. I'm not really good with children." It was an uncharacteristic admission that she made mostly under her breath.

She always told herself that the reason she wasn't good with kids was simple; she'd rarely ever been around them. But after holding baby Freddie and watching little Jinhai play, for the first time in her life, she wondered if there was more to it than unfamiliarity.

Maybe her aversion to children was a safety mechanism against someday finding out that she was innately horrible at caring for a child.

Like her mother had been.

She pushed those thoughts aside with the resolution to never be like her mother. It wasn't the first time she'd made that promise to herself, and it probably wouldn't be the last.

Jason spoke, pulling her back to their efforts to prepare for the interview. "You'll probably want to come up with a few things about me that you think are adorable," he said. "I mean, most couples have that cute stuff that they could tell people who want to know about their relationship."

A short, aggravated grunt escaped before Hannah could stop it.

Jason glanced at her. "What? You don't think that's a normal thing for couples?"

"Oh, I'm sure it's a normal thing," Hannah said. "But we don't have that kind of time. Let's focus on the basics for now. We're on our way to our first performance."

"Okay, what about affectionate mannerisms? Like, when we're near each other, do you put your hand on my arm or my shoulder? Or maybe you run your fingers through the back of my hair." Jason glanced her way as he drove. "You could try it out right now."

Hannah fought the sudden lurch in her stomach. She shook her head. "That's *so* not happening."

He chuckled. "You're a highly skilled undercover agent, trained to assume any identity in any situation, but you can't pretend to be affectionate with me?"

Hannah stiffened. "I can act friendly and flirty whenever the mission requires it. But I'm not going to practice it here in the car with you."

Jason shrugged. "Suit yourself."

"Let's just stick to the stuff we already talked about. Things we're most likely to get asked, like how we met and . . . fell in love." Hannah could hardly believe she hadn't choked on the phrase.

He must have noticed her hesitation because a smug grin spread across his face.

In previous missions, Hannah had strutted her stuff, come on strong, even pulled guys into the shadows and attacked them—romantically speaking. But they had been strangers, and the mission—not to mention her safety—had always required it. Five minutes of making out with a disgusting criminal so that later she had the satisfaction of slamming him to the ground and watching him be dragged off to jail was far preferable—and oddly satisfying—compared to a mission where she would need to play the part of the doting wife to an insensitive jerk for days or even weeks on end.

Hannah had never failed to step up when something had to be done, but she was beginning to have doubts about acting romantic with Jason. Could she pretend to be in love with him for that long without a payoff at the end?

Maybe she could rough him up afterward.

A small smile played across her lips at the thought.

They pulled into the parking lot of a long row of business suites and found an open space in front of a small office with the words *Eastern Seas Adoption Agency* above the door.

Jason jumped out of the car and ran around to Hannah's side. His face fell when Hannah opened the door and stepped out before he got there.

"I can open my own door," she said.

"Yeah, I know. I just thought a husband might . . ." He shrugged and held out his hand to her.

For a split second, Hannah stared down at it, wondering what he wanted her to do. Fortunately, her training kicked in. She took his hand, hoping that the weird sensation she felt didn't show on her face.

Relationships were usually awkward at the beginning; she'd had plenty that started that way.

But why did that have to apply to a fake relationship?

At the front door, they paused. When she glanced over at him, his eyebrows were up in a questioning expression.

"So now you want me to open *this* door for you?" Jason asked sarcastically.

The front door of the agency swung his direction. There was no way she could open it with her free hand without doing a pirouette. It would be much easier if he opened it with his free hand.

She lifted their clasped hands slightly to show him how difficult it would be. "Yeah. Obviously."

Jason rolled his eyes, muttered something unintelligible, and pasted a fake smile on his face as he pulled the door open. Hannah proceeded awkwardly next to him as they squeezed through the door.

A woman in her late twenties sat at a small desk tucked in the back of a pleasantly decorated reception area. She stood and approached when they entered.

"Welcome to Eastern Seas Adoption," she said, extending her hand to them. "I'm Sandra. How can I help you?"

Jason shook hands with Sandra. "We're the Sterlings. We have an appointment with Bethany Clark."

Sandra smiled. She was several inches shorter than Hannah, with hazel eyes and shoulder-length light-brown hair. "Wonderful. I know she's looking forward to meeting both of you." Sandra tilted her head and rattled off a quick phrase in a foreign language that sounded like it could have been Chinese.

Hannah's brow furrowed, and she glanced over at Jason to make sure she hadn't heard incorrectly. Jason looked just as confused. She turned back to Sandra, who looked at her expectantly. "I'm sorry. I didn't understand you," Hannah said.

Sandra's smile grew. "That's okay. It's just a little joke here at the agency. I asked if you speak Chinese."

"Do we need to learn Chinese for the adoption?" Jason asked. He had moved quickly to the natural concern a prospective father might feel at discovering a possible obstacle in the adoption process.

Sandra laughed lightly. "No. Not at all. In fact, we find it works better when adopting parents don't know any of their child's native language. It helps the transition to the new family go much smoother."

"Do you place many children who are old enough to talk?" Hannah asked as they walked down the short hall to an open conference room.

She may have been initially caught off guard, but she wanted to do her part.

"All of the children are under three years old, so it doesn't happen very often," Sandra replied. "But children learn to speak at all ages, so it's definitely possible."

Hannah and Jason shared a quick glance, knowing that some of the children coming through the agency were definitely old enough to speak and even remember their former lives.

"Have a seat," Sandra said, indicating the chairs on the other side of the conference table. "Ms. Clark will be with you momentarily."

After Hannah sat, Jason pulled his chair right up to hers. She shot him a warning glance, but he only smiled and winked at her.

Was he teasing her now?

A moment later, a robust woman in her late-forties walked into the room. She gave them both a broad smile. "Hello, Jason and Hannah. I'm Bethany." She held out her hand across the narrow conference table. Bethany had butter-blond hair—definitely dyed—and medium brown eyes. Based on her showy wardrobe and layers of makeup, Hannah wondered if she might have been a cosmetics dealer in a former life.

Bethany settled into a chair across from them and smiled. "I like to have couples come in for an interview, just to make sure they're a good fit for our agency."

Jason and Hannah both nodded eagerly, and Jason subtly placed a hand on Hannah's knee. Apparently, he took great pleasure in annoying her with the expectations of being a happily married couple.

Either that, or he had a death wish.

Hannah attempted to casually brush his hand off her leg, but he fought her efforts with a cool poise that aggravated her even more. Eventually, their hands came to a momentary truce, clasped and resting on her knee. Hannah actually had his hand in a death grip, which she decided was preferable to giving him free rein to affectionately touch her anywhere else. They would definitely need to review boundaries later.

Hannah might also need to punch something to let off some steam.

Bethany peppered them with questions and Jason successfully rehearsed the cover story of how they met, fell in love, and got married. The story was so convincing, Hannah might have believed it herself, except that she never would have done any of those things with the annoying jerk who was currently holding her hand.

Hannah must not have been participating to Bethany's level of expectation because the woman turned to her and said, "Tell me what you love most about your husband."

At the words *love* and *husband*, Hannah's traitorous stomach did a disconcerting little flip. Caught off guard—and because she barely tolerated Jason—Hannah struggled to come up with something. She turned her best fake smile toward her mission partner. "Oh, there's so much I love about him."

Jason squeezed her hand and subtly raised an eyebrow. The look of mild concern in his eyes made Hannah realize that she wasn't going to get away with a vague, nondescript answer. She needed to come up with something convincing, or the entire mission could be in jeopardy.

Hannah wracked her brain for something she could convincingly say about this twit sitting next to her. She imagined what she *wished* he was like. "He's so considerate. Always doing nice things for me. That's what I love the most about him."

Bethany nodded, and Jason's grip relaxed. Hannah suddenly realized that she could make up any story she wanted, and there was nothing Jason could do about it. "In fact, just the other day, he made me breakfast in bed." She smiled and turned to Jason, whose eyes had widened slightly. "And he told me not to worry about cleaning the bathrooms, that he had already taken care of it."

"Hmm," Bethany said, looking down at her list of questions.

"And he's always bringing me flowers and candy. And—"

Jason squeezed her hand and leaned in as if to kiss her on the cheek. "Cool it," he whispered sharply.

Hannah fell silent, her fake smile still firmly in place.

Apparently, Bethany wasn't the least bit suspicious of Jason's super-husband status. She smiled knowingly, as if this sort of thing happened all the time.

If she only knew.

"What's the silliest thing you've ever done together?" Bethany asked.

What kind of question was that? They had definitely not covered any stories like that on the drive over. Hannah turned toward Jason, attempting to channel her best bubbly persona into inventing something funny. He must have seen the panic in her eyes, though.

Jason smiled conspiratorially. "Definitely don't tell her about the time that we got lost trying to find the entrance to the roller coaster at Six Flags."

This wasn't so bad. Hannah could do playful banter. "Only because you refused to stop and ask for directions," she said with a laugh.

He pretended to be affronted. "Riding the sky chairs to get a better view was a solid idea. I had no idea you get vertigo above ten stories high."

Hannah frowned. "I do not get verti—"

Jason held up his hands in surrender, hiding a small wink from their interviewer. Hannah huffed and turned back to Bethany.

The smile on the woman's face told Hannah that it didn't really matter what story they told—or even apparently whether it was true. The agency director was trying to get a feel for their personalities. And they appeared to be making a good impression. Or rather, Jason's underhanded fibbing had saved them.

Would he still have that grin on his face if she spilled about his fear of elevators? Hannah wasn't willing to stoop low enough to find out.

"How about child-rearing styles?" Bethany asked. She looked pointedly at Hannah.

Why did she specifically expect Hannah to answer? Wasn't discipline more of a father thing? Of course, in her case, every parental interaction in her teens had been a father thing.

"We want our children to be well-behaved." Hannah tried to sound confident.

Jason jumped in again. "Who doesn't, right? But we think it's important that they have some freedom to express their independence as well. So, really, our biggest challenge is going to be walking that line between authoritative and permissive."

The agency director wasn't the only one impressed with Jason's knowledge of parenting styles. Hannah forced herself to look straight forward, benign smile firmly in place, to keep herself from gaping at her partner. He had clearly done his homework for this mission.

Bethany took a breath and straightened her pile of notes. "Well, assuming the income and credit inquiries turn out okay—"

"Oh, given the current balances in our various bank and investment accounts, the income check shouldn't be a problem," Jason said with an air of confidence.

Hannah saw the subtle uptick of Bethany's brow. Naturally, a client's affluence would be something of interest to the director.

"Good. Then we should have no problem finding a child for you," Bethany said.

"That's great," Jason replied. "After we've had a chance to visit the other agency, we can let you know if we're interested."

Bethany's posture stiffened. "Other agency? Who else are you considering?"

Jason gazed around the room offhandedly. "Oh, I think it's called Adoptions International."

The agency director looked ready to jump out of her chair. She recovered quickly and smiled. "Adoptions International would be a fine choice. You should have no problem getting on their lists. I don't think they've implemented any sort of screening process yet. And I'm sure they would find a child for you eventually."

Hannah knew what Jason was doing. They needed to use their leverage—specifically, the promised size of the bank account—to get access to the other influencer couples. Hannah knew the part she needed to play. She placed a hand on Jason's arm. "We don't want to have to wait that long. Maybe it's best to skip the other agency."

Bethany smiled at Hannah's intervention.

"Besides, if the adoption is going to bring more subscribers to our channel, we need the process to go smoothly." Hannah turned to Bethany. "You've worked with other social media influencers before, haven't you?" This was the moment where they would find out how well they had hooked the agency director and how deep her connections went.

Bethany's eyes lit up. "Yes. We have two very well-known couples who have recently adopted with us. We arranged for all the release forms to be done ahead of time, not to mention the camera access that would normally be prohibited. We love working with influencers."

With a reluctant look on his face, Jason turned back to Hannah. "If that's what you think is best."

Hannah nodded at him almost imperceptibly. This was going to work.

Bethany held up a hand. "Just to be clear, the discount that I gave the other influencer couples would no longer be available. I want to make sure you know."

Jason waved the concern away. "That's fine. Cost isn't really an issue."

Though she tried to hide it, Bethany's reaction to Jason's willingness to pay was predictable. She immediately slid the application papers toward Jason and Hannah.

Hannah turned to Jason. "I do wish I could talk to those other couples, though. Just to set my mind at ease," she said sweetly.

Right on cue, Bethany pulled out her phone and dialed, then swiped to send the call to the screen on the conference room wall. A few seconds later, a young woman with long, silky, honey-brown hair answered the call. She had a toddler perched on her hip.

"Hi, Bethany," the woman said.

"Hello, Lexie. How are you?" Bethany asked.

Despite the woman's obvious attention to her appearance, there were clear cracks in her facade. Lexie winced as the baby pulled hard on a handful of her hair. "I'm good. What's up?"

Bethany swept a hand toward Jason and Hannah. "This is Jason and Hannah Sterling. They're looking into doing an adoption with us. They have a social media channel, too, so I thought I'd make an introduction."

Lexie's smile immediately turned genuine. "That's great. It's nice to meet you two. How long have you had your channel?"

Hannah stared straight at Lexie, unwilling to give Jason the satisfaction of seeing that she knew he had been right. "Oh, five or six years. I started a little before we got married."

The lie seemed to satisfy Lexie. "That's great. I'll have to check out your channel." She smiled as she bounced the baby on her hip.

Hannah and Jason both asked a few mundane questions about the adoption process, and Lexie patiently answered.

"It's so nice to talk to someone who understands our situation," Hannah gushed. "I'd love to connect in person some time."

Lexie nodded absently. "Actually, your timing is perfect then. We're having some friends over tomorrow night for a barbecue. They're influencers, too. You should join us."

Jason squeezed her hand, presumably congratulating her. Hannah smiled. "That would be great. Just send us the details."

Bethany beamed.

Walking out of the agency to their car, Hannah reflected on the results of their undercover interview. She hardly cared when Jason came to her side first and opened the door. "I have to admit, you had some nice saves in there," she said.

He smiled as he closed her door, and the stupid grin continued as he rounded to his side and got in. "No problem. You did a great job, too."

"Thanks," Hannah said. It wasn't her best performance, but she'd accept the compliment as graciously as she could.

"Yeah, I used to be in an improv group, so I always had to think on my feet to save the other members of the team when they'd mess up." He grinned at her.

It was amazing really, that he could take a nice compliment and twist it into a jab at her.

With her head turned toward the window, Hannah hid a very satisfying eye-roll. "Anyway, it looks like we'll get a good chance to investigate the other influencer couples. What do you think about Eastern Seas? Could Bethany be the one behind the illegal adoptions?"

Jason shrugged. "When we were first contacted by the Phelps, we did extensive background checks on Bethany Clark and the adoption agency. We only found circumstantial evidence. No smoking gun or anything like that."

"Doesn't mean she's not the one behind it," Hannah said.

"True. We can't rule her out. But I think the influencer couples would have the ideal opportunity to push people toward this type of adoption without raising suspicions. I mean, that's what they do full-time, push people toward some product or another."

"But how would the influencer couples be involved in the process at all, except for adopting their own babies?" Hannah asked. "What could they possibly gain from encouraging illegal adoptions?"

Jason's brow furrowed. "I've been thinking about that. It would have to be at the broker stage."

"Broker?" Hannah almost regretted the question as she saw Jason preparing to launch into a long-winded explanation.

"First off, you have two adoption agencies, one in each country. The receiving agency—that's Bethany and Eastern Seas Adoption in this situation—finds the prospective parents, while the originating agency finds the children." He glanced her way. "So far, so good?"

Hannah lifted a shoulder. He must have taken that as permission to continue.

"The situation gets complicated when brokers are brought into the process. Often the originating agency will contract out to other companies or individuals to find children who need to be adopted."

"What's wrong with that?" Hannah thought it sounded like any number of her father's business transactions.

"The problem is that occasionally you'll have brokers who don't follow the law or really even care about what's best for the children. They're not looking for kids who actually *need* to be adopted; they're just looking for a way to facilitate *more* adoptions. The more kids that get adopted, the more they get paid."

Hannah thought about the Phelps. "Do you think that's what happened with Jinhai?"

Jason shrugged. "We might never know."

"So, how do the influencer couples figure in?" Hannah asked.

"If they can arrange with a broker to give them a cut of the adoptions they bring in and then push more couples in that direction through their influence, you can see how they could stand to make a fair amount of money."

Hannah scowled. "But why would they? These couples are probably already making thousands of dollars a month through their social media channels."

"They could easily do ten thousand dollars per adoption," Jason countered.

Hannah's brows shot up. "Ten thousand dollars per adoption?"

Jason nodded, his expression grim.

"Whoa." She glanced out the window at the golden-brown leaves on passing trees.

She wasn't entirely sure that meant the influencer couples would be the ones involved, but it was a definite possibility.

"You're more suspicious of the influencers, but I still think it could be the agency," Hannah said. "How do we decide who to focus on?"

"Fortunately, our cover lets us investigate both, so that's what we'll do. While still keeping an open mind about who it might be." Jason eyed her as if she had already declared the case closed.

She held up her hands. "Hey, I'm certainly willing to consider other possibilities. You're the one who seems so sure of your conclusions already."

"I have to listen to what my gut tells me," he said with a shrug. "I'm sure you can understand that, what with your women's intuition and all."

Hannah wanted to scream at him to stop being a chauvinistic jerk, but she doubted he would understand what she was trying to say. Her eyes narrowed as she considered a new possibility. "I have an idea. How about we pit my *women's intuition* against your manly *gut feel*?"

He frowned at her. "You want to turn the investigation into a game? Is this some kind of joke to you?"

"Absolutely not." Hannah bristled at the insinuation that she wouldn't still do her job. "Everything about the mission would proceed normally. This would just be a friendly tally, keeping track of who's right or wrong."

Jason's face relaxed a bit. He looked to be pondering her suggestion. A smirk tugged at the corner of his mouth. "No sabotaging each other's efforts?"

"I'm insulted that you think I would even stoop that low." Hannah folded her arms in a mock show of taking offense. If she was stuck with this guy for an entire mission, the least she could do was liven things up.

After another moment's pause, Jason said, "Sure. I'm in."

Hannah reached over and shook his hand to seal the deal. She sat back in her seat and continued to ruminate on the mission's next steps.

Obviously solving the case and preventing what happened to Jinhai and the Phelps from ever happening again was her top priority. But it couldn't hurt to serve her partner a little humble pie in the process.

It might even make the mission a little more enjoyable.

CHAPTER FIVE

"I INCLUDED THE MINI plasma cutter in your purse this time," Katie said from the doorway to the Banana Girls' dressing room.

Hannah took a calming breath. "It's a small family barbeque, Katie. I don't think I need a plasma cutter." She and Jason would be spending their Friday evening with the other social media influencer families. It was like a triple date.

Did married people even go on dates?

Apparently pretend ones did.

"What if they have trouble getting the grill started?" her friend asked innocently.

Hannah cocked her head to the side and raised a brow.

"You never know . . ." Katie replied with a smile. "And it's disguised as a permanent marker, so don't offer it to anyone. That would definitely be permanent." She grinned at her little joke.

"I could have used one of those when Leo and I went for our joyride in Port Miami," Anna called from across the room.

Hannah sighed and checked herself in the mirror again. Susan and Katie had her looking wonderful again. A little too wonderful, in fact. All of this pretending to be the picture-perfect wife and hopeful mother-to-be was exhausting. She would much rather throw on her pink fuzzy pajamas and curl up in the corner on her favorite chaise with a good book in her lap than go out to a social event.

Hannah felt a ping and checked her watch. One of her roommates must have cleared Jason to come up.

She grabbed her purse and waved goodbye to the girls as she hustled out the door. She met Jason halfway down the hall. He hesitated, looking almost reluctant to get back in the elevator again. This time on the way down to the lobby, Hannah watched him out of the corner of her eye. His breathing was sporadic, as if alternating between holding his breath and hyperventilating. And he was pacing again.

Hannah shrugged to herself. As long as his issues were confined to elevators, it shouldn't affect the mission.

Jason was back to his normal self by the time they were in the car. "What's in the purse?" he asked as they pulled into traffic.

"It has some essentials." Hannah was short with her reply. She didn't feel the need to justify her equipment—or fashion choices—to him.

Jason's brow went up as if he didn't quite believe her answer. "It's just regular girl stuff, right?"

Hannah twisted in her seat to face him more fully. "I'll give you a quick tip because I'm in a good mood right now. First off, never question a woman about the contents of her purse. Of all the injustices in the world, probably the worst one is the fact that women have half the storage space in their clothing as men, yet we're expected to carry three times as much stuff. And second, it's really none of your business." She turned back to face the road.

He hadn't reacted to her mini-tirade. Maybe they would get along okay after all. A minute or two passed in uncomfortable silence.

"The only reason I bring it up is that—"

Hannah threw her hands up. "Sheesh, you really aren't going to let this drop, are you?"

"It's just that your group of agents is sort of notorious for your crazy little gadgets. I wanted to make sure that you don't have anything in your purse that would blow our cover."

"I've got all the regular stuff a woman would have in her purse," Hannah began. She almost felt guilty when she saw Jason visibly relax. "Plus, a small plasma torch disguised as a permanent marker."

"What?! Why in the world would you need something like that?"

"You never know what might happen." Even she wasn't convinced that the plasma torch was necessary. But she wasn't about to tell him that.

Jason shook his head and drove on. He slowed when they pulled into an affluent neighborhood bordering on a beautiful golf course. He brought the car to a stop in front of a gray, two-story colonial home. "This is it," he said.

Hannah grabbed her purse and opened the door to get out.

"You're not bringing your gadgets with us, are you?" Jason asked.

"I'm not sure what good they would do out here in the car if there's an emergency," Hannah deadpanned.

"You'd better leave it in the car. They have young kids, and kids are always fiddling with things they shouldn't."

"That's why we disguise our gadgets and build in safety mechanisms," Hannah said with an exasperated sigh. "It's not like we go out in public with lasers attached to our heads." Jason opened his mouth to retort, but Hannah held up her hand. "You know what? I don't even care enough to argue about this. I'll leave it here." She tucked her purse under the seat as far as she could manage. Then she glanced back at Jason. "But if I end up needing a mini plasma torch tonight . . ." She got out of the car, leaving the threat hanging in the air.

They walked awkwardly next to each other up to the front door. Hannah could almost feel Jason's outward attitude shift from annoyed coworker to doting husband. She had no idea how he could switch gears so easily. When she was upset with someone, she usually stewed about it for days.

Channeling her best undercover skills, she smiled sweetly as the door opened and Lexie Gray invited them in. Jason stepped aside and motioned Hannah forward. Though part of her chafed at his deference, it also helped her get more into character. She faked a smile at him and followed Lexie across a bright living room straight out of a magazine. The leather couches looked brand new, as if they'd never even been sat on. Stylish pictures of Lexie, her husband, and their two children hung in evenly balanced clusters around the room. The inset shelves held collections of perfectly organized trinkets and knick-knacks. Hannah had thought this type of room only existed in architects' portfolios or on home remodeling shows—or her mother's renovation of their New Hampshire beach house.

Lexie led them to the back patio and introduced her husband, Drew. He was at least six and a half feet tall, lean and athletic. He smiled politely, but didn't say much beyond a curt greeting. There was another couple on the patio that Lexie introduced as Belle and Luke Baker. Belle was short and petite, with wavy strawberry-blond hair. Luke was only an inch taller than his wife, but he was stout. Hannah tried not to gape at the size of his arms, which were almost as thick as Belle's waist.

Hannah and Jason settled into a rocking loveseat together and made small talk while Drew barbecued the chicken on the grill. After a few minutes, Luke—apparently bored with the conversation—walked over to stand next to Drew and started talking about the World Series game the night before.

Jason had obviously never rocked on a double swing chair with someone before, because he was horrible at it. Hannah glared at him every time he changed his rocking cadence, but he was completely oblivious.

"Why don't you go visit with the guys?" Hannah whispered to him.

Jason looked over his shoulder toward the grill and pulled a face. "They're just talking about baseball," he whispered back. "I don't even like baseball."

"Then fake it." Hannah tried to push him out of his seat.

"How am I supposed to know how the story ends?" Jason tipped his head toward Lexie and Belle who were deep in conversation about that month's book club choice.

On a certain level, Hannah could commiserate with him. He would rather be part of the book club discussion, and she would happily listen to any conversation related to sports. But they had appearances to keep up.

"I'll tell you how it ends." She shoved him—a little less than lovingly—out of the rocker. Hopefully, with him gone, her swaying stomach would settle before the meal.

A pair of kids—clearly of Asian heritage—came barreling through the patio. They stopped next to Belle, both speaking at once.

"But I said he couldn't play with my tablet while I was gone," the girl said.

"Nuh-uh. I never heard her say that," the younger brother shot back.

The siblings turned to each other and started arguing about something that belonged to the older girl. Finally, Belle held both hands up, eyes fluttering shut. "Do I need to get out the Happy Camera?" She flapped her hands as if shooing them away. "Just go play nicely."

The siblings shared matching horrified looks before fleeing the patio together.

Belle sighed in relief.

"I just don't know how you do it, Belle," Lexie said. "Your kids are so well-behaved. I can't get Brooklyn to sit still long enough to even braid her hair."

With a smile, Belle waved off the compliment. "You just have to know how to motivate them."

Thinking through what a hopeful mother might want to know, Hannah asked, "What was that about the Happy Camera?"

Belle leaned forward as if sharing a secret. "They hate it when we record content for the channel because I make them act happy. In fact, I'll even re-record if they aren't smiling enough."

Lexie gasped and giggled, sharing a conspiratorial look with Hannah as if Belle had just spilled her deepest, darkest secret.

Was it not common knowledge that these influencers edited and even re-shot their videos? Maybe it was an unspoken secret.

"When I figured out how much they hate it, I started threatening them with it. You wouldn't believe the stuff I can make them do," Belle said with a wicked grin.

Lexie beamed at her. "I love it, Belle. I'll have to try it on Brooklyn and Jaxon. Of course, that won't help with Drew. He's as bad as the kids sometimes when he's sulking."

"Does his sulking look anything like his smolder?" Belle quipped.

Lexie rolled her eyes. "If only."

The two women laughed as if it was the funniest joke ever. Hannah smiled politely while trying not to look bored. As the laughter died into sighs, they both turned casually to Hannah.

Realizing that she might actually be losing brain cells during this conversation, Hannah decided to steer things in a more productive direction. "So, what were your adoptions with Eastern Seas like? Did you enjoy working with Bethany?"

"Yeah," Belle said.

Lexie nodded. "Bethany's great."

"And how did you know you'd get such beautiful babies? Did she let you pick?" Hannah asked in a tone that she hoped was casual enough.

Belle glanced around, making sure the kids weren't nearby. "Well, they said not to tell anyone, but when we went to China on our first adoption trip, the agency let us go to the orphanage the night before to see all the babies that would be available the next day."

Lexie's eyes went wide. "Is that how you got Madison?"

Belle nodded, a broad smile on her face. "We just fell in love as soon as we saw her. She was definitely the cutest baby there."

Lexie sighed like it was the most perfect thing ever. Hannah wanted to grab both women by the shoulders and shake some sense into them, or maybe yell at them for being shallow enough to even suggest that getting to pick the cutest baby was something to be hoped for.

Whatever happened to loving a child because she was your child, because she was meant to be a part of your family?

Because you were her mother?

That thought hit a little too close to home.

Hannah turned casually away from the other two women. She needed to keep her emotions in check. She watched Jason standing with the husbands, trying to act interested in their talk about the game. When Drew looked up from the grill and called to Lexie that the food was ready, Jason's silent sigh of relief matched Hannah's own.

The parents called their kids for dinner, and everyone sat down to eat. Fortunately, Jason had his hands busy through the meal, but as soon as he finished, he leaned back in his seat and put his arm around Hannah. Her body tensed at the physical contact, but she tried her best not to show it. She gave Jason a fake smile and continued eating.

She hoped that Jason had pumped the guys for information while they were talking about sports because Hannah felt like she was the only one doing any investigating. "I'm so glad we had the chance to meet all of you," she said, looking at the other couples. "Do you ever get together with other adoptive families?" The Phelps had mentioned family support groups, maybe they could find out more about those.

"Only about ten times a year," Luke said as he shot Drew a knowing look.

Drew chuckled. "These two have never been to a party they didn't like. I think they enjoy torturing us."

Lexie pointed a playful finger at her husband. "And don't forget, you two promised after last year's fiasco to be better behaved at the retreat this year."

Drew and Luke grinned at each other.

That had Hannah intrigued. "What did they do?" she asked.

Belle shook her head. "When they ran out of water balloons for the balloon toss, these two decided to throw the littlest kids back and forth."

"And they loved it," Luke piped in.

Everyone laughed.

"What retreat is this?" Jason was finally starting to pull his weight in the conversation.

"Several years ago, some of the international adoption agencies in the area got together to start an annual retreat. In fact, that's actually where we met each other." Belle indicated their two families.

"When is it?" Jason asked Belle.

"It's actually next weekend," Lexie answered with a smile. The others around the table—including the kids—looked just as excited.

Jason cast a furtive glance in Hannah's direction. They might not have been working together long, but she could tell they were thinking along the same track. This retreat would be a great place to get some inside information to continue their investigation. They would need to figure out a way to get to that retreat. Jason looked like he was about to say something, but Hannah placed a hand on his arm to stop him.

"Y'all are so lucky to have a support group like that." Hannah smiled at Belle. "I wish there was something like that for couples who are still waiting to adopt. You know, a group that understands that we have certain hopes for our child's future." She turned to Jason with a commiserating expression. He looked annoyed that she had interrupted him.

"That's exactly what this group is for," Belle said. "It's not just families who have already adopted. It's for anyone at any point in the process."

Hannah allowed her smile to brighten hopefully. "Really? It's too bad it's such late notice. I'm sure it's already full."

Belle and Lexie glanced at each other. "I bet we could get you in," Lexie said.

Hannah put a hand to her chest. "Oh, could you? That would be amazing."

"Sure," Belle added. "Especially if you're going to adopt with Eastern Seas. You're practically family already."

Hannah smiled at Jason as if this was the best news they'd had in months. His polite expression was definitely forced, and she knew why. She would count getting invited to the retreat as a point in her column on their friendly tally, and Jason knew it.

Well, he was going to have to get used to it because Hannah planned to show him exactly what an agent of her caliber could do on a mission like this.

After-dinner conversation continued for several more minutes as the topic turned back to the kids and how they were doing in and out of school—Hannah couldn't believe the number of activities Madison was participating in. The strain of acting excited about parent-teacher conferences and piano recitals was beginning to wear on Hannah. When Lexie mentioned how well Brooklyn was doing on her soccer team, Hannah knew she had to get away from the conversation. In reality, it hadn't been anything that Lexie said. It was Drew's flippant comment that Brooklyn's team had yet to lose any game where she had scored at least two goals.

Hannah saw a similar scene in her mind's eye—her father, lounging around the family pool with several golf buddies, bragging about her performance in a recent gymnastics competition. Unfortunately, his praise only ever seemed to come when she placed at the top of the podium.

Hannah stood abruptly and stepped to the edge of the large patio. "I'm going to walk a little bit. Stretch my legs," she said before striking out into the large back yard.

Half a minute later, Jason caught up to her. "What's up? You okay?"

Hannah wanted to tell him to never be an over-controlling father, that if he ever had kids, he should just love them for who they were not what they did. But she didn't think it was the right time in their partnership to bring up kids. The right time would probably be . . . well . . . never. "I just needed a break from the perfection, that's all." She rubbed her neck and rolled her head back and forth.

Jason walked along beside her. "I'm sure they're not that bad once you get to know them," he said with a grin.

They stood in silence, staring out at the manicured backyard dimming in the growing twilight.

"Funny to think that there are thousands of people around the world—sometimes millions—who are entertained by just watching a family do . . . whatever it is they do here." He waved his hand back toward the patio.

Hannah chuckled. She knew something about people's fascination with wealth and prosperity—or the appearance of it, anyway.

After another minute of silence, Jason tilted his head toward the patio. "We should probably get back to the group."

"I'm not quite ready." Hannah didn't try to hide the annoyance in her voice.

"Well, you need to be ready. They're going to get suspicious if you can't handle a half-hour dinner conversation."

"Sometimes people need alone time, Jason."

"Not these people. They're extroverts. They thrive on people, groups, and attention." He cast an appraising look over his shoulder at their hosts. "And they'd never believe an introvert could be an influencer or have the kind of online following you have."

Jason went to grab her arm. With a quick jerk, Hannah pulled out of his reach. She glanced over her shoulder to make sure they weren't being watched before glaring at him. "I don't know what types of team-up missions you've had," Hannah said through gritted teeth. "But when I say I'm not ready, I actually mean don't touch me unless you want the bones in your wrist rearranged." She shifted casually away from him.

"It doesn't always have to be about you," he said.

Hannah rounded on him. "I know that, Jason. In fact, the only thing keeping me on this mission with you is the kids we're trying to save. But you know what?" She spoke softly while keeping an eye on the others. "After seeing these kids, I wonder if we wouldn't be doing them a favor letting them come to loving families here in the states. I mean, despite being overscheduled and possibly spoiled rotten, think about the opportunities they'll have in their lives." She spread her arms wide. "Is all of this really such a bad thing?"

Jason stepped toward her but suddenly pulled up short, a cautious look on his face. Maybe her threat had done its job. "No, of course not. If the kids really are orphans, they're much better off here. But if they're being torn away from loving families . . ." He inched closer and lowered his voice. "Think about Jinhai. Think about how much he missed his family back in China. And what about his birth parents? Were they forced to give him up for adoption? Do they know he's okay? Do they even know where he is? And that's not even considering the torture that couples like Kayla and Brandon go through."

Hannah knew that he was right, and she hated it. "I'm going for a walk around the neighborhood."

"What, alone?" Jason looked through the side gate toward the dark road.

"When you were doing all of that research on the Banana Girls, did you happen to notice the type of training we undergo? Did you think I was bluffing about what I could do to someone who touches me when

I don't want them to?" Hannah didn't wait for him to respond, but she loved that look of annoyance on his face.

Pushing through the gate to the side lawn, Hannah took a deep breath of crisp night air. Once she reached the sidewalk, she looked both ways down the quiet suburban street before striking off in the direction that looked the most deserted. That usually meant peaceful.

She knew Jason was right about her behavior around others. He only wanted to make their mission a success. And he clearly felt very passionately about the Phelps and little Jinhai and the mess they were in. Truthfully, so did she.

Jason was probably a competent agent who was good at his job, but why did he have to be so bossy about things? She was usually pretty easy to get along with. Well, maybe not all the time, but Hannah tried to be rational when it was absolutely necessary.

She continued her stroll through the neighborhood, not really paying attention to which roads she took as she contemplated her situation and the mission's requirement to act like Jason's loving wife.

Hannah wasn't really sure how to be a loving spouse. She had only been eleven years old when her mother walked out on them. Even before that, she'd never seen an affectionate, loving relationship modeled in her home.

If only Jason wasn't so annoying all the time, it might come naturally.

Who was she kidding? It wouldn't come naturally.

If her parents were any indication, she'd gotten the short end of the genetic stick when it came to emotionally healthy relationships, to say nothing of parental instincts.

Up ahead, Hannah saw a figure standing next to a car, pulling intently on the handle. Though she had always wanted to be as non-judgmental as Anna, she couldn't help but think that it looked like the person was trying to break into the car. She hurried down the sidewalk, glancing around to see if there was anyone else around. Surprisingly, she saw the Grays' house. Had she walked a full circle around the neighborhood?

Turning back to the would-be burglar, she called out, "Hey. Stop!"

The man glanced up, but in the darkness—and at that distance—Hannah couldn't see the details of his face. He looked thin and close to her height. She shouldn't have any trouble making him stop.

When she was about three car lengths away, the burglar succeeded in getting the car door open. She needed to hurry. As she sprinted forward, two very disconcerting feelings struck her. First, the clunky, fashionable sandals Katie had insisted she wear were impossible to run in, and second, the sporty white coupe looked vaguely familiar.

It was Jason's car.

Hannah kicked off the sandals and sprinted barefoot along the cold cement sidewalk. The thief fished under the passenger seat and pulled out a small purse.

That was her purse, the one she would have been holding in her hand had Jason not insisted she leave it in the car.

Now in possession of the only thing of value in the car, the purse snatcher turned to make his getaway. Before he made it two steps, Hannah hooked one of his legs with her bare foot, and he tumbled headlong onto the sidewalk.

Only, he didn't end up sprawled out with a patch of missing skin on his face like she had hoped. The burglar rolled expertly and bounced back onto his feet. He spun to face Hannah and swung a fist at her head.

Still off balance from running so fast, Hannah blocked and ducked at the same time. She succeeded in avoiding the brunt of his blow, but the awkward motion tipped her over. She fell backward into the neighbor's front lawn.

The burglar lunged forward and kicked her in the ribs. She grunted against the pain and grabbed his leg, using it to leverage her own flip-kick upward. She caught him in the gut and knocked him back. Hannah tried to twist his ankle around to pin him down, but he kicked free.

They both scrambled quickly back to their feet. The burglar squared to her and lowered into his fighting stance. He had been trained in hand-to-hand combat, that much was clear. Hannah could have brought down a regular guy of his size in half this time.

She lunged toward him, testing his reactions. He didn't commit or fight back until she kicked at his knee. He deflected her attack and aimed a punch at her ribs again. This time, she was ready and blocked his fist. She swiped for her purse, but he kept it out of reach.

Hannah went for his sternum, swinging a one-two punch. He deflected the first, but with the purse in the other hand, her second punch landed true. The criminal stumbled backward, still clutching the purse. Hannah pressed her advantage and lunged forward with a kick to his knee. The guy completely lost his balance, but still didn't let go of the purse. He fell into a perfect somersault and rolled away from her, his momentum once again carrying him back to his feet.

Why wouldn't he drop the purse? She'd be willing to let him get away if he would just give it back.

Maybe.

Hannah moved closer, still on the offensive. She aimed for his chest once more, but this time, she grabbed the purse when he tried to use it to block. He held the strap tightly in his hand, still unwilling to let go of his prize. They continued the fight—each with only one free hand—alternately punching and blocking. Hannah attempted a kick, but quickly realized that he could pull her off-balance with the purse strung between them.

As they passed in and out of the weak light from nearby streetlamps, Hannah was able to get a better idea of what he looked like. He had Asian ancestry—possibly Chinese or Korean. His dark brown hair was dyed blond at the tips. And even though he was obviously in top physical shape, she could tell the fight was wearing on him.

They appeared to be at an impasse, neither willing to release the purse.

The sound of approaching footsteps caught her attention. Hannah glanced in the direction of the Grays' home.

"Hannah?" Jason called out as he came around the corner.

"I'm over here," she yelled. Though she wasn't willing to risk another glance, she heard Jason's pace increase.

The burglar's expression changed from focused determination to resigned anger. He released the purse strap and sprinted away down the street.

Hannah yelled after him. "Hey, don't run off just cuz a guy's coming!" She felt insulted enough to chase him down and make him fight her again. In fact, his tenacity for wanting to get away with her purse made her wonder if she shouldn't grab him for further questioning. She ran after him.

"Hannah," Jason called after her. He was too far behind to help at this point.

Half a block down the road, the burglar jumped onto a waiting motorcycle. A second later, the bike sprang to life with the whine of a powerful electric engine. Without any shoes, Hannah never got close enough to stop him.

She stood panting in the middle of the street as the motorcycle zipped away. Jason stopped next to her, holding her sandals. Hannah grabbed one and chucked it at the disappearing burglar.

"Feel better?" Jason asked.

"No," she said, shooting a scowl at her pretend husband. "Why did you pick up my sandals? You might have gotten here in time to stop him."

"Why did you drop your sandals in the first place? Don't you realize we have a very particular appearance we need to keep? On this mission, you're not a ninja-girl. You're a young wife and fashionable social media influencer who wants very much to adopt a child. You can't get into street-fights with shady characters."

"He was going for this." Hannah held up her purse.

"You risked our cover for your purse?" he asked.

"It wouldn't have even been an issue if you hadn't insisted I leave it in the car."

"Who cares about a purse? You should have let him take it," Jason said.

"You remember those crazy little gadgets you mentioned?"

"So?"

Hannah held up her purse and shook it at him. "Don't you think the thief would have been suspicious to find that half of the breath mints contain tracking devices?"

"All the more reason to let him take it. We could have tracked him later," he hissed, casting a glance around him before adding, "when it wouldn't have blown our cover."

Hannah glared at him. She wasn't even willing to honor his suggestion with a response. She snatched the other sandal from his hand and walked gingerly out into the street to collect the thrown one. With the sandals firmly on her feet, she marched past Jason back toward the sounds of the party.

Jason caught up with her in the Grays' driveway, glancing at her every few seconds. What could he possibly want from her? Couldn't he tell she was angry at him?

He stepped in front of her when they reached the path around the side of the house. "Hang on, Hannah. We can't go back to the party like this." He motioned back and forth between them.

Hannah huffed to a stop. "Like what?"

"Like we just had a fight," Jason replied.

"We *did* just have a fight." Hannah was trying not to yell, but this aggravating man was making it impossible.

He glared at her as if he wanted to wring her neck. Hannah would have welcomed the chance to blow off some steam. Particularly if it meant taking out some aggression on her annoying partner.

With a deep breath and a false smile, Jason continued, "I know you may not care about the challenges of social media influencers and the heartbreak of making the wrong step and losing followers. But your persona,"—he held out a hand at her—"Hannah Sterling, would. She would never act annoyed or angry or out of sorts around strangers, especially not new social media friends. A slight from them could devastate your audience."

Hannah rolled her eyes and looked away, but she didn't move or try to contradict him.

"Let's just wait here until we've calmed down a bit and then we can rejoin them," he said.

They stood there, Jason looking mostly calm, Hannah still fuming, for another minute. "Will you have to make up some excuse to save our cover?" Hannah didn't bother hiding the sarcasm.

"Maybe." Jason's reply sounded very noncommittal.

That piqued Hannah's curiosity. Or maybe it was a sense of dread. "What are you going to tell them?" she asked.

He grinned. "I'll tell them that we were enjoying one of the benefits of *not* having children yet."

Hannah's cheeks burned at the insinuation of what they might have been doing alone in the shadows. Fortunately, the dark night hid it well.

If forced to, Hannah would begrudgingly admit that would count as a point for Jason's column.

But only if forced.

CHAPTER SIX

THE BUZZ OF THE crowd in the small cafe wrapped around Hannah like a security blanket. Situated only a few blocks south of Club Banana, it was a favorite spot of hers when she needed some time to think or unwind. And after their dreadful attempt at making friends with the Grays and the Bakers the night before, she definitely needed some time to think and unwind.

From her table tucked against the back wall, she could see the activity of the lunchtime crowd while not getting swept up in its chaos. She didn't actually want to talk to anyone, after all. She simply enjoyed the feeling of blending in, getting lost in the anonymity of a busy restaurant.

For the last twenty minutes, she had tried various combinations of Internet search terms, trying to find a picture that matched the electric motorcycle her assailant had used to escape the night before. Truth be told, whoever the man was, he was a trained martial artist. If she had been more prepared for the encounter, she might have eventually gained the upper hand. Either that, or she needed to have worn more sensible shoes.

Frustrated by her lack of results, Hannah opened another search window and began investigating which models of motorcycle had keyless start. There's no way the guy could have pulled out a key in time to start the bike that fast. If she could cross reference the electric motorcycles with the models that were keyless, maybe . . .

A prickly sensation raced up her neck.

Someone was watching her.

She could feel it.

As casually as possible, Hannah turned her head and glanced over her shoulder, nearly jolting out of her seat at the sight of a looming presence.

Jason stood a few feet behind her, a thermal coffee cup in each hand and a goofy grin on his face. "It took you six seconds to realize I was standing there," he chided. "I would think that a spy girl would work a little harder on situational awareness. Maybe that should be a point for me."

Hannah's blood boiled at the insult. She wanted to show him some of the things that a spy girl could do, but she didn't want to have to explain to Stacia—or Anna—why her mission partner would have to spend a month in traction. She shrugged, attempting an aloof look, while her heartbeat returned to normal. "I'm here waiting for you, after all. How do you know I didn't notice you more than six seconds ago? Maybe I should win this one."

He shook his head and sat down across from Hannah at the small table. "I'm just trying to give you some friendly pointers. Do you always have to make it about winning?"

"Spy girls don't like friendly pointers. And we don't like to lose," she said with a false smile. "Speaking of which, I think I deserve another point for being right about not leaving my purse in the car last night."

"Then I deserve a point for being right that you shouldn't have brought a purse full of silly gadgets in the first place."

"Be careful what you say," Hannah said with an arched brow. "You might be saved by one of those silly gadgets someday."

Grinning, he shook his head then nudged her laptop to the side with his elbow before placing one of the steaming cups next to it.

She glanced down at the cup. "What's this?"

"Oh, I picked up a drink for you," he said.

Hannah stared at the cup then up at her partner. Was Jason actually being kind to her? She suddenly felt guilty for all the biting comebacks she had been planning to use on him.

"Uh, thanks," she said, still unsure what to make of this gesture. "That was nice of you."

A small part of her wondered if maybe she had judged him too quickly. Deep down, he might actually be a sweet guy.

Jason shrugged and glanced nonchalantly out the window at the passing cars. "No problem. I've been wanting to try out that new autumn spice flavor, but I didn't want to risk not liking it. So, it worked out great."

Hannah gaped at him. "You . . . drank some of mine?"

His expression turned confused. "Well, yeah. I didn't take much. Just a sip to try it out."

"Your lips were touching my cup?"

He stiffened. "It's not like I was slobbering all over it. I didn't think you'd care. I mean, we're acting like a married couple, aren't we?"

With great effort, Hannah kept her eyes from bugging out at him. "We're only *acting*, Jason. Plus, we're only acting married when we're around people." She glanced down at the coffee cup. "And we're certainly not sharing drinks. Eww."

Was he completely clueless, or was he intentionally being a jerk? Hannah stared at her partner, wishing she could figure out what was going through his head.

Jason's blue-gray eyes crinkled in a smile that quickly faded. He must have realized that she wasn't joking. "Fine. No sharing drinks. I'll remember that." He leaned back in his chair, his arms folded across his chest. "Anyway, I'll tell you that you're wasting time researching the motorcycle. I already looked into it. It's a dead end. So, I'd say that's a point for me."

Hannah opened her mouth to protest, but decided it wasn't worth it.

"Also, I was able to do some research into the Grays and the Bakers," Jason said as he sipped his drink.

Hannah lifted a shoulder to show she was mildly interested.

"I think there is definitely some sort of kickback happening between the agency and one or both of the couples." He nodded meaningfully.

Hannah considered him for a moment. "What makes you think that?"

"Both couples made several very large purchases right after they signed on for adoptions with Eastern Seas."

"So?"

"So, we're talking new cars, a boat, new houses . . ."

"So?"

Jason scowled at her. A tiny part of her loved the look he gave her when she was being difficult. Sometimes, aggravating people was just so much more rewarding than being pleasant.

"Don't you think it's suspicious that both families were living in small homes, driving old cars, then suddenly they have enough money for new houses and new cars all at once . . . at the same time?"

Hannah shrugged again, and Jason's frown deepened. She decided to cut him a break. Leaning forward, she put on her best third-grade teacher expression. "You know, if you work hard and save up your pennies, someday you can buy a new car, too."

Jason's eyes narrowed. "Is this some sort of game to you?"

"If it was, I would win," Hannah shot back.

Their staring contest stretched on—neither of them willing to admit defeat and look away—until the side door suddenly slammed. Hannah felt pleased that it had been Jason who finally flinched. She chalked up another point to herself. Or half a point anyway.

Maybe she was being silly and childish. Maybe she needed to be the one to help them get focused back on task. Clearly, Mister Stubborn-Agent wasn't going to do it.

She airily waved a hand in his direction. "Buying new cars and houses isn't the smoking gun you're hoping for. Maybe they had been saving up for the car. They probably needed a bigger house because their family was growing."

Jason opened his mouth to protest, but Hannah spoke over him.

"Not to mention the fact that posting their adoption experience would have brought in some serious sponsorships."

"Enough to buy new cars and houses?"

Hannah nodded slowly. She couldn't help a smug expression when she considered how little he really knew about social media influencers. "Mid-level earners could easily afford to buy a new car. Maybe two. Upper-level earners . . ." She held her hands out in a shrug.

"Seriously?" Jason asked, his eyebrow cocked up.

Hannah affected her normal, aloof expression. "Some of the top influencers could earn a car in just one post."

Jason just stared at her for several seconds. "Huh." After his initial shock passed, his gaze drifted out the window. "I wonder how much we could make."

"As a social media couple?" Hannah pressed.

He turned his attention back to Hannah. "Yeah. I mean, once the mission is over, I doubt the agency will care what we do with the account. It's of no use to them. I wonder how much it could earn."

"Wouldn't we have to be a couple for that to work?" Hannah deadpanned. She was sure her tone conveyed the idiocy of the suggestion.

Half a second later, Hannah saw reality flash across Jason's expression. His cheeks went slightly pink, and he turned back to stare out the window.

A few moments passed before he turned his attention from the window and muttered, "Yeah, that would never work."

Even though they would obviously never be a social media couple together, part of her wished they didn't hate each other's guts quite so much. At the very least, it would make some aspects of the mission bearable. Under normal circumstances, sitting at lunch with an attractive guy would be enjoyable, if the guy in question wasn't so insensitive sometimes.

Jason attempted a casual change of subject, though it was a bit forced. "By the way, I was able to get us an invitation to the adoption retreat next week."

It was Hannah's turn to be surprised. "Really? How?" She couldn't imagine Jason being very smooth or subtle in fishing for an invite.

"Lexie texted me after the barbecue and said she would see if she could arrange things with the agency. She must have called Bethany and talked her into it, because the invitation email came in this morning."

All of the pretending to be a couple must have started to affect Hannah's emotions because for a split second, she felt a small tinge of jealousy. She covered it with a fake smile. "That's great." Hannah chided herself for such a strange feeling. She had no reason to be jealous of other women doing favors for Jason, especially if it was helpful to the mission. After all, he wasn't her real husband.

Of course, Lexie didn't know that.

In an attempt to regain her footing in the conversation, Hannah asked, "It's next Saturday, right?"

He nodded. "Yeah, next weekend. I think we actually get there on Friday, though. Hopefully, we can use the next few days to develop a game plan for how to spend our time at the retreat."

Hannah knew that was true; they needed to be prepared.

But she couldn't focus on that at the moment. Her brain was still tripping over the part where he said "weekend." As in, more than one day together as a married couple.

As in, at least one night.

CHAPTER SEVEN

"How's your linear algebra class going?" Hannah asked Mari. Though Hannah had been awake for an hour or two, she had only just emerged from her room, preferring to spend some time alone before facing the new week and a full day of classes and mission investigation.

Mari looked up from her homework and gave a small smile. "Oh, it's good."

Hannah still didn't have a perfect read on Mari's personality. The newest Banana Girl was fiercely independent, but Hannah occasionally saw cracks in the facade. She resisted the urge to be blunt with Mari, especially given how rocky their relationship had been at the start. Hannah sat next to her on the sofa and glanced at the pages of notes spread on the coffee table. She cocked her head to the side and looked at Mari. "Is it really? Or are you just saying that?"

With a huge sigh, Mari looked sheepishly at Hannah. "I'm completely lost," she admitted. She looked both ways before leaning towards Hannah and lowering her voice. "I'm super grateful to Katie for taking notes while I was on the mission trying to save my mom, but . . ."

Hannah let out a short laugh. "Katie doesn't take very good notes, does she?"

Mari shook her head. "They're complete gibberish," she whispered. "It's like she was only half paying attention."

"I'd guess it was actually less than half," Hannah said with a knowing smile. "Most of her attention was probably on the hot guy sitting closest to her."

Mari blew out a long breath and sank back into the leather sofa. "Trey doesn't know anything about the subject, so he's no help. What's the point of having a boyfriend if I can't even ask him to tutor me?"

Hannah shook her head. "Mari." She took a breath in an attempt to soften her tone. "Mari, why didn't you ask one of us?" Hannah asked patiently.

Mari shrunk slightly. "I didn't want to be a burden. You girls have already done so much for me."

Time for the big guns.

Hannah cocked her head to the side, doing her best to balance stern and playful the way she had seen Anna do it so many times. "You've got to stop thinking that you're in this alone, Mari. You're one of us now, and we're a team. We help each other with everything."

Mari's brows furrowed. Clearly, she wasn't convinced.

"As it just so happens, I'm a whiz at linear algebra," Hannah said as she lifted her chin and performed a pretentious and obviously overdone hair flip.

A tentative smile spread across Mari's face.

Hannah looked at her, eyebrows raised in invitation.

Mari took a quick breath. "Would you help me with my algebra, Hannah?" she pushed out.

"I'd be happy to," Hannah said with a nod. She scooted closer to Mari and looked down at her notes. "What topic are you working on?"

"Well, we just covered—"

Hannah's phone buzzed. She tilted the screen and saw Jason's number. She immediately slammed it back on her leg.

Mari stared down at the phone in Hannah's lap. "Don't you need to get that?" she asked.

"No. Keep going," Hannah said with an airy smile.

The phone continued to vibrate. Mari glanced between her homework and the distracting little device. "Really, Hannah, I don't want you to get in trouble because of me."

Hannah sighed. "Fine. But we'll continue this later, okay?"

Mari nodded, and Hannah swiped a finger across the screen as she stood and walked to the enormous picture windows overlooking Midtown Atlanta. "Yes?" she said into the phone.

"Good morning to you, too." Jason's tone was way too chipper for eleven in the morning.

Reminding herself to try not to sabotage their working relationship, Hannah switched on her friendly voice. "What can I do for you?"

"We need to go back to the adoption agency this afternoon."

Hannah frowned. "What for?"

"Sandra just called and said there are some non-disclosure forms we need to sign because of social media and the other couples and something else I didn't quite catch."

"No. I have class this afternoon. I can't go back to the—"

"I know it's not great timing, but if we're going to keep our cover, we have to go sign the papers today."

Even though she was annoyed that he pretty much just assumed she would do it, he did sound like he was sorry about it. That was a step in the right direction. And ultimately, she knew he was right.

Hannah let out a long sigh. "Okay. How soon can you get here? If we go right now, I might still make my afternoon classes."

"I'm already on my way," Jason replied. The smile was back in his voice. "I'll hit a drive-through on the way. Pick up some burgers for lunch."

"I haven't even eaten br—" The line was dead before Hannah finished her sentence.

She glanced across the room at Mari, who gave a commiserating shrug. Hannah wanted to tell the young new agent that her mission experience—having a hot undercover operative infiltrate the same organization, offer to help, then fall in love with her—was not the norm. When a Banana Girl was forced to work with their male counterparts from other organizations, the guys were usually insensitive and annoying.

Hannah shook her head to herself.

No need to ruin the fantasy for her friend quite yet.

After a quick change into one of her Katie-approved influencer outfits, Hannah was down in the lobby pull-through in less than ten minutes. Jason pulled up a minute later. He waved a half-eaten burger through the window at her.

As she sat down in the passenger seat, Jason held a wrapped burger out to her. "Sorry, I should have asked what you wanted. I got the supreme. Hopefully that's okay."

"Thanks." Hannah hesitantly took the burger and unwrapped one corner to take a peek. "This wasn't a burger you wanted to test out, was it?"

Jason chuckled. "No, I try to learn from my mistakes."

He took her ribbing well. That was an improvement.

She ate as they drove, contemplating how nice it might be to have a partner who was only annoying part of the time instead of all the time.

The visit to the adoption agency was uneventful; Sandra had all of the paperwork ready for them to sign. She also handed them an invitation for a party in three weeks.

"We always have a send-off banquet for the couples before they travel to China for the adoption," Sandra said. "You're welcome to join us if it helps you make your decision."

Hannah glanced at Jason, who was all smiles. First an invitation to the retreat, then another to their send-off banquet. Bethany must have asked Sandra to pull out all the stops.

Even though Hannah hoped Jason wouldn't make small talk, it was another five minutes before they were back in Jason's car heading across town.

"Despite my chatty husband, I might make it to class after all," Hannah said, gazing out the window at the passing buildings.

"So, what are your plans after you graduate?" Jason asked. "Are you going into espionage full time?"

Hannah frowned. Was this just small talk, or did he really want to know? "Anna and I haven't talked about what will happen to the Banana Girls after we graduate. We've got a pretty well-rounded team right now, but when Anna and I leave, we might need to bring on some new girls as replacements. I guess it depends on what Stacia needs. If she has a way for me to help after college, I think I'd do it."

Jason nodded but didn't reply.

After a few moments, Hannah turned her attention more fully to him. "What about you? Did you always want to be an agent in homeland security?"

Jason's brow knit in thought. "I think I've always liked things to be fair. You know, the good guys win, the bad guys get what's coming to them." He cast a grin her way. "But the real world isn't quite so clean cut. The bad guys get away sometimes. And good people get hurt." He paused then shrugged. "I guess I just want to do what I can to make things right."

Hannah wasn't sure what she'd expected when she asked the question, but his response caught her off guard. If he'd made some flippant comment about high-speed chases, cool guns, and hot women, she wouldn't have been surprised. In fact, a devil-may-care attitude like that would have made it easier to continue disliking him.

Hannah studied him for a long moment—taking advantage of the fact that his attention was on the road. She had to admit, he was fairly handsome, certainly more handsome when he was talking about helping people than when he was acting like a jerk. She couldn't imagine the type of girl that would put up with his attitude about . . . well, pretty much everything. But she could see that there might actually be a caring guy underneath the rude facade.

Suddenly, Jason tensed, his hands squeezing tight on the wheel.

Hannah surveyed the surrounding buildings. "It's okay. You didn't miss it. The turn to campus isn't for another few blocks."

He glanced briefly in the mirror before returning his attention to the road ahead. "I think we've got a tail."

"What?" As she was about to turn around in her seat, Jason's hand flew to her leg.

"Don't look," he said slowly. "We don't want to attract attention."

Hannah forced herself to stay facing forward—and to not overreact to Jason's hand on her knee. "Then let's lose them."

He subtly shook his head and glanced at the surrounding cars. "I don't think that's a good idea."

She turned to him and very unceremoniously removed his hand from her leg. "Listen. If you don't think you can handle maneuvering a car at high speeds in this setting, we can pull over and switch. I'm more than capable of—"

"We can't just switch drivers."

"Why not? Is our tail prejudiced against female drivers, too?"

Jason's gaze jerked to her. "I'm not prejudiced against—" He stopped his retort mid-sentence, the surprise in his expression slowly fading to resignation as he turned his attention back to the road. "No. It's because driving like a madman,"—he shot a sideways glance in her direction—"or madwoman, would definitely blow our cover. We have to continue as if we were a happy couple on our drive home."

Hannah stared at the small mirror on the passenger side, trying to see which car could be the one trailing them. Suddenly, Jason took a turn into a parking lot.

"What are you doing?" Hannah asked.

"Trying to shake him," Jason said, pulling into a parking stall. "Doing something in character." He pointed at the business in front of them.

Hannah looked up and saw the pharmacy sign. She looked back at Jason, her eyebrows lifted. If he wanted her to do something, he wasn't being very clear about it.

"We're running an errand on the way home," he said with a casual glance over his shoulder. "Why don't you go inside and buy something?"

"Wouldn't a happy couple with no kids go inside together?"

"I'm not going to leave the car out here unattended. He might put a tracker on us."

"I don't even know who you think is following us." Hannah could feel herself getting testy, but she didn't bother hiding it.

"Small gray compact. I lost him when we pulled into the lot. But he might still be back there," he said.

Hannah really wanted to take the little car through a couple of high-speed turns, hit the freeway and see if their tail could do ninety. That's what a spy girl would do. Acting normal felt so . . . unnormal. "So, you're going to sit in the car while I go into the store for what?"

Jason let out a frustrated sigh. "I don't care. Go buy some feminine products. It doesn't really matter." In complete contradiction to the irritation in his voice, he pulled out his cellphone and casually began scrolling.

"That's the first thing you go to? Feminine product? Do you know how—"

"If you sit here arguing with me, that's just going to draw attention to the fact that we're not acting like a normal couple," Jason said without looking up from his phone.

Hannah gaped at him. Then with a huff, she opened the door. "If someone was a couple with you, I think arguing would be the norm," she said as she stepped out of the car and slammed the door behind her.

By the time she had walked up and down two aisles in the store, Hannah had calmed down enough to see that she might have been a little harsh. After paying for her items—a bottle of shampoo and a package of gum—she walked back to their car, wondering whether their tail was still out there.

Once back in the car, she unwrapped the gum and offered him a piece. A conciliatory gesture, she hoped. "Where to now?"

"Thanks," Jason said as he took the gum and popped it in his mouth, all while maneuvering out of the parking lot and back onto the road. Hannah wanted to tell him to floor it before their tail was on them again. He could at least drive like an impatient husband. Hannah had seen plenty of those.

"Once we've lost our tail, then I can take you to campus." Jason watched his rearview mirror. "But unfortunately, not yet."

In all the excitement, she had completely forgotten about her afternoon classes. She couldn't believe Jason had managed to remember.

Hannah glanced in her side mirror in time to see a small gray car pull out of the parking lot into a narrow gap in the traffic and accelerate after them. She took several deep breaths. Not being in control of the situation—or the car, at the very least—was going to drive her crazy.

"Where are you planning to drive?" Hannah asked. "We can't stop for errands all afternoon. That wouldn't quite be normal either."

"I'm thinking." He drove for another block as Hannah watched the gears turning in his head. "We have to drive back to our house," he said finally.

"We don't have a house, Jason."

"I know that," he shot back, running a hand absently through his hair.

Hannah watched the surrounding buildings zip past. Whether Jason was conscious of it or not, he was heading toward Midtown.

"You absolutely cannot take me back to Club Banana with a tail," Hannah said. "You're one of the few living people who knows its location."

Jason shook his head, as if clearing his thoughts. "Yeah. I know." He glanced at the surrounding streets as if considering his options. "Well, there's no way I'm driving back to my apartment with a tail either. The mission would definitely be over at that point."

Hannah stared forward. "Wait a minute. We don't have to think of a place to drive. If our tail is involved with the adoptions or our fake social media account, they would know where we're supposed to go. You need to drive to whatever address you put on our adoption application."

"I put the address of a vacation rental on it."

"You mean, like a beach house?" Hannah asked.

"No. It's a condo north of Midtown that the owner rents out by the week. The agency felt like it would be an ideal option."

"Jason, if the agency rented a unit for us to use as a fake home . . ." She took a breath, resisting the urge to knock on the side of his head. "Then let's drive there."

Jason gave her a chagrined look. "Actually, I talked my boss out of renting it."

"What?" Hannah's eyes were nearly bulging out of their sockets at this point. "Why would you do that? Were you looking for ways to make the mission more complicated?"

"I told him we could have the rental as a backup, in case of an emergency."

"It's an emergency," Hannah declared. "Drive to the rental."

Jason shook his head. "What if someone's staying there? We can't just barge in."

"We can if we need to. Haven't you ever commandeered a car for a mission before?"

Jason gave her a surprised look. "Are you crazy? That only happens in movies."

A smug little smile spread across Hannah's face as she returned her attention to the road. It didn't only happen in the movies.

"The rental unit is a bad idea," Jason said.

"Do you have a better one?" Hannah snapped.

They drove on in silence for half a minute. "Fine," Jason finally said. "But this is not going to end the way you think it will."

"Tell me about it," Hannah muttered.

Neither spoke as Jason wove his way toward the vacation condominium. Hannah hoped that it was empty and that it had one of those electronic locks. She'd loaded Katie's new lockpicking app on her phone, so as long as it had an electronic lock, Hannah supposed it didn't matter whether the unit was empty or not. They could deal with that later.

Jason's voice broke the silence. "Actually, we may not need to get into the unit after all. If I recall correctly, the rental complex has an underground garage with a security gate."

Hannah's brow went up. "That would be perfect. Do you have the code?"

Jason frowned. "Uh, no. The property owner wouldn't give it to me until we rented the unit."

Hannah's hands involuntarily clenched into fists. "By any chance, is this your first time working with a partner on a mission?" Hannah asked.

"Yeah. Didn't I tell you that already?"

"No, you didn't," she said through gritted teeth. "Call it a hunch."

"What do you mean?"

"Because you're still alive." Hannah let out a long breath and pulled out her phone. "Just drive to the condo. I'm going to call for some backup on this."

Hannah clicked the icon to connect directly to Club Banana. After a few seconds, Susan's face appeared on the screen. "Hi, Hannah, what's up?"

"Hey, Susan. We need a little help on something." Hannah tilted the phone slightly so that Susan could see she was in the car with Jason. He glanced briefly at the camera before returning his attention to the road.

Katie's lowered voice came through from the background. "I still say Hannah's partner is incredibly attractive."

Hannah quickly turned the phone back to herself and cast a glance at Jason, hoping he hadn't heard. Based on the broad grin on his face, he obviously had. Hannah rolled her eyes and focused back on the call with Susan.

Of course, Katie wasn't completely wrong. Jason was nice to look at. It was everything else about him that would drive a spy girl crazy.

Hannah cleared her throat. "We need to get into a gated garage, but we don't have the code."

Katie came into view and plopped down on her stomach on the leather ottoman. "No problem. We have a wireless bypass transmitter here in the workroom. I can double-check it and you can swing by and pick it up."

Hannah shook her head. "No can do."

Her friends waited for more explanation.

"We've got a tail."

Susan's expression went full bug-eyed.

"You? Got a tail?" Katie exclaimed.

"Just get rid of him." Susan grabbed an imaginary steering wheel and swung recklessly back and forth, in a horrible impression of Hannah's driving.

"We're just coming back from the adoption agency, so we can't break character," Hannah explained. "Do you have anything that can work from my phone?"

Susan turned to Katie. "Could you repurpose the code from the transmitter into an app for Hannah's phone?"

"Maybe, but it would take some time." Katie turned back to the camera and spoke to Hannah. "When do you need it?"

Hannah turned to Jason, eyebrows raised.

"We're about ten minutes away. Maybe fifteen if I drive slow enough to hit some red lights," he replied.

"Whoa. There's no way I can create a brand-new app in fifteen minutes," Katie said.

"Do the best you can," Hannah said. "We'll see if we can come up with more time, or a backup plan."

Katie and Susan both stood and ran off camera, Susan saying something about "tweaking the scrambler app" as she followed Katie into the workroom.

Hannah turned to Jason. "What other options do we have? Can we drive around town until the guy loses interest or runs out of gas?"

Jason shook his head. "Tails don't usually lose interest. Besides, randomly driving around town would definitely raise suspicions, don't you think?"

Hannah glanced in the mirror again. The small silver compact car was still behind them. Suddenly, their car swerved to the side. Hannah grabbed the handgrip to steady herself.

"What are you—"

"Getting gas," Jason said, pointing to the gas pumps. "Thanks for the idea."

Hannah watched their tail drive past. "He kept going. Let's just drive away."

Jason gave her a patronizing smile as he leaned over to pull the gas door lever. "You're still thinking like a spy. Remember our cover? It would be a little out of character to suddenly swerve into a gas station, then drive the other way." He stepped out of the car and unhurriedly fiddled with the gas pump before he started putting gas in the car.

Realizing that he probably had a point, she got out of the car to do her part to stall. "I'm gonna grab a snack. You want anything?"

"Thanks. Just get me whatever."

She wandered around the small, dirty aisles of the convenience store pretending to look for something for her . . . what was Jason again? Her husband? It felt weird to even think that word in her head. After spending what felt like more than a normal amount of time, she grabbed a Crunch bar and a water and paid for them.

On her way out of the convenience store, Hannah spotted the gray compact in a partially hidden parking spot across the road.

She got back in the car and offered Jason the water just as he reached for the candy bar. "This is for me," she said, quickly pulling the treat out of his reach. "Why would you assume that I wanted the water and you would get the chocolate?"

Jason opened his mouth, then shut it. Shaking his head, he started the car and pulled back onto the road. In the rearview mirror, Hannah watched the small gray car wait until they were half a block away before it pulled out to follow them.

"In my defense, it's not because I thought anything about whether a woman would want water and a man would want a candy bar. You just happened to buy my favorite kind. I thought you must have gotten it for me," Jason said.

Hannah glanced down at the Crunch bar in her lap. She'd grabbed *her* favorite without thinking. But she wasn't about to tell him they had the same favorite candy bar.

"Of course, you wouldn't have known it was my favorite," Jason said mostly to himself. "Not that you would have bought it for me even if you had . . ." his voice trailed off.

Hannah unwrapped the chocolate and took a huge, gloating bite out of it. But the normally delicious, crunchy texture felt dry in her mouth. Glancing sidelong at Jason, she could tell he was trying not to notice. She considered the candy once again, then with a huff, she broke off half—well, more than half—and handed him the rest.

His eyebrows went up in surprise. "Are you sure?"

With her mouth full of chocolate, Hannah couldn't have replied even if she wanted to. She thrust the candy closer to him and nodded.

He grabbed the last of the candy bar with a smile and took a bite. "Mmm, that's delicious," he said, glancing back at her. "And I'm happy to share my water, you know, if you're not still too grossed out."

Normally, Hannah would have politely declined, but she still couldn't swallow. And desperate times called for desperate measures. She popped the top off the water and took a quick swig. "Thanks," she said, replacing it in his cup holder.

For a brief moment, she almost felt like they could actually *be* a young married couple on their way back home—minus the twitterpated feelings, of course.

"Almost there," Jason said, eyeing an upcoming street. He glanced at Hannah with a look of anticipation.

She had almost forgotten about the call with Katie and Susan. Hannah pulled out her phone and checked the connection. An empty living room stared back at her. "Did you come up with anything?" she asked.

"Just a sec," Katie called from off-screen.

Hannah glanced at Jason. His brows went up, but he didn't say anything. It's not like they could take a drive around the neighborhood to stall for more time. Maybe they could stop at a neighboring unit and pretend to borrow some sugar.

"Okay, I think we've got it," Katie said breathlessly as she and Susan skidded to a stop in front of the camera. "I just sent a tool update to your scrambler app. Thanks to Susan's idea." She nodded to the redhead at her side.

Susan performed a very elaborate curtsey, her smile as broad as ever.

Hannah switched to the scrambler app and saw that there was a new icon called *Gate Key*. She tapped the icon. "Any special instructions?" Hannah asked, trying to act calm.

"Hold the phone against the card reader," Katie explained. "It will tell the system that there's a card there but the card has no code. Then when the system times out, it sends a crash command into the loop before the next cycle—"

Susan bumped Katie with an elbow, a common signal the Banana Girls used to tell her she was rambling.

"Actually, you probably don't care how it works as long as it gets you in," Katie finished.

Hannah smiled at her excitable friend and nodded, hoping the girls couldn't tell how nervous she was.

"Good luck," Katie said. "It will work."

Susan grinned and held two thumbs up.

"Thanks, girls," Hannah replied as she fumbled for the screen to terminate the connection.

Jason pointed to a three-story condo building and slowed the car. "That's the one."

Hannah nodded and took a calming breath. The scrambler tool would work.

It just had to.

The car slowed to a stop at the gate to the underground garage. Hannah activated the scrambler and handed the phone to Jason. He held it out the window, pressed against the card reader.

Nothing happened.

Jason looked back at Hannah. She bit her lips together and crossed her fingers.

The phone beeped.

A second went by.

The scanner beeped.

Another second went by.

Suddenly, the wide iron gate lurched to life, nearly scaring Hannah out of her seat.

"Nice job," Jason said, handing her phone back. "I'm glad you're on my team."

Apparently, her partner was full of kind surprises today.

Hannah basked in the glow of their success.

Jason pulled into a parking stall marked with a number twelve. "This spot is reserved for the rental unit. Maybe no one's staying there today."

Hannah glanced around. The parking garage was mostly enclosed, but she could still see the street through the open gaps in the walls. "We can't just sit here. Our tail will be expecting us to go into the house."

"Do your friends have an app that can get us into the condo?" Jason asked with a hopeful expression.

"Wouldn't it look silly if we're standing in front of the door to our own house, pointing a cell phone at the lock? Besides, we won't know until we get to the door whether it's a wireless lock or not."

Jason pulled out his phone. "I can check the property listing again."

"We don't have time for this," Hannah said, opening her door. "What if we go on a walk around the neighborhood? Is that in-character for our personas?"

Jason shrugged. "Sure."

"Great." Hannah slammed the door. "That will give us a chance to come up with a plan."

Together, they walked out of the parking garage and onto the street. Jason kept glancing at her as they went. Hannah was too distracted looking for the car that had followed them to have any idea what he wanted from her.

When he looked her way for the tenth time, she couldn't ignore it anymore. "Is something wrong?" She scanned the cars across the street.

He scratched the back of his head. He looked like he had bad news.

"What?" she said.

"Well, a couple on a walk would probably hold hands." He winced as he said it.

"Fine. Whatever," Hannah replied, still on high alert to everything happening around them.

It wasn't until Jason took her hand that Hannah realized what she'd just agreed to. Fortunately, he didn't try to intertwine their fingers. He simply squeezed lightly as they continued down the sidewalk.

Though she wouldn't have believed it a few days earlier, Hannah was forced to admit to herself that the warmth of his hand and the gentle pressure of his squeeze had a calming effect. She took a deep breath and tried to become her persona. They fell into a comfortable cadence of steps, arms swinging carelessly between them. She hoped it looked natural. "Do you see our tail?" she asked quietly.

"I think he's behind the white van over there." Jason subtly nodded toward a small side street they had just passed.

"If we can draw him away from the parking garage, maybe one of us can go back for the car. Then we can meet up somewhere else."

He made a satisfied sound. "Yeah. That might work. But would a married couple—"

Hannah cut him off. "We're running out of options, Jason. At some point, we both need to get home tonight. This might be the best we've got, regardless of how it looks."

Jason scowled, but he didn't seem upset with her. He was probably frustrated about the situation as well.

"What if I pretend to get a phone call and rush back home like I need to grab something?" Hannah suggested.

"That's a good idea," he said with a nod. "But what if he follows you instead of me?"

"Then you sneak back to the car and come get me," Hannah said.

"But what will you be doing? You obviously can't go to the condo."

Hannah shrugged. "I'm a spy. I'll come up with something."

Jason gave her a genuine smile. His look conveyed confidence, and for the first time in the mission, Hannah was glad she wasn't doing this alone.

They walked for another minute down the sidewalk. Jason pulled out his phone but held it casually at his side. A second later, he lifted it and checked the screen. He had taken a video of the street behind them. It was upside down, but Hannah could clearly see the gray compact car pulling out onto the road to follow them.

"Do you have earbuds with you?" Hannah asked.

Jason shook his head. "No. Do I need them?"

"If we need to split up, it would be great to be able to talk to each other. That way I know if I'm clear or not."

"Sorry. I don't have them on me."

Hannah dug out her wireless earbuds and offered him one. "Here, you can borrow one of mine."

"Are you sure you want to share an earbud?"

"Sure, why not?" Hannah said.

"Well, backwash in a drink is one thing, but earwax . . ."

Hannah held it out. "Just take it before I change my mind."

Jason put his hand out, a playful grin on his face. He was teasing her now.

She dropped the single earbud into Jason's hand. He connected it to his phone and dialed her number, a subtle nod to indicate it was time to set their plan in motion.

Hannah pulled out her phone and answered it. "Hi, how's it going?" she said, fully in character.

"I promise to wipe off all the earwax from your earbud before I give it back," Jason said quietly, his voice echoing a split second later in her ear.

Knowing that a doting wife would say something to her husband before abandoning him on their walk, Hannah placed a hand gently on his shoulder and pulled the phone away from her ear before saying, "You're lucky it would be out of character to slug you."

He chuckled and winked at her.

Was that fake Jason or real Jason?

Hannah spun on the spot and brought the phone to her cheek again. "Really? Okay, I'll be right there." She caught sight of their tail but acted like she hadn't noticed. Hoping to appear in a hurry, she picked up her pace. Ten seconds later, she passed the small gray car.

Even with only a casual glance at the driver, Hannah immediately recognized their tail. "It's the guy who tried to steal my purse the other night," she whispered into the phone as soon as she passed the car.

"Are you sure?"

"Absolutely," Hannah replied. "What is he doing now? Can you tell if he's still following you?"

"At this very moment, the role of bored husband looking at his phone while patiently waiting for his wife to continue their walk is being played by . . . me. And it just so happens that I can see the car out of the corner of my eye as he's slowly driving past me." Jason paused his running commentary for a moment. "He stopped half a block down. I think you're clear."

Hannah continued her pace as she approached the condo's parking garage. If she could get the car without being seen, all Jason would need to do was lose his tail in the neighborhood somehow and they'd be home free.

Half a dozen steps from the entrance to the garage, she heard Jason's sudden intake of breath.

"What?" Hannah asked.

"He's turning around. He's coming back your way. If you're not already in the car, I don't think you'll make it out before he sees you."

Hannah continued past the garage entrance. "I'm not in the car yet. How fast do you think I am?"

"I'm afraid any witty response I would make would only be misinterpreted, so I'll just say stay there and I'll join you. We'll try to shake him some other way."

"Hang on, this can still work. I'll lead him away from the garage, then you grab the car and come get me."

"Without a plan, you'll look like you're wandering around lost in our own neighborhood," Jason shot back.

"You're just worried I'll get the points when I pull it off," Hannah said with a laugh.

"Honestly, if you can get us out of this mess while still in-character, you deserve the points."

Hannah smiled to herself. "I think I've got an idea. Get ready to make a break for the car."

She turned at a side street leading away from their condo. As she walked, she put in her other earbud and switched to handsfree.

"He's right behind you," Jason said quietly over the call. "I'm heading for the garage now."

"Okay," Hannah replied in a whisper.

Zeroing in on the last townhouse in the row on the opposite side of the street, Hannah strode briskly toward the door. It was the farthest away she could get from the parking garage without having to walk into a different neighborhood. Hopefully, it would draw their tail far enough for Jason to be out of sight.

"Can you get into the garage without being seen yet?" Hannah could still hear ambient sounds on the other end of the line.

Jason's voice came back a moment later. "Uh, possibly. He's almost out of sight. Keep doing whatever you're doing."

As she mounted the steps to the last townhouse, she cast a quick glance back down the road. The gray compact car had pulled up to the curb next to a large SUV. Their pursuer was apparently becoming bolder. He was easily within sight of the door.

Nothing to do now but follow through with her idea.

Hannah took a deep breath and rang the doorbell. She hoped that someone would answer and be open to a little improvisation.

The door opened to reveal a stocky man in his early thirties wearing workout shorts and a muscle shirt. "Yes?"

Hannah had hoped for a kind, old grandmotherly type. Or maybe a mom with kids. But things rarely worked out the way she hoped. "Would you mind giving me a hug?" she asked.

He gave Hannah a wary look. That was not the reaction she needed.

"Like we're old friends?" She looked sideways with her eyes, hoping to communicate that something was going on. "Please," she pleaded.

Comprehension dawned quickly, and his face spread into a huge grin. The muscle guy stepped forward eagerly, arms extended like they were old pals. "How are you?" he asked before squeezing her tight.

"Thank you," she whispered in his ear.

"What's going on?" Jason asked in her ear. "Who are you hugging?" He sounded momentarily flustered.

Hannah did her best to ignore him. She gestured broadly with her hands, as if she was having a comfortable conversation with a friend. "Is your wife home, by any chance?"

"Actually, I'm not married." The man kept smiling at her. He was a natural at this. Though it did make Hannah wonder if his willingness to go along was more due to a pretty woman showing up on his doorstep than anything else.

"I need to make it look like we're neighbors," Hannah continued, gesturing with a thumb toward the rental unit's parking garage. If her disjointed hand signals confused the guy, he hid it well.

"If we're neighbors, then I would probably invite you in for a visit?" By his tone, she could tell he was asking whether that's what she wanted.

She did need a way to get out of view of their tail so she could make her escape. Would going inside this stranger's house present a whole new set of dangers?

If she had any hope of maintaining her cover, Hannah didn't see that she had any other choice. "Yes, thank you."

The nice guy stepped aside and swept a broad arm through the entryway

Hannah slid past him to the sounds of Jason protesting in her ear.

"Did you just go into a stranger's house?" Jason asked. "Are you crazy?"

She was tempted to mute Jason, but she needed to stay on the call to know when her getaway car was there.

Once inside, Hannah put a fair distance between her and the muscular stranger. The man casually closed the door, as if this sort of thing was a common occurrence. He stuffed his hands in the pockets of his basketball shorts and leaned against a nearby wall.

Hannah held her hands out. "I'm sorry to barge in on you like this. It's sort of complicated."

The guy shrugged. "Whenever gorgeous women show up on my doorstep asking for hugs and begging to be let inside, it's my policy not to ask for any explanations."

"Thanks," she said as she glanced around the entryway, trying to determine if there were other ways out. "As long as you don't mind helping out the good guys," she added absently.

"Always. Although my brother is better at it than I am." The man tilted his head toward a framed photo on the entryway table showing a young Marine in full-dress uniform.

Hannah nodded her understanding, and some of her worry lifted.

His gaze settled on her again. "Are you okay, though? Do you need any help?"

"Hannah, are you still okay?" Jason's voice came in loud in her earbud. "I'm in the car. Where are you?"

Cupping her hand against the earbud, she said, "Yeah, I'm fine. I'm with . . ." Hannah glanced at her host.

"Nate," he said, pointing to his chest.

"I'm with Nate. His house is the last one on the next street."

"And you're good?"

Hannah smiled at the concern in Jason's voice. "Yeah." It felt nice to suddenly have so much concern for her welfare.

"How am I going to get you?" Jason asked.

Hannah walked to the back of the townhouse and glanced out the window. "There's an alley behind the townhouse row." She turned to Nate. "Is there a way to access the lane behind your house without driving onto the main street?"

"You can come around the lane from that way." He pointed away from the direction Hannah had come.

She pulled out her phone. "Jason, I'm sending my location. You'll have to drive a few blocks past us to get here without our tail seeing you. I'll meet you in the lane behind the townhouses."

"Got it. I'll be there in a minute."

Hannah turned back to Nate. "My partner will be here in just a minute, but I could use another favor."

"Sure," Nate said with a big smile.

"We have a sort-of stalker."

Nate frowned at that. "Do you want me to go get rid of him?"

"No," Hannah said with a smile. "I just need you to watch for him. He's in a small gray compact car about two houses down."

Nate moved to the window and peered through the half-opened blinds. "I see him."

Hannah hurried to the back of the townhouse and checked the lane. It was clear. "Jason, if you can get here before our stalker loses patience, I think this might work."

"I'm just coming around the next block. I should be there in half a minute."

A few moments later, Jason's car turned down the access lane. "I see you. I'll be right out," Hannah said. Before she could reach the door to the back patio, she saw Nate pull back from the blinds.

"He's leaving," Nate called out. "He just drove by. He might try to check around the back."

"Hang on, Jason. He's on the move," Hannah said.

"Yep, he's turning toward the back lane," Nate said.

"Jason, stop. You have to get out of there. He's coming right for you." Hannah watched out the back window as Jason's car screeched to a halt.

"How? It's not like I can make a three-point turn."

"Put it in reverse." Hannah checked the side window. Their pursuer was halfway around the block. It wouldn't be long before he reached the alley.

"You want me to go in full reverse down a narrow parking alley?" The annoyance carried clearly over the phone connection.

"I don't know. Just do something!" Hannah cried. They only had a matter of seconds.

"Got it. That's perfect," Jason said.

Hannah frowned in confusion. She hurried to the back and peeked out at the alley. Jason's car had disappeared. A second later, their pursuer pulled into the empty lane and drove slowly past. "Jason, where are you? How did you get away?"

"The garage. That was perfect timing."

Hannah turned back down the hall and saw Nate standing by the door to the garage, a big grin on his face.

"These townhouses come with two-car garages, but it's just me and my MINI," he said.

Hannah hurried to the door and looked in. Jason's car was neatly wedged next to a small blue hatchback. She looked back at Nate and smiled. "You saved the day again."

"All in the line of duty," he said with a grin.

Hannah gave him a quick hug. "Thanks again, Nate."

He nodded. "I'll tell you when it's clear."

She hurried into the garage and jumped into the car with Jason. "That was close," she said.

"Too close." Jason nodded to Nate. "If I had been the one trying to pretend to be neighborly, I doubt he would have let me in, no matter how I begged."

A small smile curved Hannah's lips. "Not so smug about spy girls' *intangibles* anymore? That's refreshing."

He shrugged, a somewhat sheepish expression on his face. "My opinion of your skill set may have improved since we first met."

Coming from him, that was a monumental admission.

Nate stuck his head into the garage and pressed the garage door button. "It's all clear," he said as he waved them away.

Jason and Hannah both waved back. "Thanks, Nate," she called out.

They pulled slowly out into the parking lane and then proceeded out of the townhouse neighborhood. Hannah was on-edge at every intersection, expecting to see their tail pull up next to them. But the farther they went, the more she was able to relax.

Suddenly remembering her afternoon classes, she checked the time on the car dash. "Well, I guess I missed my statistics quiz," she said with a huff.

"I'm sure your professor would let you retake it." Jason grinned. "Does the university not offer a spy girl accommodation?"

"Sure. But this particular professor requires me to produce a dead body as proof. Are you volunteering?"

Jason chuckled and shook his head. "You are a piece of work, Hannah. You know that, right?"

Hannah smiled. She did know.

And she was proud of it.

CHAPTER EIGHT

"**G**OT IT!" SUSAN HELD up her tablet triumphantly. She stood up and started dancing around the couches of Club Banana as if she had just won the lottery.

From her seat in the corner, Hannah couldn't help but smile at her friend's antics.

"What's she got?" Anna asked from the kitchen. "Happy feet?"

Susan suddenly stopped and stared at Anna. "That's not my happy feet dance. This is my happy feet dance."

The excitable redhead started dancing again with more vigor. But truthfully, the dances looked the same to Hannah.

"She was doing a search for the car that chased us yesterday," Hannah explained. "She must have found it."

Susan landed back on the couch and picked up the tablet. "Yep. The crazy chaser-guy rented his vehicle from Palmetto Car Rentals. It's a small regional rental company based in Charlotte, North Carolina."

"Can we hack their system and figure out who the guy is?" Hannah asked.

Susan shrugged and pointed across the room at Katie.

"Not from here," Katie answered with a shake of her head.

"Don't you have some hacking magic wand that you can wave and get access to their network?" Hannah asked.

Katie struck a defiant pose. "I know we're amazing enough to make this look easy," she gestured between herself and Susan, "but it's no cakewalk. Just because you can't see it, doesn't mean software doesn't have rules and limitations."

Hannah furrowed a brow at her. "You and Susan aren't just angling for a new server or router or whatever, are you?"

Katie huffed. "You could buy us a room full of servers and we still wouldn't be able to hack their network remotely."

"But we wouldn't mind if you still bought us the servers," Susan added.

"So, how do we get the information?" Hannah asked.

"We could do it above board for a change," Anna piped in from the kitchen.

"That'd take, like, ten days," Susan said. "A month if they're feeling uncooperative."

Hannah shook her head. "We can't wait that long." She turned back to Katie. "What are our options if it needs to be faster?"

"We would need to have someone onsite," Katie said.

"In Charlotte?" Hannah asked.

Katie offered an apologetic shrug.

Susan threw both fists in the air. "Road trip!" she yelled triumphantly.

"Hang on," Anna said. "Let's not be hasty." She came and sat across from Katie.

Susan's enthusiasm deflated as she sunk back down on the couch.

"Do you need to be at a computer in the headquarters location for this to work?" Anna asked Katie.

Katie scrunched one eye closed. "Not technically. I could probably get the information if I was on any computer on the company's system. You see, if I can use the new interface drive that Susan helped me work on and Hannah built the mechanical case for, then I can—"

Anna held up a hand. "I don't need all the details right now."

"Sorry," Katie replied.

"Is there a Palmetto Car Rental location in Atlanta?" Anna asked.

Susan grabbed her tablet again and started searching. She whistled and nodded vigorously. "Oh yeah. Definitely. There are at least a dozen."

Anna turned back to Katie. "How long do you need to hack the system?"

"Ten, maybe fifteen minutes," she replied.

"And do we have a way to get you into one of these rental locations for more than a minute or two?"

"We could try the fumigator trick," Susan suggested.

The girls all groaned.

"What's the fumigator trick?" Mari asked as she walked into the living room.

"We show up at a location pretending to have an order to fumigate the building. Then we get the job done," Susan said.

"That sounds like the exterminator trick you used trying to rescue my mother," Mari said.

Susan nodded in agreement.

"Except the fumigator trick wouldn't have required me to strap a live mouse to my leg," Mari added drily.

Susan's eyes went wide, and she mouthed a silent "Sorry."

Anna shook her head. "Don't feel bad, Mari. The fumigator trick wouldn't have worked at Keating Mansion. It only works in small buildings with minimal security protocols. Plus," she turned to Susan, "even then, it doesn't always work."

Susan's exaggerated frown was comical.

"What about a computer on the same network as Palmetto's?" Hannah asked.

Katie squinted at nothing in particular. "Yeah, I think I could make that work. Why do you ask?"

"I have a friend who works at the airport rental car center. Those computers are most likely connected to a common network hub."

Katie stood and began pacing excitedly. "Yeah, this could work. We'd need to have two of us there so that one of you distracts—I mean helps—anyone who comes to the counter while I hack the system. Of course, we'll need to get outfits that match the counter employees' uniforms. But I should be able to handle that." She stopped and looked at the girls. "Who's going with me?"

Anna held a hand out, indicating Hannah. "It's Hannah's mission and her contact at the rental company. I think she should go."

Hannah sighed. She had expected as much.

Katie spun and looked at Hannah. "When should we go?"

"Not in the morning," Hannah said.

"Not tomorrow morning? Or not any morning?" Katie asked. She sounded far too innocent for it to be a serious question.

Hannah glared at her. Katie knew Hannah's distaste for anything before eleven.

Katie held up her hands in surrender. "Fine. How about tomorrow afternoon?"

"I'll check with my friend, but I think that should work." Hannah pulled out her phone and scrolled through her list of contacts, considering what time of day would work best for her friend's schedule. "Actually, as much as I hate to start a mission at any time that ends in A.M., we might need to be in position before she goes on her lunch break."

"Send me the name of the car rental, and I'll get going on the outfits," Katie said.

"Shouldn't you be prepping the hacking fob?" Hannah asked.

Katie swatted away Hannah's suggestion like a pesky fly. "I'll have Susan help me."

"With the hack or the outfits?" Mari asked.

"Both," Katie and Susan said simultaneously.

CHAPTER NINE

S TANDING BESIDE A LARGE pillar situated between the escalator and a tall wall of windows in the airport car rental center, Hannah and Katie tried to keep themselves relatively hidden without making it look like they were trying to stay hidden. Hannah used the reflection in the windows to check the rental counter of the Beat the Heat Rental Car agency. Her friend, Tenesha, had agreed to send her coworker on her lunch break and then leave immediately after. The plan was that Katie and Hannah would be done before Tenesha's coworker could get back. No one would be the wiser, and Tenesha would get two lunch breaks.

Katie and Hannah were dressed identically to the two women behind the car rental counter—thus the need to stay hidden until the switch. Just when Katie was starting to get antsy, Hannah saw Tenesha's coworker walk past and out of sight.

"That's our cue," Hannah whispered.

As Hannah and Katie walked toward the rental counter, Tenesha left her computer, subtly nodding at Hannah as they crossed paths. Nothing needed to be said.

"Take this one," Hannah indicated the first computer terminal as they came around the rental counter.

Katie sat and inserted the small flash-drive device into the computer. She hunched down over the keyboard and, within a few seconds, was completely engrossed in her task, oblivious to anything around her.

Hannah decided that was probably a good thing when she caught a glimpse of the guy working the rental counter next to theirs. His rental uniform fit extremely well across his bulging shoulders and arms. He had medium-brown skin and close-cut hair and beard. But Hannah decided that his smile was the most dangerous thing about him.

"Hey," the guy said. "You must be new here."

Hannah nodded briefly before facing forward to the non-existent line of customers. Then she remembered that she couldn't simply ignore him. It was her job to run interference while Katie hacked the system, and if this guy got too suspicious, it might blow the whole thing.

Taking a deep breath, Hannah slid casually toward him and switched into flirtation mode. "Yeah. We're just here on a temporary assignment to do some training." She let her eyebrow tick up slightly as she considered him. "But I might be tempted to ask for a permanent transfer." Every time she flirted with a guy for a mission, she was sure they'd see right through it. Permanent transfer? For someone she'd just met? No guy would be dumb enough to believe that.

A broad grin spread on her neighbor's lips. "You definitely should transfer over permanently." His voice seemed to have dropped half an octave and doubled in huskiness. "I'm Drake," he said, raising a brow.

Resisting the urge to shake her head in disbelief that it had worked again, Hannah kept up the charade. "I'm Hannah." She took a step closer to the half-wall that divided the two companies' counters. "And what's so great about working here? Besides the view," she added with a suggestive wink.

Drake's chest puffed out even more, and he nodded, probably congratulating himself. Men's egos never ceased to amaze her.

"So, besides the view," he paused for emphasis, waggling his eyebrows, "Airport rental is great because when it's busy the time flies by, and when it's not," he put an elbow on the counter and leaned back against it, "you can just kick back and relax with neighbors."

"I definitely like the relaxing part," Hannah said, taking a small step closer.

Drake grinned, and Hannah forced herself to stay focused. He did have a dazzling smile.

He must have noticed Katie sitting at the computer on the other end of the counter, because he leaned to the side and asked, "What's your friend up to?"

As casually as she could, Hannah shifted to block his view. "Oh, she's new with the company, so she's working on some training."

With a short grunt of understanding, Drake nodded and refocused his attention on Hannah. She hoped Katie wouldn't take too long, because she couldn't be able to keep up this level of flirtation for much longer without taking a break. Or a very solid eye-roll.

After a moment of simply grinning at her, Drake's expression suddenly changed. He looked up at the ceiling. "Incoming."

Hannah followed his gaze, but couldn't see anything out of the ordinary above them. She did hear a very faint rumbling sound followed a few seconds later by the swoosh of automated doors and a growing din of scattered conversation.

"Well, it was good talking to you," Drake said as he moved back to his computer terminal.

Hannah decided to follow his lead and took up position at her own computer. She glanced down at the screen, completely unfamiliar with how the rental system would work.

She was haphazardly clicking through menu options in a vain attempt to figure out what she was doing when the first wave of travelers arrived. A man in his early thirties stepped up to the counter. He had obviously run to beat the rush.

"Parker Headly," he said quickly, pointing to her computer screen.

Hannah fumbled around the menu system until she found a screen that listed the reservations. She quickly located the man's name, but struggled to figure out what to do next. The system wanted her to verify a bunch of things. She clicked *OK* on everything that popped up until the screen showed which car he had reserved. She bent down and found the key cabinet under the counter. After a few minutes of searching, she figured out the organization of the keys and plucked the correct one from its hook.

Standing back up, she handed the man the key to his car. He gave her a funny look like she had done something wrong. "Bring it back the way you found it," Hannah said cheerfully before pointing vaguely in the direction that might be the rental car garage. "Next," she called as the confused man started moving away.

Though this car rental company wasn't as large as some of the national brands, it apparently could still attract a crowd. At least a dozen people stood in her line; many of them kept casting disapproving looks at Katie, probably wondering why she wasn't doing her fair share of the work.

If those people only knew the truth.

Hannah pretended to be an obnoxiously cheerful employee as she helped people get their rental cars. The looks of confusion slowly faded into looks of gratitude as she quickly doled out keys. She wasn't technically racing her new neighbor, but Hannah couldn't help but notice that her line shrank much faster than Drake's line, and he was supposedly an expert at airport rental car stuff.

Hannah's next customer was a middle-aged man in an expensive suit. She scanned the cabinet for the key to the car he'd reserved only to discover that it wasn't there. She double checked the dwindling stock of keys to no avail.

"Don't you have a car for me?" the man asked impatiently.

Hannah clicked on his reservation one more time to confirm the car he was supposed to have. The key definitely wasn't there. "Sir, it would seem that the S-Class sedan is not here." Hannah checked one more time and caught a glimpse of a Corvette key fob. "How about a Corvette instead?"

The businessman started to complain about his missing luxury car when her suggestion stopped him mid-sentence. His eyebrows rose a fraction and a broad smile spread across his face. "Actually, a Corvette would be acceptable."

Hannah grabbed the Corvette keys and handed them to the man. "Make sure you watch your speed. This one handles so smoothly that you may not realize until it's too late."

The businessman nodded his appreciation and walked away, an additional spring in his step.

Hannah glanced over at Katie. She couldn't tell if her friend was any closer to finishing the task or not. Fortunately, Hannah's line of customers was almost gone.

Three customers later, she finally had a chance to take a breath again.

"How's it going?" she whispered to Katie.

Katie didn't respond, but her fingers continued to fly wildly across the keyboard.

As Hannah moved closer to ask again, she heard Drake's voice behind her. "That's one of the only drawbacks of working airport rental."

It's not that Hannah disliked making small talk with handsome guys, but she really wanted to hurry Katie along, and she couldn't do that if she also needed to keep distracting Drake. If only she hadn't drawn his attention so easily. Maybe she should have insisted that one of the other girls come in her place. Of course, all the Banana Girls were beautiful and could attract men's attention in their own ways, so maybe it wouldn't have mattered; Drake would have flirted with any of them.

Hannah glanced back at Drake, and he motioned her over with a crook of his finger. Mentally turning on her bubbly persona, she stepped closer to where he leaned against the dividing wall.

"I'll let you in on a little secret," Drake whispered.

Hannah braced herself for some pickup line or come on.

"You'll work through the line of customers faster—and keep them happier—if you're both at the rental counter." He peered around Hannah at Katie, still typing away on the other console.

What excuse could she come up with for Katie's behavior? "Uh . . . that might be true . . . under normal circumstances. But she's still in training," Hannah said.

"Shouldn't you be training her to do the actual job?" Drake sounded genuinely confused.

Hannah glanced casually around, trying to come up with a reason that wouldn't draw too much undue attention to Katie. "Uh . . . it's a new kind of training. You know, she just listens to how I interact with the customers and takes detailed notes on the computer. It's helpful for employees who are extra shy. That way, she won't get flustered by interacting with customers before she's ready." Hannah knew she was grasping at straws, but she only needed to put this guy off for a few more minutes and they could make their escape.

Drake's brows furrowed. "Why would your company even hire a rental counter employee who gets flustered working with people?"

Why couldn't this guy just believe Hannah's lie and leave her alone? "Oh, it's part of our outreach initiative, we go into—"

"Done!" Katie declared.

Hannah whirled around to see Katie's beaming smile. She stood from her chair and shook out the stiffness in her arms and hands. Hannah saw the moment that Katie noticed Drake. The petite girl's entire demeanor changed. She went from accomplished engineering student and world-class hacker to ditzy beach girl in half a second flat.

"Ah, that was so hard," Katie whined. Her voice had also gone up half an octave. She glided over toward Hannah and Drake. "Hey, who's your new friend?" she asked Hannah.

"This is Drake," Hannah replied drily.

"Hi, Drake. I'm Katiana." Katie held out her hand.

"That is a beautiful name." Drake suavely took her hand, his voice dripped with charm.

Katie's giggle lasted twice as long as it should have.

Hannah pulled on Katie's arm. "If you're done with your training,"—Hannah drew out the last word—"then we should probably get going."

"It looks like your program for shy employees is really working," Drake spoke to Hannah, but he still hadn't taken his eyes off Katie. "In fact, would it help your coworker's shyness if she just stood here and visited with me for a bit longer?"

Katie nodded vigorously.

Pulling harder, Hannah was finally able to separate her friend from their dangerously handsome neighbor.

"Bye, Drake. I'll see you later," Katie called out.

"No, you won't," Hannah whispered as she dragged Katie away from the rental counter.

On their way past the escalator, Hannah's friend Tenesha walked by right on cue, her head dipping slightly as they passed. Hopefully, Tenesha would be able to come up with a viable explanation for Hannah and Katie's brief presence there.

"Were you flirting with Drake the entire time?" Katie asked once they were out of the building.

Hannah couldn't help but smile at Katie's very predictable question.

Katie let out an exasperated sigh. "I knew it. Why do you always get to flirt with the hot guys, and I'm stuck doing the hard work?"

"Katie, I promise if there's ever a mission that is specifically about flirting with all the hot guys, you can have it."

"Really?" Her friend's brow ticked up in a skeptical look. A second later, she deflated. "Yeah, but what are the chances we'll ever get a mission like that?"

Hannah smiled and shrugged. "You never know."

Chapter Ten

"Are you sure you don't want any of these flash bombs Katie and I made?" Susan asked as Hannah stuffed the last of her clothing for the retreat into a suitcase.

"Sure, go ahead." Hannah wasn't really paying attention. The weekend of the adoption retreat had finally arrived, and she had far more important things on her mind.

"I don't know as much about mechanical design as you do, but I took a shot at building the casing with your new 3D printer," Susan added.

"Uh-huh," Hannah said, more focused on whether her new tan sweater would look good with the navy slacks she had already packed.

"Also, do you mind if I use a few of your quadcopters to hoist myself up off the roof and take an aerial tour of the city?" Susan asked.

Hannah definitely wanted to bring the red blouse. She would get plenty of attention in that—not that she necessarily wanted attention from anyone in particular. In fact, now that she didn't quite hate Jason as much, she'd need to be on her guard around him. "What did you say, Susan?"

Susan giggled. "Your mind is about a million miles away. Are you super nervous for the retreat or something?"

Hannah absently shook her head. She wasn't really nervous at all. But for some reason, she couldn't wait to get back to solving the case and maybe even beating Jason at their friendly little competition. She'd love to prove to Jason that she could be a beautiful woman and an amazing spy at the same time.

Anna walked in with a tablet. "Suze, I'll take it from here. I don't think Hannah's paying attention to you anyway."

Susan shrugged and flashed a bright smile before walking out of the room.

"Sorry, Susan," Hannah called after her. "What was she asking about the quadcopters?" she asked Anna.

Anna ignored her question. "How are things going on the mission?"

With a lift of her shoulder, Hannah proceeded to bring Anna up to speed on their leads and suspicions.

"How are things going with Jason 'I'm-a-man-so-I'm-a-better-spy' Briggs?"

Hannah laughed. "Still extremely clueless sometimes."

Anna responded with a lifted brow. It was an obvious invitation to elaborate, but Hannah wasn't sure how to explain, so she opted for a distraction. She turned and surveyed her suitcase. "I think I've got everything." Anna opened her mouth, but Hannah grabbed the suitcase and headed for the living room, cutting off whatever Anna was about to say. "Besides, the retreat is only two nights, so I won't be gone long."

In the living room, she waved goodbye to the other roommates and headed out.

Her tall friend followed her out into the hall. "Good luck," Anna said as they walked toward the elevator. "And try to be nice to your partner."

Hannah was about to say she was always nice, but the elevator dinged and her partner spilled out, nearly bowling the two ladies over.

"Speak of the devil," Anna whispered with a giggle.

"What are you doing here?" Hannah asked. "You could have waited in the lobby." She still wasn't sure what Jason's issue was with elevators, but she felt bad that he'd had to ride fifty-three floors up to get her, only to get right back in a few seconds later.

Jason's chest heaved as though he had just been holding his breath. "Oh . . . it wouldn't be polite to . . . uh . . . I thought you could use some help with your luggage." He pointed down at her rolling suitcase.

She smiled at the gesture. "It's just one bag, so I think I can manage. But thanks anyway." She stepped into the elevator and cast a sidelong glance at Anna, who was still eyeing her partner with curiosity.

Jason stood outside the doors of the elevator, still carrying on the conversation. "One bag, that's great," he said. "I actually thought with all the gadgets that you girls usually have that you'd—"

Hannah skewered him with a withering glare that cut off whatever sexist thing he was about to say. She glanced back at her friend. Anna's broad smile said it all. Two years working together on the team they cofounded meant that they often didn't need to use words to communicate.

"Call me," Anna mouthed, miming a phone to her ear.

Jason gave Anna a half-wave of greeting and farewell before taking a deep breath and stepping back into the elevator. He grabbed the rail on the side wall and offered Hannah a forced smile.

As soon as the doors closed and the elevator began its rapid descent, Jason started pacing again.

"Can I do anything to help?" Hannah asked.

He forcefully shook his head but continued doing tiny circuits back and forth in the small space until they reached the lobby.

Hannah watched him as they made their way to his car. With each step away from the elevator, he seemed to return more and more to his normal self.

A few minutes later, after Jason had found his way to the interstate, he turned to Hannah. "So, you mentioned a quick mission at the rental car center. Did you find out anything?"

Hannah blew out a long breath. "Our purse-snatcher turned stalker guy is listed on the rental car agreement as Eric Chen. The picture on the license is definitely the guy who I wrestled my purse from. Unfortunately, it's pretty much a dead end."

"He's not really Eric Chen?" Jason asked.

"He might be, but the license is definitely a fake—not state issued. And the credit card he used doesn't have any traceable personal information. And none of the agency databases have any Eric Chens that match our guy. We need to know more about him."

Jason nodded in thought, his gaze focused on the road. "Maybe after the retreat, we can try and find out more about him. He's shown up twice when we've been undercover together. He must be related to the mission somehow." Jason paused in thought. Finally, he shrugged. "Anyway, good job on what you did get."

"Thanks." Hannah was grateful for the compliment, even though it didn't really feel like a win for her or her team.

They drove on in silence for several more minutes as the wide, divided highway walled by tall manicured trees gradually turned to a narrow country road surrounded by farmland and wild forest. Hannah wondered just how rustic this adoption retreat was going to be.

"I don't know exactly what types of activities they'll have us do, especially considering we don't have children," Jason said. "But let's find out whatever we can about Bethany Clark and the Grays and the Bakers. It would be great if we could spend time with them, but even just talking to other people about them could help."

Hannah nodded her agreement. "And we need to stay open to other suspects. We know Eric must be involved, but he can't be the only one."

"Definitely," Jason said.

Hannah was glad they were making some progress in the investigation. Pretending to be Jason's wife for an entire weekend made her extremely nervous, but it would be worth it if they could solve the case.

Half an hour later, after navigating through a handful of adorable towns, they pulled onto a narrow, well-manicured country lane which wound its way through tall groves of trees. The last orange rays of the setting sun dappled the forest canopy around them. It felt like they had stumbled onto the opening scene of a Hallmark movie. All they needed was a heroine on the side of the road with car trouble and a hunky mechanic that could fix anything—including her conflicted emotions about her career in the big city—to pick her up and sweep her off her feet.

Either that or it was the opening to a horror movie where the reclusive mountain man finds the stranded woman and drags her back to his shack in the woods to imprison her until she falls in love with him.

Hannah glanced at Jason. She mused on whether their fake-relationship would be a better fit for the feel-good romance or the psychological thriller, laughing to herself when she realized that it would probably be somewhere in between.

As she was about to share this humorous insight with her partner, the lane came over a rise and opened up to a broad meadow with a large mansion in the middle.

It was beautiful, like something out of a postcard.

A tall, wrought-iron gate barred the road as it exited the forest. Hannah glanced along the fence and saw it disappear into the trees on both sides. At least they wouldn't worry about security during their stay.

Jason held out their invitation to a scanner at the gate control box. After the gates opened, they drove up the quaint lane to a turnaround in front of the mansion, passing an ornately decorated board saying "Welcome Adoption Families!"

Jason parked behind a minivan being unloaded by retreat attendants.

A woman approached from the mansion doors. "Welcome to Sweetwater Falls Retreat."

Hannah put on a friendly smile. "We're the Sterlings—Hannah and Jason," she said awkwardly. Maybe with a few more weeks of practice, she could get used to introducing herself and Jason as a couple. Actually, it might take a few more decades to get used to something like that. Hannah wondered what Jason would look like in twenty or thirty years.

That thought sent a wave of goosebumps up her arms.

Better to not think about that.

"If you'll continue into the main house, a representative from your adoption agency will meet you there," the woman said with obvious practice. "Don't worry about your luggage or your car; our attendants will get your car parked and your luggage brought to your suite."

Jason and Hannah walked up the steps to the mansion's large front doors. The interior of the house had all the amenities Hannah would have expected, but it seemed that everything had been repurposed to serve the needs of a corporate retreat.

"Jason. Hannah."

Hannah turned to see Sandra, Bethany's assistant, moving toward them, holding out two small gift bags.

"Hi, Sandra. It's nice to see a familiar face," Jason said as they accepted the welcome totes.

Hannah glanced over Sandra's shoulder. "Is Bethany here?"

Sandra's brow furrowed. "Unfortunately, she couldn't make it to the retreat this year. You'll have to make do with me instead." She gave a self-deprecating smile.

Hannah tried to make up for her gaffe. "No, that's fine. I'm sure everything will be wonderful, especially knowing you'll be here."

She and Jason shared a subtle look, both knowing that Bethany's absence would put a major damper on their investigation during the retreat.

"Actually, I'm only here until tomorrow morning," Sandra said as she guided them farther into the mansion. "I need to get back to the office. I still have so much to get ready for the send-off gala in a few weeks."

Poor Sandra sounded entirely overworked. Maybe Bethany should consider hiring another assistant to help with the agency.

Sandra led them through wide halls, past converted dens and dining rooms, to a large meeting room overlooking the back patios. "After the orientation, I'll be back to take you to meet your weekend group." She indicated that they should enter.

Hannah really wanted to ask who was in their group, but it didn't seem like the time.

A family of four sat on one of the couches. It might be more correct to say that the parents sat on the couches while the two children—a girl about six and a boy about four—bounced around them.

Jason took Hannah's hand and led the way to a comfortable sofa. Hannah smiled at the family, which caused the children to immediately become shy. Jason and Hannah introduced themselves to the parents and did their best to make small talk.

After a few moments, the boy began inching toward them. He would slowly peek his little head above the tall arm of the couch, then quickly retreat down again. Hannah had so little experience with children that she didn't know what else to do besides continue smiling at him.

Jason pretended not to notice at first until the boy's head was almost entirely above the arm of the couch. Then he suddenly swung his attention to the boy and took a dramatic breath, sounding genuinely surprised. The boy squealed and quickly ducked out of sight. By the time he ventured to peek again, Jason was casually looking out the windows as if nothing had happened. He waited until the boy's grinning face was entirely visible again to repeat his earlier reaction.

Despite being completely expected from Hannah's point of view, the boy seemed to be even more thrilled by Jason's attention the second time. He giggled and squirmed as he hid himself again. Jason and his new little friend repeated the exercise half a dozen times; each time, the boy grew bolder as Jason would wait for him to peek higher above the edge of the couch.

Amidst all this, Hannah tried to find out where the couple was from and which adoption agency they had used, but they were nearly as entertained by Jason's antics as their son was.

A few minutes later, a young couple holding a baby walked through the door followed by a woman in her mid-forties. "Right in here," the woman said as she guided the couple to another sofa.

The woman was trim and tall, with light skin and green eyes. Her brown hair was pinned up in a tight bun at the back of her head. She wore a dark gray pantsuit that looked business and casual at the same time.

The woman stood in the middle of the room and faced the small group. She clasped her hands together enthusiastically. "Well, I had thought we'd get another family or two, but we'll go ahead and get started. My name is Shannon Mills, and I'm the director of the annual International Adoption Retreat."

The gathered families nodded and smiled.

"For those of you who have been here before, most of this will be a review. You new families will want to pay attention, though."

Ms. Mills proceeded to tell the group about the activities for the next two days as well as give some general rules to follow. During the explanation, Jason continued making faces at the little boy. Hannah wasn't sure whether to be embarrassed at his lack of attention or annoyed that he was clearly not following his own advice to make friends with the people in charge.

After Ms. Mills finished her well-rehearsed pitch and dismissed the families, Hannah stood and moved toward her, hoping to get a chance to introduce herself. She could still do her job even if her partner wasn't willing to do his. Unfortunately, the director slipped through the group and out the door before Hannah had a chance to catch her.

Hannah returned to Jason's side, ready to glare daggers at him, but his continued antics with the small boy softened her ire somewhat. She plopped next to him on the sofa. "You were no help there."

"We don't want to appear too eager. Best to start out making connections with people," he said quietly as he made a crazy face that sent the boy into another fit of giggles.

Hannah was usually the laid-back one, especially among the Banana Girls. It was strange to be told that she needed to relax and be patient.

Sandra arrived and guided Hannah and Jason out onto the back lawn. The early November air was crisp, but not cold, and smelled of the surrounding forest. They walked across the grass to a nearby pavilion where a lively activity was already in progress.

"You'll be part of group three." Sandra indicated the families gathered playing an egg relay race. "You can join in as soon as there's a lull in the action." She smiled and nodded toward a nearby table. "Oh, and here's the packet for your suite." She handed Jason a narrow envelope with two door keycards. "You'll be in number twenty-two. The retreat staff has already put your luggage in the suite. After your group is finished with games, you'll go to dinner and then settle into your cabin."

"Thanks, Sandra," Jason said as he and Hannah found seats at the nearest empty table.

The families in their group continued their raucous competition until everyone—with the exception of Hannah and Jason—had run back and forth across the pavilion's open space with an egg balanced on a spoon in their mouth.

As the game wound down and the winning team congratulated each other, one of the mothers approached their table. "Come join the fun, you two."

Just as Hannah opened her mouth to politely decline, Jason grabbed her arm and pulled her forward. "Thanks," he said, smiling broadly at their new group.

Jason made the introductions, and within a few minutes, they were engulfed in another activity, children swarming all around them as she and Jason were selected to lead a rousing game of Simon Says.

Hannah was initially unsure how to interact with the children around her, but they didn't seem to care that she didn't know. Plus, their enthusiasm for the games made it that much easier. By the time the activities were over and it was time for dinner, Hannah was almost disappointed it had to end. She had been so distracted by the games that she hadn't even thought about the mission. Maybe she shouldn't be so hard on Jason when he got caught up playing.

Dinner was held in a large banquet hall that had obviously been a barn in a former life. Red gingham tablecloths covered dozens of round tables. Jason and Hannah found the Grays and Bakers sitting at a table together, but there were no empty seats. The two families seemed perfectly content just visiting between themselves, so they didn't make any offers to squish in two more chairs for Jason and Hannah. In the end, Hannah said hello to Lexie and Belle while Jason tried to make conversation with the husbands. But standing there balancing their plates of food led to an awkward and abrupt end in the conversation.

Eventually, Hannah and Jason found spots with the family they had met in the orientation. Hannah tried to focus on the family they were eating with, but her mind continually drifted to the Bakers and the Grays. There had to be a way to find out more about them. She began to realize the true scope of their task, to find out the details of an ultra-secret illegal adoption scheme by making small talk with possible suspects. And what if it wasn't either the Grays or the Bakers? It could be any number of other individuals who had gone through the adoption process and saw an opportunity to skirt the law and make a few thousand bucks.

Hannah's shoulders sagged as she pushed the sauteed vegetables around on her plate. Finding the mastermind of the adoption ring in this group—assuming the person was even present at the retreat—would be like finding a needle in a haystack.

As the dinner wound down, Shannon Mills entered from a side door and stopped at a nearby table to chat with some of the participants. Hannah tensed. Ms. Mills would know quite a bit about the attendees at the retreat. In fact, she'd probably know about the adoption process itself. This would be a great opportunity to question her.

When Hannah went to stand, Jason put a firm hand on her leg. "Nope," he said.

"What?" She tried to act innocent.

"Now isn't the time," he whispered.

"What do you mean? It's the perfect time."

Jason leaned over and spoke in her ear. "You're not an investigative reporter and you're definitely not a tenacious spy girl—at least you're pretending not to be." The nearness of Jason's lips to her ear did funny things to Hannah's insides. "She's probably making the rounds to all the tables," he said.

Not only did having him that close throw off her focus, but she was forced to admit that he was probably right. She leaned back and tried to act like a normal woman at a banquet. After a few moments, she noticed that Jason hadn't removed his hand from her thigh, even though he had already gone back to making faces at the little boy.

Hannah could feel the warmth of his hand through her jeans. She scooted her chair forward so that his hand was covered by the tablecloth then casually pried it away from her leg. When he immediately grasped her hand, she looked over at him. Was he really so engrossed playing with his little friend that he didn't realize what he'd done?

She firmly extricated her hand and pretended to be busy fiddling with her silverware.

A moment later, the director stopped at their table.

Jason had been right.

"How is everything here?" she asked.

The small group mumbled various answers indicating they were enjoying themselves.

"This has been absolutely amazing, Ms. Mills," Jason said as he swept a hand to indicate the crowded dining hall. "It's so wonderful that you put this all together for us."

Ms. Mills dipped her head. "Thank you. We try very hard to make the experience a positive one. And please, call me Shannon."

Jason nodded. "And you must be proud that something you started has grown so large."

With a thin smile, Shannon said, "Actually, I'm not the founder of the group."

"Really? How did you become the director if you didn't get everything started?"

"A few years ago, the couple that started the retreat decided that they weren't enjoying the experience as much as they had at the beginning. Rather than discontinue the event, they asked me to step in."

"That must have been daunting. Had you attended before?"

Shannon shook her head. "No, I don't have children. I'm an event planner."

Hannah decided she wanted to help out. "Do the founders still attend?" She glanced around as if she might find them.

"They do. But their role is one that happens behind the scenes. Having any extra attention on them would take away from their experience."

Her tone sounded like she was wrapping up the conversation, and the rest of the table nodded accordingly. The director smiled at the group before moving to another table.

When Hannah and Jason left their table a short time later, Jason insisted on taking her hand as they crossed the room. And he continued holding it even after they left the dining hall.

"You can let go now," she said once they were outside walking across the dark meadow toward their cabin.

Jason glanced down at their clasped hands. "Oh," he said absently before releasing her hand.

Hannah refused to acknowledge—even to herself—that she missed the warmth of his hand in hers. Instinctively, she hugged her shoulders, fighting off a shiver.

Jason looked over at her. "If you're cold, I could put my arm around you. We are still supposed to be pretending, after all."

"I'm not that cold," Hannah lied. "Let's just get to our suite."

Behind the main house, two rows of cabins flanked the lawn and pavilion where most of the activities took place. When they reached the second row of suites, they walked along, counting the numbers on the doors until they reached twenty-two. Jason swiped his keycard and pushed the door open.

They stepped into a comfortably furnished sitting area. Despite the outward appearance of a rustic, backwoods cabin, the interior was quite modern. A sturdy sofa sat facing a large flat screen TV mounted on the wall. Behind the sofa, a small oak table and two chairs marked the beginning of a tiny kitchenette.

Jason nodded as he walked around the sofa toward the only other door from the living area. Hannah followed, a sinking feeling knowing what was through the door. Or more precisely, what wasn't.

Hannah immediately saw that her fear had been completely justified. Jason appeared quite pleased with the arrangements until his gaze landed on their luggage. Apparently, the sight of their clearly mismatched suitcases standing neatly side by side brought to Jason's attention what Hannah had already realized.

There was only one room.

And that one room only had one bed.

Jason turned to Hannah and opened his mouth to say something. When no words came out after several seconds, Hannah lifted a shoulder. "As you so frequently remind me, we're pretending to be married. What kind of accommodations did you expect they would put us in?"

Jason looked at the bed again, then back at Hannah. His gaze briefly roamed the room, perhaps searching for another bed hidden in the wall. He stared at the bed again before letting out a long, dejected sigh. "I suppose I need to be a gentleman and say that you should take the bed and that I can just sleep out on the sofa." His voice carried a tone of resignation mixed with a little whining.

"I guess we could take turns," Hannah offered. She didn't sound very convincing.

He gave her a skeptical look. Then with a mirthless laugh, he grabbed his suitcase and started lugging it back into the living room.

"Seriously, I'm sure we can figure something out." She really tried to sound like she wanted to take turns on the bed, but it still came out flat.

"Nope. I may not have everything figured out when it comes to women, but I know the gentleman always offers the lady the bed." He moved out of the bedroom, but Hannah could still hear him mutter, "Even if the lady does always gripe about everything needing to be equal. Then sometimes she doesn't want things equal. How's a gentleman supposed to know when to make things equal and when not to?"

Hannah wasn't going to let him get away with misrepresenting her opinion like that, even if he was just grumbling to himself. "Ladies want to be treated as equals. They don't need men assuming they can't do things for themselves," she said as she followed him into the living room.

Jason hefted his suitcase up onto an end table with a huff.

Hannah leaned against the doorframe, arms folded. "And just because a lady wants to be treated as an equal, it doesn't mean that she minds if a gentleman would like to do something nice for her. Unless he's condescending about it; then the gentleman can take a hike."

Jason flung the lid of this suitcase back and started rifling through his clothing. "Yeah, it's still pretty confusing, you know?"

"It's not confusing," Hannah declared adamantly. "Just be a nice guy. It's not that hard."

"I *am* a nice guy," Jason countered, wielding a pair of pajama pants at her like a weapon.

Hannah held her hands out in an attempt to diffuse the situation. Jason *was* giving up his claim to the bed, after all. "Yes, that's true. You've always tried to be nice . . ." She paused, not quite sure how to finish the statement.

"But . . ." Jason raised his eyebrows in anticipation.

Hannah cringed. She didn't really want to hurt his feelings, but it might be good for him to hear it.

"But . . .?" he prompted her again.

"But . . . you sometimes come across a little . . . arrogant." She winced as she said the last word.

Jason didn't immediately react to her claim; his eyes shifted down, unfocused, looking at nothing in particular. After a moment, he huffed and, with a nod, finally said, "Okay."

Once he had snapped out of his reverie, he glanced up at her.

He didn't look offended, only a little surprised. But his expression soon turned back to normal, maybe even a little mischievous.

He stared at her for a moment then tossed his pajamas back on his clothing pile and started unbuttoning his shirt.

"What are you doing?" Hannah asked.

Jason looked down at his hands. "I'm taking off my shirt?" It came out like a question, as if he thought he knew what he was doing but suddenly wasn't sure.

"Why?"

"It makes my pajamas more comfortable," he replied with a teasing grin.

"You can't change now. I'm standing right here," Hannah said.

Jason slowly undid another button. "I don't see why not. As you just pointed out, we're supposed to be acting like we're married."

A blush crept up Hannah's neck as Jason revealed the top of his surprisingly well-defined chest. She looked back at his face. His smirk told her that he knew the effect he was having. She lifted her chin defiantly. "You can't get rid of me that easily. We're in the middle of a conversation."

Jason waggled his eyebrows suggestively as he continued down the row of buttons, slowly, methodically undoing each one. "Bet," he said.

So that's how it was going to be? Who would flinch first? Well, she had no intention of losing this game of chicken.

Jason's gray-blue eyes danced with mischief. Hannah glared right back. She wasn't willing to let him win on this one.

She'd seen plenty of men without shirts on. Surely, he didn't think his chiseled physique would affect her that much.

Without taking his eyes off her, Jason undid the last button and slowly slid his shirt off over one toned bicep, then the other. Hannah made the mistake of stealing a quick glance at the rest of his newly uncovered torso. The definition of his abs matched his chest.

She quickly looked back at Jason's face.

Swinging the shirt around his head like a lasso, Jason proceeded to strut—cowboy-style—around the small sofa.

He was having way too much fun with this, which only made Hannah all the more determined not to yield.

From across the room, he flung the shirt at her. Hannah grabbed it out of the air and threw it on the ground in front of his suitcase. "Will you stop being so juvenile," she said.

"Juvenile?" He sauntered confidently back toward her. "I'm just changing my clothes in the privacy of my own sleeping area."

Hannah shook her head. "So, you think you've won this one?"

Jason grinned. "Did you think I was done?"

He stopped right in front of her and reached for the button on his pants.

Hannah's eyes went wide, and her cheeks burned in an uncontrollable blush. Without a word, she turned and stormed back into the bedroom, slamming the door behind her.

"Hey, where are you going?" he called through the door. "We were having such fun."

Hannah loved a dramatic exit just as much as the next spy girl, but in that moment, what she really needed was some distance from her surprisingly athletic-looking partner and some time to allow herself to cool down and get her heart rate in check. And perhaps even do some thinking about it.

No. Best to think about it later.

Hannah quickly found her own pajamas and put them on. When she was done, she cracked the door open a few inches but didn't look through. She sat on the edge of the bed and faced the partially open door.

After a long silence, Jason spoke again, his voice more serious this time. "Back to what you said before, I know your explanation probably made sense to you, but it just sounded confusing to me."

Hannah reached out with her foot and nudged the door farther open. "What's confusing about it?" she asked.

"Women in general are confusing," he declared.

"How are we confusing?" Hannah countered.

"I can't figure out how I'm supposed to act around them."

Hannah felt silly continuing this conversation out of sight through a doorway. "Are you finished changing?"

"Yeah," Jason replied.

"Seriously, though."

He chuckled. "I am fully clothed again."

Hannah peeked into the living area. Jason had pulled out the sofa bed and had a small pile of sheets and blankets that he was attempting to fit on the thin mattress. Hannah walked over and attached one of the corners of the fitted sheet before sitting down on the arm of the couch, a leg folded underneath her.

She watched as he spread the rest of his bedding. "So, you're a highly trained government agent that can take on any number of dangerous missions, discovering clues and deciphering codes," Hannah began. "But you can't figure out how to interact with women?" She kept her tone light and playful.

Jason lifted a shoulder. "You remember our first meeting, when I texted you the wrong time and you didn't get any lunch?" He fiddled with the sheets, refusing to look up at her. "I still feel bad about that, by the way," he added quietly.

She remembered being so angry at the time. It seemed silly now.

Jason continued. "I didn't know how to admit I'd messed up without looking like an idiot. So, I faked extra confidence to make up for it."

Hannah shook her head at his convoluted thought process. "Okay, so you're not great at interacting with women in mission scenarios." Hannah observed. "Maybe you'll need to draw on your experience with women in your personal life."

Jason let out a long sigh. When he looked up at her, his expression was open and honest. "I've never had a third date."

Hannah frowned. "What? You've only been on two dates? In your entire life?"

Jason bristled. "No. I've been on plenty of dates, just not with the same girl."

"That's not so strange," Hannah said. "I'm sure plenty of people date around until they find someone they want to get serious with."

"Yeah. It wouldn't be strange if I dated around until I got into a relationship. But I've never been in a relationship because I've never gotten past the second date; I've never gone on three dates with the same girl." Jason tossed the last blanket on the bed and stared at Hannah.

"Never?" Hannah found it difficult to believe.

He plopped onto the edge of the sofa bed, staring at the wall. "The really nice girls sometimes give me a second chance, but then I get so excited about the second date that it usually goes worse than the first."

Hannah tried to hide her shock, but she was completely at a loss for words. She wasn't exactly a dating machine, but she'd had her share of boyfriends and almost-boyfriends in high school and college.

Jason rubbed his forehead and turned to Hannah. His eyes held an uncertainty that she'd never seen there before. "I honestly have no idea how to pretend to be your husband because I've never even had a girlfriend."

He'd *never* had a girlfriend.

That actually explained a lot.

His focus on silly things like how to hold hands. His complete lack of understanding of how to share things like drinks and food. His fixation on how a couple should appear to others.

No wonder.

Honestly, she sort of understood. Jason was definitely handsome, but sometimes his personality could be insufferable. He wasn't that bad to be around after a person got to know him. Women just needed to give him a chance.

Hannah suddenly felt extremely guilty about her initial interactions with him. If she hadn't been assigned to this mission, Hannah wouldn't have given him a second chance, much less a third. She might not have even given him a first chance.

Hannah picked up his discarded blanket and started unfolding it. "You know, for not having any experience, you're not doing so bad at it."

Jason let out a short, mirthless laugh.

"Seriously, though. Your preoccupation with our fake relationship has saved the mission several times when I would have blown our cover because I wasn't focused on how a couple would act."

He shrugged. "Unfortunately, one mission pretending to be married doesn't really help me figure out women."

"Probably not. But maybe I can help a little," Hannah said.

Jason turned his hopeful gaze on her. "Really?"

Hannah slid down the arm of the couch onto the newly made sofa bed. "Sure. What kind of partner would I be if I let you keep screwing up?"

"I'll take any advice you've got."

"Well, first off, don't focus so much on doing the right thing. Each girl is different, so there really isn't one *right* thing you can do."

Jason nodded, willingly accepting what she said.

"And speaking of things being just right, if you think you can follow some formula that will sweep a girl off her feet, you've been watching too many movies. Women might eat up those Hallmark movies where the handsome doctor or the lawyer-turned-car mechanic says exactly the right thing to make the heroine fall madly in love with him, decide to give up her high-power career in the city, and settle down with him on a tree farm. But it rarely works that way in real life. If a real guy said half the things they say in movies, the girl would run away."

"I can vouch for that," Jason added with a wry smile.

Hannah watched him for a moment as she considered what else she could say. He really was nice to look at. Especially this side of him—real, down-to-earth, and smiling.

"Just be yourself," she finally said.

Jason's brow furrowed. "You know, girls keep using that phrase, but I don't think it means what they think it means."

Hannah laughed. "It means that you need to stop worrying about being the perfect guy, and focus on being a regular, nice guy. Think about things from the girl's perspective. Are you treating her like a person or like a stereotype?"

"It can't be that easy," Jason said.

"Listen. If we had been on an actual date that time we met for lunch before visiting the Phelps, I would have left halfway through."

"A half date," Jason said with a laugh. "That's a new one."

Hannah started ticking off reasons on her fingers. "You started eating before I got there. You didn't bother to find out where I was when I didn't show up on time. And when I pointed out that you were wrong, you made me feel like it had been my fault."

"I didn't say it was your fault. I said—"

Hannah held up a hand. "And all I got to eat was your leftover tater tots." Jason opened his mouth to say something, but Hannah cut him off again. "I know you feel bad about it. But I think you felt justified at the time because of some broad stereotype of women you've come across."

She paused a moment before continuing. "We like food, too, you know. We're not always like the women you see on TV."

He looked away, obvious embarrassment in his expression.

Hannah waited until she had his attention again. "And you know what else I've discovered from being forced to spend time with you?"

"Do I want to hear this?"

She smiled. "Under all your bravado and pretentiousness, you're actually not that bad."

"Gee, thanks."

"You know what I mean," Hannah insisted.

Jason rubbed the back of his neck. "I do try to be a nice guy."

Hannah leaned forward and put her hand on his. It was warm under her fingers. "I know you do. But you might need to stop trying to follow a formula. Stop treating women like the stereotypes you see in movies. Just be more casual about it. Give the girls a chance to get to know you—the nice you, not the trying-too-hard you—and things will start working out better."

Jason looked down at their hands. "Thanks," he said quietly. His gaze drifted up to her face. A moment later, his expression turned slightly awkward. He stood and cleared his throat, looking around the room.

Hannah smiled to herself. Maybe she could have an effect on him, too.

It would be so fun to tease and flirt with him, especially knowing that he was so inexperienced with real attention from women.

But that would be mean, and she couldn't bring herself to do it.
Much.

"I'd better get to bed." Hannah stood and padded lightly back to the bedroom. As she closed the door, she paused and gave him a small smile. "Goodnight, Jason."

The coy farewell had the desired effect. Her last glimpse was of Jason's silly grin as he awkwardly waved goodnight.

After all, she'd never promised to be a saint.

Chapter Eleven

THE NEXT MORNING, AS Hannah started returning to consciousness, a soft knock sounded on the bedroom door.

"Hannah, are you awake?" The closed door muffled Jason's voice.

"Mm-hmm," she croaked. "Gimme a minute." She slid out of bed and dragged herself to the door. Fumbling with the knob, she noticed that she hadn't locked it the night before. As she groggily chided herself for letting her spy girl vigilance slip, she realized that she had forgotten because she felt safe with Jason. She trusted him.

Of course, if she had known the door was already unlocked, she could have yelled for him to come in while still comfortably snuggled under the covers.

"Good morning, sunshine," he said with a smile. The smell of fried eggs and pancakes wafted in from the front room.

"If you say so." Hannah took a few steps backward and slumped onto the bed, content to be horizontal again.

"I didn't think you'd be up in time for breakfast, so I brought you some food back."

She cracked an eyelid open.

He swept a hand toward the kitchenette. "Care to join me?"

Hannah scowled at him. "I've decided this marriage is never going to work. I think you might be a morning person."

Jason laughed.

She squinted at the clock next to her bed. A few minutes past nine. She supposed that was acceptable during a mission.

Brushing the long blond hair out of her face, she got up and shuffled out to the table.

"I didn't know what you'd like, so I just got a couple different things." Jason pulled several takeout containers from a bag.

"You didn't sample any of them, did you?" Hannah eyed him suspiciously. She was surprised to realize that it wouldn't have annoyed her half as much as it did the first time it happened.

"I might have devoured one of the French toast sticks I grabbed for you," he said with a grin. "But I definitely didn't take a bite out of your blueberry muffin."

Hannah laughed and pulled an orange juice container out of the bag. She leaned over to the counter, grabbed two glasses, and poured some for each of them.

As they ate breakfast and visited at their cozy little table, Hannah couldn't help but think how different it was from her first interaction with him. He was obviously much more comfortable with her than he had been at the beginning. And for her part, she wanted to strangle him much less. He was even fun to joke with now that they understood each other's sense of humor.

After breakfast and showers, they headed out to join their group for the day's activities. The seminars on bonding as a new family, adjusting to adoption, and honoring birth heritage were broken up throughout the day with a variety of games and activities. At one point, Hannah and Jason even got volunteered to compete against several pre-teens in a go-kart racing video game. Despite his boasting before the race, Jason didn't even finish in the top three. Fortunately for their team, growing up as an only child meant Hannah had spent plenty of time on this particular game. She knew all the tricks and shortcuts and ended up winning three out of four races. Jason was so excited when their team won that he wrapped Hannah in a huge bearhug.

"That's one more for me," she said, giving him a sly wink.

"You deserve it," he replied as he let her slip out of the hug.

During the calmer activities, Hannah and Jason did their best to meet as many families as they could. At each break in the day's schedule, they took turns checking up on the Bakers and Grays. Unfortunately for their mission, the two families never did anything suspicious; they stuck together like glue and it was becoming more and more awkward for Hannah and Jason to insert themselves into their conversations. Visiting with them at the resort wasn't anything like visiting at their backyard barbecue.

Hannah arrived late to one of the classes after tailing the influencer families to the video game room. As she slid into the back row with Jason, she saw a woman a few rows ahead of them that—from the back—looked almost exactly like Carissa. When the woman glanced to the side a few moments later, Hannah saw that it clearly wasn't her. But it had been close enough for a serious double-take.

Hannah wondered what had become of Carissa and baby Freddie. Were they safe from Eddie's boss? Would Carissa ever get to see Eddie again?

The clear love that Carissa had for her baby and her devotion to Eddie were such foreign ideas to Hannah. She'd never had a well-functioning family, so she thought it was completely natural that she'd never had the desire for a family herself. But she could no longer deny that a small corner of her heart longed for what Carissa had—or her own version of it, anyway. And that small bit seemed to be growing bigger and bigger lately.

And the bigger it got, the more it scared her.

The last activity before dinner was in the craft room, and unsurprisingly, Jason was down at the kid table making turkeys and snowmen with the young children. As Hannah watched the kids respond so well to Jason's attention, she couldn't help but wonder what her life might have been like if she'd had a more attentive father. Or if her mother hadn't left them.

Jason brought a very ugly looking cornucopia over to Hannah. "I bet you didn't realize what an amazing artist you married." His eyes held a teasing look.

"Just don't quit your day job," she said with a laugh. Her gaze strayed back to the children, unable to shake thoughts of her childhood.

Jason nudged her with his shoulder. "You okay?"

Hannah didn't respond for a moment. Finally, she lifted her chin toward the group of children and their attentive parents. "I want my children to be loved like that. I want my family to be a happy family," she said quietly, hating the catch she heard in her voice. "I didn't have that growing up." Hannah almost never spoke about her home life. She wasn't sure what made her do it now.

She took a deep breath and cast a sidelong glance at Jason. She didn't see judgment or joking in the eyes of her pretend husband. All she saw was understanding and compassion. He put his arm around her shoulder and pulled her close. Rather than fighting his embrace, Hannah let herself lean into his chest. She felt safe and even a little bit understood. And somehow, she knew she could trust him with that secret from the back corner of her heart.

Hannah tilted her head back slightly. "If you ever tell a soul, I'll break three large bones in each of your limbs."

Jason chuckled and whispered, "Your secret's safe with me, crazy spy girl." He squeezed her a little closer.

Hannah knew it was true.

A wiry man in his mid-forties suddenly stepped into her view. Hannah flinched, instinctively wanting to punch or kick. Fortunately, Jason had his arm tightly around her shoulder. The man must have just passed behind them. Hopefully, he hadn't overheard her whispered secret.

"Forgive me for eavesdropping, but I couldn't help but hear you say 'my children' and 'my family.' As counselor at the retreat, I can't hear something like that and not step in. It's important that we break these old habits"—he made a motion like breaking a stick—"and replace them with good new habits."

Now that he mentioned it, Hannah realized he looked a little familiar from one of the sessions on family unity.

The annoying man continued. "You need to change the 'my' and 'me' to 'us' and 'we'."

The phrase rolled off his tongue so easily—despite not being grammatically correct—that Hannah guessed he must have used this same spiel hundreds of times.

He held out his hands to Jason and Hannah, clearly expecting their participation. "Our family." He over-enunciated the words, cartoonishly so. "Say it with me. 'Our family'."

Jason belatedly joined him. "Our family."

Jason shifted slightly so that he was facing Hannah.

Were they ganging up on her now?

The man nodded at Jason encouragingly and looked at Hannah with raised brows.

She shrugged. "You know, it was just an old habit, I'm sure it won't—"

"Our family," the man said very slowly and succinctly.

"Our family," Jason added.

Hannah could tell from the look on Jason's face that he was only egging her on. Was she willing to let him win this one? She glanced around the room. Most of the kids were completely oblivious, but some of the parents were starting to notice.

"This is important, and I need you to say it," the man said. "Our. Family."

"Come on, babe," Jason said. Butterflies fluttered in Hannah's stomach with how sincere the nickname sounded. "We don't want our family to be broken before it even starts." He was clearly enjoying himself, and it took all of Hannah's willpower not to tackle him to the ground.

The counselor turned suddenly on Jason. "No sir, that's not correct, either. Your family has already begun." His voice had an intensity that felt incredibly overdone. "The two of you are a family now, even without children."

Jason's triumphant smile faded quickly now that he had stepped out of line, too.

Hannah suppressed a grin.

The man turned his attention back to Hannah. "But you must get that family back on the right track. Can you say it to your husband? Our family."

Hannah could tell that they would never get rid of this guy unless she gave in. She looked at Jason. "Our family," she ground out.

"Good." The counselor exuded enthusiasm. "I think if you can remember the little things, your family will be on the right track." He patted them each on the arm. "You can go back to hugging if you'd like."

The man stood there as if waiting for them to hug. Hannah caught Jason's smug grin and decided she wasn't going to give him the pleasure. She turned to the man and smiled her sweetest smile. "Thanks for your help."

It only took him four or five seconds to get the hint that they were done. Despite his obvious disappointment, the counselor nodded his approval and finally left them alone.

Hannah's attention returned to the children doing their crafts and Jason shifted back to her side, though she could feel his occasional glances in her direction. She folded her arms and pointedly did not look at him. He deserved a few minutes of cold shoulder for ganging up on her.

His hug had been quite enjoyable, though.

After a few minutes of thinking about how silly the family counselor was, Hannah couldn't help a small giggle. Jason glanced at her. She giggled again. The man had been so ridiculous. Jason chuckled.

"That guy was certainly a piece of work," he said.

That only added to Hannah's laughter. She clamped a hand over her mouth, reminding herself that she was still annoyed at Jason. "You were no help," she said drily.

"I do my best." He added a gentle shoulder nudge.

One of the children at the table, who looked about six, finished his construction paper turkey and stood. He waved it at his mother who was helping his younger sibling on the other side of the table. "I want to show daddy," the boy said.

"He'll be right back," his mother answered. But before she could even finish her sentence, the boy was halfway to the door. "Sweetie, just wait!"

The mother obviously couldn't leave the younger child unattended, but if someone didn't intervene quickly, the older child would be out the door. Before Hannah even thought of what she could do to help, Jason stepped forward and blocked the boy's path to the door. Hannah wondered how he was going to corral the boy without frightening him. As a kid, she would have freaked out if a stranger had tried to stop her like that. Come to think of it, she probably still would.

In an instant Jason was down on one knee at the boy's level. "Did you make one of the fancy turkeys?" he asked the boy in an eager voice.

The boy nodded shyly. He peeked around Jason, obviously still hoping to reach the freedom of the hallway. Hannah glanced back at the mother, who was visibly relieved not to have to chase down her older child.

"Can I see your turkey?" Jason asked.

The boy held it up.

"Wow. That's amazing!" Jason's reaction was over exaggerated, but the boy ate it up. "I love how you colored this part pink instead of red."

The boy nodded. "Uh-huh. And look at his eyes." He pointed to a set of googly eyes that were much too large and made the turkey look a little cross-eyed.

"I know," Jason replied. "He looks like such a happy turkey."

The boy nodded again.

"I really like happy turkeys," Jason said.

The boy smiled. Hannah was amazed at how naturally Jason interacted with children. She could easily imagine him as a father corralling a wayward child by distracting him. For a split-second—standing there watching Jason care for the young boy like a father would—Hannah pictured herself as the mother. The brief vision was so vivid that it momentarily took her breath away.

For obvious reasons, she had never seriously imagined herself as a mother, but there in the craft room, this small glimpse into family life—and the feeling that had come with it—told her that maybe she might feel differently someday.

Had her feelings about motherhood really changed that much? Maybe attending this retreat, pretending to be married to a handsome fellow agent, was playing tricks on her brain.

Hannah shook her head, pushing those feelings aside to deal with another day. Besides, this was Jason who was crouched down interacting with the little boy. She could never handle the idea of being married to Jason in real life. True, they had started to develop a camaraderie, almost a friendship, but it could never be anything more than that. She had hated him from almost the first word he spoke.

How could that ever become something romantic? It was impossible.

Jason turned to smile up at Hannah, hopefully oblivious to the swirl of emotions she had just experienced. But something about the gleam in his eye told her that he was up to no good. "You know who else likes happy turkeys?" he asked the boy, his eyes on Hannah the whole time.

The boy glanced at Hannah then shrugged.

"My wife loves happy turkeys." Jason indicated Hannah.

The boy's face broke into a huge grin. He ran to Hannah, holding the funny-looking paper turkey out to her. She still felt incredibly awkward but tried to imitate some of the things she'd seen Jason do.

She squatted down next to the boy. "Let's see this happy turkey," she said in what felt like an overly childish way. The boy handed the paper to her. "I like the way you put glitter on his feathers."

"Uh-huh. I wanted it to be sparkly."

"Well, I think it looks great," Hannah added with a smile.

The boy beamed back at her and nodded vigorously. A second later, something caught his attention. "Daddy!" He ran past Hannah and Jason to a man coming back into the room.

The man bent down and grabbed the running boy. "Hey, buddy. Did you finish?"

The boy held the turkey nearly touching his dad's nose.

Hannah stood and Jason joined her as they watched the dad take his son back to the craft table. The mother caught their attention and silently mouthed, "Thank you."

Jason smiled and nodded.

Maybe having a family of her own someday wouldn't be such a bad thing.

It definitely wouldn't be with Jason. But there had to be someone out there who would love her despite all her flaws.

And who would love their kids; that was non-negotiable.

Once the families had finished their crafts, the group was ushered into the dining hall again. The other groups who had finished their activities early were already there, eating and visiting. Jason and Hannah once again stopped near the Grays and Bakers' table, attempting to engage them in conversation, and it ended in a similar way as the night before. The influencer couples hadn't snubbed them, but they hadn't invited Hannah and Jason to join them either.

As she ate her meal, Hannah watched the influencer couples. They seemed just like any other families at the retreat; nothing sinister there unless you counted Belle's red highlights. Hannah doubted those were natural. The night before, she had been sure one of the influencer families was behind the illegal adoptions. Now, after interacting with others throughout the day, all she saw was two happy families—with very overly-energetic children—enjoying a vacation together. The idea that one of them could be the mastermind of an illegal international adoption ring just felt so wrong.

Jason must have noticed where her attention was because he leaned over and whispered, "Still having doubts about the influencers?"

Hannah shook her head. "They seem just like any of the other families. Maybe a bit more attractive," she added with a shrug.

"You're not still trying to get out of the mission, are you?" His smile told her that he was teasing.

"It's not the mission so much as the marriage." She smiled back, still speaking low. "My husband is driving me crazy." She added a light punch to his leg which elicited a deep chuckle from her partner.

After dinner, Jason and Hannah joined a small group in one of the gazebos for some casual visiting. The scattered fire pits cast flickering orange into the shadows. In their conversations throughout the day, Jason and Hannah had discovered that there was no traceable connection between any of the adopting families and the two influencer families. Most of them hadn't even heard of the Grays or the Bakers until after they began attending the annual retreat.

Even though that poked some serious holes in their theory that the influencers steered couples toward illegally arranged adoptions, Jason didn't seem worried about it. He continued easily making friends with all of the couples in the vicinity—usually by playing with their kids first.

Hannah leaned back in her chair, watching the conversations going on around her. Jason sat at a nearby bench talking to the family of the boy with the happy turkey craft. Hannah didn't mind letting him take on most of the conversations. He had a talent for asking casual questions that didn't make people feel like they were being interrogated. Hannah, on the other hand, had a talent for interrogating people. And when she wasn't interrogating someone, she was most comfortable in the solitude of her corner at Club Banana.

Jason excused himself from his conversation and walked toward Hannah. She scooted over to make room for him next to her on the wide wicker patio chair. Jason slipped into the seat and made himself comfortable, their shoulders brushing lightly against each other.

Before their forced proximity made her say something awkward, Hannah fished in her jacket pocket and pulled out the Crunch bar she had bought that afternoon. "Look what I picked up at the retreat's gift shop."

"Ooh, that looks delicious." He reached for the candy but stopped himself. "But it's your favorite, too. Are you offering to share it with me?"

"I'm not sharing. It's for you." She held the bar out for him to grab.

"Really? That's sweet of you." He took the candy and started to unwrap it.

Hannah shrugged. "I'm trying to be a considerate wife."

Jason chuckled. "Well, just for that, I won't even take a bite of the half I'm going to share with you." He broke the bar and handed half back to her.

They munched their chocolate in silence—except for the crunching candy bar noises. With a very fluid, casual motion—almost as if he was simply shifting into a more relaxed position—Jason stretched his arm out behind her and settled it around her shoulder.

A shiver ran through Hannah's body that had nothing to do with the chilly air.

"You're good with kids," Hannah said matter-of-factly. She was actually just looking for some kind of distraction from his arm resting softly around her.

"I'm the oldest of four, so my parents left me in charge a lot as a teenager," he said with a shrug. "Plus, I had two sets of younger cousins who lived around the corner, and I was the one who had to babysit when my mom would go out to lunch with her sisters."

He seemed so casual about it. Maybe he didn't realize that his ability didn't come naturally to everyone.

"But you're doing great, too. Especially with little Jake this afternoon." Jason jutted his chin toward the small boy from the craft room.

Hannah shook her head. "That was so awkward. I'm sure it's obvious to everyone that I'm really not good with kids."

He chuckled. "I may have noticed that a little. But you're definitely getting better."

"I've always been a little jealous of people who were that comfortable with kids. The other Banana Girls all have siblings or cousins or nieces and nephews." She blew out a sigh. "I'm the only child of two only children. No siblings or cousins. Kids are sort of a foreign thing to me."

"At least you don't seem scared of them anymore." Jason offered. "Maybe this has been good spy training. Now you'll be impervious to the next horde of toddlers sent to attack you."

Hannah burst into laughter at the absurdity of that mental image. Jason joined in, pulling her closer as they laughed together. The whole moment just felt so right, like it was the most natural thing in the world for them to be sitting there cuddling in that chair.

As their laughter slowly died down, Hannah studied her handsome faux-husband—his strong arm tucking her nicely against his chest—and considered how far she wanted to let this conversation go. It could very easily stray into dangerous territory about her family life—a topic she usually avoided like the plague. But for the first time in years, Hannah didn't feel the need to change the subject or avoid talking about her family. Based on the hints she'd given him that afternoon, Jason must know she hadn't come from an ideal home environment. She'd trusted him with a small part of that secret already, and surprisingly, she wasn't afraid for him to learn more.

Jason's tone turned a little more serious. "Of course, I can see how being at an event like this could be really difficult if it's hard for you to be around kids."

She nodded. "Being around kids. And pretending to be married."

"Really?" Jason could have easily made a snide remark or joked about their disastrous beginning as a fake couple, but he didn't. He seemed to be taking their conversation seriously.

Could she really do it? Could she really tell someone what had happened between her and her mother all those years ago?

Hannah took a deep breath and forged ahead. "My mom left us when I was eleven years old." She tried to say it casually, but it felt like she was shouting it through a megaphone.

Jason wrapped his other arm around her and pulled her close. She melted into his arms, her head against his shoulder, and reveled in the genuine compassion she felt from him.

"Oh, I'm sorry, Hannah," he said. "We don't have to talk about it, if you don't want to."

Hannah shook her head. "No, it's okay. I actually don't mind telling you."

She explained her father's obsession with work and his hands-off style of raising her. She recounted her mother's mood swings and the way she would alternate between smothering attention and borderline neglect. She told him about her parents' arguments over cars and vacation houses and money. And especially their fights about her—how she was doing on her soccer team, how her grades were, what college she would go to.

"It's almost like I was a show dog they were training for a competition," Hannah said. "I hated it."

He gave her shoulders another squeeze. "That sounds awful."

Hannah continued with her story. "I came home one day from school to find my mom packing her bags. She refused to explain or even tell me where she was going." Hannah swallowed against the lump in her throat at what she had to say next. "I had seen how they fought. I knew how her leaving would affect my dad. So, I blew up at her. I told her that we didn't need her. I said I hated her and that she should leave and never come back." Her breath shuddered as she fought back the guilt of what she'd done.

She waited for Jason to say something. He would have every right to tell her she had been wrong. That she'd acted childish. She already knew it, of course.

"Now I wish I could take it back," she added softly. "I wish I'd never said it. It wasn't true anyway. I didn't hate her." Her voice caught at the end.

Jason rested his head gently on top of hers. "I've noticed that most of what we call hate fades away with time, if it was ever even hate to begin with."

They cuddled for a minute, the lull in their conversation offset by the hum of visiting happening around them.

Finally, Jason spoke again, "It makes sense that pretending to be married isn't fun because of what you saw in your parent's marriage. But what about being around kids?"

Hannah watched the children playing around them in the large pavilion as she tried to organize her feelings. "I think it's because I'm afraid," she said eventually.

"Now we're back to being afraid of the kids?" he said with a chuckle.

She poked him playfully in the ribs. "I'm not afraid of kids." She paused and took a breath. "I'm afraid of how I might feel about them."

"How so?"

Several seconds passed before Hannah could bring herself to answer. "What if I hate them?" she whispered.

The hum she felt rumble in Jason's chest was one of understanding. "You're worried you'll be like your mother, aren't you?"

With that one question, Jason cut to the core of that niggling doubt in the back of her brain. All the years of avoiding kids, of refusing to allow herself to get sucked in by their cuteness, of coming up with excuses for why she didn't want to be around them. Hannah realized now that it all came down to that simple question.

But it wasn't a question she was ready to answer. Not seriously, anyway.

"Well, obviously," she said, affecting a self-deprecating tone. "I'm kinda self-centered, I don't like to be around people who can't seem to solve their own problems, and I'm not a particularly patient person. I'm already at least halfway to becoming my mom."

Jason shook his head, his tone still somber. "I don't think you'll ever be like your mother. You're only looking at the flaws that you have in common. You're not seeing all the good things about yourself. You're kind. You're patient—especially with me. You're understanding and forgiving. You're—" He paused, almost like he wanted to say more but wasn't sure if he should. "Anyway. I think you'll be a great mother someday."

Hannah smiled at the compliment. She even wondered what he had been about to say, though it might have been more than she wanted to hear at that point. She wasn't sure if she dared stay in this position much longer. Her heart was already beating out an irregular rhythm at the warmth of his body under her hand and the feeling of his muscles through the fabric of his shirt.

Hannah patted his chest softly. "Thanks, Jason. That means a lot."

She tilted her head to look up at him. He stared back at her with those captivating gray-blue eyes.

She needed to put some space between them.

But she didn't really want to.

Her stomach lurched as he suddenly leaned several inches closer.

Was he going to try to kiss her right there in front of everyone?

Had he not been paying attention to her advice the night before?

Jason grabbed his phone out of his back pocket and glanced at the screen.

Hannah let out a tense breath. He had only been shifting position to reach his phone. He hadn't been leaning forward to kiss her.

That was a relief. Mostly.

He held the phone out to her. "It's Brandon Phelps," he said. "Hey, Brandon," Jason said when Brandon's face appeared.

Brandon looked tired. "Hey, guys. I have some news."

"Hang on just a second." Jason looked pointedly at the crowd around them as he dug into his pocket. They clearly didn't want anyone else listening in on what Brandon was going to say. Jason produced a pair of wired earbuds and plugged them into the phone.

"Still using wired earbuds," Hannah teased. "Aren't you a little behind the times?"

Jason waved the earbuds at her. "The wired ones never need to be charged. They just work."

Hannah's brow went up. "Your wireless ones died, didn't they?"

Jason nodded. "They're back in the room charging."

"We can sync mine to your phone again," Hannah made to reach for her back pocket, not really trying to hide her grin.

Jason waved her off. "We don't have time. You'll just have to settle for the lowly wired version." He offered her one side, his tone still playful. He turned back to his phone screen. "Sorry about that, Brandon. What's up?"

Hannah looked at the earbud in her hand. Jason had given her the wrong side. Their heads would have to be right next to each other to use it in the correct ear. Had he done that on purpose? Considering his general cluelessness about relationships, probably not. She glanced at the phone screen and realized she was already missing part of the conversation. Completely ignoring the sudden case of butterflies in her stomach, Hannah leaned in close to Jason—their cheeks nearly touching—and put the earbud in.

". . . investigator finally sent his report," Brandon said.

"What did he find out?" Jason asked.

"He first checked with the agency in China that coordinated the adoption," Brandon explained. "That led him to the village where Jinhai was living right before we got him."

"Did the investigator find his parents?" Hannah asked. She really needed to know if Jinhai had been an orphan or not.

Brandon shook his head. "He found an extended family member that Jinhai had been living with, a great-uncle, I think. Apparently, about a year ago, Jinhai's mother got very sick. He must have been too young to understand what was happening, but his mother sent him to another village to stay with her uncle while she was sick. She died not long after that."

"What about his father?" Jason asked.

"According to the investigator, the father worked away from the village most of the time. Apparently, he was killed in a mining accident shortly before the mother got sick."

Hannah exhaled. "Jinhai really is an orphan."

Brandon nodded slowly.

"And does that mean you get to keep him?" she asked.

Brandon sighed. "The great-uncle relinquished all custody claims when he signed the adoption papers. The investigator searched for any closer relatives, but wasn't able to find any." For the first time, Brandon's expression lightened just a little. "So, yes, I think we get to keep him."

Brandon graciously accepted congratulations from both of them. Hannah felt a sudden weight lifted from her chest. Knowing that Jinhai would get to stay with Brandon and Kayla made all their efforts that much more meaningful.

"Did the investigator give you any more details?" Jason asked. "Anything that might help us with our investigation?"

Brandon rubbed a hand over his face. "Sure. From what the investigator was able to find out from the family, shortly after Jinhai's mother died, there was an American woman who came to the great-uncle's village looking for small children. The great-uncle was offered two thousand dollars for Jinhai."

Jason let out a low whistle.

Hannah wanted to look over at Jason, but she was still keenly aware of how close they were. "What? Is that too little? How much did you pay the agency to manage the adoption?"

"Fifty times that," Brandon answered.

"But it isn't the amount that matters," Jason added.

"How can the amount not matter?" Hannah asked.

"Offering any amount of money for an adoption is illegal," Jason said.

Hannah frowned. "That doesn't seem right. If Brandon and Kayla paid for the adoption, somebody must get the money. Who deserves it more than the family?"

"They may deserve it," Jason said. "But think about how dangerous it would be to let people pay parents for their children."

"Dangerous how?" Hannah asked.

"If a family is struggling financially or overwhelmed—like Jinhai's great-uncle probably was—they could easily be exploited by someone offering large sums of money. To say nothing of unscrupulous parents who would have children just to sell them."

Hannah hadn't really thought about it that way. She nodded in understanding.

Brandon continued, "You got it exactly right, Jason. The investigator said the great-uncle was desperate for money and completely exhausted caring for an energetic little boy. He knew Jinhai would have a good life in the U.S. so he agreed to the adoption."

"Did he know who the woman was?" Jason asked.

Brandon shook his head. "The investigator asked if he had a way to contact her, and the great-uncle shut him down cold. The investigator had a hard time getting any information after that, but his best guess is that the great-uncle was told to never attempt contact with the woman or Jinhai."

"Did the great-uncle give any description of her?" Hannah asked.

"The only description was that she was a tall, beautiful American woman who spoke fluent Mandarin."

Jason and Hannah waited, but Brandon didn't say anything else.

"Okay, thanks for the information, Brandon," Jason said. "We'll be in touch."

Brandon said goodbye and hung up.

Jason and Hannah simultaneously turned to face each other, so close that their noses bumped. They both hastily pulled out their earbuds and leaned back. Hannah gave her earbud back to Jason, glad to finally put some needed distance between them.

"That doesn't give us much to go on, does it?" Jason said.

Hannah absently shook her head. "Yeah. I mean, how many of our female suspects would fit the description of a tall, beautiful American woman?" She kept her voice low, though amid the commotion of other visiting, no one seemed to be paying them any attention.

"You would fit the description," Jason said with a short laugh.

Hannah rolled her eyes. "Suspects. Not just anyone around you." A smile tugged at the corner of her lips when she realized that he had jumped straight to her when he thought of someone tall and beautiful. "What about Lexie?"

"She's medium height. I wouldn't really call her tall," Jason replied.

"And Belle?" Hannah offered.

Jason laughed. "She's shorter than Lexie."

Hannah's eyes went wide. "Bethany Clark is tall," she said.

Jason scrunched one eye closed as if trying to picture her. "I guess it's possible that an old guy in a small village in China might call her tall and beautiful."

"Sandra, the agency receptionist?"

Jason shrugged. "Yeah, she's attractive. But I wouldn't necessarily call her tall."

Hannah's brow went up at this evaluation, but she didn't comment on it. "From the perspective of the great-uncle, she might be tall."

"Yeah, but if we use that criteria, we'd have to include most of the women here." He waved a hand at the surrounding retreat.

"There's always Shannon Mills," Hannah suggested. "She's the definition of tall and beautiful."

"We can add her to the list," Jason said. "But she doesn't really have anything to do with the actual adoption, except for organizing this retreat."

Hannah pulled her feet up on the bench and hugged her knees to her chest. "Shannon might lead us to the founders of the retreat, though. She seemed pretty intent on protecting their identities."

Jason shrugged. "It could be something. Without knowing who they are or what they look like, it's hard to say if they would be suspects."

Hannah sighed and looked out across the darkening grounds. There were so many other families they hadn't even met, much less considered as possible suspects. She turned back to her partner in earnest. "Tomorrow's the last day, Jason. How are we going to figure out who this mystery woman is in just one morning? Not to mention the fact that we're only two weeks from the next adoption trip. We have to catch her before she steals away another kid like Jinhai."

Jason nodded, his expression grim. "We'll just have to do our best with the time we have. Honestly, we don't even know if the woman who arranged the adoption with Jinhai's great-uncle is even at this retreat."

The partners sat in silence for several minutes, each pondering the situation. Finally, Jason spoke again. "I bet this woman—whoever she is—has been making trips to China to find vulnerable families who are desperate enough to sell their children."

Hannah had a sudden idea. She grabbed Jason's arm and said, "Jinhai's great-uncle also said that the woman spoke fluent Mandarin. Tomorrow at breakfast, I could ask some of the women if they speak Chinese," Hannah suggested.

Jason's brow went up. "Can you be subtle about it?"

Hannah tried to act hurt, but there was no point. They both knew she was as subtle as a freight train ringing a doorbell. "What if I promise not to waterboard any of them?"

Jason's mouth cracked in a smile. "I'll hold you to that."

For the next several minutes, they discussed ways that they could each bring up language abilities in a casual conversation the next morning before the retreat ended. The most non-threatening would probably be to ask about their adoption trips to China.

They continued brainstorming ideas as they made their way across the dark meadow to their suite. As they approached the door, a flicker of movement through the curtains caught Hannah's eye.

She grabbed Jason's arm before he scanned his keycard. "Someone's in our room," she said softly.

Jason tensed and looked at her. "You sure?"

With a small lift of her shoulder, Hannah said, "Pretty sure."

The keycard in his hand hovered over the security reader. "When I unlock the door, we rush them," he said firmly and quietly. "Make sure whoever it is doesn't get away."

Hannah nodded, her body tensing for combat.

In one quick movement, Jason swiped the card and shoved the door open. They burst through the doorway, and Hannah flipped on the main lights.

There, in the middle of an incredible mess of scattered clothing and upturned furniture, stood her would-be purse napper and their one-time stalker, Eric—or whatever his name really was. His surprise at suddenly being caught lasted only a second. He made a move toward the front window, apparently ready to crash through the glass to escape. Hannah was already halfway across the room, and she lunged at Eric, tackling him in the midsection before he could get away.

Eric rolled away from her and back onto his feet like a cat. Jason jumped forward and grabbed his arm. The guy twisted, breaking Jason's grip, and delivered a quick punch to Jason's chest. Jason flew backward over the sleeper sofa and landed next to the kitchen table.

Hannah was back on her feet, prepared to launch another attack, but Eric was ready for her. She moved forward quickly, kicking and punching every time she saw an opening. He gave up very little ground as he easily deflected her attacks.

After a quick feint forward, Hannah backed off slightly, giving Jason a chance to get to his feet again. Jason stepped sideways into the kitchenette area, forcing Eric to continuously glance back and forth to keep them both in sight. He shifted nervously as they closed in on him.

As Hannah got closer, Eric rushed toward her. Hannah blocked and dodged, but he nearly had her against the wall. With Eric's attention fully on Hannah, Jason charged forward and wrapped the guy in a headlock. The burglar spun, grabbing Jason by the head, and flung him off. Jason clipped the edge of the sofa and cartwheeled to the ground.

Hannah aimed a kick at the guy's leg. He easily blocked her attempt, pushing her away in the process. She staggered backward and stopped to take a breath. "Remember when you thought he ran off because he was scared to fight us at the same time?"

Gathering himself off the floor, Jason stood and turned back to their attacker. "Yeah, that sounds like something I might have said." He grinned at her. His lip was swollen and there was a small cut above his eye. Hannah knew she probably had similar bruises.

"You might need to revise your brilliant theory," she said.

With an intentionally wild but sloppy series of kicks, Hannah forced the burglar to back up toward the bedroom door. If they could trap the guy in the room, the smaller space might allow them to get in closer and grab him.

Jason must have guessed Hannah's plan because he also stepped forward and took a few crude swipes. His efforts almost worked.

Unfortunately, Eric saw right through their attempt. He swung a lightning-fast punch at Hannah that caught her in the shoulder and knocked her into Jason's mostly empty suitcase. Then he spun and rushed Jason. Despite Jason landing a few good punches, the intruder quickly had him on his heels. The decisive blow was a roundhouse kick to Jason's middle that slammed him into a nearby wall.

The burglar leaped over the coffee table and grabbed the handle to the front door. Hannah couldn't reach the door in time to stop him, and if he made it outside, they would never catch him. Without even thinking, Hannah grabbed Jason's suitcase and flung it across the room like a frisbee. It struck the intruder in the side of the head, just as he was about to disappear through the door. The timing was perfect—the impact slammed his head into the partially opened door.

In three strides, Hannah was across the room, picking up one of Jason's shirts on the way. She put a knee between the burglar's shoulder blades and quickly hog-tied his wrists behind his back.

Jason scrambled back to his feet and looked down at her. "Nice job," he said.

"Grab his feet. Let's move him out of the doorway."

With her partner's help, they had the stalker sprawled across a small loveseat. Twenty seconds later, his ankles were tied, too.

"Now," Hannah began, her breath still coming in ragged bursts. She flipped an errant strand of long blond hair out of her face. "You're going to tell us why you've been following us and what you're looking for." She placed her hands on her hips.

"I now have what I need," the guy said with a sneer. His English was accented, but still quite good.

Hannah and Jason glanced at each other. Jason looked as confused as she felt. What could he have meant by that? Did they need to search his pockets?

She turned back to Eric, prepared to continue the interrogation, when a soft knock sounded at the door. "Hannah, Jason, are you okay in there?" It was Stephanie, their next-door neighbor. "I thought I saw you wrestling in the doorway; not that I'm opposed to a couple getting a little wrestling in every once in a while." Their neighbor laughed lightly at her joke. "But I thought you might have been fighting with someone."

If they didn't open the door, Stephanie would start to get suspicious, and who knew where that might lead. On the other hand, if they let her in, she would wonder why they had a guy tied up in their suite. The explanation could get sticky. Hannah hardly remembered what it was like to be a regular civilian. Would a normal person tie up an intruder and interrogate them for half an hour before contacting the local authorities?

Jason must have read her mind. He tilted his head toward their captive. "We need to call the police and report a burglar," he said in a loud voice, clearly for Stephanie's benefit.

Hannah nodded and moved quickly to open the door. As best she could, Hannah switched from spy girl to suburban housewife. "Oh, Stephanie," she said with a hand to her chest, "I'm so glad you're here." She stepped back and motioned her neighbor inside the small suite. "We came back and found a burglar." She pointed an accusatory finger at their attacker.

"I'm calling the police right now," Jason said, holding his phone up.

Stephanie's eyes went wide when she saw the burglar tied up on the love seat. "I can't believe this." She stepped closer to Hannah. "Are you two okay?"

Hannah glanced at Jason. He heaved a huge sigh and looked like he was pretending to be shaken up by the experience. Hannah didn't know if Stephanie could see through the poor acting job, but she had no doubt that their attacker could. She and Jason hadn't tried to hide their fighting abilities. He would definitely know that they were trained in hand-to-hand combat. That meant all the effort they had gone through during the car chase was for nothing. He knew they weren't a normal couple investigating adoption choices.

Hannah wondered again who Eric really was and who had hired him. And what had he seen in their cabin before they caught him?

Making sure he didn't deliver this newfound information to whoever had sent him was now of paramount importance.

As they waited for the police to arrive, a small group began to gather in the doorway—mostly because Stephanie would stop every passerby to have them come in and look.

With some strategic body presence, Hannah finally had them corralled outside the doorway. She hoped Jason would take the hint and close the door behind her. Maybe he would get a chance to interrogate the guy.

Unfortunately, Shannon, the retreat director, chose that very moment to approach their group. "What's all the excitement about?" she casually asked.

Before Hannah could stop her or even come up with a diversion, their neighbor blurted out, "Jason and Hannah had a break-in. And the guy's still in there."

Shannon's eyes went wide. Without making too much of a scene, Hannah tried to place herself between Shannon and the door. The retreat director dodged her and swept into the suite. She glanced around for the burglar, eyes narrowing when she found him tied up on the love seat.

"Have you notified the authorities?" The question was directed at Jason, but she continued to glare at their intruder.

"Yes, the police are on their way," Hannah said.

Shannon stayed in their suite, alternating between apologizing profusely and describing how shocked she was, until the police arrived. Hannah wanted to pull the officer aside and ask him to hold the guy at the station until they could come interrogate him. But Shannon's presence made that impossible.

After the burglar was safe in the squad car, they each gave their statements to the responding officer. Of course, they had to omit the part about being trailed on their way back from the adoption agency. Hannah considered telling the officer that the guy had tried to steal her purse the week before, but decided against it because she worried that it would only bring up more questions. Not from the officer—she could handle that—but from Stephanie and their gathered fans, not to mention the ever-present retreat director.

The officer asked them to look around to see if anything valuable was missing. Hannah didn't know what Jason might have brought, but she definitely had some Banana Girls gadgets that she didn't want anyone to see. She went back into the room and found the secret compartment in her suitcase open. Her gadgets were all still there, but the lid of the permanent marker was off—the plasma torch end.

Once the officer was gone, Shannon stayed after to talk to them. The crowd of onlookers, including Stephanie, was now gone. Shannon must have shooed them away.

"I'm so sorry this happened," Shannon began. "I can assure you that you're perfectly safe. But if you decide you'd like to change rooms, just come find me, and I'll make the arrangements."

They both smiled and thanked her for the offer.

After Shannon finally left, Hannah shut and locked the door before turning to face Jason. "He found some of my secret gadgets."

Jason picked up an errant shoe. "Yeah, he apparently found plenty of our stuff."

"No, I mean I think he figured out that they weren't innocent travel items."

Jason's brows went up. "Did he take anything?"

"No," Hannah replied.

Jason picked up his suitcase and started tossing his scattered clothing back inside. "Well, if you're worried that he knows we aren't a typical married couple, we can be pretty sure he figured that out during the fight."

Hannah blew out a frustrated breath.

Jason stopped near the end table and picked up the book he had been reading. "Aw, man. Look at this. He pulled the bookmark out of my book." In his other hand, Jason held up a flimsy piece of paper that looked like a store receipt. "What kind of monster would do something like that? Now I'll have to figure out where I was."

Hannah's eyes narrowed. "That's not a bookmark."

"What do you mean? It's a perfectly good bookmark. It marks my place in the book—as long as nobody messes with it," he muttered.

Hannah snatched the small piece of paper out of his hand.

"Oh, come on. Not you, too. Can't a guy just use his bookmark in peace?"

"This isn't a bookmark," Hannah repeated as she thrust the printed side back in his face. "It's a library due date receipt."

Jason shrugged. "So? That's what I have on hand when I start reading my library books. I just use it as a bookmark. Is that a crime now?"

"No, but it might cause problems for an undercover agent when it has his name on it." Hannah waited for her comment to sink in. "His real name."

Comprehension slowly dawned on Jason's face. He grabbed the receipt and examined it closely, muttering an expletive that Hannah couldn't quite make out. He pulled his phone out of his pocket. "We need to make sure that guy stays in police custody."

Hannah sat on the edge of the sofa bed while she listened to Jason talk to the police dispatcher of the nearest small town. He hung up after twenty minutes of making no progress. He sat down next to her and blew out an exasperated breath.

Hannah patted him on the knee. "Maybe I should see if my team can use some of those special skills you said we had." Hannah tried to keep her tone playful. There would be plenty of time to gloat about it later, if her girls came through for her.

"If it can help the mission, go for it," Jason said.

His response surprised Hannah a little. She half expected him to dig in his heels to prevent her from winning this one.

With a satisfied smile, Hannah pulled out her phone and connected to Club Banana. A few seconds later, the familiar living room appeared on the screen, Susan lounging happily on one of the wide couches.

"Hi, Hannah. How's the retreat?" Susan asked as her eyes searched for details of the room behind Hannah.

Hannah took in her solitary figure. "Where is everyone?"

"Mari's out with Trey, and Katie wanted to show Anna a new dance club she heard about. Plus, there was a guy involved." Susan spread her hands out wide on the couch. "What, am I not enough?"

Hannah shook her head. "You'll be fine."

Susan put both hands together under her chin and dipped her head. "Thank you for the vote of confidence." The gesture was silly and overdone.

"I need you to call the local police," Hannah began without any additional chit chat. "They apprehended a guy—"

"And you need me to bust him out of the clink?"

Hannah had no idea why Susan's imagination ran so wild sometimes. "No. I need you to make sure they don't release him."

"Lock the door and throw away the key?" Susan mimed twisting a key then tossing it over her shoulder.

"Something like that."

"What did the guy do?"

"We think he might have found out our identities," Hannah replied.

"You brought evidence of your identity on a mission?" Susan's eyes became even wider, if that was possible.

"No." Hannah fought the urge to glance across the room at Jason. "Anyway, it doesn't matter. Just see what you can do." Hannah gave her the information they had on the local police department.

Susan saluted.

Hannah couldn't help but shake her head as the call disconnected.

As soon as she finished, Jason began pacing the small living area. "I don't think we can afford to just sit and wait. We need to get to the police station ourselves to make sure Eric doesn't get released."

Hannah shrugged. "Won't they keep him in jail until he can see a judge?"

"Maybe. But you never know in these small towns. Do we want to risk it?"

After considering him for a moment, Hannah asked, "How do we get out of here without blowing our cover?"

Jason continued pacing, his brow furrowed. "Could we fake an emergency?"

"One that doesn't involve them calling an ambulance?" Hannah pressed.

"Hmm." More pacing. He turned to her with a mischievous grin. "It's too bad we didn't think ahead to say you were pregnant. We could have pretended you were going into labor."

"Again, they would call an ambulance." Hannah shook her head at the obvious absurdity of his suggestion. "Besides, if I were pregnant, why would we be at an adoption retreat?"

He laughed. "Good point."

They sat for another minute, both deep in contemplation.

"We'll have to sneak out," Jason finally declared.

"Did the attendant give you back your car keys?" she asked.

"No, but I have a spare." He considered her for a moment. "What are our chances of getting past the gates without anyone knowing?"

"Let's get the car first, then we can worry about getting out." Hannah stood and moved toward the door.

"Do you have a plan already?"

She turned and gave him a half-shrug. "Sure. Get the car. Get through the gates."

"Pretty elaborate plan," Jason said with a wink. He moved to join her at the door.

Before they set out, Hannah peeked through the blinds. Even though Stephanie had been forced out of the suite, she and a small group had continued visiting just outside the door.

"We'd better go out another way," she suggested.

Jason nodded. They moved to the bedroom and looked out the windows that faced the surrounding forest. Hannah carefully opened one and removed the screen. Sticking her head out, she checked both directions. Behind the row of suites, a narrow strip of manicured lawn faded into the wild grass of the surrounding forest. Hannah shimmied through the window and crouched against the wall while Jason climbed out. They crept slowly behind the row of cabins, careful to duck below windows as they passed.

When they reached the last suite, Hannah paused. They weren't far from the path that led back to the mansion house, but the walkway was lined with small lights every few feet.

The sound of footsteps warned them of an approaching couple on a walk. She ducked behind the corner, pushing Jason with her hand. After a few moments, the couple passed by their hiding place. She suddenly became aware that she had forgotten to remove her hand from his chest. She dropped her hand and turned her attention back to their goal, chiding herself for becoming so physically comfortable with her partner. That was a dangerous path.

Jason leaned in close behind her, obviously trying to see around the corner. "We could just sneak out onto the path and pretend to be on a walk."

"Good idea. But we have to avoid Shannon. She'll think we came to switch rooms."

Jason nodded his agreement. They checked again to make sure the path was clear before sneaking out of the darkness. Jason fell in step next to her and casually took her hand. Before she realized what she was doing, Hannah intertwined her fingers with his. Fortunately for her—and him—he didn't make a big deal about it. He barely even seemed to have noticed.

They followed the path along the back of the mansion house. Given that the main building was only used for classes and indoor activities—plus some administrative offices—Hannah wasn't surprised to see that the windows were mostly dark.

As they continued around the house, they came upon a solitary lit window. A one-sided conversation drifted out through the inch-wide gap open to the night air. It was Shannon's voice.

". . . had an intruder." There was a long pause. "Yes, I understand. But it's been taken care of." Another long pause. "Yes. Yes, I know. I'll inform them personally." Pause. "No, I think we can continue with the original plan."

Jason and Hannah shared puzzled looks. What plan? Who was she going to inform?

They didn't have time to stop to figure it out.

When the phone call ended, they snuck by the window toward the dining hall building. Noise from the converted barn filtered through the open door. It sounded like there was some sort of evening social happening. A poster pinned to the door frame said it was a couples-only dessert. They hurried past the open door, but Jason slowed, craning his neck to see inside.

"They never told us there was an evening social for couples," he hissed as they plunged into the darkness again.

"Yes, they did," Hannah whispered back.

"When?"

"During the orientation meeting," Hannah said. "You were too busy playing with that cute little boy."

"Well, if I had known . . ."

Hannah stopped abruptly, causing Jason to bump into her. "We can go back, if you want. I'm sure Eric wouldn't dare get out of jail before we get there, especially considering there's dessert involved."

Jason huffed and nudged her forward. "You can joke all you want, but now we'll never know if it might have been delicious."

They alternated between walking casually and sneaking in the shadows until they reached the industrial sized carport. Hannah followed Jason as he crept along the first rows of cars. If his car was on this row, they could just jump in and drive away.

They weren't so lucky.

Given that they were some of the last attendees to arrive, his car was one of the last ones brought into the carport. Unfortunately, they must not have been the very last to arrive, because a green Jeep was parked in the spot right behind it. There was no way to get his car out without moving at least one other vehicle.

Crouched next to Jason's car, the partners stared at each other. "What now?" Jason asked.

Hannah glanced around at the nearby vehicles and shrugged. "I could probably figure out a way to hotwire the cars we need to move, especially if they have remote start systems."

"And then what? Wouldn't it be a little obvious if half a dozen cars have been rearranged, and ours is the only one missing?" Jason replied.

Hannah scowled. "We could just take the Jeep and bring it back."

Jason gaped at her. "Just steal someone's car? If we got caught, it would not only blow our cover, it could land us in jail."

"So, we wouldn't get caught," Hannah suggested, not really appreciating Jason's condescending look. "Do you have a better idea?"

He rubbed a hand across his face. "I don't know. If we could get out of the compound, I guess we could walk back to town."

"That's at least three miles," Hannah said.

"Yeah. But it's either that or give up on our cover and call for backup." He eyed her, probably waiting for a reaction.

She shook her head. "After what we've been through to keep our cover, I'm not giving it up that easily. We can walk."

Crouching low, they moved to the far end of the carport and slipped into the darkness of the open meadow. The entrance gate was at least a hundred yards down the small road that led from the mansion house. They set off across the grassy meadow, parallel to the road, skirting the pools of light that marked the drive.

Halfway across the broad field, Jason grabbed Hannah's arm. "Get down," he whispered.

Hannah had trained long enough to know not to question an order like that. They dropped quietly onto the cool grass. Hannah was close enough to her partner that she could feel the warmth of his arm against hers. She lifted her head to look around. Jason pointed away from the main gate along the fence line. A solitary flashlight bobbed and swung slowly along. It looked like someone was walking the perimeter of the retreat grounds.

Had there been a guard on duty earlier?

Jason brought his face close to her ear. "Why would they have a guard patrol at an adoption retreat?"

Hannah shook her head. As they watched the light get closer, she could make out the figure of a member of the staff wearing an official retreat jacket. He didn't seem to be searching for them—or anything for that matter. He almost looked bored as he walked along the fence, periodically shining his flashlight into the dark trees beyond.

"He's not looking for us," Hannah whispered.

"I don't care," Jason hissed. "Now I feel trapped."

Hannah squinted at him in the dim light from the distant carport. From the hard-set expression on his face, she could tell he wasn't joking about how he felt. She could hear his breathing become shallow and quick. He'd hyperventilate soon if he wasn't careful.

Could this be related to his pacing in the elevator?

Realization dawned. "You're claustrophobic, aren't you?" she said.

Jason took a deep breath and quietly let it out. "It's agoraphobia, actually. The fear of being trapped." His whisper sounded strained and anxious.

Hannah nodded. That made a lot more sense, especially for a guy like Jason who always liked to be in control of situations.

She reached over and touched his arm. "Hey." She waited until he looked at her. "We're highly trained agents. We could get over that puny fence anytime we want." She tried to sound encouraging. "We're not trapped in here. We're *choosing* to stay because of our cover."

Jason considered her for a moment, glancing back at the solitary security guard walking away along the fence line. "Yeah, that's true." He nodded, and his breathing began to slow. His normally gray-blue eyes, darker in the dim light, locked with hers. "Thanks," he said softly.

She squeezed his arm in acknowledgment. Hopefully, he understood her unspoken promise—that she would guard his secret just as fiercely as he had promised to keep hers.

With the immediate danger passed, they stood and moved toward the nearest walking path. Their hands found each other almost instinctively as they made their way back to their cottage.

"Besides, they probably only sent that guy to wander around the property to help us feel safe," Hannah said.

Jason shrugged. "Unless Shannon's in league with Eric and wants to keep us from getting out."

"She *was* acting suspicious in our suite. Not to mention the phone call." Hannah nodded toward the mansion house and the slightly open window. "Let's definitely run a check on her when we get back."

"First thing Monday morning," Jason said with a smile. He squeezed her hand—either intentionally or subconsciously—and Hannah found that she didn't mind.

CHAPTER TWELVE

THE NEXT MORNING, BEFORE sunlight had even touched the blinds in her room, a call sounded on Hannah's phone. She squinted at the clock on the nightstand as she fumbled for the phone. It was a secure connection from Club Banana.

"Hello," she croaked once the phone verified her identity.

"Hi, Hannah. Did I wake you?" Susan's chipper smile was even more annoying before seven in the morning.

Hannah tried to say no, but it came out mumbled. She couldn't give Susan the glare she deserved because her eyes were barely open.

"Sorry, I don't have good news," the redhead said with an exaggerated shake of her head.

That had Hannah suddenly much more alert. "What's up?" she croaked.

"I called the police station last night. And they had the most annoying night dispatch controller that you could imagine. All he could do was hit on me. Even when I tried to give him my agency identification, he wouldn't listen."

"What are you saying? Do they still have our burglar?" Hannah asked impatiently.

"I never found out. I called back several times, hoping to talk to someone else, but I think that only encouraged the dispatch guy. He thought I was calling back to talk to him."

"So, what happened?"

"I finally had to get mean." Susan looked both ways to see if anyone else at Club Banana was listening in on the conversation. Hannah couldn't imagine anyone else would even be conscious this early on a Sunday morning. "I called him a naughty name," Susan whispered.

"Susan, you need to tell me whether or not our guy is still in prison." Hannah's patience, which, given the hour, was already in low supply, had nearly run out.

"I don't know. When I finally convinced him that I was serious about breaking his arms, he got all defensive and said they didn't have anyone in their jail cell anyway."

Hannah sighed. "Thanks for trying. But next time, call me as soon as you find out instead of waiting until the morning."

"Oh, I didn't know any of this last night. I just got off the phone with him a few minutes ago."

Hannah's eyes went wide. "You've been at this all night?"

"I told you, he thought I was hitting on him. I had to call back every half hour or so to see if he was still there."

"Oh, Susan, that stinks. I didn't mean for you to be awake all night."

Susan shrugged. "It's okay. I worked on other projects in between." Her smile was as chipper as ever. "Plus, I had a long nap yesterday."

"We'll head over there this morning to see what we can find out," Hannah said.

"Great idea." Susan nodded. "And if you see a guy named Vern, tell him I might still come over there and break his arms just for the trouble he caused me. Or better yet, you could go ahead and do it while you're there. Sort of save me the trip."

Hannah chuckled. "Will do. And get some sleep, Susan."

She disconnected the call and hurriedly threw some clothes on. She opened the door into the living area, expecting to find Jason still asleep, but was surprised to see him on the floor doing pushups.

Without a shirt.

Hannah skidded to a stop and glanced away. Then she forced herself to be professional. He was just a fellow agent keeping himself in top physical shape for the mission.

And it was a nice physical shape, at that.

She focused on his face as he stood up and smiled at her. "Hey, we have a problem," she said quickly, trying not to notice the contours of Jason's chest and abs.

"Good morning to you, too."

"We need to get out of here," Hannah said.

"Seriously. That's what I've been trying to say," he said with a smile. "Just knowing there's a guard walking around the perimeter makes me feel trapped."

"No, I mean we need to get out of here now. I just heard from Susan that Eric might not still be in police custody."

Jason's face clouded over. He glanced around the small living space at the contents of his luggage. "Give me a few minutes to pack, and then we'll grab breakfast and get checked out."

"We don't have time for breakfast," Hannah declared.

Jason stopped stuffing clothes into his suitcase and looked at her. "If we leave before breakfast, we risk blowing our cover. Again."

"If we don't leave before breakfast, we risk losing Eric."

Jason folded his arms over his bare chest.

Hannah caught herself staring and glanced away. "Don't you have a shirt or something you could put on?" She grabbed a random item of clothing from the back of the sofa and threw it at him.

She stalked back into the bedroom. Her rising frustration with him certainly helped fight down the increasing physical attraction she was feeling.

Jason might not be worried about Eric knowing his real identity; he was just a regular agent after all. But her training as a Banana Girl told her that secrecy was paramount. As important as their cover story might be, not letting Eric get away to tell his boss about them seemed much more important at the moment.

Hannah had her suitcases packed and sitting by the door in seven minutes—another benefit of spy girl training. Jason took three minutes more than that. Hannah mentally chalked up a win on that one.

Six minutes later, they were eating breakfast with a few other families in the converted barn. Hannah kept glancing at the clock above the buffet table. How long was long enough before they tore out of the retreat for the police station?

Thirty seconds after Jason finished his glass of orange juice, they bid hasty goodbyes to the friends at their table and hurried over to the mansion house's circular driveway. The attendant took an incredibly long time to bring Jason's car around—probably because they were the first to leave that morning and the car was still blocked in.

Back out on the country road leading away from the retreat, Hannah navigated them to the police station. Once there, it took four minutes of explaining to the front desk receptionist what they needed her to do. Finally, she begrudgingly called the sergeant on duty for Sunday morning, and he came out to chat with them.

"These folks want to know about a criminal that was arrested on the night shift," she said in a heavy drawl.

The sergeant turned to Jason and Hannah, puffing out his chest with self-importance. "I'm sorry, but we're not at liberty to share arrest histories with the general public."

"That's not actually true," Jason said. The sergeant shifted stance, clearly taking offense at Jason's tone. "Arrests are part of the public record. Anyone who wants—" Jason stopped and held out his hands. "Actually, it doesn't matter. We're not part of the general public anyway." He held out his agency identification for the sergeant to inspect.

The sergeant frowned and hiked up his belt. "Well, this does change things." He gave the receptionist a sidelong glance before turning back to Jason and Hannah. "Why don't you come on back into the office."

They followed the now-helpful officer around the reception area to a small, generic office. He sat at the desk and began typing on the computer. "We did have a burglary call last night around ten." He looked up at Hannah and Jason expectantly.

"Yes, that was us," Jason replied.

"You were the ones who called in the complaint?" he asked, eyebrows raised.

"It's an undercover mission, and we think the burglar might have discovered our identities when he was going through our suite." Jason was getting antsy.

"Well, we booked him." The sergeant looked up from the computer, rubbing his neck. Hannah could tell it wasn't going to be good news. "But he didn't stay long."

Jason leaned forward in his chair. "What?"

"He posted the standard bail and was released," the sergeant said with a shrug.

"He was caught in the act of burglarizing our home," Jason said.

"Was it your home?" The sergeant squinted at the computer, though he obviously knew the answer.

"Well, it wasn't our home, but he entered and ransacked our cabin."

"Do you have evidence that the intruder stole anything?" the sergeant asked.

"No, we don't think he took anything," Jason replied.

The sergeant leaned back in his chair. "Then without a prior record, the best we could get him for would be first degree burglary that would probably be reduced to misdemeanor criminal trespassing."

Jason gaped at the sergeant for a moment. He opened his mouth to say something back when Hannah intervened, putting a hand on his arm. "Jason, if the guy's already gone, let's not waste any more time arguing about it. The damage is done. The crime last night wasn't enough for them to hold him."

Jason leaned back in his chair, grumbling under his breath. "Pulling someone's bookmark out of its place ought to be enough of a crime to hold someone."

Hannah turned her charm up a notch. "Could you give us the booking information, sergeant? Then we'll be on our way."

The sergeant printed out a page and handed it across the desk with a smile. Jason deftly pulled it out of reach before Hannah could grab it.

The sergeant escorted Hannah and Jason out of the small police station, wishing them well in their investigation. Once they were back in the car, Jason pocketed the police booking sheet.

"So, I take it you're going to investigate our attacker," Hannah said as they drove off.

"Let's not argue about who has the best resources. Let me see what I can find on him. If I come up empty, then I'll send the info your way." Jason seemed to be in a grumpy mood.

Again, it was a strange feeling for Hannah to be the opposite of her normal role with the Banana Girls. "Are you saying you need a head start?" Hannah didn't try to hide her gloating.

Jason glanced over at her, and his shoulders slumped. "C'mon, Hannah. Just give me a chance to win this one."

She held up a finger. "One day. That's it."

Chapter Thirteen

A FTER BEING SO RUDELY awakened by Susan the day before, Hannah relished the chance to sleep in late enough for the rays of the low autumn sun to find her sleepy eyelids. She might have slept even longer except for the mouth-watering smells wafting under the door into her room. She rolled over and repositioned the covers to block the sunlight. But a few minutes later, her stomach grumbled that it was time for breakfast.

As she sleepily padded out into the hall, her mind began turning over the case. How did the intruder get onto the retreat property in the first place? Admittedly, the rustic compound wasn't built for high security, but he couldn't have come in at the front gate without being seen. And even if he had scaled the small fence, someone would have noticed.

But what if he'd had help getting in?

Hannah yawned as she plopped down next to Anna at the kitchen table.

"Good morning, sleepyhead," Anna said.

Hannah leaned over to look at Anna's half-empty plate. "What smells so good?"

"Aebelskivers," she replied.

"Aebelskivers?" Hannah thought they looked like little pancake balls.

"Yeah. Leo gave me a special pan for our three-week anniversary," Anna said with a smile.

"Such a hopeless romantic." In truth, Hannah knew that Anna's favorite gifts usually involved cooking.

"It's only slightly selfish on his part. He says my breakfasts are his favorite."

Hannah envied the wistful look in Anna's eyes. What girl wouldn't want a handsome prince to come in and sweep her off her feet? Though Anna was the one who had done the feet sweeping.

"You want some?" Anna asked.

"If they taste as good as they smell, I would love some," Hannah said.

Anna eyed Hannah for several moments before her brow arched up. "Well, your legs aren't broken. The bowl's in there. Go grab it." Anna gestured to the kitchen counter.

Hannah dragged herself out of her chair with an exaggerated grumble. She loved to be pampered, but deep down, she knew Anna was good for her.

"How's the mission going?" Anna asked as Hannah prepared her plate of breakfast puffs.

"Our leading suspect got released from police custody yesterday," Hannah said from the kitchen.

"Oh, yeah, I heard that from Susan. Three incidents with the same guy. Sounds like you've got a fan," Anna said with a wry grin. "What'd you think's going on?"

"The first time he was going for my purse as if it were the most valuable thing in the world. The second time he tailed us home. The third time he ransacked our cabin suite but didn't take anything." As Hannah spoke, Anna nodded in acknowledgment. "We don't really have any reason to think he's the mastermind. Our best guess is that whoever he's working for is suspicious about our cover identities."

"Makes sense," Anna said. "Do you think he figured it out?"

Hannah didn't want to throw her partner under the bus about the bookmark with his name on it, but couldn't just gloss over the answer. "Between our fighting ability and what he probably found in our suite, we're pretty sure he knows we're not a regular influencer couple."

Anna nodded slowly. They both knew things didn't always go perfectly on missions. "So, what now?"

Hannah swallowed another bite of Anna's delicious breakfast. "Jason's checking into some possible suspects. We'll just have to see what turns up."

Anna leaned back in her chair. "Speaking of Jason, how are you two getting along?"

"Fine," Hannah replied. That was true; they were getting along much better. She just hoped her friend didn't ask for more details.

Hannah took another bite, but she could sense Anna still watching her, trying to be casual about it. Finally, Hannah glanced up at her friend whose face had a small grin.

"What?" Hannah asked with more accusation than she meant.

"You didn't complain about him or say what an idiot he is," Anna said.

"Did I ever say he was an idiot?"

"Maybe not in so many words." Anna gave her a long look. "But until about a minute ago, I was pretty sure that's what you *thought*."

Hannah stood and took her empty plate back to the kitchen, attempting to affect an air of casualness in her reply. "Oh, well, he might not be as bad as I thought at the beginning."

"Really? Do tell." Anna leaned forward as if Hannah was going to spill her secrets.

Hannah had no intention of telling Anna how her feelings for Jason had changed. The last thing she needed was her friend goading her on. Anna's look of anticipation only grew, and Hannah knew she wasn't going to drop the subject.

Fortunately for Hannah, Mari and Katie chose the perfect moment to hurry through the living room, backpacks slung over their shoulders, on their way out the door. "We're taking Teen Banana," Katie said as they swept past.

"Put some gas in it this time," Hannah called back. The last time she had used the compact car, Katie had left it with the fuel light on.

Katie waved airily over her shoulder.

"Hey, Mari," Hannah called out.

Mari skidded to a stop. "Yeah?"

"Why don't we meet on campus this afternoon and go over your algebra?"

A small smile spread across her face. "Sure. That'd be great. I have a research meeting until two, but any time after that. Maybe in the library?"

Hannah nodded and waved Katie and Mari out the door, all the while inching across the room away from Anna and toward the hall. Before Anna had a chance to press for more details about Jason, Hannah slipped through the door into the privacy of her bedroom.

She wasn't cofounder of a top-secret, highly trained group of spy girls for nothing.

Later that afternoon, Hannah sat on campus with Mari in the library's first floor reading room. As Mari worked through one of the equations, Hannah stared out the giant windows at the small grove of trees in the courtyard below. Some of the leaves were just hinting at changing color.

Hannah knew she should probably be working on her own homework sprawled out in front of her, but her heart wasn't in it. In fact, her heart was in full betrayal mode at the moment. She found her thoughts continuously wandering back to Jason and the crazy, aggravating weekend they'd spent together at the retreat.

"Hey, Hannah?" Mari said, pulling Hannah's wandering mind back.

"Hmm?" Hannah looked back at her.

"You didn't hear my question, did you?"

Hannah frowned. "Did you ask me something?"

Mari cocked her head to the side. "You've definitely got something on your mind."

Unwilling to tell Mari what she had really been thinking about, Hannah grabbed for the next best thing. "It's my mission." She sighed dramatically, though not as dramatically as Susan might have. When that didn't elicit anything more than a raised eyebrow from Mari, Hannah continued. "So, there's this guy—"

"I knew there was a guy involved," Mari said hastily.

Hannah scowled. "No, not like that. I mean, there is the other guy, my partner, but we're not talking about that right now. There's a guy that's been stalking us on the mission. We're pretty sure he's been trying to find out our real identities."

"Do you think someone knows about your mission?" Mari asked. She lowered her voice. "Do you think we have a mole?"

Hannah tried not to laugh at the new agent's intensity when it came to mission security. "I don't think it's a mole." But Mari's question did force her to consider the times Eric had found them or tailed them. "If the stalker guy, Eric, already had inside information about our identities or the Banana Girls' operation, he would have found Jason and me at the coffee shop or when Katie and I were at the airport car rental. But he's only ever found us when we're undercover doing things related to the adoption." Hannah paused to make sure she had everything straight in her mind. "That can't be a coincidence. I think Eric must be working for someone involved in the adoptions. Could be one of the other influencer families. Or . . . my money has always been on Bethany."

"Who's Bethany?" Mari asked.

"The adoption agency director." Hannah glanced out the window again. "She's always seemed too smooth. I've never trusted people like that. Too many of my father's associates turned out to be snakes."

"I've known a few of those myself," Mari said grimly, most likely referring to the men who kidnapped her mother a few months ago and catapulted her into the Banana Girls' world.

Hannah considered Mari for a moment. She had grown into her role as a spy girl rather well. And despite her occasional shyness, she made an incredible contribution to the team. "By the way, you're doing a great job."

Mari smiled and looked back at her scribbled equations. "Thanks. I've always been good with numbers, but this class is harder than I thought."

"No. I mean, you're doing a great job as a Banana Girl."

Mari's smile grew, and her cheeks pinked slightly. "Thanks."

Hannah smiled back. As Mari's gaze continued on her, Hannah glanced away.

"You know, you're not as mean as I thought you were when we first met," Mari said.

Hannah's eyes shot back her direction. "Oh?"

"You can certainly be prickly," Mari said with a smile. "But I've lived with you long enough to know that you're a softie underneath."

Now it was Hannah's turn to blush. She glanced down at her jeans, fiddling with a few loose strands. She looked back up at Mari with a smile. "Just don't tell anyone my secret, okay?" she said.

Mari nodded once, a conspiratorial smile on her lips.

"What secret?" a voice behind her said.

Hannah whirled around, ready to fight, flirt, or finagle to secure the person's silence.

Jason stood over her, a goofy smile on his face.

"What are you doing here?" Hannah asked.

"I have news," he replied.

"Couldn't you have just texted?"

He grinned. "I believe my latest effort warrants a win for my column, so I wanted to tell you in person."

Now he had Hannah's curiosity. "I'll be the judge of that. What did you do that's so amazing?"

Jason scanned the crowded study room. "Shouldn't we go somewhere more private?"

Hannah wasn't sure if he meant to put emphasis on the last word, but it caught her off guard. She looked immediately at Mari, who had suddenly become very interested in her linear algebra. Maybe that's who Jason had been referring to. "You met Mari at our place, right? She knows about our assignment."

Mari looked up and gave him a small wave.

Jason smiled politely before sitting down next to Hannah. "I ran the booking information on Eric," he said quietly.

Hannah nodded. "What'd you find out?"

After a pause, Jason glanced around the large reading room again. "Are you sure we shouldn't talk about this somewhere else? This is a library, after all."

Hannah brushed off his concern with a casual wave of her hand. "This isn't an elementary school library. Here on the first floor, you're allowed to make some noise. You don't really have to be careful about talking too much until you go up to the top floors."

Jason looked around suspiciously and lowered his voice. "Well, if we're allowed to be talking, why am I getting so many strange looks?"

Hannah shrugged. "Sometimes attractive guys get noticed." The observation was out of Hannah's mouth before she had even thought it all the way through. She caught a glimpse of Jason's growing smirk before turning back to face Mari.

Her roommate did an admirable job of hiding her smile at Hannah's blunder by immediately focusing back on her homework assignment.

Hannah decided to try and salvage the situation. She stood. "Sure, we can head up to one of the study rooms. That's probably smarter anyway."

Hannah led Jason to the stairs and up to the group study room. His smug grin continued unabated. He was going to be insufferable if she didn't distract him somehow. She found an empty pair of high-backed sofas tucked in the back corner and dragged him over.

"What did you find out?" she asked.

"Eric Chen might not be his given name, but it's the name he uses here in the states." Jason unfolded a computer printout and slid it halfway across the table.

Hannah scanned the entries which ranged from apartment complex rental applications to department store credit card verifications. All had the name Eric Chen. "Nice job." She went to grab the page, but Jason quickly pulled it out of reach.

"You're willing to admit that I won this one?" he asked. His eyes had a teasing glint to them.

Hannah folded her arms and leaned back in her seat. "Sure. Why not? You're so far behind in our tally that I can afford to concede a point or two."

His smug smile grew as he waved the paper back and forth, taunting her with it.

She couldn't let him gloat about it, though, not when she was so far ahead of him in their little competition. Besides, if she could get her hands on that printout, she could use the information to show him what her team could really do.

Fortunately, Hannah wasn't a world-renowned spy girl for nothing. She knew how to get what she wanted.

Very slowly, she shifted up onto her knees and put her hands on the table, ready to climb on top. Like a panther stalking its prey—all the while keeping her eyes locked with Jason's—she crept across the table toward him. Hannah reveled in the look of terror and elation on his face as she prowled closer and closer. She moved slowly forward until she had one knee up on the edge and their faces were only a few inches apart.

When she was close enough to feel the warmth of his breath, she stopped and held his gaze for several long moments.

She flitted a glance down to his mouth.

That trick never failed.

Jason's eyes went wide and a nervous mumble slipped out as his gaze dropped to her lips.

This was too much fun.

But she probably shouldn't torture him much longer.

Her lips spread in a wide grin as she snatched the paper from his feeble grip.

"Thanks," she whispered in his ear before slinking slowly back into her seat.

Jason's glass-eyed gaze lasted at least a minute as Hannah perused the rest of the document, looking up occasionally to see when she would be able to have a reasonable conversation with her partner again.

"That was a dirty trick," he finally said, though his broad smile told her he didn't really mind all that much.

Hannah laid the paper in her lap and shrugged. The information would be useful, but probably nothing that Susan couldn't have discovered in ten or twenty minutes of combing corporate databases.

Jason spread his arm across the back of the bench and took a deep breath. Hannah could almost see his bravado coming back. "Of course, even if you do find out anything else, we'll both know that I won first." He nodded at the page.

Hannah leaned back, her arms crossed. "You know, all of this tallying of wins doesn't mean anything if nothing's on the line."

He raised a brow. "Oh really?"

"Yeah. There needs to be a prize for the winner." Hannah stared into his gray-blue eyes.

"Dinner," he said finally.

"Dinner?"

"Yeah, a *nice* dinner." He folded his arms across his chest.

Hannah considered her chances. She was already far enough ahead that she almost couldn't lose. Besides, even if she lost, she'd be using her father's credit card for something like that anyway. "Fine." She held out her hand to him.

His mouth spread in a broad grin as he shook her hand to seal the deal. "I look forward to having dinner with you." He held her hand—and her gaze—longer than necessary.

Hannah felt her skin start to tingle, and she pulled her hand away. It was fine when she was having an effect on him. She didn't like the power shifting in his favor. "You'll be having dinner with me either way," she pointed out.

"I know." He waggled an eyebrow.

He was starting to lay it on pretty thick. Maybe being alone with him in the corner booth wasn't such a good idea. She moved to stand, but Jason held his hand out.

"Wait. I have more information," he said.

Reluctantly, Hannah sat down. She leaned back, arms folded, and nodded for him to proceed.

Jason tapped the screen of his phone and slid it across the table. It showed a video of a large wooden desk taken from above. She could see a pair of hands opening an envelope. Hannah looked up at Jason and lifted a shoulder. "What am I looking at here?"

"This is Shannon Mills' desk. The warrant approval came through this morning, so we acted fast."

"You went and opened her mail?" Hannah asked, a little confused.

"No. Although I suppose the warrant might have let us. This is in Shannon's office here in Atlanta. She's opening her own mail."

Hannah looked back at the video, scrutinizing it for details. "This must be shot from the ceiling. Did you use a climbing micro-bot with internal vacuum features?"

Jason looked at her like she had just arrived from another planet. "No. We just waited until she went out to lunch and snuck in and taped a camera inside her light fixture."

Hannah nodded. Old-fashioned, but passable.

"Look at what she's reading." Jason reached over and paused the video then zoomed in on the letter.

Hannah couldn't read all of the words, but it looked like a thank you card. She could just make out the words *retreat* and *great success*. "Who's the card from?"

Jason's shoulders sagged a bit. "Well, you can't really tell on the small screen, but it's a note thanking Shannon for all her hard work organizing the event. We think it's from the founders of the adoption retreat."

Hannah looked back at the words on the card. His conclusion sounded plausible. She rewound the video to a point before Shannon opened the envelope.

"1455 King's Court Circle," Jason recited the address, clearly anticipating what Hannah was looking for.

She squinted at the enlarged envelope. "Does that say Birmingham?"

He nodded.

"As in, Alabama?"

"Yep."

"Who lives there?" Hannah asked.

Jason pointed to the screen. "Someone with the initials 'D. J.' obviously. Or maybe it's two people: 'D' and 'J'."

"No, I mean, who owns the house? Did you do a records search?" Hannah asked.

"Of course. It's owned by a trust."

"And who owns the trust? Who's the trustee?" Hannah couldn't believe she was having to coach a fellow agent on basic investigative techniques.

Jason stared back at her, a deadpan look in his eyes. Hannah thought back to what she'd just said. Had she gone too far?

"We're not amateurs, Hannah. We looked into all that. It's a series of layered, anonymous trusts. We can't tell who owns the home, or at least, we can't tell what *person* owns the home."

She stared at the paused video for several moments.

Jason seemed to shake off his annoyance with her. "But the more important question is, Why would they feel the need to have such levels of protection for their identity? What are they trying to hide?"

"The adoption retreat organizers," Hannah said with a slow nod. "Maybe Shannon was being evasive about their identity because they're the ones calling the shots and she's the one making trips to China to find the children."

Jason cocked his head to the side, looking apologetic. "Well . . ."

"What? Do you have a better theory?" Hannah asked defensively.

"I ran the travel check this morning," Jason said. "Shannon Mills hasn't left the country in three years."

Hannah's brow furrowed in thought. "Long before Jinhai's adoption."

Jason nodded.

Hannah shrugged. "Well, Shannon could still be in on it. We need to figure out who these mysterious founders are."

"We'll know soon enough," he said with a self-important smile. "I put in a request for a stakeout."

"You have agents in Birmingham?" Hannah was impressed.

"Unfortunately, no. At least, none that are available. If it gets approved, an agent from our office will leave tomorrow morning."

Hannah waved her hand dismissively. "Oh, don't bother."

Jason frowned in confusion. "What?"

She pulled out her phone and mapped the address. "Birmingham is about 150 miles away. I can have a drone there in about . . ." Hannah's voice trailed off as she did the quick calculations in her head. Sunset was definitely going to complicate things. "Eight hours."

"A drone? What are you, the CIA?" Jason said with a laugh.

Her brows went up in feigned offense. "Hey, now. There's no need for insults."

Jason smiled, considering her. "So, what are you going to do, land a model airplane on their front lawn?"

Hannah leaned across the table, staring her partner down. "This is one of those—what did you call it?—intangibles that you said we have. You'll just have to wait and see how I work my spy girl magic."

Jason held her gaze for several moments before a wry grin spread across his face. He held out his hands in surrender. "Okay. You do your thing, but I'm still sending someone for the stakeout."

Hannah's lips curled in a coy smile. "Why bother? My drone will get there first. It's just going to be another win for me. And I'm so far ahead, I don't think you'll ever catch up."

Jason smiled back, eyes locked on her. "Are you hoping I'll just give up and let you win?"

"There's no shame in losing to a beautiful spy girl," Hannah said with an overly exaggerated hair flip.

Jason stared at her, his expression becoming more serious. "We might need to up the ante to dinner and a movie," he said finally.

Hannah had planned to return to help Mari with her algebra, but she might have to do that later. She needed to get back to Club Banana to launch the drone if she was going to stay ahead of Jason in their competition.

Chapter Fourteen

Hannah watched the sped-up recording from the camera outside the house in the suburbs of Birmingham. That large city in the center of Alabama was too far for one of her quadcopters to reach, so she had been forced to use her large, fixed-wing sailplane. It had taken the drone most of the evening and into the night to fly the 150 miles from Atlanta. It had loitered in the air over the target house long enough to confirm that the dropped camera pod was operational and transmitting video. When Hannah had rolled out of bed that morning—earlier than normal because of her excitement to see the video feed—she had found the drone perched on the landing apparatus on the roof of Club Banana. Another perfect recovery by her automated system.

So far, the video from the house in question was nothing more than an occasional car crossing the picture as the sun slowly rose. Hannah leaned forward when she saw a pedestrian enter the screen, but it was just a neighbor strolling past.

A few minutes later, Anna walked by the door to Hannah's flight workshop. She stopped and leaned against the doorframe. "Don't think I couldn't tell that you were avoiding me yesterday," Anna said.

"Oh, you know, busy with . . . school. And mission stuff." Hannah waved a hand absently at the screens of video feeds above her workbench.

Anna stepped into the room and looked up at the screens. "Hmm. Yeah."

After a moment, Hannah could feel her friend's eyes on her. She focused on the screen, trying not to let her friend's scrutiny rattle her. After all, she hadn't spent years practicing her cool exterior for nothing.

Unfortunately, Anna had always been able to see right through it. That's what made her such a good friend.

Hannah risked a glance at her friend. Anna tapped a finger on her chin, a look of concentration on her face.

That was never a good sign.

"What's up?" Hannah asked with as much innocence as she could manage.

"I'm just trying to figure out why you're avoiding me," Anna said. She didn't sound upset, just matter-of-fact. "I have a hunch, but it's almost too crazy to even consider."

Hannah didn't trust herself to pull off a convincing argument at the moment, so she merely shrugged her response. It was fortunate that nothing was happening on the screen, because Anna's scrutiny was throwing off Hannah's concentration.

After a few moments, Anna spoke again. "Mari said y'all saw Jason at the library yesterday."

"Mm-hmm," Hannah answered.

"And she made it sound like he was being a nice guy," Anna added.

"I guess," Hannah said vaguely.

Anna paused for another long moment. "At the beginning of this assignment, I would have put money on the fact that you wouldn't make it a week without wringing his neck. And now, after spending the weekend at the retreat with him, things seem . . . different. If I didn't know any better, I'd say you're—"

Fortunately for Hannah, the front door of the house in the video feed opened at that very moment. She paused the playback and turned to

Anna, pointing to the screen. "You know what, I really should call Jason about this. We need to get an ID on whoever this is."

It was a marginally weak excuse, but she needed something to throw Anna off of that particular line of questioning. Anna nodded and walked out of the workshop muttering, "That's exactly what I'm talking about."

Hannah dialed Jason's number and linked it to one of the side monitors above her workbench. Jason's face filled the screen, his lips spread in a lazy smile. "Good morning, bright eyes."

Hannah felt a small jump in her stomach that she quickly tamped down. "I've got a feed of someone coming out of the house."

Jason's brow went up. "What? Already? My agent barely left an hour ago." His expression turned from surprise to obvious resignation at having lost again. "Can you link me in?"

Hannah nodded and entered the commands to share what she was seeing with her partner. They watched as a woman in her thirties or forties walked out the front door and down the sidewalk to the curb. She was dressed in workout clothes. At the curb, she stopped and stretched. A minute later, another woman joined her.

"Okay, I'm sending it through our facial recognition database," Jason said.

"We have a pretty good database of—"

Jason held up a hand. "I've got this one."

Hannah leaned in closer to the screen. "This woman looks Asian." She zoomed in the video feed onto the face of the first woman—the one who came out of the house. "If she's originally from China, she might have contacts there. I wonder if she's fluent in Chinese."

"Hannah. We're looking for an American woman."

"She is American." Hannah held a hand out toward the screen. "Suburbia. Yoga pants. She's as American as they come."

"Sure, she looks American to you and me," Jason said. "But she wouldn't look American to Jinhai's great-uncle."

Hannah frowned. Even though she didn't like it, she knew he was right.

He glanced away from his camera, probably checking a second screen. "We got something on facial recognition. Juliet Motts. Married to Daniel Motts. No arrests. No convictions. No citations. It doesn't even look like she has a passport." He looked up at the camera. "I can do some more digging, but I don't think she's the one behind any of this."

Hannah leaned back in her chair, considering everything she'd had to do—programming the drone flight to Birmingham, wasting a disposable video pod, not to mention waking up early. "A whole lot of work for nothing," she said with a sigh.

"It's not a complete waste. We can cross the mysterious adoption group founders off the list," Jason said.

"What do we do now? Who are we left with?" she asked.

"We got a little distracted by Eric's break-in, plus following up on the founders. I think we need to refocus."

"So, it's back to the Bakers or the Grays," Hannah said. "Or it could still be Bethany Clark."

Jason nodded slowly. "Actually, I've been watching the Grays' and the Bakers' video content, and I can't find any reference to which agency they used for the adoptions. They don't even tell people to contact them if they want a reference. Nothing."

Hannah's brow furrowed in thought. "So, what are you saying?"

"If either of the influencer couples is trying to use their platform to funnel people into the adoption system so that they can skim money in the process, they're doing a horrible job of promoting it."

Hannah could see where he was going with this. "And this from people who would supposedly be experts at promotion."

"Of course, they could be making those contacts in person . . ."

Hannah picked up where he trailed off. "But as we saw at the retreat, they don't socialize with others much."

Jason nodded.

Hannah stared absently at Jason's image as she mulled over the case in her head. "I don't think trying to catch Eric was a distraction," she said. "Eric's the only one that we can definitively say is involved in all this. Shouldn't we be focusing our efforts on him?"

"If there was some way to track him down, then yeah, we'd definitely bring him in for questioning." Jason gave her an expectant look.

Hannah knew she was amazing, but she wasn't a miracle worker.

"I have my drones scouring the city, but there's a limit to what they can pick out from hundreds of feet in the air. If we could geographically narrow the search, I'd fly the drones much lower, and the facial recognition algorithms would have a better chance of identifying him."

Jason dipped his head in acknowledgement.

After a moment's pause, Hannah said, "So if we can't find Eric, we're back to square one on our suspects."

"Pretty much," Jason replied.

Hannah tapped her fingers on the workbench as she pondered the ways they could get close to the other suspects. "Our best options at this point are probably a stakeout or a confrontation," she said. "And given that the send-off party is next weekend, I think it needs to be the confrontation."

Jason nodded. "Would you rather confront Bethany or the influencers?"

"Considering what we've learned about the influencers, I'm not sure they should be our focus right now," Hannah said.

"True."

"Besides, can you imagine actually confronting them?" Hannah laughed at a sudden mental image. "What if the cameras were rolling?"

"That would certainly get us more views," Jason added with a grin.

As their laughter ebbed, Hannah realized that meant they would need to confront Bethany. "Actually, it makes more sense to talk to Bethany anyway. She has to talk to us if she wants to keep us happy. And scheduling another visit with her would be much less suspicious than inviting ourselves over to the Grays' or the Bakers' again."

Her partner seemed to contemplate that idea for a moment or two. "Yeah. I think you're right. I'll call Sandra to set something up."

CHAPTER FIFTEEN

As Hannah had expected, the appointment with Bethany for two days later was easy enough to set up. Most people didn't turn up their noses at that much money, regardless of how annoying the rich people were.

Hannah had just finished a late lunch when a message appeared on her phone that she had a visitor coming up from the lobby. Despite the fact that she was already expecting Jason, she couldn't help but smile at the quirky face he made on the video feed. She wasn't concerned about him coming up to the penthouse at the moment—the other girls were all on campus for classes or studying.

Stopping briefly in front of a full-length mirror, Hannah double-checked her appearance. It was only because she needed to play the social media influencer part for the visit with Bethany. It had nothing to do with the small bubble of excitement at getting to spend the afternoon with Jason. That was absolutely not the reason at all.

The penthouse's front door chime echoed down the hall. Hannah grabbed her phone and purse and walked into the living room.

"I got it." Anna's tall figure swept across the entry toward the door, long black braids streaming behind her.

Hannah's stomach lurched up to her throat. She'd forgotten that Anna was still home. Should she bolt for the door and drag Anna away to keep her from talking to Jason? That might be a little suspicious. Plus, there wasn't really any reason to do that.

They hadn't done anything wrong.

Yet.

"Hi. Anna, right?" Jason's voice came around the corner as Hannah moved into view of the front door. He stood there with a half grin that could easily be mistaken as cocky but was actually just part of his awkward attempt at friendliness.

Anna nodded. "Yeah. Come on in. I'll go get Hannah."

Jason looked over Anna's shoulder, and his eyes lit up when he saw Hannah. Despite her best efforts, Hannah couldn't keep from smiling back.

"Hi," Hannah said. Why did that simple greeting sound so awkward all of a sudden?

"Hey. You look terrific, as usual," Jason said.

"Thanks." Hannah fiddled with the pocket on her pants in an attempt not to blush.

When she looked back up, she saw Anna's suspicious gaze alternating between her and Jason.

"Should we get going?" Hannah asked, hoping to make an escape before Anna started to piece together the truth about their relationship.

Whatever that was.

"Yeah," Jason said with a grin.

Stepping up next to him, Hannah deftly grabbed his arm and ushered him back out the door. She offered Anna an innocent smile as they breezed past into the hall.

They had made it three steps toward the elevator before Anna's voice called out, "Jason, be a dear and hold the elevator, would you? There's something I forgot to mention to Hannah." With lightning speed, Anna moved forward, grabbed Hannah by the arm, and dragged her back into the condo entryway. Hannah knew better than to resist her friend when she was in one of these moods.

"What's up?" she asked casually.

Anna considered her for several long moments, employing the penetrating gaze she had learned from her mother. "What's going on between you two?"

"Nothing," Hannah answered quickly.

Anna stuck a hand on her hip and cocked her head to the side.

"What? I'm trying to get along with my mission partner."

"Uh-huh." Anna wasn't convinced.

Hannah sighed. "Look. We got to know each other a little better over the weekend, and that's helped me not want to strangle him."

Anna let the silence stretch even longer before she spoke again. "I would have thought you'd be the last person I'd need to remind about Rule Number One. Particularly on this mission. With this guy." Anna nodded toward the hallway.

Hannah waved a hand at her friend. "Oh, you definitely don't have to worry about that. We're not going to get involved with each other. We might've called a truce, but I'm sure I drive him as crazy as he drives me."

Anna arched a brow at her. "You sure about that?"

Their silent staring contest lasted for several seconds.

"We're fine. Really. There's nothing to worry about," Hannah insisted.

Anna's stern expression softened. She shrugged and smiled. "I like this new version of him. He seems nice."

Hannah allowed a tiny grin. "He's not bad."

Anna opened the door and shooed Hannah out into the hall again. "Have fun, you two," she said with a wave.

When she caught up to Jason, she hooked his arm and pulled him along.

"What was that all about?" Jason asked.

Hannah shook her head and pushed the elevator button. "Just some Banana Girls stuff."

"Hmm," Jason said with an absent nod as the elevator doors opened.

As the lift descended, Jason began pacing back and forth. His behavior made much more sense now.

"Is there anything I can do?" Hannah asked quietly.

Without stopping his movements, Jason replied, "Elevators are the smallest spaces I regularly have to deal with. It's not so bad if I can distract myself."

Hannah reached out and caught him by the hand, bringing his pacing to an abrupt halt. "Have you ever tried other kinds of distractions?" she asked as she rubbed her thumb back and forth along the back of his hand.

Jason looked down at their clasped hands then up at her. He released the breath he'd been holding. "That's kinda nice, actually," he said with a hesitant smile.

When the elevator dinged and the doors opened on the lobby, Hannah noticed that Jason lingered a half a second longer before dropping her hand and hurrying out into the freedom of the open space.

She smiled to herself. At least her ability to have an effect on him was being put to good use.

Jason still hadn't said anything by the time they were in the car, so Hannah decided to kickstart the conversation on the way to the adoption agency. "So . . . we might need to press Bethany pretty hard during the visit, maybe trick her into letting something slip about buying children from poor villagers."

"Did you have anything in mind?" he asked.

"I'll probably need to act like a spoiled brat," Hannah muttered, mostly to herself.

"Ooh, that could be a stretch for you," Jason said with a good-natured wink.

Hannah nodded, accepting the jab—and the challenge. "I think I can handle it. But if the mission calls for Reformed Jerk, then we'll know who can fit the role."

Jason's brow went up. "I'm reformed now? When did this happen? I thought I'd be the Clueless Chauvinist for the duration of the mission."

Hannah fought back a grin. "You were on track for much longer than that."

Jason smiled as he glanced between her and the road, his expression still playful. "And what changed?"

"It's probably because you've gotten so good at taking my advice," Hannah declared.

"It must have been an accident, because I can't imagine ever doing something like that on purpose."

Hannah smiled despite herself. "See, you're acting more naturally, more like yourself. That's exactly what I told you to do."

"Given how much I annoyed you when we first met, I was sure that acting more like myself would be a recipe for disaster."

She turned toward him and faked cluelessness. "You could tell I was annoyed with you?"

Jason laughed. "I was so intimidated by you and your team, I figured I needed to project confidence—"

"You mean arrogance?"

"—or you'd chew me up and spit me out."

Hannah reached out and put her hand on Jason's leg. "Wait. You thought that by acting like—"

Jason looked down at his leg.

Hannah's cheeks flushed, and she pulled back her hand. "—like an arrogant pig, that you'd be projecting confidence?"

Jason must have had a brain hiccup—it took a couple seconds before the dazed look on his face faded. "I admit, I may have gone a little overboard."

Hannah let out a short laugh.

"But you've got to understand my predicament. I was given the assignment to recruit an agent from Stacia Keller's top-secret, handpicked team of beautiful, intelligent, highly trained spy girls. What was I supposed to do?"

"Talk down to us and berate us, apparently." The sting of his initial insults was lessened by his description of the Banana Girls as beautiful, intelligent, and highly trained.

"I'm actually kind of embarrassed about the way I acted," Jason said between glances at the road. "Can you forgive me?" He reached out and placed his hand over hers.

Flinging her chin up at a jaunty angle, Hannah assumed a regal air. "Perhaps you forgot to include 'gracious and merciful' in your description." She cast him a sidelong glance.

"Yes, that's true. Beautiful. Intelligent. Highly skilled. Plus gracious and merciful. It sort of flows, doesn't it?" He squeezed her hand.

Unfortunately, her hand was resting directly over the ticklish spot on her knee. She let loose a high-pitched squeal and pulled her leg out of his reach. Maybe he would think she was being playful.

A mischievous grin began to spread across his face. "You're not ticklish, are you?"

"No!" Hannah said a little too quickly.

"I think you are." Jason reached for her leg again, not absentmindedly or unintentionally, but slowly and purposefully.

She deftly swatted his hand away. "Keep your eyes on the road." She tried her best to sound serious, but her traitorous voice came out playful.

"I can watch where I'm going and tickle you at the same time." He pretended to reach for her leg again.

"No. You can't." Hannah grabbed his hand and held it down against the center console. He pretended to struggle against her grasp, but Hannah could tell he wasn't trying very hard.

When his struggling stopped, Hannah considered letting go of his hand, but unlike the times they had held hands for show, this felt different.

They stopped at a traffic light. "You know what? You're not that scary." Jason turned his full attention to her. "Once you give a guy the chance to get to know you, you're actually really fun to be around." His grin tipped to one side.

Hannah wasn't entirely sure that the car wasn't tipping, too. It certainly felt that way to her stomach. She released his hand, patting it for good measure to make sure it stayed in place, and turned to face forward. As much as she hated to admit it, she enjoyed spending time with him, too.

They drove in mostly comfortable silence for a few more minutes before arriving at the Eastern Seas Adoption Agency. Jason took her hand as they walked toward the door. Except for her increased heartbeat, it was the most natural thing in the world. He smoothly switched sides and grabbed the door as they walked in.

Hannah wondered if all couples went from awkward to comfortable as their relationship progressed. Maybe most other couples hadn't been forced to pretend not to hate each other at the beginning.

The reception desk was empty, but they heard footsteps coming down the hall from the direction of Bethany's office.

"Hello, Hannah and Jason. You're right on time." Bethany's attitude was civil, but not as warm as before. "Come on back."

"Where's Sandra?" Jason casually asked as they followed Bethany past the reception desk.

"Oh, she's off making preparations for the send-off banquet next Friday." Bethany waved a hand as if to say it was nothing out of the ordinary. Hannah wondered if Bethany helped her assistant with any of the planning or if the poor woman was left to do everything herself.

They sat across from Bethany at the conference table. It was the same room where Hannah and Jason had first met with the agency director, but the mood was decidedly different this time. The woman didn't offer them any drinks or refreshments or attempt to make small talk. She sat in the chair across the table and stared, apparently waiting for them to explain the reason for the meeting.

Bethany's mood wouldn't make Hannah's job any easier, but it had to be done. She took a breath and focused on her influencer persona. "We were just wondering"—she spoke in her practiced, airy tone—"if there will ever be a chance that the birth parents will try to contact us, you know, for money or something." Just saying the words made her feel so shallow.

Bethany gaped at her for a moment before recovering. "Perhaps I didn't explain things well enough during our previous visits. There aren't any birth parents." She waved her hand as if to erase her comment. "I mean, there are obviously parents, but this isn't like an unwed, teenage mother wanting to find a good home for her child. The children that we place are either orphans or they've been cast off by their families so that they might as well be considered orphans."

Either Bethany was an extremely good liar or she wasn't the one responsible for the families being offered money for their children.

Hannah cast a glance at Jason. He very subtly lifted one shoulder. That meant she needed to press on. "And that brings up a very good point," Hannah continued in her fake, superficial voice. "Is there something wrong with the children that they were abandoned by their families? Should we be concerned about deformities or health problems?"

Bethany looked at Hannah as if she was a slug that just crawled out from under a rock. In a flash, she schooled her expression. "The children chosen for placement are healthy, and we make sure they receive the very best medical care prior to the adoptions."

Jason placed an arm protectively around Hannah's shoulder. "We're only concerned with what's best for the child," he said.

Hannah glanced over at him, grateful that he was willing to bear some of the blame for the distasteful comments she was forced to make.

She sniffed dramatically, as if wounded by Bethany's words, and for a moment, she thought she smelled something strange. Like a newly paved street or the shooting range in the basement below Club Banana. She figured it was just her imagination.

If Bethany had taken offense to Hannah's earlier question, she really wouldn't like this one. "You know, we saw the kids at the adoption retreat, and none of them were as cute as the children placed through your agency, especially Belle and Luke Baker's daughter. She's adorable." Hannah hoped that hinting at the tidbit Belle had mentioned—that they had been able to see the children before the others—might be enough to crack Bethany's facade. "We just want to make sure that our child will fit in with our family aesthetic." Hannah wanted to scream at the superficiality of it all.

Bethany's posture stiffened, and it was clear that she had reached the end of her patience. "I'm very grateful that you two have been willing to consider Eastern Seas, and I'm sure the additional exposure you could bring would have been very helpful to our business, but I don't think we are a good fit for each other. You clearly have the wrong impression of what our agency can do."

Jason jumped into the conversation. "We really don't mean to pester you with all these questions, but we feel like this is such a big decision for us."

Bethany's smile didn't falter. "Yes, I can appreciate that. But I think this relationship"—she waved her hand between herself and them—"has gone as far as it can. Thank you for considering our agency." She stood up, clearly firm in her decision to end the interview.

Hannah glanced at Jason and shrugged. They did the best they could.

As they stood, Hannah was struck with a smell that this time reminded her of a busy city road. Jason frowned, sniffing the air.

"You can smell that, can't you?" Hannah asked. The smell was suddenly much more pronounced. She glanced back at Bethany, wondering if the agency director had also noticed.

The woman blinked and stared at them, looking very unsteady on her feet.

"Something's wrong here." Hannah frowned and looked around. With each additional breath, the air smelled more and more like a congested bus station. "Let's get some fresh air."

She pushed her chair away and hurried into the hall then past the reception desk. With a few sniffs, she noticed that the smell wasn't quite as strong in the reception area. She grabbed the handle on the front door, ready to throw it open. The door wouldn't budge. She jiggled it harder, but it was solid.

Looking closer, Hannah saw that the deadbolt lock was engaged, but the interior lever arm was missing. Only a small stub of metal was left, not nearly enough to grab and twist—though she did attempt it.

"What's wrong?" Jason asked.

"We're locked in." She indicated the broken lock.

Jason stepped up and pulled hard on the handle then jiggled it just like Hannah already had.

She stared at him. "Don't you think I just tried that? Why do men think they're the only ones strong enough to unstick things?"

"Can we talk about this later?" Jason's chest heaved rapidly. "I'm feeling a little trapped."

They hurried past the empty reception desk and down the hall toward the back of the building. As they passed the conference room, Hannah saw Bethany sitting in her chair again, looking dazed. The smell was much stronger near the conference room.

Hannah moved to Bethany and helped her up. "We need to get out of here. Are there any other exits besides the front door?"

Bethany looked at Hannah like she had asked about the temperature on Mars. "Well, I think so. There's a back door." Her words were coming slower.

"C'mon." Hannah half dragged Bethany down the hall away from the front reception area. They found Jason banging his shoulder against the back door. With each jolt, the door moved enough to let in a sliver of light, but then immediately slammed closed.

"I think . . . there must be something . . . jammed against the door." He spoke between impacts.

Hannah considered his efforts. Whatever was blocking the door wasn't moving. They needed to find another way out.

Bethany put her hands to her head. "Why are you banging against our door? And why does my head hurt so much? I feel sick."

She tried to sit down right in the hall, but Hannah grabbed her arm and held her up. "No. We can't stop here. Let's get out the front."

Together, Hannah and Jason helped—and somewhat dragged—Bethany back to the reception area. They set her unceremoniously on one of the sofas. Jason stepped toward the door and reached inside his jacket for his gun.

"Jason! We still need to . . ." She jerked her head toward Bethany, though the woman hardly seemed to be noticing anything at the moment. "Besides, what were you going to do, shoot out the lock?"

"Uh . . . no," he replied.

She could tell by his guilty expression that shooting out the lock was exactly what he'd planned to do. "Are you crazy? There could be people on the other side of the door!" she hissed.

He lifted his chin arrogantly. "I might have planned to use the butt of it on the window."

Hannah cocked her head to the side. "Standing right in front of the door?"

He gave her a sheepish look and shrugged.

With a quick glance around the reception area, Hannah's gaze settled on the substantial-looking coffee table in the center. She dragged it toward the large front window, spilling magazines as she went. Jason must have guessed what she had in mind. He grabbed the other side, and they hefted it to the window.

"Ready?" Hannah asked.

Jason nodded, and they started swinging the table.

"What are you two doing?" Bethany's voice was weak.

"Throw!" Hannah yelled.

The sound of crashing glass was accompanied by Bethany's wail of protest. A rush of humid, fresh air came in through the jagged opening. Jason kicked at the remaining glass shards, clearing the way for them to step through as Hannah went back to the sofa.

"C'mon, Bethany. We need to get out of here." Hannah grabbed her by the arm and lifted her onto wobbly feet.

With Jason's help, they stepped gingerly through the shattered window and into the fading sunlight. Hannah guided Bethany to sit on the curb.

She turned to Jason. "Watch her. I'll be right back."

Without waiting for Jason's response, Hannah took off down the office suites' front walk. At the end of the building, she rounded the corner and headed for the service alley. She needed to know where the exhaust smell was coming from.

Skidding to a halt where the service alley met the street, Hannah saw immediately what had caused their near-asphyxiation. Halfway down the alley, a boxy pickup truck sat idling next to the adoption agency's back door. Hannah approached cautiously, wondering how the exhaust could have gotten into the building so efficiently.

Suddenly, the truck's idling engine roared to life. The hulking vehicle jolted forward, barreling down on her. Hannah dove to the side. The weathered front bumper clipped her leg, sending her spinning into a pile of garbage.

Tossing garbage bags out of the way, she rolled back to her knees and reached under her arm for her gun. Her brain took half a second to remember that she hadn't worn a holster for this particular meeting.

As the big pickup rumbled out the end of the alley, Hannah grabbed her cell phone and pressed record just as the truck turned onto the main road. The adrenaline surging through her body made it difficult to think straight.

After a few seconds, she sank from her knees to her butt and took a breath. She stared at her phone for a moment before she stood to investigate the agency's rear entrance. The first thing she saw was a long, flexible tube hanging from the roof. It ran up the side of the building to the rooftop air conditioner. The free end had probably been attached to the pickup's exhaust pipe.

That was a pretty efficient carbon monoxide delivery method.

She walked around the building to tell Jason what she'd found.

Back in front of the agency, she found her partner trying to calm Bethany down.

"That was our only way out of the building," Jason said. "If we stayed—"

Bethany waved her hand. "I don't care if it was your fault or not; this is the end of our relationship."

Hannah gaped at her. "Bethany, we just saved your life."

"It was probably your fault in the first place," Bethany shot back. "Don't think I don't know about the scene you made at the retreat last week. Such an embarrassment to my agency. You two have been nothing but trouble from the start."

Hannah opened her mouth to protest, to make a case for their innocence.

Bethany closed her eyes and held up her hand. "My mind is made up. You are no longer welcome at my agency or at the send-off party next week. Consider yourselves officially uninvited."

Jason shook his head, heading off Hannah's argument. There wasn't anything they could say to change her mind.

Back in Jason's car, Hannah waited until they were out of the parking lot to share her news. "It was Eric that nearly asphyxiated us."

"Why am I not surprised?" Jason said.

"And he almost ran me down when I caught him."

"What?" Jason's brows shot up. "Are you okay?"

"Just some scratches and maybe a bruise on my hip, but I'll be fine."

Jason heaved a deep sigh. "First, we get uninvited to the send-off, then you nearly get killed. We're definitely worse off than when we got here."

Hannah smiled. "Actually, I'd say we're way better off."

"How?"

"Because my drones are amazing at finding cars." She waved her cell phone at him. "And now we know what we're looking for."

Chapter Sixteen

T HE NEXT AFTERNOON, AFTER wasting an exceptional amount of time pretending to do her homework, Hannah found herself driving Posh Banana into the parking lot of the regional Homeland Security Investigations office.

When she finally had gotten around to unpacking from the retreat, she found a bottle of lotion in her suitcase that wasn't hers. Given their haste to pack up and leave the retreat, she figured some of Jason's stuff must have gotten mixed up with hers.

At least, that's the excuse she was using to drop in on him at work. If not for this unplanned visit, she wouldn't see him until next week. She didn't like that idea.

The front desk receptionist buzzed Jason's office and told him that Hannah was there.

When Jason came out to meet her, he looked confused. "Hi, Hannah. What's up?"

Hannah suddenly wished she had sent a warning text that she was coming. Or maybe that she'd fought the idea to come at all. She held out the bottle of lotion to him.

"Thanks," he said. "I could always use more"—he glanced at the bottle and his smile grew wider—"Eucalyptus Tea body lotion and face moisturizer," he read from the label.

A flush crept up Hannah's neck. Clearly, the lotion wasn't his after all. In her defense, the bottle was a very manly dark blue.

What else could she do now besides play dumb? "Oh, sorry, I thought that was yours."

Jason grinned and leaned toward her, lowering his voice. "I guess it might be, but I definitely wouldn't admit it at the office."

Hannah appreciated his attempt at humor. Still feeling awkward, she glanced around the small entry area, doing her best to avoid Jason's gaze and the receptionist's obvious interest in their conversation. She opened her mouth to try and salvage the situation, but Jason spoke first.

"Why don't we go for a walk?" he said, pointing out the front door.

"Sure," Hannah said with a lift of her shoulder. She hadn't really planned anything specific with her visit except that it would give her a chance to see him.

They ventured out into the early afternoon sunshine. The weather was still mild enough to be completely comfortable in her light jacket. In fact, after the embarrassment in the reception area, she was feeling rather warm. They walked together toward a nearby city trail.

"So, have you found anything about the truck?" he asked.

Hannah was glad to have something to talk about. Normally she didn't mind silence, but suddenly she was feeling awkward about it around Jason. "I did. It's registered to a Sunny Phillips in east Atlanta." She shrugged. "Obviously, it could be an alias or just some random person, but we've got some drones set up in that area watching for the truck."

"That's great. Let me know what you find out."

The cool autumn breeze twisted around them as they walked. After a few moments in silence, they stopped on a wooden bridge over a small stream. Jason leaned back against the rail, smiling at her. Hannah wasn't sure why he suddenly seemed so smug, but the look on his face gave him away.

She leaned against the rail next to him. Not too close as to be obvious, but still close enough. "What?" she said with a nudge against his shoulder.

"I'm not sure what our current tally is, but I think we can add one more to my win column."

"What? Why?" Hannah asked.

"You were obviously wrong about Bethany," Jason said.

"Well . . ."

Jason cocked his head to the side. "She was nearly killed by carbon monoxide poisoning. Do you really think she did that to herself on purpose?"

"I guess not," Hannah reluctantly admitted. "Plus, even before the sabotage, I would have moved her lower on the suspect list just based on our chat with her."

Jason nodded. "She did seem incredibly shocked by your insinuations."

Hannah chuckled at the outlandish things she had said to Bethany to get that reaction. They stood in silence for a minute. Hannah inhaled a deep breath of the thick autumn air, savoring the strong smell of leaves and cool weather. "We're running out of time, aren't we?" she asked even though she knew the answer.

"A fact that is particularly complicated by being uninvited to the farewell party on Friday," he added with a mirthless laugh.

There must be some angle they weren't considering, some way to trap the mystery woman who had paid for Jinhai or find Eric and question him. Hannah was sure the two were connected somehow.

"Hannah, I probably should have mentioned this earlier, but it would be really great if we could solve this case. I know I sometimes project a very confident persona—"

Hannah laughed. "Is that what we're calling it now?"

He gave her a friendly glare and continued. "—but this would be a huge boost to my career. It's just that . . ." His eyes locked with hers and he pushed out a breath. "Aw, who am I kidding? You've always been able to see through my hot air. I've had a lackluster track record on solving cases, and with rumors of upcoming staff cuts . . . let's just say solving this case might keep my neck off the chopping block." He stared, eyes unfocused, at the nearby trees.

"Hey." She put her hand on his arm. "We'll figure it out. I'm not quitting until we do."

Jason smiled, but it didn't look like his heart was in it. A moment later, he laughed. "I guess if we fail in this case, you'll finally be rid of me."

Hannah wondered how she had gone from wanting to strangle him so she could avoid being anywhere near him to wanting to save his job just for the slight chance that they might see each other on a future mission. "You know, I said some stuff at the beginning of our mission—heck, I said some stuff a few days ago—that I don't really feel anymore."

He turned to face her more fully, giving her his undivided attention. "Oh yeah? Do tell."

With a deep breath, Hannah pressed forward. She might as well get it off her chest. "I shouldn't have said that you were a conceited egomaniac and that I never wanted to work with you."

"I don't remember the egomaniac part."

Hannah blushed. "I might have just been thinking that. Forget I mentioned it."

His broad smile slowly faded as the silence stretched on. When he turned to look at her, his face was serious. He held her gaze for several long moments before he spoke.

"I would miss you," he said softly.

Hannah's insides felt like they were doing somersaults.

She'd had plenty of guys tell her she was pretty. She'd even had guys say they didn't care how much money she had.

She had never believed any of them.

This was the first time a guy had gotten to know who she really was—warts and all—and he still wanted to spend time with her. Sure, it wasn't a declaration of love. But despite her flaws, Jason said he would miss working with her—miss *her*.

And she believed him.

Hannah leaned toward him. She wasn't teasing this time or trying to see what reaction she could get out of him. This time she wanted to be close to him—for him.

She wanted to tell him how he made her feel, that she would miss him, too. But before she could even open her mouth, her phone buzzed. It was a call from Club Banana.

With a mounting feeling of disappointment at a moment lost, Hannah leaned back, holding out the phone to show him who was calling.

When she answered, Susan's happy, smiling face popped up.

"Hi, Hannah," she said brightly. Her eyes moved quickly back and forth, scanning the feed from Hannah's phone that would be showing up on the wall at Club Banana. "Where are you?"

"Oh, I'm just out on a walk," Hannah said.

"It looks beautiful," Susan said before scrunching her face. "Since when do you go on walks?"

A low chuckle escaped Jason's lips, and he tried to cover it with his hand.

"Who's that?" Susan asked suspiciously. "I have an update, but you need to be alone." Susan mimed zipping her lips.

Hannah rolled her eyes. As a general rule, she avoided letting the other girls know about any interactions she had with guys. Maybe it was the teasing that inevitably followed. She turned the screen briefly toward Jason. "Jason and I are talking about the mission." She put particular emphasis on the mission part. "So go ahead."

Susan's brow furrowed momentarily as if she didn't quite believe Hannah's explanation. Finally, she shrugged and continued, "We spotted the truck that nearly ran you over." Susan paused to make a terrified face. "We caught it several times coming and going from a particular townhouse. And guess who the townhouse belongs to."

Hannah frowned at her excitable roommate. She hated guessing games.

Susan pouted melodramatically. "You might have actually gotten this one. It's Sunny Phillips."

"If the truck is registered to Sunny Phillips, then why are we surprised that it's been spotted near her house?" Hannah didn't think this was anything to get excited about.

"Actually, Sunny Phillips is a man," Susan said.

Hannah shrugged as if that didn't change much.

"I think it's one of those cases where someone picks a new name when their real name is unfamiliar to people speaking English. His real name is Mùyáng—"

"Which doesn't sound anything like Sunny." Hannah's deadpan tone continued. Sometimes Susan dove a little too deep into the detail.

Susan continued as if she hadn't been interrupted, "It means *bathe in the sun* which is probably why he picked Sunny for his English name. He's enrolled in the International MBA program at Georgia State—"

Hannah cut in. "Susan, where is Sunny, or Mùyáng, from?" Maybe with a little prompting, they could cut to the chase.

"He's from Shandong province in China. I could look up the actual village name, but it's a mouthful, and I'm not sure I would pronounce it right."

Hannah perked up. "Why didn't you say he was from China in the first place?"

"Well, I was getting to that part." Susan gave her an overly exaggerated—and overly aggravating—pout. "You have no appreciation for the big reveal. Besides, that wasn't even the best part."

Hannah felt a headache coming on. "Tell me the best part, Susan, or I'm going to hang up."

Susan stuck out her tongue at Hannah. "You're lucky I'm feeling in such a happy mood—"

"You're always in a happy mood," Hannah muttered under her breath.

The redhead's perky smile brightened. "I know. Aren't you lucky?"

"Susan." Hannah drew out the name so her friend would know she was serious.

"All right, all right. The best part is that the truck has been seen at Sunny's townhouse since the attack on you yesterday."

"Why does that matter?" Hannah knew the answer was probably obvious, but between Jason leaning so close to her and Susan's antics, she was having trouble thinking straight at the moment.

"Means it was borrowed, not stolen," Jason offered.

Susan put a finger on her nose and pointed straight at her camera. "Ding, ding. The handsome and surprisingly less arrogant agent from Homeland Security wins a prize."

Hannah leaned slightly farther away from Jason as she fought the heat creeping up her neck. "Was that the big reveal, or do you have something else?" Hannah asked in an attempt to regain her calm exterior.

Susan smiled. "Nope, that was it. I just figured you'd want to know what I found out."

"I did." Hannah gave her friend a sincere smile in return. "Thanks for the info."

After ending the call, Hannah turned to Jason. Fortunately for her frazzled brain, speaking directly to him required that she shift away from him. He was certainly too close for her comfort. "What do you think? Could Sunny Phillips actually be Eric?"

Jason stared off into the nearby woods. After a moment, he shook his head. "Susan has Eric's mugshot. She would have connected the two once she found Sunny's information. But I bet if we watch Sunny's townhouse, we might eventually track down Eric."

Hannah grinned. "This calls for a stakeout," she said.

Chapter Seventeen

"There. That's perfect." Susan stepped back and admired her handiwork. They had been in Club Banana's salon for almost an hour, hard at work on Hannah's disguise.

With a quick spin, Susan turned Hannah to face the mirror. The face of a stranger stared back at her. No matter how many deep-disguise missions she went on, she would never get used to that moment of staring at herself for the first time.

Hannah primped the wavy, dark-brown hair of the wig. "It looks good, Susan. But do you think I need a darker hair color to go with the makeup?"

"Since when have you ever cared about how well the disguise matches your makeup?" Susan asked, her brows raised comically.

Hannah ignored her. "Or maybe we could have Katie give the color in my cheeks a little touch up." Hannah turned her head side-to-side, checking the contrast.

Susan frowned. "I think we might have a security breach," she called loudly toward the door to the hall. Stepping in front of Hannah, Susan put her hands on her hips. "Who are you, and what have you done with Hannah?"

Mari hurried into the room. "Did you say there was a security breach?"

Susan widened her eyes and pointed toward Hannah. "She cares about her makeup."

Mari stifled a giggle and considered Hannah in mock seriousness.

"Okay, Susan, that's enough." Hannah turned from the two ladies and considered herself in the mirror once more. "I just want the mission to go well." After all, she and the other girls had spent their entire Saturday morning planning it.

"Yeah . . . but how is this mission any different from the dozens of others I've gotten you ready for?" Susan asked.

Hannah caught the sly grin that flashed across Mari's face, so she decided to head off the conversation. "I convinced Jason to let the Banana Girls take the lead on the stakeout this evening by telling him that we were better suited for this type of mission. I told him we had better equipment to monitor the mission and better vehicles for nabbing the bad guy."

"This is just about the mission?" Susan didn't look convinced.

"Our reputation among the agencies for perfect execution of operational missions is on the line. That ought to be enough reason to want things to go right," Hannah said with her best air of importance.

Susan shook her head and glanced at Mari. Their newest agent simply shrugged.

For obvious reasons, Hannah wasn't willing to concede that she also wanted to look good for Jason. Besides, that was only a small, small part of it. She really wanted the mission to succeed because it would save children from becoming trafficking victims. Plus, it couldn't hurt if the other agencies knew the Banana Girls got their stuff done.

Anna walked in, holding the purse that Hannah had packed. "Han, I don't think you'll need the quadcopters' mini controller." She looked up at Hannah and froze. "Wow! You look terrific. I see that Katie and Susan have worked their magic again."

"Why won't I need it?" Hannah asked.

"That's what I'm for," Katie said as she bounced into the room. "And did I hear someone say that Susan and I are wonderful and amazing beyond compare?"

As if on cue, Susan executed several elaborate curtsies to an imaginary audience.

"Yes, you two are wonderful," Anna said, patting Katie's arm. "But help me convince Hannah that she should just take a flashpod and some zip-cuffs in the pocket of her coat." She turned to Hannah. "A purse is only going to weigh you down."

"You definitely need to travel lighter. We'll all be there as backup anyway." Katie glanced around the room. "Mari and Anna will be in the park waiting to help you nab the guy. And Susan and I will be in Fat Banana waiting to whisk him away."

Susan held up her hand. "I'm driving so Katie can fly your little copters."

Hannah scowled at Susan's imprecise reference before turning her scrutiny on Katie. "Are you sure you know how to fly them? They can be finicky sometimes."

Katie cocked her head to the side and stared at Hannah. "Have you forgotten who retrofitted them with new differential GPS chips? Not to mention reprogramming the guidance software?"

Susan's hand shot up again. "I helped on that part."

Hannah let out a long breath. "I know, I know. I'm just trying to anticipate everything that might happen tonight."

Katie tilted her head to the other side, now intent on Hannah's new hair color. "Speaking of anticipating stuff, I wonder what Agent Critical-of-Everything will think of you as a brunette."

Hannah glanced back at the mirror to imagine what Jason might think. Quickly she caught herself and shrugged. "What Agent Briggs thinks about my hair is not mission-critical."

"Hmm," Katie said as she moved behind Hannah. She looked at Hannah's wig in the mirror, fluffing it on one side.

Susan mimicked Katie's motions on the other side. Her expression suddenly turned sour. "It's too bad your partner is such a jerk because he is incredibly attractive."

Anna and Mari shared a look that made Hannah nervous. When Anna looked back, she raised a brow, almost challenging Hannah to disagree with Susan's assessment.

She lifted a shoulder. "Yeah, I guess he's okay to look at."

Katie's sigh was followed a second later by Susan's echo.

"I'd be willing to put up with some pretty big character flaws for someone who looked like that," Katie said wistfully.

"I'm pretty sure you have," Hannah said under her breath.

Katie continued. "But he can't be a jerk. I can't handle that."

Hannah stared at her reflection, contemplating how she felt about Jason. "Me neither," she finally said.

They had dropped off Mari and Anna three blocks east of the park that bordered the front of Sunny Philips' townhouse row. That would allow Mari time to stroll into the park from the opposite direction than Hannah and Jason. Anna would wait about fifteen minutes before she made her way there as well. They had to give the appearance of happenstance.

"You were definitely right about a stakeout vehicle being too obvious," Jason said as they slowly ambled toward a nearby park bench, their hands clasped.

He subtly nodded toward the row of townhouses lining the far end; its narrow lane was much too small for any cars to park on, much less a stakeout van. Hannah nodded in acknowledgment, swinging their hands playfully as she scanned the park. They were posing as a young couple in love out for a walk. Pretty much what they'd been doing for the last three weeks.

The early evening air was crisp with the change of seasons, but not overly cold.

Jason pulled her down to sit on the bench next to him. "And I like this," he said, playing with the curly brown hair of her wig. "But not as much as the original."

Hannah smiled and snuggled into his shoulder, placing her hand on his chest. She positioned her head against his neck in such a way that she could still see the entrance to Sunny Phillips' townhouse. One of her quadcopters—perched on a nearby rooftop—had matched the face of a man entering the house to Eric's mugshot. They were fairly certain he didn't live there, so the plan was to tail him to his own place when he left his friend's house.

Hannah shifted a little to give her butt a break from too long in the same position. In doing so, she ended up leaning even more against Jason's chest.

"You know, you're kinda in my space," Jason said, shifting to rest his chin against her head. "Can a guy not sit on a park bench in peace?"

"Considering how helpful and accommodating I've been during this mission, I would think you'd be a little more grateful." Obviously, they both knew she had been anything but accommodating.

He chuckled, and the vibration rumbling through her hand made her stomach do a little flip. "I should be grateful that you're willing to follow orders and do your mission?"

Hannah clenched her hand on his chest to give him what she hoped was a flirtatious pinch.

"Ow," he said playfully.

As Hannah snuggled back against him, she heard Katie's voice over the comm.

"Do we need to rescue Hannah's mission partner again? It sounds like she's about ready to murder him, and you know how I hate having to write up the incident report afterward." Katie's tone was one of humorous resignation that Hannah wasn't sure her past conduct really deserved.

"I think they're okay," Anna said, a laugh in her voice.

Hannah glanced across the park and saw Anna leaning against a tree, staring back at her. Despite Hannah's ability to fool the girls on the comm, she was pretty sure Anna saw right through her act.

"Is that your man?" Mari asked over the comm.

As Hannah was about to protest that she and Jason weren't technically in a relationship and that if they were, it would definitely be too complicated to refer to him as "her man," Jason's reply stopped her.

"Yep, I think that's Eric."

Hannah felt her face heat with the embarrassment of what she'd almost said.

"Jason and Hannah, it looks like he's moving your way," Mari added.

With her head tucked against Jason's neck, she couldn't really see Eric's face as he walked through the center of the plaza. As he approached, Hannah could feel her muscles tighten. Would their disguises be enough to fool him? Particularly when they were looking straight forward, faces fully visible?

When their attacker was only a few dozen steps away, Hannah's nerves got the better of her. All it would take was one glance directly at Jason's face for Eric to recognize him. Without thinking, she grabbed Jason by the back of the head and pulled him down against her neck. She didn't know what else to do to avoid being recognized.

Jason initially tensed at her trick, but quickly made himself comfortable.

Hannah's line of sight—and therefore her own face—were partially blocked by Jason's head, so she assumed that Eric didn't have a clear view of her either. Jason's breath tickled her neck, which made it very difficult to concentrate on Eric's walking cadence. If their disguises worked, he would just continue right past.

"Is he looking at us?" she asked quietly.

"How would I know?" Jason's voice was muffled.

Hannah smiled. "I'm not talking to you."

"He's specifically avoiding looking your direction," Anna said quietly over the comm. "Some professional he is if he falls victim to one of the classic blunders."

"Getting involved in a land war in Asia?" Susan quipped.

She heard chuckles from the other girls on comms.

Hannah let out a slow breath as Eric walked past them. After a few seconds, he was far enough away that they needed to start tailing him. She eased her hold on Jason's head, but he didn't pull back. She nudged his shoulder. "Jason, don't you think that's enough with the vampire impersonation?"

"No. He might glance back any second," Jason mumbled against her skin.

Hannah had a sudden urge to wrap her arms around his neck and completely forget about the mission. That thought surprised her out of her daze. She pushed harder on his chest. "Don't make me get a wooden stake."

Katie's voice crackled on the comm. "See, I knew she was going to kill him."

Jason pulled back, a crooked smile on his lips. He glanced at Eric out of the side of his eye before standing and playfully pulling her up next to him. Intertwining their fingers, he turned and started walking slowly after Eric.

Hannah tried to appear like any other romantic couple on an evening stroll, but it was difficult to stroll at such a quick pace. Eric had reached the edge of the park before they had even covered half the distance.

"We need to catch up," she said under her breath.

They both increased their strides, trailing him down a narrow road away from the park.

"Can we get him with the van yet?" Anna asked.

Hannah glanced back to see her tall friend moving quickly across the park. She was only about a minute behind them.

"He didn't go the way we predicted, but I can be there in two minutes," Susan said.

"Come around the block," Hannah instructed. "But don't move in until we have a clean grab."

Eric glanced casually over his shoulder then his pace picked up.

"Did he see us?" Jason asked.

"Maybe," Hannah replied.

Jason and Hannah matched his speed.

At the next corner, Eric disappeared behind a small barbecue shop. Had he seen them, or was Hannah just being paranoid?

Hannah began to panic. "Katie, do we have eyes on him?"

"I'm on it."

Hannah hated feeling out of control of the situation.

Jason must have read the concern on her face. "We're going to lose him, aren't we?"

Hannah shook her head and gripped his hand tighter. "Not if we run while he can't see us."

She pulled her partner forward at a run until they reached the barbecue shop. Once they were around the corner, Hannah expected Eric to be less than half a block ahead of them. Instead, he was nearly two blocks away and at a full sprint.

Without a word to each other, she and Jason immediately pelted after him.

"Don't worry about being stealthy with the van; he knows we're on him," Hannah said through labored breathing.

Eric tossed a glance behind him but kept up his pace.

"He's headed for the Metro station," Jason said.

"I've got eyes on him," Katie announced. "He's heading north about to go under the train overpass."

The Metro station was just on the other side of the tunnel. They would never catch him before he made it to the station.

"Katie, is there a train in the station right now?" Hannah asked. As long as they made it there before he got on a train, they might be able to nab him.

"Nope," Katie replied. "But a Blue Line train is about to arrive."

"Is he going to make it before the train leaves?" Jason asked. He sounded out of breath, too.

"Probably so," Katie said. "He's just coming out of the tunnel, and the train is about a minute from the station."

"The question is whether *we* can get there before the train leaves," Jason muttered.

"Anna, how far behind are you?" Hannah asked.

"Just passing the barbecue," she replied. "And it smells like I forgot to eat dinner." Anna could always be counted on to bring food into a mission.

By the time they reached the station, Eric had already disappeared inside. The rumble of the tracks overhead and the whine of the electric braking system meant the train was just arriving.

Jason and Hannah leaped the fare gates and raced up the stairs. Hannah's legs burned as they mounted the steps, but she refused to be the reason they lost him. At the top, they ran out onto the train platform just as the chime announced an eastbound Blue Line train.

Hannah caught sight of Eric moving through a nearby car toward the front of the train. She pointed, and they ran forward, fighting through the passengers on the platform.

Jason reached the car first. "Watch him from the outside."

Hannah continued along the side of the train, watching through the windows as Eric moved down the train. Several exiting passengers stared at her as she wove back and forth, trying to keep her eyes on him.

She glanced back to check Jason's progress. He was not-so-politely pushing through a clump of passengers standing in the middle of the aisle. Fortunately, even if Jason was delayed a few seconds, they'd still easily catch Eric. Where could he go now? He was trapped on a train and he had just stepped into the last car.

When Hannah looked back, Eric was gone.

She skidded to a stop and frantically checked up and down the platform. No sign of him.

She backtracked along the last car to make sure she hadn't missed him. Jason stared at her through the windows, his brows up expectantly.

Hannah shrugged. "He disappeared," she mouthed.

Movement above the train caught Hannah's eye. As she backed up and stood on her tiptoes, she caught sight of Eric jumping onto the train on the other track.

Hannah motioned to Jason then pointed above the train, trying to pantomime what she had seen.

But how had Eric even gotten on top of the train? Hannah was fairly certain she would have noticed him climbing up the side.

She moved in parallel with Jason as they approached the junction between the last two train cars. The gray rubber connector boot looked intact. Could Eric have peeled it back and squeezed through?

Her question was answered almost immediately when Jason's hand pushed back the top of the accordion-looking buffer.

"He must have climbed up this way." Jason wriggled through the flexible connector, but it trapped his lower body right away. Immediately, his eyes went wide, and he nearly tore the rubber boot in half as he fought to escape from it. After a short struggle, he scrambled up onto the train car, relief evident on his face.

"Nice job," Hannah said, relieved for him. "Can you make the jump?"

Still breathing hard, Jason surveyed the gap between the trains. "Sure. It's about seven or eight feet."

That sounded doable. Now all she needed to do was shimmy through the rubber accordion connector to join him. But when she stepped forward to board the train, all the doors slid closed. She looked up at Jason, as the reality of the situation sunk in for both of them.

If the mission was to succeed, he would have to continue alone.

"Go! The train's about to leave. We can't lose him." She smiled at her partner. "You can take the win for this one."

Jason glanced at the other train then back at Hannah and shook his head. "I can't do this by myself." He motioned upward with his hand.

Did he want her to jump on top of the train?

Without thinking, she took three fast steps and leaped for the upper lip of the train car roof. She got her elbows over the rounded aluminum edge, and Jason was there in an instant, hauling her the rest of the way up just as the train jolted into motion.

They exchanged grim expressions.

The train was gaining speed.

It was now or never.

They simultaneously hurtled themselves across the wide gap. Hannah landed squarely in the middle of the other train—which began moving in the opposite direction—and slid to a stop. Jason landed a split second later and skidded dangerously close to the far edge.

Hannah plastered her body flat against the top of the train and grabbed his hand. With their mismatched body weights, he would slide off the edge if she didn't do something quick. Using her other hand, she reached for his midsection and grabbed a handful of his shirt.

He thrashed a few times as she pulled him away from the edge.

"I won't let you fall," she said.

"I know, but you grabbed me where I'm super ticklish," he said with a look of chagrin.

Hannah smiled mischievously. Big, tough Agent Briggs was ticklish, too. Now she had ammunition for their next tickle battle.

They both searched for handholds as the train began picking up speed.

Eric was in a similar situation—pinned against the roof of the train—about three cars ahead of them.

They clung to the metal surface as the train rocketed toward downtown, trees and buildings flashing by. The overhang of a tunnel entrance loomed ahead, and Hannah pressed her cheek against the cool metal as the train plunged into darkness.

Half a minute later, the train began to slow, and the roof opened up to the vaulted ceiling of the downtown station. Eric was already standing again, heading for the front of the train. Jason and Hannah scrambled to their feet, crouching low for balance, and moved slowly forward.

Despite drawing a few curious glances, most people simply went about their business. Maybe agents chased fugitives across the tops of trains all the time in downtown Atlanta.

Before the electric whine of the braking system stopped, Eric leaped from the train onto the platform. Hannah and Jason quickly hopped down, too.

"Stop!" Jason yelled. But it was too late; Eric was already halfway across the dimly lit platform, heading toward one of the tall escalators. Jason and Hannah pushed forward, elbowing their way through the crowd. Jason ran ahead, yelling something incoherent as he rounded a wide column at the base of the escalator.

Out of nowhere, a leg swung around the column and caught Jason square in the face, knocking him onto his butt. His gun clattered over the cement and off the edge of the platform onto the tracks. Eric dashed away from the ambush as Jason scrambled to his feet and ran back to the edge of the platform. The light of the train on that track grew brighter as it entered the station.

Hannah grabbed Jason just as he was about to jump onto the tracks. "What are you doing?"

"My gun," he said, looking from the looming train to his firearm lying in the dirt below.

Hannah watched Eric dash across the platform toward the far end. "Forget about your gun. We're going to lose him."

"But—" Jason's shoulders sagged as the train rolled to a stop with his gun underneath.

"We can't wait for the train to move. Besides, we can't shoot him in a crowded train station." She slapped her own gun into Jason's gut. "But you can borrow mine if it makes you feel better."

Jason reluctantly followed as she barreled along the platform, scaring passengers out of the way and dodging the rest.

"We're pursuing the suspect in the lower level of the downtown station," Hannah announced to her teammates. "How soon will we get some backup?"

"We're in traffic right now," Anna answered. "Jason's backup team could probably get there sooner."

"Send them," Hannah said. She didn't even care who got credit anymore. They just needed to catch him.

They dashed through a labyrinth of utility access halls and dimly lit work rooms until Eric ducked through a side door that opened onto a mini train platform strewn with rags and tool boxes. A single train track disappeared into the darkness in both directions. It smelled like a mechanic shop.

A dim overhead emergency beacon bathed the platform. Faint footsteps echoing from the left caught their attention.

"Did he really go that way?" Jason pointed. "The main line is the other direction."

"Pretty sure." Hannah said.

They jumped down onto the dark tracks and moved toward the sound of the footsteps. The crunch of the gravel under Hannah's feet echoed noisily off the round tunnel ceiling. Jason pulled out a small flashlight, and Hannah used the light from her phone.

Even after the footsteps stopped, they crept slowly forward, light beams sweeping back and forth, until they reached the end of the tunnel. A brown, metal girder marked the end of the track line. Crates and boxes littered the enclosed space.

There was no other way out.

The cadence of Jason's labored breathing increased slightly.

Hannah leaned over and whispered, "He's not trapping us; we're trapping him."

A loud scream reverberated off the cement walls as Eric stood from behind a crate and charged. Jason fumbled with the flashlight as he tried to switch Hannah's gun back to his dominant hand. Before Jason could get a solid grip on the gun, Eric kicked him in the chest, sending him sprawling backward, flashlight and gun banging along the railroad ties into the gravel.

Hannah sprang forward and kicked Eric in the back of the knee. His legs buckled, and he rolled away from her.

Jason grunted as he scrambled back to his feet. "Not again," he grumbled, searching the dark tunnel for Hannah's gun.

"Forget about the gun," Hannah yelled. Eric was back on his feet and coming at her. She dodged a punch, blocked a kick, but took a blow to the ribs at the same time as she landed a hit to his shoulder. Hannah stumbled over the steel track and caught herself against the far wall.

"So, the two stupid government agents have come back for more punishment." Eric's taunt, though slightly accented, came across clearly.

"If you want to make this easy for yourself, you'll give up now," Jason said. He always did have a little more bravado than he should.

Eric's mouth spread into a wide leer. "You are idiots."

Jason rushed forward, swinging hard at Eric's head. He landed a few glancing blows, but took a jab to the gut that sent him backward. Seeing her chance, Hannah lunged forward, striking quickly for Eric's exposed side. He absorbed the impact easily, then swung for Hannah's face. She dodged the strike just in time, but his follow-up knocked her on her butt.

Hannah scrambled back to her feet. She glanced at Jason, trying to read his expression in the dim shadows. Like her partner, Hannah was breathing heavily, trying to recover, watching for an opportunity to strike again.

Their opponent seemed barely fazed at all. He was trapped at the end of the train tunnel, but he shifted back and forth like a hunting tiger waiting to pounce.

They had to catch him, and this was the best chance they would get.

Eric lowered into his stance and positioned his fists to fight. "When you are ready for more punishment, please try to attack me again."

It would make the most sense to move around him, have one of them attack from the back. But they couldn't risk him breaking free.

Hannah moved forward, attempting a feint to his dominant side. Jason must have read her intention, because he crossed behind her and launched at Eric. The ninja-guy punched Hannah off balance and side-stepped Jason's attack.

"What are the chances we could get some back-up?" Jason called loudly into the comm.

The connection was garbled and choppy.

"Anna? Katie? Can you hear us?" Hannah said.

No response.

"It's these tunnels. We can't get a good signal," Hannah said. "It might take them a while to find us down here."

"I guess we're on our own." Jason moved toward Eric again.

"We need a plan, Jason." Hannah knew what they were doing so far wasn't working.

When he got knocked on his butt again, she resisted the urge to rub it in.

Fishing around in her jacket pocket for something that might help, her hand found the small flash bomb. She would only have one chance at it.

Hannah lunged at Eric to keep him at bay as Jason stumbled back to her side.

"Keep your eyes shut," she muttered to him.

Jason gave her a skeptical look. "What?"

She could tell he had understood her; he just wasn't sure if he wanted to do it.

Their eyes connected, and Hannah tried to convey in a look what she couldn't explain out loud. "Trust me," she said softly.

Jason's gaze softened, and he nodded. Turning back toward Eric as if nothing was different, he closed his eyes in a long blink.

Seizing the opportunity, Hannah aimed the flashbomb, scrunched her eyes closed, and mashed the activation switch.

The inside of her eyelids lit up brighter than noon on a sunny beach.

When she opened her eyes again, she could barely make out Eric rubbing his eyes and shaking his head. "Now!" she yelled at Jason.

Together, they closed in on him, ready to seize their prey. Despite his momentary blindness, Eric swung and kicked in the direction of their footsteps, but the clumsy blows were easily dodged. Hannah grasped a flailing wrist. Jason grabbed Eric's other arm and wrenched it behind his back. Eric grunted and wildly swung one of his legs. Jason deftly swept his other leg out from under him, landing Eric face-down on the railroad bed.

Hannah pulled two zip-ties from her jacket and cuffed his ankles then his wrists. Eric writhed and kicked against them, but couldn't free himself.

Hannah straightened and took a deep breath. Given how well Eric had fought them, even blind, they were lucky to have him in custody at all. She retrieved Jason's flashlight and used it to locate her handgun.

Weapon in hand and eyes glued to their captive, Hannah sat on a nearby crate. Her body felt ready to collapse. Jason sat next to her, his breathing returning to normal.

The nearness of his body was reassuring. Hannah didn't know what came over her—there was no need to act like a couple—but she leaned against him, her head resting on his shoulder. Hopefully, he wouldn't think anything of it—just a pair of agents relying on each other for support at the end of a difficult mission.

"See. I told you I couldn't do it alone," Jason said.

Hannah nodded against his shoulder. "Thanks for not leaving me behind."

They sat in peaceful exhaustion for several minutes.

"He's not so arrogant when he's all tied up," Jason remarked.

Hannah grunted but didn't say anything. She was too worn out for words.

Jason raised his voice toward their prisoner. "You don't have to talk right now. But if you tell us who you're working for, we might be able to cut a deal."

"You understand nothing of loyalty or devotion," Eric mumbled into the dirt.

"I certainly know excellent teamwork when I see it." He nudged Hannah's elbow.

"How could you know devotion," Eric continued as if Jason hadn't spoken, "if you've never loved such pure beauty?"

"Well, I've seen some pretty girls here and there." He glanced at Hannah, but quickly looked away.

"Pretty girls? Ha!" Eric's tone had turned arrogant again. "I love a *woman,* not a girl. And her beauty shines brighter than a thousand suns. And her intelligence is beyond your comprehension. She has suspected you from the beginning." His voice became muffled as he shifted his face back into the dirt. "It is my shame that I failed her."

Jason's brow ticked up. He was about to say something else when the sound of footfalls echoed around the bend of the tunnel followed quickly by half a dozen spotlights. Jason's team had finally arrived.

Agents swarmed around Eric, lifting him to his feet. Jason and Hannah stood and watched as the other agents removed his ankle restraint and applied regular cuffs.

"Take some time to think about where this beautiful woman has landed you," Jason said as they dragged Eric past. "But don't take too long."

"I will pay for my disgrace with my silence," Eric said.

"You may end up in prison for a very long time," Jason replied.

"I would rot in jail for a thousand years for the slightest hope that she could be pleased with me again," Eric replied, his chin high.

Jason jerked his head for the agents to take him away.

Hannah stepped up next to her partner and watched the gaggle of arms and flashlights recede down the dark tunnel. "Wow. Love can make a person do crazy things, can't it?"

Jason turned to look at her, and something in his expression shifted. He gave her a sheepish smile. "Yeah, it can."

Chapter Eighteen

"Are you sure I can't rough him up a bit?" Hannah asked. "I have been known to be very persuasive." Hannah knew that was stretching the truth a bit, but Jason didn't need to know that. And given that they were lounging next to each other on the couch in his apartment, far away from the risk of having to follow through on her bluff, she felt safe enough.

Jason chuckled. "We got pretty physical with him down in the tunnels. It didn't seem to loosen his tongue." He rubbed the back of his head where he'd been slammed to the ground at least once during the altercation. "Not that he wouldn't have deserved more for what he did with my bookmark," he added under his breath.

It had only been three days since the fight in the train tunnel, and Jason wasn't the only one who had bruises that hadn't healed yet. Hannah had a few doozies herself.

"Besides," Jason continued, "he's in official custody now. You know we can't do that sort of thing."

Hannah made a big show of grumbling about it. Jason laughed a little louder, and that put Hannah on the defensive. "What? You don't think I could do it?" she asked.

Jason held up his hands. "Oh, I have no doubt you *could* do it." His smile turned lopsided. "But I think we've spent enough time together for me to know that you wouldn't want to."

Hannah huffed and folded her arms, acting annoyed. But inside, she smiled at the idea that he really was getting to know her.

"Anyway, I got some stuff on Eric from my research team," Jason offered.

Hannah sat up. "Yeah?"

He nodded. "We're still not sure about his real name, but we found an Erick Cheung that matches our Eric. Apparently, he's here in the states on a student visa. He was previously enrolled at Georgia State, which is probably how he met his friend Sunny."

Hannah's enthusiasm sagged. This wasn't anything exciting.

"And . . ." Jason leaned forward and waggled his eyebrows, a cheesy grin on his face.

"You saw how much I enjoyed it when Susan dragged out her big reveal?" Hannah asked in a deadpan voice. "I'm not allowed to hurt her because she's my roommate."

Jason laughed. "He's from the same province where Kayla and Brandon adopted Jinhai. Just a few towns over, actually."

Hannah whistled long and low. "That can't be a coincidence."

Jason shook his head dramatically.

"And you're sure I can't—"

Jason held up a hand. "The answer's still no."

She leaned back into the couch cushions. "Fine. He won't talk. We'll just have to pull clues from what he *did* say." She tapped her chin with her finger. "First off, who could have suspected us from the beginning? And second, do any of our tall, beautiful American suspects also fit the description of 'a thousand times brighter than the sun'?"

Jason shrugged. "With as love-sick as Eric obviously is, it could probably be any of the women on our list."

Hannah's brows went up. "Bethany could have known about us from the beginning. Does she fit that description?"

"Sure," Jason said.

Hannah rolled her eyes. "We're not going to get anywhere if you can't be serious."

"I am being serious. I know it's not likely, but Eric could have fallen for an older woman like Bethany. It's not impossible."

Hannah waved away his assertion. "It doesn't really matter; she's already off the list. Unless we think she was willing to risk killing herself to get rid of us."

Jason shook his head.

"Then who else could it be?" Hannah asked. "What about Lexie or Belle? We met them near the beginning, and they're both extremely beautiful." She scrutinized Jason's response. Not that she cared if Jason thought the women were extremely beautiful or not.

He cocked his head to the side, his face scrunched in concentration. "Yeah, I suppose they could fit the description of a beautiful American, though neither of them are as beautiful as . . . uh . . . I mean, neither of them are as *tall* as you." Jason hid the adorably flustered look on his face by grabbing his can of soda from a side table.

Hannah smiled, but decided not to tease him about what he had almost said. "Hmm, but I don't think Lexie and Belle seem like the type."

"You mean they don't seem like international criminal masterminds? The real ones tend to hide it pretty well," Jason said.

Hannah ignored his teasing. "Eric's madly in love with whoever this woman is. There must be some sort of physical—or at least emotional—relationship going on between them. Would either Lexie or Belle do that sort of thing?" She paused, trying to figure out what didn't seem right about it.

Jason nodded for her to continue.

"Wouldn't it be so easy for them to get caught in a relationship like that?"

"Well, Eric's clearly not going to blab about it," Jason quipped.

"Yeah, but think about the risk. Their videos are scrutinized by millions of people. They could be recognized in public at any moment. How could they ever pull off a dalliance like that?"

"That's true." Jason nodded, deep in thought.

"Plus, like you said before, in their videos, they've hardly said anything about the adoption agency, or international adoptions in general. If they're trying to convince people to adopt the kids they're buying, they're really bad at it," Hannah observed.

The partners sat in silence for several moments, each contemplating what they could do to puzzle out the problem.

"I wish there was a way we could figure out if they speak Chinese," Hannah finally said. "That would settle it once and for all."

"We could just ask them," Jason offered.

Hannah scowled. Maybe he failed to appreciate the power of a well-crafted deception. "Wouldn't they just lie about it?"

"Do you remember what Sandra did at our first interview? She asked you in Chinese."

Hannah frowned. "We'd have to learn how to ask 'Do you speak Chinese?' in Chinese."

Jason smiled and turned his head toward the kitchen. "Alexa! How do you say 'Do you speak Chinese?' in Chinese."

A moment later, the smooth automated voice replied, "In Mandarin, 'Do you speak Chinese?' is *'Nǐ huì shuō zhōngwén ma?'*"

Hannah's frown deepened, and she pulled a sour face. "That doesn't sound right."

Jason grinned at her. "What, now you're an expert linguist?"

Hannah shot him a dirty look. "No. But that's definitely not what Sandra asked me that first day."

His grin grew. "Oh, so now you have a photographic memory, too?"

Hannah turned her world-famous glare—the one she learned from Anna, who had learned it from her mother—on her partner. His grin faded, though she could tell he was still amused at her expense.

"Do you still have the audio recording from that first day?" she asked him.

"Sure. I've saved all the audio recordings from our mission," he said.

Hannah's brow ticked up. "All of them? How much of the mission have you been recording?"

A slight pink flush crept up Jason's cheeks. "Uh, pretty much everything." he answered.

"What about our private conversations? Have you saved those?" she asked.

"I, uh, wanted to hold on to them for some personal research." He nervously rubbed the back of his neck.

"What kind of personal research?" she pressed.

Jason looked around, apparently hoping for a way out of his predicament. Hannah folded her arms across her chest, waiting.

Finally, he let out a long breath. "I usually fall pretty hard for girls—and pretty fast, too. Once that happens, I always mess things up. No matter how hard I try, I get so nervous that I end up saying or doing the wrong thing."

Hannah waved a hand impatiently. "You told me that already. What does that have to do with recording our conversations?"

"At first, it just made sense for the mission, but then I figured if I could review everything I said to you, I might be able to catch myself before I messed things up." Jason suddenly made himself busy scrolling through his phone, presumably looking for the recording of Sandra.

"But why would you care about messing things up . . . with me?" Before the question was all the way out of Hannah's mouth, she knew the answer.

Jason had fallen for her.

And if his explanation was to be believed, it must have happened early on in the mission.

Hannah played with the idea of Jason being in love with her from the beginning.

He had acted like such a jerk so many times. Had those been clumsy attempts to get her attention or show that he liked her? Two weeks ago, she would have said no, but now that she had gotten to know her partner, she realized the answer might actually be yes.

And how did she feel about him?

They had certainly grown closer in the last few days, and she was much more comfortable around him. But did she feel more than that?

Was she falling for him, too?

"Here it is," Jason said, placing his phone on the coffee table in front of them.

Hannah dragged her mind back to the present. She'd have to deal with her feelings for Jason later.

The muffled greetings between Jason, Hannah, and Sandra on that first day emanated from the small cellphone speakers. She heard Sandra's question in Chinese again and felt justified at how clearly different it was from the phrase they'd just been told by the home device.

"Wait. Turn up the volume and play it again," Hannah said.

Jason nodded and grabbed the phone.

"Alexa, what does this mean?" Hannah nodded for Jason to start the playback.

The blue light on the smart device twirled. "In English, '*Yòuyì zhi zhīzhū pá shàng nǐ de tuǐ,*' means 'There's a spider on your leg.'"

Hannah's brow furrowed. "Why would she tell me there was a spider on my leg?"

She glanced back at Jason. He shook his head slowly, but it looked like the gears in his brain were working overtime. Hannah stifled a giggle.

After a few moments, his face brightened. "It's terrific," he declared.

"What?"

"It's the perfect way to find out if someone speaks a language, even if they're trying to hide it. Think about it. As agents, we're trained to lie at a moment's notice, especially when we're in character. But there's no way a person—trained or not—could resist looking down at their leg if they knew a spider was crawling on them."

Hannah scowled. "A professional could do it."

"Oh yeah?" He said with a teasing smirk. "What if I told you there was a spider on your arm right now?"

Hannah shook her head in disappointment. He'd have to do a lot better than that.

Jason's eyes went wide in mock surprise. "Yeah! Oh! It's just crawling up on top of your shoulder."

Hannah fought the desire to glance down or to brush at her shoulder. It was almost instinctive.

"Ooh, it's one of those huge, hairy ones." Jason was really getting into it now.

His eyes were lit with an almost gleeful excitement, and he stared, unwavering, at a spot on her shoulder. She wasn't willing to let him win this, though.

"I can't believe you don't feel that," he continued. "The fuzzy legs must be tickling your neck." He drew out his words, slowing them to a painful crawl. "It's so close now . . . almost . . . to your . . . ear. Just a few . . . more . . . steps."

Hannah's hand moved of its own accord to slap at the empty air against her neck. Relief and chagrin washed over her.

Jason laughed. "See. It works. Maybe we should try that on Belle and Lexie."

Hannah had to admit, it was a sneaky technique.

She stiffened. "Wait. Why would Sandra need to secretly find out if we speak Chinese?"

Jason scratched his head. "She said it was to help the adopted children adjust."

Hannah frowned. "But that's not such a huge deal, is it? Would it ruin an adoption if the kid spoke Chinese during the transition period? Or more to the point, would that be a good enough reason to risk freaking out a potential client who might understand Chinese?"

Jason considered then shook his head.

The niggling of a suspicion was beginning to grow in the back of Hannah's mind. "Then why would she go to such an extreme?"

"Only if she needed to make absolutely certain that the parents wouldn't understand anything the child says." Comprehension spread across Jason's face. ". . . to make sure the child couldn't tell his new parents about his old life."

The weight of their discovery hung thick in the air around them.

Sandra was the mastermind.

Pieces of the puzzle started clicking into place.

"Sandra could've made the trips to China," Hannah said. "In fact, when we went to the agency last week, didn't Bethany say she was out of the office arranging the details for the next adoption trip? I wonder if she was actually out of the country."

Jason nodded. "And I'm no linguist, but she certainly sounded pretty fluent."

"Would she fit the description of a tall, beautiful American?" Hannah asked.

He gave her a short, sidelong glance. "I wouldn't really call her tall, but someone in China might. And she's certainly pretty."

Hannah chose to ignore the flash of jealousy she felt. Sandra wasn't *that* pretty.

"We met her at the beginning of the mission," Hannah said. "She must have suspected we weren't really a couple."

"I can't imagine why," Jason said with a deadpan expression.

"She would have known about the barbecue at the Grays. She must have sent Eric to spy on us."

Jason's eyes grew wide with a sudden realization. "And she was the one who asked us to sign those additional release papers. That's when Eric tailed us home."

Hannah nodded. "Plus, she was at the retreat. She could have let Eric onto the grounds to snoop around our suite."

"And that last visit with Bethany was scheduled through Sandra, too." Jason paused in thought. "By that point, I'm sure Eric had told her who we really are. She must have told him to get rid of us."

Hannah frowned. "Would Sandra have risked killing Bethany just to get rid of us?"

"I doubt it, but maybe Eric was freelancing, or Sandra didn't know the details of his plan. Either way, he sure messed up," Jason said with a grin. "We'd never have found him without the connection to his friend's truck."

Hannah blew out a breath as she sat back on the couch. She could hardly believe that Sandra was the criminal behind the illegal adoptions and the attempt on their lives. She had always been so kind and sweet. She turned to Jason. "We need to figure out where Sandra was traveling this week."

"Unfortunately, I don't think we can just call up Bethany and ask. We sort of burned that bridge."

He was certainly right on that count, but Hannah had an idea. "Eric might have made more than one mistake when he tried to gas us to death."

Jason's brow went up. "Oh yeah?"

Hannah nodded. "Maybe he actually did us a favor."

"This is what you call doing us a favor?" Jason hissed as Hannah peeled back the plastic tarp covering the adoption agency's broken front window. It had taken less than an hour to drive across town, but they had waited another half hour to make sure the dark office was empty.

"At least it's not breaking and entering," she replied with a grin. "I'm pretty sure you have to break something for that."

Jason groaned. "That will not stand up in court, and you know it."

Hannah shook her head. "I don't know it. That's what's called plausible deniability."

She held the tarp aside for Jason to slip through before dropping it back in place. Jason stood in the waiting area, looking very uncomfortable.

"C'mon. Let's see if we can access Sandra's travel schedule." Hannah sat down at the reception desk.

"Are you sure we're not going to trigger the alarm system?" Jason asked, glancing around the office.

Hannah shook her head. "That's why we're here right now. The alarm system won't arm if the windows aren't closed." She nodded toward the broken front window. "That sort of qualifies as not closed."

Hannah considered the login screen. How many attempts would she get? She opened the desk drawer and rifled around for sticky notes.

"Hey, make sure you leave everything the way it was." Jason sounded ready to scrub the mission any minute.

She glanced up at him. "How many people do you know who catalog the layout of their miscellaneous drawers?"

Jason mumbled something about "smart people" and looked back toward the tarp flapping in the light evening breeze.

"What are you even looking for?" Jason asked.

"I'm hoping Sandra has her password written around here somewhere."

"You think the mastermind of an illegal secret operation would leave her passwords lying around?"

Hannah frowned. Jason was right. Which meant they were going to have a hard time finding the information they needed.

"But I know where Bethany keeps her passwords." Jason volunteered.

Hannah's brows shot up. She considered him for a moment. "Do I want to know how you know where her passwords are?" she teased.

Jason gave her a deadpan look. "Very funny. Do you want my help or not?"

Hannah switched to Bethany's user name. "Fire away."

"I don't actually have her passwords memorized," he replied with a scowl. "Hang on."

He walked toward the back offices and returned a minute later. He held out his phone, showing a picture of a collection of sticky notes. Hannah nodded in appreciation of his keen eye. She scanned the various login credentials until she found the one she wanted.

She typed in Bethany's password and hit *Enter*. The login screen disappeared, replaced by a wallpaper image of dozens of baby pictures. Hannah ignored the adorableness and went straight to work.

"Not even an 'ah' or a 'how cute'?" Jason said.

"I don't have time to stare at pictures of other people's babies." She focused on navigating to the default email client folder. "Besides, mine will be much cuter."

Jason didn't say anything, but Hannah got the distinct impression that he felt smug about something. With a few clicks, she found the email archive file and opened it. She scrolled down the list of messages.

"Wait. Right there." Jason pointed at a string of messages with Chinese subject lines.

Hannah pulled out her phone and opened the translate app. She aimed the camera at the computer monitor and watched as the app changed the Chinese characters to English phrases in real-time on her screen.

The email was from an adoption agency in Shandong province.

Jason knelt next to her chair and studied the translation over her shoulder. She couldn't help but notice his closeness. Her traitorous body leaned into his chest while her brain tried to stay focused.

"Looks like she was meeting with some of the agencies involved in the next round of adoptions," Jason whispered.

Hannah suppressed a nervous tingle at the sound of his voice near her ear. "Yeah, but it doesn't look like there's anything nefarious there." She scanned the rest of the email translation.

They read through several more emails from various agencies with no luck. Hannah hadn't really assumed Sandra was dumb enough to leave incriminating evidence for anyone to find.

"Nothing that would stand up in court," Jason said as he rose to his feet.

Hannah nodded, but she wasn't willing to give up yet.

"Which is probably for the best, considering how we would have obtained the information." Jason swept his hand around the reception area.

"Hang on, I found something. It's an automated message from an airline website." Hannah scanned the itinerary. "If she kept to this schedule, she flew to Beijing a week ago, and she's flying back"—Hannah looked at the return flight—"tomorrow. Or actually, right now, considering the time difference."

"That means whatever she had planned for this trip is already done," Jason said.

"True." Hannah tapped a finger to her lips as she thought through their options. They were too late to catch Sandra in the act, and if they waited until her next trip, they risked another round of children being torn from their families. Sandra would get back tomorrow, and the send-off banquet was in three days.

Was that enough time to set a trap?

"Do you think the Phelps would give us the name of their investigator in China?" Hannah asked her partner. "I think I might have an idea."

CHAPTER NINETEEN

HANNAH CLOSED HER EYES and patiently waited for Katie to work her makeup magic. She heard footsteps come to the door of the Banana Girls' salon. Given that Susan was already putting the finishing touches on Hannah's hair, it could only be Anna or Mari.

"I remember when you did this on me," Mari said to Katie and Susan.

"I know." Katie said it almost like a squeal. Susan actually did squeal. "I can't believe you've been with us all these months and we haven't had a chance to get you dressed up for another fancy event."

Mari shrugged. "I kinda prefer my regular look anyway."

Katie continued applying blush to Hannah's cheeks. "It's a shame that all of this work is going to waste," she said with a sigh.

"Thanks a lot." Hannah did occasionally enjoy teasing her roommates. Plus, it helped calm her nerves, which were already on edge because of the send-off banquet.

Katie inhaled sharply. "Oh, that's not what I meant. You look gorgeous. But you're going with Agent Briggs, and you hate his guts. That's why I say it's a waste."

Hannah's eyes flew open, and she had to fight the urge to say something in Jason's defense. She wasn't entirely sure how she felt about him or where their relationship might go, but she certainly didn't want to discuss it with her two most excitable roommates.

"It's not going to waste, Katie," Hannah insisted. "It will help me blend in at the send-off gala."

Katie heaved a deep sigh, and Susan echoed it times six.

"I know," Katie said. "I just like to imagine I'm putting on just the right amount of make-up and choosing just the right ensemble—"

Susan cleared her throat.

"—and Susan is doing your hair just right so that you'll catch the guy's eye and he'll have no choice but to fall madly in love with you." Katie said it like it was the ending to a romantic fairy tale.

Hannah rolled her eyes. "Meanwhile, back in the real world, I just need a disguise that will get me into a party where I'm not on the guest list."

"Speaking of that," Mari said from the doorway. "I was able to make a sweep through the reception hall this afternoon—thanks for the hotel attendant outfit, Susan."

Susan smiled, her hands posed daintily under her chin.

"—and I disabled the lock on the hotel's south auxiliary door," Mari said.

"A time delay on the electronic actuator?" Hannah asked.

"Duct tape," Mari answered with a grin.

Hannah nodded. "That works, too."

"Here's your gear for tonight." Mari extended a shimmery green clutch. "It's all the standard stuff."

"Does it have my grappling hook brush?"

Mari nodded.

"What about my nail file lock picker?"

"It should have everything you'll need," Mari said, an impish smile tugging up the corners of her lips. "We even included some truth serum, in case your partnership could benefit from a little honesty."

Hannah felt her neck heat, but she refused to break eye contact with Mari. The girl had certainly gotten cheeky lately. Hannah almost regretted being nice to her. She never would have acted this way when she was intimidated.

"Anna and I have to go get in position." Mari waved and walked out.

Katie turned to Susan, a puzzled look on her face. "We have truth serum now? I might need to get some of that."

Susan shrugged theatrically.

"We don't have truth serum, Katie. I'm pretty sure Mari was just joking," Hannah said.

"Hmm. Well, it wasn't a very good joke." Katie went back to applying Hannah's makeup. "It didn't even make sense."

Despite her efforts to keep her friends in the dark about Jason, Mari and Anna were well on their way to figuring it out. Hannah had no doubt that's what the truth serum jab was meant to convey.

"Of course, if we *did* have some truth serum, using it on Jason wouldn't be a bad idea," Katie said. "Maybe you could find out why he's such a jerk."

"And, while you're at it, maybe he knows why the hottest guys always seem to be so shallow," Susan added enthusiastically.

Katie grinned. "And why they always act so tough and dumb."

"Yeah." Susan came out from behind the salon chair and strutted around with her arms wide and her chin jutted out. "They're always like 'I'm so manly. Look at all of my manliness in the manly things I can do.'"

Katie joined in with her friend, though her attempt to imitate a low, masculine voice ended up rather squeaky. "'And I'm so tough on the inside, too. I never need to share my feelings or talk about emotions.'"

Katie and Susan laughed, and Hannah couldn't help but smile at their silliness. Their laughter ebbed as they both went back to work.

"You know. It's actually okay that Jason's a jerk," Katie announced. "Because it never would have worked between you."

Hannah stiffened at the insinuation that she couldn't have made a relationship work, even though that's probably not what Katie meant.

Katie continued, "I mean, can you imagine two agents trying to date? Much less get married and have a life together. It would be a disaster. You'd never be able to talk to each other about your assignments."

"Unless they did missions together," Susan piped in. "You know, like Mr. and Mrs. Smith."

"Oh, I love that movie," Katie gushed.

"Me, too." Susan bounced up and down.

Hannah let out an exasperated breath. "You do know that the two agents in that movie were hired to kill each other, right?"

Katie and Susan looked at Hannah, expressions crestfallen. Katie shrugged. "Well, I guess it applies all the more to you and Jason since you've pretty much wanted to kill each other from the start."

Susan giggled.

Hannah was ready to be done with this. "Are you two almost finished?" she asked.

"There." Katie stepped back. "If you're not careful, someone might fall head-over-heels for you tonight."

"Too late," Hannah muttered.

Katie's brow furrowed, but before she could say anything, the bell for the front door chimed.

"Thanks, ladies." Hannah was up out of her chair before they had a chance to beat her to the door.

She swept down the hall and through the living room, feeling for all the world like a princess ready for a ball—a modern ball anyway.

The door swung open to reveal Jason in a finely tailored black suit, his dark blond hair slicked back. The tension in his jaw made those chiseled features stand out even more. And if that wasn't enough to make her go weak in the knees, his gray-blue eyes quickly took in her long, green, form-fitting gown.

"Wow," he said, almost breathless. "You look amazing."

Hannah tucked a stray blond strand behind her ear, doing her best not to blush. "Thanks," she said.

Jason brought his arm out from behind his back.

In his hand he held a single, red rose.

If Hannah wasn't careful, she was going to break Rule Number One right there in the middle of the hall. She smiled and closed the door behind her, glancing over her shoulder to make sure Katie and Susan hadn't been watching.

She held the rose to her nose and inhaled the intoxicating scent. Looking up at him through her lashes, she smiled again. "Thank you."

Jason held out his arm, and they walked together down the hall. "Despite the fact that we're going to be sneaking our way into a gala banquet and possibly fighting our way back out, I thought you might want to enjoy a little elegance at the beginning."

As they faced the elevator door, Hannah turned to look at him. "All these times, you came up the elevator. I could have just met you in the lobby."

He gave her a warm smile. "A gentleman meets the lady at her door if at all possible." He pushed the elevator call button.

"Even when it makes the gentleman miserable?"

He nodded stiffly. "Even then."

Hannah looked over at her partner. He suddenly seemed like every woman's dream man—strong, thoughtful, handsome, kind, good with children. She could hardly believe she hadn't seen it before.

The elevator doors opened and Jason took a deep breath, no doubt preparing himself for the next sixty seconds of torture.

Hannah slid her hand down his arm. "We tried a distraction last time. Shall we try one again?" She intertwined her fingers in his.

He nodded as they stepped onto the elevator. Hannah pushed the lobby button and turned immediately toward Jason. Very slowly and deliberately, she took one of his hands and slid it around her waist. Switching her purse and rose to her free hand, she took his other hand and repeated the process. With calculated motions, she inched her way up his arms and draped her arms over his shoulders. In a low, husky whisper, she asked, "How's that for a distraction?"

Jason's mouth spread in a lopsided grin as his eyes went to her lips. "I've never enjoyed an elevator ride quite this much."

His hands tightened against her back, pulling her ever closer. He tilted his face down toward hers.

Hannah's eyes fluttered closed as she felt the warmth of his approaching skin.

The elevator dinged its arrival at the lobby.

Hannah opened her eyes and saw the expression of longing and regret on her partner's face.

"I suppose that's our cue to get to work," Jason said.

Hannah nodded.

It was the first time she had ever wished that the condo tower had a slower elevator.

From the first level of the parking garage behind the hotel, Hannah watched the south auxiliary entrance door—the one Mari had rigged with duct tape. "We're in position, Anna," she said. "Just let me know when we can go."

The sound of Anna coughing or clearing her throat came over the comm. Hannah waited for some additional response, but all she heard was background conversation.

"Anna's up in the A/V booth," Mari whispered. "She must not be able to talk."

"Mari, can you see if the back hallway's clear for us to sneak in?" Hannah asked.

"Hang on, I'll go check." There was a long pause. "The main hallway has one security guard," she whispered. "And I don't see anyone in the back hallway, but it's hard to know—"

Another voice—someone near Mari—carried through the comm. "Excuse me. All catering attendants are supposed to be in the preparation area."

"Sorry," Mari said, clearly not to the team. "I must have gotten turned around coming back from the bathroom."

That was quick thinking on Mari's part to say she had gotten lost. After several seconds, Hannah dared to inquire. "Are you still good, Mari?"

"Mm-hmm," she replied.

Hannah turned to Jason. "That might be as good as we'll get. What do you think?"

Her partner nodded, determination in his expression. "Let's get in there, the guests are already arriving."

Together, they exited Jason's small car. They were probably the only guests not arriving via the hotel's valet parking. Hannah shrugged to herself. In some cases, it didn't matter how the princess got to the ball. She just needed to get there.

The alley between the parking garage and the back of the hotel was empty. And thanks to Mari's skillful use of duct tape, the auxiliary door was unlocked. They easily slipped through the door, and Hannah pulled off the tape before letting it close softly. No need to leave any evidence of their entry.

She looked at Jason, handsome as ever in his suit. "Now all we have to do is join the rest of the party," she said.

He smiled and offered her his arm. Hannah felt like a debutante ready for her big entrance. She slipped her hand into the crook of his elbow, and they started walking down the empty hallway toward the main part of the hotel.

"Are you two in the back hall?" Anna asked over the comm. Her voice sounded uncharacteristically nervous.

"Just barely," Hannah said as she strode confidently down the hall.

"Security coming. Hide!" Anna sounded frantic now.

Hannah looked around for somewhere to hide. There was a small alcove with a door labeled *Linens*. Jason grabbed the handle, but the door was locked.

"Do you think we have time to pick the lock?" Hannah asked drily as she looked over his shoulder.

"Hey! Stop right there." A voice boomed from the end of the hall. "What are you doing?"

Hannah turned to see a very beefy security guard, his extremely tanned arms bulging against the sleeves of this uniform. Jason flattened himself against the door. Fortunately, it appeared the guard's attention was entirely on Hannah, so hopefully Jason had stayed out of sight.

Hannah made a quick motion with her hand, hoping to convey to her partner that he should stay put. Maybe she could lure the guard close enough for Jason to incapacitate him. They needed it to be a clean grab, though, or they risked alerting other security personnel.

The bulky guard stopped about ten feet away. "Ma'am, if you'll come with me, I need to escort you to the check-in."

That was exactly what Hannah needed to not do. She attempted to channel her inner flirt. Actually, she wasn't sure she had one of those, so she imagined what Katie might do to get the guy to not drag her to the check-in desk and discover she was actually a secret undercover agent who had been strictly forbidden from attending and was thus forced to crash the party.

She waved her hands down dismissively and added a playful lilt to her voice. "Oh, aren't you just so sweet, but there's no need for that. I already checked in."

The guard took another step toward her. "I'll need to double-check, if you don't mind. I'm just doing my job."

The guard was still a good five feet short of Jason's hiding spot. "Oh, yes. I understand what an important job you must have, with those huge rippling muscles defending this hallway from dangers like me." Hannah giggled playfully at the end. Did Katie use sarcasm to underhandedly insult the guys she was flirting with? Hannah made a mental note to suggest a flirtation training class. Of course, she might be the only one who needed it.

"Why don't you just come with me?" The guard sounded like he was genuinely wondering why she hadn't come toward him yet. Maybe she could work with that.

"Well, at first you told me to stop, so I stopped." She tilted her head and smiled innocently at him.

The guard scanned the hallway, suddenly nervous. The muscles in his shoulders tensed, and his hand moved to the holster at his hip. In an attempt to act scared at his sudden change, Hannah let her eyes go wide. Unfortunately, Jason must have mistaken her reaction for real fear, because he sprang from the alcove. The guard wasn't close enough for a sneak attack, but it was still a surprise.

Jason's kick caught the guard in the gut. The large man stumbled backward, too off balance to pull his weapon. Hannah ran forward and grabbed his arm. He tried to fling her aside, most likely underestimating her because of her size. She clung to his forearm and elbowed him hard in the ribs. Jason swung for his head, but the guard dodged awkwardly.

Noisily fighting a guard in a side access hall was not the best way to make a discreet entrance. They needed this guy out now.

Hannah climbed onto his back and wrapped her arm around his neck. He jerked backward in an attempted head butt, but Hannah tucked her head low, her other hand pulling hard against the sleeper hold.

The guard flailed his arms over his shoulders, trying to dislodge her. Jason punched him hard in the stomach, and Hannah welcomed the distraction. Finally, the guard stopped swinging and teetered backward.

"Stop hitting him," Hannah yelled at Jason. "I don't want to be crushed." The guard wasn't pro-wrestler-massive, but he probably weighed twice as much as she did.

Fortunately, the guard's oxygen-deprived brain overcorrected his balance. He tipped forward and crumpled to the floor. Jason helped

Hannah back to her feet, and she checked to make sure her gown was all still in place.

"I know you probably could have taken care of that, but I thought I'd help out," Hannah said.

"No, I'm glad you did. That was perfect." He smiled and touched her arm.

His gaze locked with hers.

Hannah's middle did a little flip.

She took a half step forward, wishing she could pull his strong and quite capable arms around her again.

As Jason moved toward her, he bumped against the unconscious guard. They both looked down.

"I guess we can't leave him here, can we?" Jason said.

Hannah shook her head, both in answer to his question and in an attempt to clear her frazzled mind. "Let's put him in with the linens."

Jason dragged him over as Hannah used the nail file lock-picking tool on the door. Half a minute later, they had the guard slumped against a soft pile of tablecloths. Jason zip-tied his wrists and ankles while Hannah gagged his mouth with an elegant cloth napkin.

With the door securely locked again, the pair crept to the end of the hallway and assumed a more casual demeanor as they entered the main part of the hotel.

"Looks like a clear shot all the way to the hotel lobby," Jason said.

"Mari, are they checking invitations at the entrance to the hotel or the ballroom itself?" Hannah asked.

"Hmm," was all they heard from Mari. The sound was distinctly non-committal.

"I guess you have to ask yes or no questions," Jason said.

"Okay. Are they checking—"

"Don't bother," Anna piped in. "I saw a pair of attendants at the ballroom doors. You'll need to find another way in. But luckily for you, there's still plenty of dancing happening thanks to the tunes being spun by yours truly." There was a laugh in Anna's voice, and Hannah could picture the self-satisfied smile on her face.

"Let's use the back-of-house access," Jason said out of the side of his mouth.

Despite both their minds being preoccupied with the mission, Jason took Hannah's hand through his arm. She had never really stopped to think about how considerate he was most of the time. Sure, he had his moments of cluelessness, like any guy, and he definitely put his foot in his mouth occasionally. But deep down, he really was a sweetheart.

Hannah did her best to drag her focus back to the mission. They ducked down a narrow side hall before reaching the main atrium. They slowed as they approached a pair of facing double doors. "I think we're between the kitchen and the ballroom," Hannah said quietly into the comm. It didn't hurt to keep her teammates apprised of the situation.

Hannah stepped up to the double doors going into the ballroom and peeked through the gap between them. "I can't see anyone standing in the way." She turned back to her partner. "Should we go for it?"

Suddenly, a voice behind them yelled, "Coming through!"

Hannah's eyes darted to the kitchen doors. She lunged for Jason, pushing him flat against the wall just as the access doors banged open. She had the presence of mind to grab the handle to keep one of the doors from swinging closed again.

An entourage of plate-wielding servers moved across the narrow hall toward the ballroom as Hannah wedged Jason and herself between the wall and the kitchen door. Attendants continued through the door unabated, and Hannah watched Jason's anxiety rise as they held perfectly still, trapped in their hiding place.

Hannah used her other hand, which had fortunately landed on Jason's chest, to soothe her restless partner. "Hang in there," she whispered. "Focus on me."

She could feel his heartbeat through the expensive fabric of his shirt as she stared into those gray-blue eyes she had grown so accustomed to. They stood hidden behind the door, gazing at each other. Several carts loaded with food trundled past on their way into the ballroom, but Hannah barely noticed. She was lost in the electric feeling of Jason's nearness.

He leaned into her, and a thrill shot through her body. He glanced down at her mouth and smiled. Hannah slowly rose onto her tiptoes, bringing their lips closer and closer.

A whisper came through the gap above the door's hinge. "Are you two okay?" Mari asked as she peeked into their small hiding place. "I'm the last one, if you wanted to . . ." Mari's voice trailed off, presumably because she saw that they were fine. Her face disappeared from view. "Anyway, you're probably clear to sneak in after me." Mari said, a laugh in her voice now.

Hannah finally released the kitchen door and when it swung shut, the partners shifted apart ever so slightly.

"Thanks for the distraction," Jason said with a knowing smile. "I might have to take you with me on all my missions." A look of chagrin stole across his face as soon as the words were out of his mouth. He rubbed the back of his neck and glanced at the ballroom doors, still swinging slightly. "Shall we?" he asked, holding out a hand to her.

Hannah smiled as she took his hand. Together, they slipped through the side doors into the dimly lit ballroom. Jason led her toward a cluster of dancers and pulled her into a dancing position, if it could be called that. His hand awkwardly held the side of her back, putting far more space between them than necessary. If they were going to blend in, this wouldn't do at all.

A small smirk crept across Hannah's lips. "Why don't we try this again." With her free hand, she grabbed his arm and pushed his hand to the small of her back. The simple movement forced them much closer, and he didn't appear to mind.

"We're in position, more or less," she whispered into the comm. She looked up into Jason's face. "Wouldn't you say this is about the right position?" She nodded toward his arm around her back, unable to resist the urge to tease him with the double meaning.

"Definitely," he whispered as he pulled her a little closer. Then he cleared his throat and spoke more seriously over the comm. "Yes. I'd say we're in just about the right position. Anna, let us know when you're ready for the next phase."

"Uh-huh," she said quietly.

"So, I guess we don't have much to do but wait," Hannah said to Jason as her arm crept farther up his shoulder.

There wasn't any fancy spinning or twirling around the dance floor, but Hannah enjoyed the feel of her hand in his, the firmness of the muscles in his shoulder, and the touch of his hand on her back.

Jason's expression of utter bliss slowly faded as his mouth stretched in a serious line. He cleared his throat. "Hannah?"

She gazed at his handsome face. "Mm-hmm?"

"You remember when I told you that I always seem to mess things up with the girls I fall for?"

"Yeah," she said.

"And you told me you'd be happy to give me pointers if I needed help knowing what to say or do to not mess things up?"

"I think I remember that," she replied with a flirtatious smile. Hannah was fairly certain she knew where this was going, but she couldn't help playing coy.

"So, there is actually this one girl that I've been spending some time with. But I'm a little worried that I'll mess it up."

"Oh yeah?" Hannah squeezed his shoulder.

"Well, at the beginning we didn't really hit it off that well," he said.

"Not love at first sight?" she asked playfully.

"Oh, it totally was on my part. She's absolutely gorgeous."

Warmth spread through Hannah's core.

"But I must have said the wrong thing," Jason continued, "because she made it pretty clear that she wasn't interested."

Hannah smiled at the reminder of the way she had acted when she first met Jason. He had been annoying and conceited and full of himself. She couldn't believe how close she'd come to missing her chance with this amazing guy. "Sounds like you're out of luck, I guess," she teased, giving him a quick wink.

He laughed nervously. "Yeah. That's what I would have thought, too."

"Did something change?" she asked.

"Well, circumstances keep bringing us together—"

"Like fate," she interjected with wide eyes.

"It could have been fate." His chuckle was more comfortable now. She was pretty sure he could read her playful banter. They'd certainly spent enough time together.

Several seconds of silence passed as they gazed into each other's eyes.

Finally, Jason picked up the earlier thread, "And I think now maybe she and I have sort of become friends."

Hannah nodded, all the while holding his gaze. "But you're hoping for more?" she asked softly. She knew what she hoped the answer was.

Jason laughed. "Honestly, I'm just happy she doesn't hate me anymore."

Hannah grinned back at him.

Then his face became serious. "But if there's any chance it could be more, I definitely can't mess it up. She just might be the best thing that's ever happened to me."

Hannah's breath hitched. She'd had plenty of guys who were interested in her, even a few boyfriends here and there. But no one had ever said something like that about her. The rest of the ballroom faded away. All she could see was Jason's hopeful eyes staring back at her.

A small click sounded in her ear. "Who's he talking about?" Katie must have switched over to a direct comm link with Hannah. "You have to find out what girl he's falling for. I'm dying to know."

Katie's interruption brought Hannah back to what they were meant to be doing there at the banquet in the first place. She blinked and glanced around the ballroom, trying to refocus.

When she turned her attention back to Jason, it was obvious he was expecting a response from her. Maybe something to give him some hope.

"Do you remember when I told you to just be yourself and everything would work out fine?" Hannah asked.

"Yeah?" he said.

Leaning forward on her tiptoes, she whispered quietly in his ear. "Trust me. It's working." She let her lips linger against his neck for an extra second.

Jason drew her closer, and Hannah was quite content to ignore anything and everything.

Until a fleeting motion up on the stage caught her eye.

She pulled back and stared across the ballroom. Anna was standing next to the stage's main curtain, holding a thick bundle of black wiring while a tech attendant knelt down and adjusted the connection on one of the large speakers. When she caught Anna's attention, Hannah lifted her shoulders and scowled. "What are you doing?" she said into the comm.

"Well, I'm sort of spilling my heart to you," Jason replied.

Hannah smiled. "Not you." She lifted her chin in the direction of the stage, and Jason spun them halfway around to see what was happening.

Anna shrugged back and nodded to the tech guy next to her.

"That must be her boss," Hannah said.

Anna nodded and held her hands out helplessly.

"Has the call come in yet?" Hannah asked.

Anna shook her head.

Hannah turned back to Jason. "Should we go up to the tech booth to hook up the call when it comes in?"

"Will you still be able to get back down here to the podium?" Jason asked.

Hannah grinned. "No problem."

Jason grabbed her hand and pulled her away from the dance floor. They moved toward the wall where the audio-visual control booth overlooked the ballroom from the second floor. Hannah steered them to what looked like a small closet. "Anna, is this the door up to the tech booth?"

"Mm-hmm," Anna hummed her affirmative.

They reached the door, and Hannah glanced over her shoulder to make sure no one noticed them. Most of the guests were either dancing, eating, or watching a slideshow of happy families on the big screen behind the podium. Jason pulled the door open just enough for them to squeeze through.

Mari must have found a safe place to talk because she started whispering instructions over the comm. "Those stairs come out on the mezzanine level right next to the control room," she said. "The tech room door is just around the corner to the left. Right, Anna?"

"Right," Anna half-whispered, half-coughed.

Jason looked over his shoulder as they climbed the narrow stairs. He winked at Hannah as if sharing an inside joke. "So, it's on the right?" Jason asked.

"No, I said on the left," Mari said.

"But Anna said right," Jason said, sounding genuinely confused, though his face held a broad grin.

"She said right, because she meant I was right." Mari's frustration carried easily through the comm.

"Wait. You're right, or the door is right?" Jason looked like he was about to burst with laughter.

Hannah couldn't help but smile at his antics, though she certainly didn't want to encourage him. She heard a muffled giggle that must have been Anna.

Mari let out a long sigh and took a breath.

Hannah felt obligated to intervene and save her friend. "Mari, don't bother. He's just teasing you; it's sort of his thing."

Jason stopped at the top of the stairs. "Aw, Hannah. Why'd you have to go and ruin it? We were having so much fun." Tears were starting to leak from the corners of his eyes, and the suppressed laughter was evident in his voice.

Mari muttered, "You can find your own way next time."

Jason glanced back at Hannah, sharing a broad smile with her as he stepped out of the stairwell onto the mezzanine. She simply shook her head at his silliness.

"Excuse me, sir," a deep, stern voice said.

Jason's head whipped around. Hannah froze. She ducked to the side, hiding herself behind the doorway. She could tell by the look on her partner's face that it wasn't good news. He took several more steps away from the stairs as he clumsily turned around.

"Hi, there," Jason said with a jovial wave. His face looked casual and innocent, but his body was tense, coiled and ready to spring.

Hannah could hear the guard's steps just on the other side of the open stairway door, but she couldn't see him, and hopefully he couldn't see her. She was amazed the guy couldn't hear her heart pounding.

If Jason could only get the guard to step a little closer to him, Hannah might have a chance to jump him. She really felt for Jason at the moment. It was an exact role reversal.

"You're not supposed to be up here, sir. Guests need to stay in the ballroom." The guard inched far enough forward that Hannah could just see his nose.

Jason smiled at him again, almost overly happy. Hannah could tell he wanted the security guard to think he was drunk.

The guard gestured at Jason with a meaty arm. "You need to go back down stairs, sir." Jason ignored him and started a wobbly turn away from him. The guard let out a resigned sigh and stepped forward.

That was all Hannah needed.

She sprang from the doorway and hooked the guard's ankle, sending him stumbling forward in a heap of tangled limbs. Hannah was immediately on top, pulling his arms behind his back and cranking his head forward into the carpet.

The guard grunted and tried to roll Hannah off his back. Jason was on his legs a second later as he pulled zip-cuffs from inside his jacket pocket and handed one to Hannah. Like a team of calf ropers, they had the guard tied in under seven seconds.

"What do we do with him?" Jason asked, looking around their small corner of the mezzanine. "We can't really leave him here. Someone's bound to find him."

"We'll have to take him into the tech room," Hannah suggested.

Jason nodded, and they each grabbed an end of the struggling guard. They burst through the control room door, surprising the one remaining tech worker.

"What's going on here?" he said, standing quickly.

"If you cooperate with us, you won't end up like this," Hannah nodded at the guard she and Jason lugged into the room and dropped on the floor.

The techie nodded, holding his hands up.

Jason locked the door and leaned against it. "Probably better work fast," he said.

The frightened techie suddenly ran toward the door. "Let me out of here!"

Hannah lowered a shoulder into him, knocking him onto the floor next to the bound guard. She stepped over to Jason, reached into his jacket pocket, and grabbed another pair of zip-cuffs. The techie was still rubbing his butt by the time she had his ankles bound. She grabbed his free wrist. "Are you going to cooperate, or do I have to cuff you behind your back?"

The techie's eyes went wide, and he held out both hands, wrists together. Hannah zipped the cuffs tight and stood back up.

"Don't be too hard on him," Jason said with a wry grin. "I know how he feels being trapped in here."

A loud bang shook the door, and Jason's body shuddered with the sudden jolt.

"What was that?" Hannah asked.

"Probably the other guard," Jason answered casually as another impact shook the door.

Hannah eyed him suspiciously. "What other guard?"

"The one who saw us coming in here. Why do you think I'm leaning against the door?" Jason answered calmly.

Hannah rolled her eyes. "I still need to get out and commandeer the podium when Bethany starts her presentation. How am I going to do that if we're both stuck in here?"

Jason grimaced. "Thanks for the reminder."

Hannah scanned the small room but quickly discovered there weren't any other exit doors.

"I'm sure we'll figure something out," Jason said. "And technically, you only need to commandeer the podium before Bethany *finishes* her presentation and people start leaving."

"That's extremely helpful," Hannah said drily. She turned her attention to the large windows that opened out onto the ballroom. She looked down toward the stage where Anna had been helping the other tech attendant. "Anna, can you get up here and help us out?"

"Nope," Anna muttered under her breath.

"Mari, are you free to help without spoiling your cover?" Hannah asked as she gazed down at the servers flitting back and forth across the ballroom floor.

"Mm-mm." The fact that Mari had to hum her response meant the answer was no.

"Is it time to bring in the cavalry?" Susan asked over the comm.

Hannah considered their situation. If they called in backup now, the mission would be a bust. Their plan to ensnare Sandra with the video calls they'd orchestrated would fail, and she would go free.

Unacceptable.

"No," Hannah replied curtly. "We're going to make this work somehow."

She scanned the ballroom below. Anna was probably backstage somewhere, which could come in handy later if things went south. Mari would be in a great position to video Sandra during the confrontation. Jason was in the tech booth, ready to go. She glanced back at Jason, his shoulder still against the door.

Well, sort of ready to go.

Bethany's voice suddenly filled the ballroom. "Welcome, everyone, to our send-off banquet. This is a momentous time for each of your families."

They were out of time.

Hannah stepped toward Jason. She realized that the banging had stopped. "Is the guard still there?" she asked.

"Probably, but a few seconds ago I heard someone yell to get the key."

"That doesn't give us much time." Hannah was frantically trying to figure out a way to salvage the situation.

Suddenly, Jason grabbed his phone and checked the incoming call. He nodded to Hannah. "It's time."

This was the call from the investigator in China.

The one that would indict Sandra.

And Hannah was the only one not in position.

Hannah couldn't get out the door without the guard grabbing her. Maybe Jason could distract the guard, but then he wouldn't be in the control room to broadcast the call to the ballroom video system.

Either way they were stuck. The plan couldn't proceed unless she could get down to the podium. She looked out the window at the stage. It was so close, but very much unreachable from the second floor.

Unless . . .

Hannah scampered onto the audio control deck despite the whimpered protest of the bound techie. She grabbed the latch on the center window and slid it to the side. Bethany's speech about the upcoming trip to China filled the small booth.

Hanging from the ceiling right above the control room window was a narrow catwalk that led down the middle of the room to the stage lights behind the curtain. Could Hannah really crawl across the ceiling of the ballroom—in a gown—and reach the stage in time?

What other options did she have?

She turned back to Jason. "Can you stall the investigator until I'm in position?"

He gaped at her, leaning forward so he could see the catwalk. "Are you serious?"

"Do I have any other choice? They'll be here with the key any minute. I have to get to the stage before the speech is over so you can broadcast the call from China. The plan depends on that."

Jason shook his head. In the end, he sighed and nodded. "Please be careful."

As if his words weren't enough, the look of longing and concern in his eyes could have convinced her not to go. But she knew that the safety of dozens of children like Jinhai hung in the balance.

Just like she was about to be hanging in the balance—quite literally.

"Don't start broadcasting until I'm in position," Hannah said. She shimmied through the window and grabbed the end of the catwalk, careful not to cross in front of the video projector. She considered going back for the mini grappling hook in her purse, but there just wasn't time.

She heard Jason answer his phone and ask the Phelps' investigator to hang on.

With a hard shove against the wall, Hannah heaved herself onto the narrow gantry. She hiked her gown up to her knees and began crawling across the metal grating. After a few seconds, she settled into a rhythm of short, easy movements that minimized the amount she had to stretch her dress while also avoiding pain in her knees.

"Jason, have the security guards come back with the keys yet?" Hannah whispered.

"Not yet. But I can't imagine it will be much longer," he replied.

"You might have a few extra minutes," Mari said quietly, a smile in her voice.

"What happened?" Hannah asked.

"I asked the front desk attendant for the hotel's health code inspection certificate. Then while she was in the back room, I intercepted the guard looking for the keys and sent him on a wild goose chase for the janitor."

"Mari, there is way more to you than meets the eye," Hannah said.

"I learned from the best," she replied.

"Yeah, I taught her everything she knows," Katie announced over the comm.

When Hannah reached the midpoint of the catwalk, she was forced to crawl over several bundles of cables coming in from the spotlight supports. Shortly after clearing that obstacle, she felt something tugging her backward. She glanced down and saw the lower edge of her gown pinched in the tangle of wiring. She tried to dislodge the cabling with the tip of her shoe, but it wouldn't budge. She pulled on the material of her dress. It stretched a little, but didn't slip free.

Jason must have heard her quiet grunting over the comm. "Hannah, are you alright? Mari or Anna could probably get to the stage faster. I'm sure you could coach them through what to say."

"Hang on. I haven't lost this one yet," she gritted through her teeth.

While pulling firmly on her dress, she pushed against the cable with her foot. A gap opened up and her dress abruptly slipped free.

Suddenly untangled, she tumbled forward against the catwalk grating. The impact reverberated through the ballroom and caused the spotlights on the gantry to sway violently. Bethany's voice faltered in her presentation, and an eerie silence settled over the crowd as dozens of faces stared up at the catwalk above them.

All Hannah could do was flatten herself against the metal paneling and hope that her emerald-green dress looked mostly black in the shadows above the guests' heads. After a few seconds, Bethany's well-practiced monologue continued, and everyone's attention returned to her.

Hannah let out a quiet sigh.

That was close.

She continued crawling forward, cautious to not snag her dress on anything else. She hadn't really been paying attention to Bethany's speech, but it sounded like she was winding down. Hannah increased her pace.

"Uh-oh," Mari said.

"What's up?" Jason asked.

"The guard is coming back to the front desk, and there's not much I can do to stop him," Mari said. "Besides, I need to find Sandra for the next part of the plan. I think you're on your own up there, Jason."

"That means you only have another minute or two before security gets through your door, Jason," Anna said.

"Shouldn't be a problem," Jason said confidently. "I built a barricade."

Hannah glanced over her shoulder toward the tech room windows. Jason stood surveying a collection of equipment and chairs piled in front of the door. He looked quite proud of his handiwork. Hannah shook her head. "It's okay, I'm almost there," Hannah said. "Get ready to broadcast the call."

"Plugged and ready," Jason replied.

"What about the auto-caption for the translation?" Hannah added.

"All set up. Just say go," he said.

Hannah had always felt like a team with Anna and the other Banana Girls, but she was surprised to find that she felt nearly the same way about Jason.

She reached the ladder that dropped down behind the stage curtain and descended quickly. When she finally touched solid ground again, she startled at a voice behind her.

"Nice job," Anna whispered.

Hannah whirled around to see her friend standing in the shadows. "I thought you were trying to keep the other tech guy busy."

"Oh, I'm sure he's busy," Anna quipped. "Busy regaining consciousness." She tilted her head toward the podium, brows raised in anticipation.

Hannah smiled. "You're the best," she whispered.

"Happy to help," her tall friend replied.

"Mari, did you find Sandra?" Hannah asked.

"Mm-hmm."

"And did Jason link you into the conference call? We need the families in China to see her."

Jason jumped in. "Roger that. She's connected."

"Then it's showtime." Hannah pushed through the curtain into the bright stage lights. It took her eyes a second to adjust to the sudden brightness.

Bethany spun around and stared. "What are you—"

Hannah stepped up next to her at the podium. "Thank you, Bethany. There's been a slight alteration to the agenda."

Anna appeared and pulled Bethany off-stage.

Hannah squinted as she looked out into the audience. Sandra sat at a table near the front, staring in confusion as Bethany was led away. Mari sat nearby, cellphone at the ready.

Hannah smiled at the crowd. "No production would be complete without the individuals who work tirelessly in the background, and this adoption trip is no exception. We'd like to recognize Sandra Till for all the work she's done." Hannah motioned an arm toward Sandra and started a slow clap.

A smattering of awkward applause echoed through the mostly silent ballroom. Mari moved closer and pointed her phone at Sandra, who frowned at the sudden attention.

"Go ahead," Hannah said, waving up at the control box.

The image of Bethany's slideshow was immediately replaced by a video conference call. It showed a man in a light blue dress shirt standing in a rural village somewhere. He nodded. "I talk to the first family now," he explained to the camera in accented English before flipping the phone around as he approached a small hut.

"This call is coming live from the town of Da Zhang in eastern China," Hannah announced to the audience.

A man in his mid-forties answered the door. He might have been younger, but his face showed the wear of a long, hard life. His clothes were ragged and old. The investigator said something in Chinese that the video conference software automatically translated into subtitles on the screen. "I need to ask you about the adoption," the investigator said. "The broker is concerned that you will not go through with it."

The man's face went slack. "That is not true," he said. His fearful expression shifted to resolve. "I will not speak to you about this."

"Why not?" the investigator asked. "Is there some problem with the child?"

The man shook his head firmly. "She told us to never speak with anyone else about the arrangement."

"And have you disobeyed those instructions?" the investigator pressed. "She will want to know."

The ragged man's image grew as the investigator held the phone toward him. He stared at the phone's screen, clearly surprised to see Sandra's face staring back. When he spoke again, the software continued its translation. "Please, madam, without your promised help, our family will be in ruins. Please honor our arrangement."

Sandra stood abruptly. "What is going on here?" She moved away from the table toward Hannah at the stage. Anna approached from the side, cutting off Sandra's path in that direction. Mari followed, keeping the phone camera trained on her. Sandra turned back to face the crowded ballroom. "I don't know what they're talking about. I've never seen this man in my life."

The Phelps' investigator adeptly translated Sandra's outburst for the man at the door.

The man took a half step forward and inclined his head slightly. "Madam," he spoke softly, "we have never divulged to anyone that the child will be sent to you. We will bear our own shame, but if you do not pay us for the child, she will starve with the rest of us."

A gasp rose from the ballroom audience. Hannah glanced up at Jason in the tech booth and nodded. A few seconds later, another device was connected to the call, and the first investigator's connection was muted. The new scene looked much like the first—a rural Chinese village, rows of tiny dilapidated homes.

The new investigator made a similar delivery to a tattered-looking husband and wife at the door of their home. But this time, the reaction was very different.

The husband swept his hand through the air. "The money can never replace the bond with our child." He stared at the camera, clearly recognizing Sandra. "Do you hear me, American lady? You cannot buy our baby," the subtitles translated. Then the father switched to English. "My baby." He slapped his chest forcefully. "Mine."

Tense silence settled around the ballroom. Dozens of rich, prospective parents whispered to each other and cast furtive glances at Sandra. Despite her projected air of calm, Hannah could tell Sandra was nervous. She shifted like someone preparing to run. Hannah jumped down from the stage on the other side from Anna. Together, they had Sandra boxed in.

Jason must have known to move to the next call, because a third connection from China popped up on the screen.

A man in a smart, gray business suit stood framed in the picture.

"Is the call coming through?" an offscreen voice asked in Chinese.

"Yes, yes, I can see her," the business man replied. Then he switched to very well-spoken English. "Miss Till, it is good to speak to you, although I am surprised at your call."

Sandra vigorously shook her head. "No."

The business man continued. "Your associate insisted that the call was necessary to give you an update about our latest arrangement of children."

Sandra looked almost frantic. "*Bù. Bù. Tíngzhǐ*," she said in Chinese. "No. No. Stop!" appeared in the subtitles.

Oblivious to Sandra's obvious rising panic, the business man continued, "They will be delivered to the orphanage tomorrow morning with the same instructions to hold them until your group arrives next week. There are some very beautiful little ones; your clients will be very pleased."

At that, the ballroom broke into chaos, accusations hurled to the front, shouts of disapproval and boos.

Hannah made a subtle cutting motion to the control room, and Jason quickly muted the calls.

Sandra scowled at the crowd as the murmurs abated. "What do you expect?!" she shrieked. "You're all so determined to have perfect babies to match your perfect lives." Her voice dripped with disdain. "Do you even care about where these children come from? They're born in poverty, they'll suffer their entire lives, and then they'll die. I am saving these children. Giving them a better life, even if it is with you," she spat out the last word like a mouthful of poison.

"You can't make this about saving the children," Hannah said to Sandra as she held a hand out toward the video screen. "You're stealing them from their parents."

"Parents who use them as menial labor, working them to death in the fields," Sandra sneered.

"They're desperate for survival! And you take advantage of them in their weakness," Hannah shot back.

"Any parents who would give up their child so easily don't deserve her!" Sandra yelled.

The din of the ballroom continued, but to Hannah, all sound faded away as Sandra's words rang in her ears.

Her mother hadn't given her up for survival—at least not in the physical sense—but she had given her up all the same.

Did her mother still deserve to be her mother?

Hannah felt a catch in her throat. She glanced up at the video screen where the families in China—though muted—continued arguing with the investigators.

Despite all the pain her mother had caused her, Hannah realized she still wanted her.

She wanted her mother to still be her mother.

Her eyes began to blur and she rapidly blinked away the tears, shaking herself back to the present moment.

"This is all your fault!" Sandra yelled at Hannah. "You and that stupid husband of yours!" Her face turned red, and she clenched her hands into fists.

Despite their marital arrangement being completely fake, Hannah felt defensive for her sort-of-husband.

Sandra screamed and bolted for the nearest exit, but Hannah caught her by the arm as she tried to escape. Sandra wheeled around and took a swipe at Hannah's face. Sandra's fingernails caught Hannah in the neck, forcing her to release Sandra's arm and duck away. Sandra lunged for Hannah, but this time Hannah was prepared. She blocked the woman's clumsy attack and kneed her in the gut. Sandra stumbled backward, but the energy of her rage brought her to her feet again.

She ran at Hannah, blind with hatred, swinging wildly. Hannah caught hold of one of her wrists and wrenched it behind her back. She sideswiped Sandra in the back of her leg, forcing the woman onto her knees. Hannah grabbed her other arm, brought it behind her back, and slammed the crazed woman onto the floor.

With a knee against Sandra's back, Hannah leaned down and spoke in her ear. "There are enough motherless children in this world. I won't let you make any more."

After Hannah had Sandra's wrists tied, Mari and Anna lifted the former adoption agency assistant to her feet again and waited for their backup to arrive.

A minute later, Jason was at her side. "You were amazing," he said, enfolding her in his strong arms.

"Don't sound so surprised," Hannah said with a light laugh. "It's not like you haven't seen me in action before."

Jason grinned. "True. I guess I just never found it quite so irresistible."

Hannah felt her attraction toward this aggravating man blossom inside her. She stared at Jason, wondering where in the last four weeks her feelings had changed from loathing to longing.

Jason took her hand. "I have to go with them." He jerked his head toward the agents dragging Sandra across the ballroom. "But hopefully after the case gets wrapped up . . . maybe we can see each other again."

Hannah nodded and smiled. Should she say more than that? Should she act flirty? That didn't seem right. Would he still know how she felt if she didn't come on stronger? Why was she suddenly unable to formulate a plan for talking to him?

Jason tilted his head and considered her. He opened his mouth to say something, but then shut it and simply nodded back. "Bye, Hannah. Thanks for everything."

It took a full minute before Hannah could process rational thought again. She should probably do something instead of standing in the spotlight in front of the stage.

"Hannah, it sounds like the mission is pretty much done." It was Katie's voice over the comm. "We're going to sign off."

Hannah had nearly forgotten they were monitoring the mission. "Uh, yeah. Thanks, ladies."

How much had they heard of Jason's goodbye? How much had he said that would have sounded suspicious?

Good thing Katie hadn't invented an interest-o-meter yet.

Hannah's heart would have already given everything away.

CHAPTER TWENTY

A FTER CHECKING THE CLOCK on the wall for the fifth time in two minutes, Hannah forced herself to take a calming breath. Her dad was a busy man, after all. He almost never made it to appointments on time, especially not their monthly lunch date.

Hannah looked at the time once more before burying her face in her hands. It's not like this particular lunch was that important. But if the conversation turned in the direction she hoped it might, Hannah planned to ask him about her mother.

Her experience on the adoption mission with Jason had opened her eyes to so many aspects of parenting and relationships that she just hadn't considered before. Even though her dad might not know all the reasons, Hannah wanted to know why her mother had left.

Had they struggled getting along with each other? Had they really gotten to know each other before getting married? Had they talked about how they planned to raise their kids? Had they even wanted kids?

Hannah's throat went dry at that last thought. Despite her new-found courage for talking about her mother, she wasn't sure she could handle the answer to that question. At least, not if the answer was no.

Fortunately, her dad rescued her from her spiraling thoughts by sweeping into the cafe and making a beeline for their usual table. "Hey, Scoots. Sorry I'm late."

Hannah smiled at her father's nickname for her. "It's okay."

He leaned across the table and gave her a quick peck on the cheek. "What's new with school? And your roommates? You still getting along with them okay? I think you have a new one, don't you?"

"Yeah. Two months ago." Hannah said with a wry grin.

"Good. Good," he said absently as he waved the waiter over.

The lunch proceeded as usual—her dad asked lots of questions and only half listened to her answers. All too soon, the meal was done, and Hannah still hadn't asked him about her mom.

"Dad, before you go," Hannah began nervously, "could I ask you a question?"

"Sure thing," he said as he waved for the waiter to bring the check.

"This is serious, Dad," she added.

He glanced back at her, probably to make sure she actually looked serious. He set his phone down and looked at her—really looked at her.

"What's up?" he asked, a note of concern in his voice.

"Did you and mom ever really love each other?" she blurted out.

He considered her for several long moments before he finally nodded. "Yeah. We did. Still do, in a way."

Hannah tilted her head. "Really? Even after all she put us through?"

He blew out a long breath and sat back in his chair. "Love, not to mention marriage, can be complicated sometimes."

"Tell me about it," she muttered. Thoughts of Jason and their mission reminded Hannah of her other burning question. She looked at her dad and hesitated. But she'd come this far; she might as well get it all out. "Did mom even want me?" Hannah asked, a small hitch in her voice.

Sadness filled her father's eyes. "Hannah, despite what happened, you should know that your mother loved you very much. She was so excited to be your mother."

"Just not enough to stay," she said quietly.

He tilted his head, considering her for several long seconds. "You know, there were times after your mother left that I wanted to tell her to come back. To tell her it didn't matter what had happened, that we just wanted her back."

Hannah looked away, trying to hold back the tears that were threatening. If only that were possible. Her mom hadn't had any contact with them since the day she left. "Me, too," she whispered, not looking up.

"Hannah," her father said gently, waiting until he had her full attention. He slid his phone across the table toward her. The screen showed a phone contact with her mother's name. It was enough of a surprise that he still had an entry for his ex-wife of over ten years, but there was an unfamiliar picture in the corner. It sort of looked like her mother, only older.

"You have . . . her phone number?" Hannah picked up the phone. She hadn't seen a picture of her mom in over seven years, not since the day she had rampaged through the house, shredding and burning every picture of her mother she could find. And there was her mom's face, staring back at her. Hannah glanced down at the phone number.

Her mom's voice could be just one touch away, assuming the number was still hers after all these years. She felt a sudden longing for the mother she might have had.

Hannah scrolled further down on the contact page, wondering what else her dad had saved about her. At the bottom, she saw the call log and her stomach jumped into her throat.

"You had a fifteen-minute conversation with her last spring?" She looked up at her dad, unsure whether she wanted it to be true or not.

He simply nodded, his expression a mixture of hope and empathy.

"But . . ." Hannah squeezed her eyes shut. Her brain seemed unable to process what was happening.

When he spoke, her father's voice was soft. "Your mother reached out to me a few years after she left. At first, I didn't answer her calls. When I finally did, I yelled at her and hung up before she could even say anything."

Hannah realized her mouth was hanging open, so she shut it. But her eyes remained riveted on her dad.

"Eventually, we started talking," he admitted with a casual shrug. "More than anything, she wanted to see you again."

Hannah felt a lump in her throat, and she didn't dare try to speak.

"I wanted to make sure that having contact with your mother wouldn't make things worse. I didn't want you to slip into the spiral of anger and resentment that you'd already gone through. So, every once in a while, I casually mentioned your mother to gauge your reaction."

Glancing back down at her father's phone, Hannah replayed in her mind dozens of conversations where she'd blown up at her dad or stormed from the room whenever the topic of her mom had come up.

"I didn't react well, did I?" she said without looking up.

"You were justified," he replied.

They sat in silence for a while. Finally, Hannah handed the phone back to him. "She's wanted to see me all this time, and you never said anything?" Hannah was too shocked to be hurt yet.

Her dad ran a hand over his face. "I know I should have. I'm embarrassed to say that once you got to college, I was so worried about keeping our relationship on good terms that I didn't want your mother to come between us. I didn't want to lose you to the anger again . . ." he glanced up at her, an ashamed expression on his face. ". . . or to your mother, if you decided to reconcile."

Hannah reached across the table and touched her dad's hand. "You stayed when mom left. No matter what happens, you will never, ever lose me."

Her dad nodded.

Hannah took a breath and considered all that had happened. Despite the lingering hurt over what her mother had done, as the anger had faded over the years, it left a gaping, mother-sized hole in her heart.

Was she ready to have her mother back again?

What would she say if she could talk to her again? If she could see her again?

Her father picked up his phone and tapped the screen, casting a furtive glance at Hannah. A dial chime sounded from the phone. Was he calling her mother?

A lump rose in her throat at the possibility.

The call connected, and Hannah heard a voice that she hadn't heard for almost half her life. One she thought she'd forgotten.

Hannah brought a hand to her mouth, smothering a sob that threatened to escape.

"Hey, Rob. It's been a while. How are things? How's Hannah?" her mother asked.

Her dad smiled at the screen. "Hi, Jen. Hannah's good." He glanced across the table. "She's sitting right here."

A gasp echoed from the phone as Hannah's dad handed it across the table to her. Or maybe that was Hannah's own gasp. As she reached for the phone and caught the first glimpse of her mother in nearly a decade, Hannah felt a tear course its way down her cheek.

"Mom?" she squeaked.

"Hannah?" Her mother's face was a little older, but fit almost perfectly into Hannah's memories of her. Tears streamed down her mother's cheeks as well. "Look at you! You're so grown up."

Hannah took a shuddering breath, not trusting herself to do anything more than nod.

They just stared at each other in silence for a while. Hannah's tears continued.

"Oh sweetie, I'm so sorry. So, so sorry. For everything." Her mother's voice pinched off with emotion.

Hannah nodded again, the lump in her throat expanding. Apparently, neither of them would be able to do much talking. Her mother alternated between nodding in approval and shaking her head in disbelief.

Finally, Hannah gathered enough strength to venture to speak.

"I missed you," she whispered.

Hannah knew there would be time to ask why she had left, time to process the pain and anger she'd felt all these years, but for now, all she could feel was the ache in her chest of finally having her mother back.

And that was a start.

Chapter Twenty-One

IT HAD BEEN A week since the send-off banquet and Sandra's arrest for international adoption fraud. Hannah stared, eyes unfocused, at the numbers above the elevator keypad as they steadily increased. She remembered standing in that same elevator with a red rose in her hand and Jason's strong arms around her waist.

Her part of the mission was complete the night they caught Sandra. She'd had to submit a brief report explaining the events from her perspective, but otherwise she was done. It was nice to have all that time back to spend on things like school and testing her quadcopters. But as she stepped off the elevator on the condo tower's top floor and walked toward Club Banana, she couldn't help but feel like something was missing. She considered everything that had happened in the last month.

She and her mother had traded text messages several times in the last few days. They were planning to meet for lunch soon.

A few days earlier, she'd received word that Eddie had agreed to turn state's evidence in the case against his boss. Arrangements were being made for him to join Carissa and Baby Freddie in a small town in eastern Tennessee. Maybe there was hope for that family after all.

And Kayla had sent her a holiday card with a picture of their small family. Jinhai looked happier than ever.

But Hannah still couldn't shake the feeling that something was missing.

Three weeks earlier, she had checked into an adoption retreat as a married woman. The memory caught her off guard and nearly took her breath away. The entire mission had been a whirlwind of emotions, from her dislike of Jason to her awkwardness around children to her resentment for her own parents. She had her mother back in her life, sort of. And there would be plenty of time to worry about kids later, once she found the right guy.

The right guy.

That's what was missing. She liked Jason, and she was pretty confident that he knew and that he felt the same way about her.

So why hadn't he texted or called?

Sure, he was probably busy tying up the loose ends of the case, but that was during the day. What had he been doing these last seven evenings?

An annoying thought played in the back of her brain. Jason wasn't using some weird, convoluted interpretation of women wanting to be treated equally to justify not calling her. Was he? Did he expect her to make the first move? That was *so* not happening.

As she pushed the door open, Hannah heard voices coming from the living room, at least one of them male. It wouldn't be Mari's boyfriend, Trey. Hannah had just left Mari studying at the library. She supposed it could be Prince Leo, but Anna normally mentioned it they were expecting a royal visit.

Katie probably had one of her boys over.

Coming around the corner into the living room, she saw Jason sitting on the wide leather couch across from Susan. Hannah stopped in her tracks, letting her backpack slump to the floor.

After a whole week, he finally decided to do something.

He stood slowly, a crooked grin on his face. How easily Hannah had mistaken that smile for arrogance the first time they had met. She realized now that it was the bravado he used to cover his uncertainty.

"I thought you didn't like to lose," Jason said. He waggled his eyebrows, taunting her. "I beat you here by"—he checked his watch—"fifteen minutes at least."

Hannah narrowed her eyes. So that's the game he wanted to play. They could get to the serious topics—like why he hadn't called her—after the teasing.

Katie rushed over to Hannah, looking apologetic. "He already had clearance, so we didn't know . . . I mean, he *is* your partner. Or was anyway." Katie grabbed Hannah's arm. "Please don't kill him," she whispered. "He's actually not that bad once you get to know him."

A slight tinge of jealousy shot through Hannah. Maybe Jason was taking her advice and acting more like himself around women. She should be happy for him, but instead, she felt possessive. She suddenly wanted the casual, charming Jason all to herself.

She gave Katie a patronizing smile. "It's not your fault, Katie." Then she turned her grim game-face on Jason. "You can't possibly think you beat me here. I've been waiting for seven days."

Jason flashed his cocky grin. "If this is a race, you could say I was pacing myself. I'd hate to make a mistake—like going too fast—that would cost me the gold medal." His gaze bored into her.

A small smile tugged at her lips. She loved this double-speak banter. "Are you sure you even deserve to win this race?" Hannah took a few sauntering steps forward, toying with him.

His grin broadened. "I do. And I'm telling you right now that I'm going to prove it."

They were still separated by the long leather couch Susan occupied. In fact, Hannah's redhead friend sat looking back and forth from Jason to Hannah, eyes wide, like she was watching a tennis match and enjoying every minute of it.

The straight line of Hannah's mouth curled into an irrepressible grin. She stared across the couch at his handsome face and sigh-inducing eyes, wondering how she could have been so lucky to have gotten stuck with him on his mission.

"Oh, and it's only been six days," Jason countered. "You can't count the day we finished the mission."

"I can if I want to."

He rolled his eyes theatrically. "Just like a woman to give herself a head start."

Katie and Susan's heads jerked in Hannah's direction, probably trying to gauge her anger at his comment.

An unbearably tortuous silence stretched between them.

He smirked at her with those irresistible lips.

Hannah's eyes narrowed. Did he have any idea the retribution he'd suffer for taunting her like this?

In a flash, Hannah took two bounds forward, stepped onto the back of the couch, and launched herself through the air straight at Jason, tackling him onto a nearby sofa.

Katie and Susan both screamed.

Hannah stared down at him for only a moment, his strong lean body lying under hers, his soft gray-blue eyes surrounded by the cascading curtain of her golden hair. She didn't even ask if he wanted to kiss her.

She just knew.

As she lowered her mouth to his, Jason's arms were immediately around her back, pulling her closer. She savored the taste of his lips and the smell of his skin. But most of all, she was overwhelmed with feeling safe and wanted. Despite her flaws, he hadn't run away. She could feel him, solid under her.

Someone grabbed Hannah's shoulder and pulled, attempting to extricate her from Jason's arms for some reason.

Suddenly, the pulling stopped. "Oh," Susan said. "I thought you were . . ." She trailed off with a giggle.

Katie laughed nervously. "Uh, Susan, maybe we should . . . uh . . . work on that project thing," she said, confusion clear in her voice.

Hannah dragged herself, reluctantly, out of Jason's arms and pulled him into a mostly sitting position; she was still on his lap with no intention of getting up. Katie and Susan both gave her cautious looks, as if they were unconvinced she wouldn't still try to strangle him.

Hannah wrapped her arms around Jason and nuzzled down against his shoulder. She couldn't care less about what her friends thought at the moment.

Jason leaned his head back and looked at her, stroking his fingers through her long, blond hair. "I know it's probably late notice," he said. "But would you like to go out to dinner with me?"

Hannah cocked her head to the side as if contemplating his offer. "Are you conceding my victory?"

"Maybe." Jason grinned. "You mostly won fair and square. Consider it your just desserts."

"Just dessert?" Hannah repeated with a playful pout. "I thought it was supposed to be dinner and a movie."

He grinned. "It'll be more than that."

Hannah's gaze flitted to his lips. "I've thought of a few new ways to distract you on the long elevator ride down to the lobby," Hannah said innocently.

"Can we ride it twice?" he asked suggestively, eyes smoldering.

Hannah smiled and took his face in her hands. "You are the most handsome second place winner I've ever seen," she said before planting a kiss on his lips.

He pulled back. "What do you mean *second* place?"

A mischievous grin spread across Hannah's face. "Because I'm about to win our race to the elevator."

She jumped up from Jason's lap and sprinted for the door, squealing as he tried—unsuccessfully—to grab hold of her.

She might let him catch up.

Eventually.
Because losing to *him* wouldn't be half bad.

ORIGIN STORY AND NEXT BOOK

THAT'S THE END, BUT the Banana Girls action continues with Spies Never Play, where Katie has to go undercover at an eSports championship tournament to catch a high-tech thief before he compromises national security.

If you've already read the rest of the Banana Girls series (Spies Never Quit and Spies Never Swoon), but you somehow didn't grab Spies Never Share, the Banana Girls' origin story novella—including Anna and Hannah's first mission and the first guy they fought over—you can sign up for it here: www.myleschristensen.com/banana3.

And if I could ask one big favor—it would really help my book succeed if you would leave a review on Amazon and Goodreads. Thank you so very much!

ACKNOWLEDGMENTS

Thanks to my readers. Your feedback keeps me going.

I appreciate the early feedback that I got from my beta readers: BingeingonBooks, Maddy216, and Ashreads. Thanks for keeping the character arcs on track.

Thanks to Courtney at Courtney Larkin Editing. Last time I had too many commas. This time, not enough.

I appreciate my youngest sons allowing me to read the final proof copy out loud to them (again). Sorry there was so much mushy stuff in this one. I'll see if I can do better next time.

As always, my biggest thanks goes to my sweet wife. You inspire me to work harder and write faster (and fly higher). Also, I didn't pull all of the traits for these characters from people you know. Only some. :)

$\mathbf{M}$YLES CHRISTENSEN LOVES TO write exciting adventures because he loves to read exciting adventures. The hopeless romantic in him will usually sprinkle a teensy bit of romance into his stories. While writing, he listens to music that matches—and sometimes inspires—the storyline.

His mild-mannered alter ego is a product development engineer, university professor, and game inventor.

He lives in Utah with his wife and children. He writes cozy thriller/suspense under the name M. Taylor Christensen.

www.ingramcontent.com/pod-product-compliance
Lightning Source LLC
Chambersburg PA
CBHW060906210726
48293CB00006B/1986